A Seed for the Harvest

Greg M. Dodd

ISBN-10: 0991533208
ISBN-13: 978-0-9915332-0-6 Paperback
Library of Congress Control Number: 2014906771
Harvest Chronicles

Printed in the United States of America

To Caroline, Hampton, family and friends…

"I write these things to you who believe in the name of the Son of God so that you may know that you have eternal life."

- 1 John 5:13

Acknloweldgements

Immeasurable thanks to Caroline, my loving, patient wife and volunteer editor, whose encouragement, interest, and support helped me press on to the end. A pat on the head to our dog, Desmond, my faithful writing companion all those ridiculously early mornings. Most importantly, thank you to my Lord and Savior, Jesus Christ, who saved me, gave my life purpose and meaning, and gave me a story worth telling.

Prologue

The pen ran out of ink. Jon Smoak scratched it back and forth across an offering envelope just to be sure it was dry. Returning it to the small hole in the back of the wooden pew, he grabbed the pen next to it. Testing the new pen, he scribbled a small circle of black ink on the back of his worship bulletin. Now he could get back to work.

When the old man in the light blue seersucker suit and bow tie finished praying in front of the congregation, Jon placed a check mark in the bulletin next to the words *Offertory Prayer – Ralph Henderson, Deacon.* As Mr. Henderson found his seat again on the front pew, Jon yawned as he watched the men and women of the choir, draped in shiny green robes, rise in unison from their chairs in the loft behind the pulpit. The sanctuary was quiet as the choir director pointed his stick at the old woman seated at the piano. He waved the stick several times in the air and the woman's hands sprang into action. The piano played loudly as the choir began to sing.

I know not why God's wondrous grace
To me he hath made known,
Nor why, unworthy, Christ in love
Redeemed me for his own.
But I know Whom I have believèd,

And am persuaded that he is able
To keep that which I've committed
Unto him against that day.

As the choir sang, Jon looked at the watch his grandmother had given him for Christmas and wrote the time, 11:31, in the bulletin next to the words *Offertory – I Know Whom I Have Believed, Celebration Choir.* Jon tapped his foot absently beneath the pew as he drew a picture of Mr. Henderson in the margin of his bulletin.

I know not how this saving faith
To me he did impart,
Nor how believing in his Word
Wrought peace within my heart.

Jon set his pen and bulletin down next to him as a brass offering plate, containing several small white envelopes and a folded five-dollar bill, made its way down the pew towards him. He received the plate in his hands and slid himself slowly along the pew, without standing up, towards an elderly woman wearing a yellow dress and a white lace hat. Her head nodded with the music as she sang softly along with the choir. "Here you go, Mrs. Wilson," Jon whispered to the woman. She smiled at Jon, as she did every Sunday, and placed a white envelope in the plate before handing it to the usher. Jon slid quietly back to his bulletin and pen as the choir finished their song.

I know not how the Spirit moves,
Convincing men of sin,
Revealing Jesus through the Word,
Creating faith in him.
But I know Whom I have believèd,
And am persuaded that he is able
To keep that which I've committed
Unto him against that day.

When the music stopped, some of the choir members sat down in their chairs, while others quietly slipped through the doors on either side of the choir loft. Jon placed a check mark beside the offertory song in the bulletin and read the next line. *Sermon – Living Right in a Wrong World, Reverend Edwards.* As Reverend Edwards stood up from his chair on the stage and took his place in the pulpit, Jon looked at his watch and wrote *11:35*. The black-robed reverend opened his Bible on the lectern and looked sternly at the people seated around the sanctuary. Jon wondered if Reverend Edwards was mad about some of the choir sneaking out early.

Since he started wearing his watch to church, Jon knew the reverend's sermons usually lasted about twenty-five minutes. He had heard people say that Reverend Edwards loved professional football, which was why his sermons always ended right at five minutes to twelve. The reverend needed time to get home, change clothes, and have lunch before the games started at one o'clock, they said. Not that anyone appeared to mind his short sermons. "At least we always beat the Baptists to lunch," he heard one man say.

If the reverend wanted his sermon to end before noon today, he would have to talk fast. Earlier in the service, the Children's Choir had taken forever – thanks to Tommy Loftis – to arrange themselves on the stage, sing their song and get back to their seats. Jon was sure Tommy was in trouble with his mom for knocking over the large fern and candle stand near the baptismal font on his way to the stage. She was sitting directly in front of Jon and had been scolding Tommy quietly for the last ten minutes as Tommy hung his head from his shoulders.

Jon knew nothing else would happen for at least another twenty minutes while the reverend talked. He flipped his bulletin over and began to draw a dog in the blank section reserved for note taking. Jon had been asking his parents for a dog as long as he could remember. He carefully drew the head and ears, coloring in everything but the two round eyes. Jon was happy he had chosen a pen with black ink. Whenever he got a real dog, he wanted it to be black.

"Try and pay attention, Jonny," his father whispered, elbowing him in the shoulder. "You're in third grade, now. You're old enough to listen."

Jon sighed, laid the pen and bulletin down next to him, and leaned forward to rest his face in the palms of his hands. He watched the tips of his black Sunday shoes tap the red carpeted floor, as they swung back and forth underneath the pew, and wished he were somewhere else.

Part I

Smoak And Mirrors

"Anyone who listens to the word but does not do what it says is like a man who looks at his face in a mirror and, after looking at himself, goes away and immediately forgets what he looks like."

- James 1:23-24

one

Missing

"In the beginning was the Word, and the Word
was with God, and the Word was God."
- John 1:1

Jon was missing something. The green numbers on the microwave clock read *9:28 a.m.* as he stood in his kitchen shaking his keys, grimacing in thought. It was time to be leaving, but he couldn't go without it. "I can't walk in there empty handed," he mumbled, staring past the bowl of fake red apples on the kitchen center island. Only when he'd begun to walk out the door did he feel its absence. He circled the room aimlessly as he tested his memory, the heels of his black dress shoes knocking loudly against the hardwood floors. He was at a loss for his Bible's whereabouts.

Dropping his keys on the black granite kitchen counter, Jon began looking around his house in all the plausible places. On his nightstand and under his bed, for starters. But there just weren't that many possibilities. Since he last went to church two Sundays ago, Jon had spent most of his time in the bonus room over his garage, where he liked to watch television or movies on his large, flat screen TV or work on his MacBook. But after searching the room, Jon made his way back downstairs empty handed. A simple walk-through of the den, living room, and dining room also proved fruitless.

Stumped, Jon began to search the more unlikely places – Holly's room, the guest bedroom, and laundry room. Still no Bible. He simply had no recent memories of having the Book anywhere in the house. Maybe he'd left

3

it at church two weeks ago, possibly under a chair in the sanctuary or in his Sunday school classroom. But, if so, surely someone would've returned it to him by now. "It's got my name on it, for Pete's sake."

Jon returned to the kitchen and snatched his keys off the counter. "Maybe Elvis took it," he said to himself, glancing once more at the time. Sunday school started in sixteen minutes. He was going to be late. "Great," he said. He opened the door to his garage, pressed a button on the wall and impatiently endured the metal screeching of his overhead door slowly exposing his garage to the world. He slipped under the rising door and walked out onto the driveway. "Elvis!" called Jon, clapping his hands as he walked into the front yard. "I don't have time for this," he mumbled. He looked for any movement in the bushes on either side of the front steps before giving up.

Jon walked back into the garage, opened the door of his white BMW and plopped into the tan leather driver's seat with a huff. Pressing his foot against the break, he pushed the ignition button and felt the car vibrate smoothly to life as he checked his mirrors for Elvis. Though it had been a year since he rolled over the dog's tail while backing out of the garage, the sound of the puppy shrieking in pain still haunted him. And calling his daughter at college to say he'd run over her dog again was not something he cared to do.

Before lifting his foot off the break, Jon threw his arm around the passenger seat and twisted his body to see fully out the rear window. "Where is that dog?" As he turned himself forward, Jon's eyes caught a glimpse of something on the floor behind him. His worn, black, leather-bound Bible lay behind the passenger seat, nestled under several pieces of junk mail and two empty bottles of Diet Mountain Dew. "Seriously?" Jon asked in relief and frustration. He shook his head and let his car inch backwards, keeping an eye on his rearview mirror. A large yellow and white dog flashed across the driveway behind him. "There you are."

Jon stopped the car, put it in park, and got out, leaving his door open behind him. Elvis danced around him, knowing what would come next. "Hang on," Jon told the dog as he walked back into the garage. He opened the cabinet door where he kept his tools and dug his hand into a bag of bacon and cheese-flavored dog treats. Elvis sat patiently behind Jon, sweeping his white tail back and forth on the painted concrete floor. "Here you go," said Jon, holding the treat above Elvis' black muzzle. "You didn't think

I'd forget, did you, boy?" Elvis caught the treat in his mouth and ran out of the garage, coming to rest under the basketball goal just a foot away from the boundary of his electric fence.

Jon walked back to his car, placed himself in the driver's seat, and closed the door. His eyes fell on the Bible resting on the floor behind him. His forehead wrinkled with conviction as he looked up to see Elvis licking the remains of his treat off the concrete driveway. "I remembered to give my dog a treat every day, but God's Word never crossed my mind once for two weeks." The thought failed to find a comfortable home in Jon's conscience. He pressed his lips firmly together as he looked over his shoulder and let his car roll slowly down the driveway. "I guess I'm a better dog owner than I am a Christian," he said, hoping to make himself laugh. But it just wasn't funny.

Stopping the car at the end of the driveway, Jon reached for his Bible. He lifted it onto his lap and brushed dust off the cover before moving it onto the passenger seat. Looking down at the thick Book, Jon rubbed his thumb lightly over the faded remnants of his name embossed on the cover. He remembered when the gold letters shined new on the black grain leather. And with the memory, a small subtle emptiness crept into Jon's heart. He'd been missing more than his Bible.

two

Holly's Wish

*"As a father has compassion on his children, so the
Lord has compassion on those who fear him."*
- Psalm 103:13

"Dad, can I have a puppy?" asked Holly.

Jon glanced at his daughter's brown eyes staring into his rearview mirror from the back seat as he turned his new white 4Runner into their neighborhood. He smiled into the mirror. "No, you don't need a puppy, honey."

"But you got a new car. Why can't I have a puppy?"

Jon laughed gently at the comparison. "A car and a puppy aren't exactly the same thing, sweetie. Besides, we already have a dog. Jo-Jo's your dog."

"Jo-Jo's *your* dog, Dad. Even Jo-Jo knows that. I want my own dog." Holly pushed the red button on her seat belt and let it slide back across her body as the SUV neared their driveway.

Jon turned his head to see his daughter inching forward in her seat. "Holly Elizabeth Smoak, you have to wait until we stop to do that, OK, honey? You know that." He stretched his arm to the back seat and rested his hand on her knee. Turning into the driveway, he pushed the button on his garage door opener and waited for the door to open. A black Labrador Retriever, sporting a yellow scarf around its neck, appeared lazily from the bushes around the corner of the house. Shaking the sleep from its body, the dog trotted up to Jon's door, stood on its hind legs, and placed its front paws on the window next to Jon's face. A wide pink tongue hung from its white muzzle, producing a smile on the dog's aging face.

"Hey, Jo-Jo," Jon said through the window. "Down, boy. Get down."

"See what I mean?" asked Holly.

"We'll talk about it later," said Jon, trying to escape the topic one more time. "OK, sweetie?"

Holly sighed. "I know what that means."

"Oh, you think so, huh?" asked Jon, smiling into his rearview mirror. He parked in the garage and fended off Jo-Jo's excited greeting as he walked around to help his daughter.

Holly climbed down out of the 4Runner holding her father's hand. "It means I'll probably be in college before you let me get Elvis."

Jon strained to lift Holly's book bag from the back seat. "You still want to name your dog Elvis, huh?"

"Yep. From *Lilo and Stitch*. Remember that movie?"

"Of course, I do." Jon tried to imagine himself standing in his yard, clapping his hands, and calling for a dog named Elvis. "But why not name him Lilo? Or Stitch?"

"Nah, I like Elvis. Do you think Mom would have liked that movie, Dad? You said she liked Elvis songs."

It had been a while since Holly had asked about her mother. "Oh, absolutely," said Jon, holding her hand as they walked up the stairs to the door. "It had Hawaii, aliens, and Elvis songs. What's not to like about that, right?" He unlocked the door and pushed it open as Jo-Jo slipped past them into the kitchen. "How was your first day of school?"

"It was fine. Ms. Watkins gave me a red."

"Uh-oh. What happened?"

"A red's good, Dad."

"I thought a green dot next to your name was good." Jon set her book bag down on the kitchen table with a loud thud.

"That was only in Ms. Mitchem's second grade class. In third grade, you get a red if you're good."

"Ooh, I see. Well, good job, sweetie." Jon rubbed the hair on the top of her head, careful not to disturb her favorite white bow.

Holly sat down at the table and began pulling papers out of her book bag while Jon sifted through junk mail on the kitchen counter.

"I got a bunch of things for you to sign and look at, Dad. Ms. Watkins said they were for our moms, but Mary Beth Roberts told her I didn't have one."

Jon looked up from his stack of mail to see Holly's brown eyes searching his face for a reaction. Now he understood why Holly's mom was on her mind. He dropped the mail on the counter and sat down next to his daughter at the table, gently rubbing his hand across her back. The fragile illusion he worked so hard to maintain – that the two of them were a normal family – had been shattered by a third grader named Mary Beth Roberts.

"Hey, you have a mom, honey. You know that. And I hope one day we'll see her again."

"I know," said Holly, looking down. "I just wish…." She leaned her head into Jon's chest and closed her eyes. "It's just that all the other girls…."

Jon stroked her long dark hair as she sniffed her running nose. "Hey," he said, lifting her chin so he could see her watery eyes. "Don't worry about the other girls. And Mary Beth's your friend, isn't she? I'm sure she didn't mean anything by it."

"OK," said Holly, pushing her forehead against Jon's white dress shirt.

Jon wiped a tear from her cheek. "Besides, we've got each other, right? And you know I'll always be here for you." He smiled as his daughter looked up at him. "And so will Jo-Jo," he added, tickling her ribs.

"Aaah!" Holly squealed as she squirmed to get away. "I want a puppy!" She giggled as she tried to break free from her father's arms. Jo-Jo barked and hopped around the kitchen table, joining in the excitement.

"One day," Jon said, pulling her close for a hug. "I promise."

three

The Picture Of Jon Smoak

"Does a maiden forget her jewelry, a bride her wedding ornaments?
Yet my people have forgotten me, days without number."
- Jeremiah 2:32

Elvis reclined next to the basketball goal, his eyes fixed on Jon's BMW as it sat at the end of the driveway. Jon usually felt a touch of guilt whenever he saw his dog's expressive brown eyes watch him leave. But on this cool late September morning, Jon felt guilty for an entirely different reason. He backed his car slowly onto the street and shifted into drive. His Sunday school class started at ten o'clock and he liked to get there on time. He could make it in as few as twenty-five minutes, if he hurried. But this morning, despite running late, Jon suddenly felt no rush to get there. His car rolled up the street from his house at idle speed, his foot resting lightly on the accelerator. At the stop sign leaving his suburban neighborhood, Jon plugged his iPod into the car stereo and selected his *Worship* playlist, as he usually did for the Sunday morning drive to church. But after turning onto the main road, he continued along without pressing play. "Not today," he told himself and drove on in silence.

Jon stared blankly over his steering wheel as he guided his car down the familiar road, which cut through a dense mixture of hardwoods and pines. Beams of bright morning sunlight slipped through the trees and striped the asphalt road ahead of him. Feeling his Bible's presence on the seat beside him, Jon struggled to fend off his growing unease. He slid his hands to the top of the steering wheel and gripped it tightly as he guided the car around a wide curve.

The undeveloped woodlands to his left opened to several acres of exposed, red clay soil behind a large blue and white commercial Real Estate sign, facing the road. "What the heck?" he said, passing the clear-cut property. "When did *that* happen?" He traveled the same road every day and had somehow failed to notice the change taking place. "I must be getting old and senile."

Lifting his foot off the accelerator, Jon coasted uphill to an intersection and rolled to a stop under a red light. He let his head fall against his headrest and waited with indifference for the light to turn green. Sighing as he rolled his head slightly to his right, he caught a glimpse of his eye in the review mirror. He quickly looked away and focused his attention on passing traffic. The fact that eye contact with himself made him uncomfortable only added to his distress. He knew something was wrong.

When the light finally changed, Jon eased the car through the intersection, turning left as a familiar ring tone sounded from the iPhone in his right front pocket. He lifted himself above his seat, pulled the phone from his jeans, and touched the screen. "Hey, Mom. Is everything all right?"

"Oh, hey, Son. How are you this morning?"

"I'm fine. Just on my way to church."

"You're such a good boy."

Jon didn't feel either description fit him at the moment. He wasn't good and he certainly wasn't a boy. "I'm 43, Mom."

"Well, you're still my boy. And you're sweet to call your mother."

"You called me, Mom."

"Hmm? I did?"

"Yes, ma'am. Was there something you needed this morning?"

"No, I don't think so. I'm just sitting here watching an old movie on the television."

"Oh, good. Which one?"

"Oh, let's see...what's it called? I've forgotten the name of it. And it's one of my favorites. Hang on, let me find the TV guide in the paper."

"Just push the info button on the remote, Mom."

"The what, honey?"

Jon felt his usual patience with his mother lacking. "Never mind, Mom. I hope you have a good morning. I might come by to see you this afternoon, OK?"

"Hang on. It's right here. Oh, goodness gracious. Let me find my glasses."

"Mom?" Jon sighed as he heard his mother put down her phone to search for her glasses. As he waited, he toyed with the idea of hanging up, knowing she wouldn't remember the call, anyway.

"That's better," she said. "Let's see…it says, *The Picture of Dorian Gray.*"

"Oh, that's what you're watching? You and I watched that once at my house, remember?"

"I haven't seen this since I was a young girl in high school."

"No, Mom, we watched it at my house a few years ago."

"We did?"

"Yes, ma'am. It's a good one."

"Oh, well I don't…."

"You just enjoy your movie, and I'll talk with you later. OK, Mom?"

"OK, Son. Thanks so much for calling. I love you."

Jon smiled. "I love you, too, Mom."

Jon placed the phone in his drink holder and returned his focus to the road ahead. The thought of sitting in his den, years before, watching *The Picture of Dorian Gray* with his mother gave him a brief reason to smile. He remembered her dozing intermittently as she rested in his recliner with a blanket over her legs. Whenever her eyes opened from napping, she would tell him, "I recall seeing this picture with my mother in the theater on Front Street in Georgetown when I was just a young girl." He watched most of the movie alone while she slept.

Jon remembered being curiously absorbed in the old black and white film, with its odd premise and witty British dialogue. He had never read the Victorian era book by Oscar Wilde, on which the movie was based. But the story of a beautifully painted portrait slowly transforming into a hideous, disfigured image with every sinful act committed by Dorian, the painting's subject – who, by contrast, remained forever young and attractive in appearance – managed to hold Jon's interest while his mother napped.

As he drove, Jon let his mind wander through his memory of the movie. He tried to imagine himself as the story's protagonist, the subject of the cursed painting. What if he could stay young and let some mystical portrait show the ugly effects of age and sin instead of him? Jon wondered just how grotesque his painting would look. It couldn't be as bad as the portrait of

Dorian. He felt his eyes pulled down to his Bible, which he'd found that morning covered with trash on the floor of his car. What about his apathy towards God? How would that sin show in the painting?

A harsher question then surfaced in Jon's mind: Had his faith become just a façade, like Dorian Gray's youthful appearance in the movie? Was his identity as a Christian simply a veneer for others to see, hiding a darker truth? Jon shook off the self-accusing thoughts. "Absolutely not. I know who I am…or at least I thought I did." His guilt still tugged at his conscience. "But if I'm such a big Christian, why didn't I even realize I was missing my Bible for two weeks? *Two weeks?*"

Jon felt uncomfortable and cornered by his own question. A desire to simply dismiss the concern and get on with his morning began to take hold. He was just being too hard on himself. "Why do I always beat myself up over stuff like this?" Jon looked for distractions in the passing scenery, hoping to clear his mind. As his car glided across the Gervais Street Bridge into Columbia, sunlight bounced into his eyes off the mud-colored water of the Congaree River below. The scene gave him a brief moment of peace before his gaze settled back on the road to church.

"Still," he thought, "you'd think I would have at least noticed at some point over the last two weeks that my Bible wasn't on my nightstand where it always is." The thought echoed in his head for a moment. "Where it always is," he said, out loud. A painful truth began to push its way through Jon's mind. He searched his memory hoping he was wrong, but he knew he wasn't. And he forced himself to admit it. "The only times I move my Bible anymore are when I dust the furniture or give it a ride to church." With the admission, the weight of Jon's body pushed deeper into his car seat. "How long has it been like this?"

Jon tried to remember the last time he read his Bible, outside of simply following along with his pastor's sermons in church. Nothing came to mind. Keeping an eye on the road, he stretched his hand to the pages of his Bible. His fingers found the laminated bookmark Holly had made for him on Father's Day when she was in kindergarten. Pulling on the frayed, blue yarn attached to the bookmark, Jon opened the Bible on the seat hoping to jog his memory of what he'd last read. He glanced at the open pages, noting the bookmark's place in the Old Testament. "The Book of Zephaniah?" he said out loud, glancing back at the road. The prophet's name failed to ring any bells in Jon's mind. On the left page, he saw a verse underlined in blue ink. "Seek the Lord, all you humble of the land, you who do what he commands. Seek righteousness, seek humility; perhaps you will be sheltered on the day of the Lord's anger."

"When did I underline that? For Pete's sake," he said. The obvious hole in Jon's memory left him feeling as though someone else had been reading and marking in his Bible, though he knew it wasn't the case.

Jon's car rolled to a stop behind several others at a large intersection in downtown Columbia. While he waited for the light to change, he flipped the thin pages of his Bible back and forth with his right hand. It was stuffed with old worship bulletins, church announcements, notes, and copies of prayer requests from his Sunday school class. He unfolded one of the prayer request sheets and held it up against the steering wheel. Looking over the copy of handwritten requests, Jon realized he'd never prayed for any of them. "I never even looked at these." He tucked the sheet back into the Bible and closed the Book. "When was the last time I really prayed for anyone? Or just prayed at all, besides saying grace over food?" And he knew he didn't do that consistently, either, unless he was eating with someone from church. The sound of a car horn behind him let him know the light had turned green. "What's happened to me?" he asked as he stepped on the accelerator.

Jon knew he was a Christian. He was confident in his salvation through his professed faith in Jesus Christ. But he found the sudden lack of evidence in his everyday life disturbing. He wasn't reading his Bible. He wasn't praying. He wasn't really doing anything besides going to church most Sundays. "Am I just going through the motions now? How could I not see that?"

Jon was getting closer to his church, but felt compelled to slow down. He wanted to resolve the conflict inside him before he arrived. After everything his faith had meant to him over the years, he couldn't accept that it had become just an empty exercise.

It couldn't be as bad as he was making it out to be, Jon hoped. He scrambled to comfort himself. "I'm in church almost every week and Sunday school, too. I even went to that Wednesday night men's group back in the spring." Jon thought about the men's group for a moment. It consisted of six to eight men, who did nothing together socially outside of meeting on

Wednesday nights. During each ninety-minute session, discussion usually alternated between members sharing too much about themselves or nothing at all. Either way, it made Jon feel uncomfortable. "But at least those guys were trying. That's more than I could say. I didn't even want to be there." He winced at his unintended confession.

Jon turned on the radio and played with the stations for a moment, before turning it back off. There had to be more to his faith than just show-ing up for church on Sunday mornings. He thought about his Sunday school class. "I lead the class in prayer, whenever Phillip asks me to. That's in front of everyone." And he remembered the positive comments class members had shared about his prayers, how "moving" they were. Jon smiled briefly and allowed himself to feel better for a moment. But as the memories of those prayers played back honestly in his mind, the positive feelings left him.

Phillip, the director of the Sunday school class for single adults, seemed to have a short list of class members whom he would ask to pray before their teacher, Steve, began his lesson. Jon knew that being asked to speak in front of twenty or thirty people could be stressful and potentially embarrassing if you didn't know what to say. In his workplace, Jon was known as a skillful public speaker and took pride in conveying ideas through careful preparation and natural delivery. If Phillip ever asked him to pray, he was determined to be ready.

Each Sunday morning over the last two years, Jon had run through ideas for prayer on his drive to church. He listened to praise and worship songs on his iPod and borrowed phrases and themes from the lyrics. He made sure to change the wording so no one could accuse him of prayer plagiarism, if there were such a thing. After arriving in the church parking lot, he would settle on a few thoughts and practice the prayer in his car before walking in. The routine had paid off, as Phillip had called Jon's name several times over the last year. Jon remembered how he had enjoyed appearing able to offer heartfelt prayers on demand.

But as Jon sifted the memories of his Sunday school prayers through a newly humbled conscience, the reality of his motivation became painfully clear. A feeling of self-indicting shame warmed Jon's face. "Practicing prayer so I'll sound good? Are you kidding me?! Who *am* I?" Jon pressed hard on his brake, turned his car quickly into an empty San Jose's restaurant parking lot and stopped. He put his hands over his face and rubbed his fingers slowly up and down against his forehead. Dropping his hands into his lap, he looked hard into the troubled blue eyes staring back at him in the rearview mirror. "You're a *phony*. That's who you are."

four

Storyin'

"Train a child in the way he should go, and when he is old he will not turn from it."

- Proverbs 22:6

Climbing up the three weathered plank steps, Jon felt a warm, salty, Saturday morning breeze from the open overhead doors, which spanned the width of the corrugated metal building facing the ocean on Pawleys Island. His family had been vacationing on the quiet three-mile-long strip of sand every June since he was a baby, and the arcade was always the first place Jon wanted to go. Separated from the South Carolina mainland by a broad salt marsh, Pawleys' only attractions were a wide beach, aging rental houses, a long fishing pier, one tiny fireworks store, and the arcade – King's Funland. King's sat on Pawleys north end, nestled behind tall dunes – its low-angled metal roof barely visible from the beach – just a block down Atlantic Avenue from their usual vacation rental. And after enduring a torturous thirty-minute wait, while his father unloaded the family station wagon for their weeklong stay, Jon finally felt the arcade's sandy concrete floor beneath his bare feet.

The sound of pinball machine bells and ricocheting air hockey pucks filled Jon's ears as he stood next to the change machine with his father. From the jukebox in the far corner, *Something About You,* by Boston, played loudly over laughter from a group of kids swarming around the two large air hockey tables. Jon's eyes widened as his mind raced with anticipation. "Come *on,* Dad," said Jon.

"I'm trying, Jonny," said his father as the machine rejected his dollar bill for a third time. "Oh, for Pete's sake."

"Try a different one," said Jon. "That one's all wrinkled."

"There's nothing wrong with this bill. You just have to be patient."

Jon watched closely as his father tried to insert the bill again. The paper dollar finally disappeared into the machine, filling the metal tray full of dimes.

"One more," said his father. The machine accepted another bill, and ten more dimes spilled into the coin return. Jon cupped his hands expectantly in front of his father as he glanced over his shoulder at a girl standing by the air hockey table. His father poured the dimes into his hands. "If you need me, I'll be right over here, Jonny."

"Dad, I'm twelve years old. I'm not a baby," said Jon as he walked away.

"Thanks for reminding me. That's twenty dimes. Make them last, OK?"

"Yes, sir," said Jon, without looking back. Jon dumped the coins into his bathing suit pocket, leaving one dime in his hand. As his eyes scanned the arcade, he felt the weight of the coins pulling the shorts off his right hip. Jon tightened the drawstring around his waist and shuffled his feet across the green painted floor to the Skee-Ball games. Rubbing the dime between his thumb and forefinger, he walked past four identical lanes before making his choice. The lane to the far right would allow him to see the air hockey table without turning all the way around.

Placing his dime in the slot, he pulled back on the metal lever and released the wooden balls, which rolled loudly, single file into the holding compartment. Jon picked up a ball and looked over his left shoulder at the air hockey table to see if she was watching. She was. He quickly looked back to his lane and took a deep breath. He fought the urge to turn his head again and then rolled his first ball. It hit the lane loudly, rolled quickly up the incline, bounced off the top corner, and disappeared into the bottom 10-point hole.

"Crap," Jon said to himself, staring wishfully at the 50-point hole at the top.

"Can I try?" the girl said, now standing next to Jon.

Startled, Jon quietly reached down for a ball and placed it gently in the girl's open hand, trying hard to maintain his composure. As she took a step back, she blew a bubble with her pink gum and popped it in her mouth. Jon watched her tanned arm swing slowly backward, then forward, and release the ball smoothly onto the lane. It rolled quietly up the center, took flight off the incline, and landed neatly in the 50-point hole. Three prize tickets slid out and hung from the slot beneath the coin return.

"That's good," said Jon, regaining his ability to speak. "What's your name?"

"Amy," she said, pulling her sun-kissed blonde hair back into a ponytail and securing it with an orange rubber band from her wrist. "What's yours?"

"Um, Jonny. I mean, Jon," he said, trying to sound older than he was. "Wanna try another one?"

Amy held out her hand, palm-side up, and wiggled her fingers. "Where you from?" she asked as Jon placed another ball in her hand. She swung her arm casually and rolled the ball straight into the 40-point hole. Two more tickets appeared from the slot.

Jon realized he hadn't answered her question. "Oh, uh, I'm from here, actually." He felt bad for telling a lie, but he'd spent too much time on Pawleys Island every summer to be labeled a tourist.

Amy cut her eyes at Jon and revealed a subtle grin that made him nervous. "Really?" she asked. "I've never seen you before." She helped herself to another wooden ball as Jon stood watching.

"Oh, that's because I'm usually out surfing or something, you know." Jon's lie grew bigger. He had seen boys surfing near the Pawleys Island pier every summer. They'd carry their boards in from the waves like conquering heroes, always to a group of admiring girls. He wished he could be one of them, but he'd never even touched a surfboard. It wasn't fair.

Amy studied Jon's face and popped another bubble in her mouth. "You ain't storyin' are you?"

"Storying?" asked Jon. He guessed she meant *lying*. Which he was. "Uh, no. I'm not storying."

"So then, you must know those boys over there." Amy pointed and waved to a group of five tanned surfer boys with long hair and no shirts. She turned back to the lane and rolled another ball. Another 50 points and three more tickets.

"Um, yeah," said Jon, now trapped in his lie. He looked across the arcade and waved slowly to the group of non-smiling strangers. "Wanna play a different game?" Jon asked quickly, trying to divert Amy's attention from the boys. "I've got lots of dimes." Jon dug his hand into his pocket, made a fist around several coins, and pulled, turning his pocket inside out in the process. The remaining dimes spilled from his bathing suit and bounced loudly onto the concrete around his feet. Jon dropped to his hands and knees, desperately trying to keep the change from rolling under the Skee-Ball lanes and across the arcade. He looked up to see Amy's tanned legs walking away towards the group of laughing surfer boys, the string of prize tickets dangling from her hand.

"Great," Jon said to himself, dropping his head in humiliation. He noticed his father suddenly on the floor next to him picking up dimes. "Dad, I can do this myself," he said, already embarrassed enough. Dropping flat onto his stomach, Jon pressed his face against the sandy floor and peered under the lane. Seeing two dimes, he stretched his arm underneath the game and pinched them between his fingers.

Jon's father ignored his son's pride and continued picking up coins. "Jonny, listen to me for a minute."

Jon pulled his arm out from under the Skee-Ball lane, rolled over into a sitting position, and brushed the sand off his right cheek. The tone in his father's voice was softer than what Jon was used to, particularly when he had done something wrong. "I'm sorry about the dimes, Daddy."

"Don't worry about the dimes, Son. I want you to remember something."

"Yes, sir?"

His father looked squarely into Jon's curious blue eyes. "Don't ever try to be something you're not. OK, Jonny?"

"You mean…you heard all that?" asked Jon, turning his head to look across the arcade at Amy.

"Pretty much."

Jon looked up at his father and fearfully searched his face for signs of disappointment.

His father placed his hand gently on Jon's shoulder. "Just remember, Son, there's nothing worse than being a phony."

five

The Actor

"So, because you are lukewarm – neither hot nor cold –
I am about to spit you out of my mouth."
- *Revelation 3:16*

During his drive to church, Jon's disposition had devolved into a sour angry mood. What started with frustration over his misplaced Bible had become a looming judgment on the integrity of his faith. By his own assessment, he had become a Christian pretending to be a Christian without doing what a Christian is supposed to do. But he knew there was more to his faith than just pretending. At least there used to be. And he didn't understand how or when he became an actor instead of a Believer. But thinking about it had given him a headache.

Jon turned his car into the church parking lot and steered his way to the half-empty overflow lot a good distance from the building. Despite being late, the comfort of knowing his car was safe from careless kids swinging their parents' car doors open was worth the walk. He grabbed his Bible off the passenger seat, got out of his car, and headed slowly towards the main church entrance.

A scowl grew on Jon's face as he imagined the next two hours. By now, he thought, Phillip would be in the middle of his weekly announcements, recycling his stale jokes and reminding members about the need to be on time. Anyone arriving after his reminder would make him a target for Phillip's humor and invite laughter from those already seated. In a few minutes, Phillip would ask someone to pray, and then Steve would begin his lesson. After the lesson, the class would divide into its usual small groups where members would share thoughts about what they learned and make prayer requests about their kids, jobs, parents, pets, or people with cancer. Then they would leave for the worship service, trading stories about their week or debating options for lunch. Everyone would find their usual seats in the sanctuary, sing the same familiar songs, and listen to an entertaining sermon from the pastor. After the service, they would go eat lunch and spend the rest of the day feeling good about themselves for giving two hours of their week to God.

Every week was the same comfortable routine, Jon thought. Maybe that was part of the problem. "Is this all there is?" he wondered as he walked. "Did Jesus die on the Cross so I could spend two hours a week being social and entertained? Is that it?" He thought it was the right question, but the lack of an answer left him feeling empty.

As he approached the church entrance, Jon knew he was in no mood to be around other people. He considered turning around and going home, but his feet carried him closer to the glass double doors. "I'll just keep my mouth shut and figure all this out later," he told himself.

At the main entrance, two familiar volunteers with nametags and smiling faces opened both doors and waited to greet him. The weight of Jon's Bible swung heavily in his hand by his side.

"Good morning!" said both greeters in unison.

Jon acted out a smile and shook one of the volunteer's hands. "Good morning!" he said with complete insincerity and entered the church.

six

The Real Thing

*"Blessed is the man who does not walk in the counsel of the wicked or
stand in the way of sinners or sit in the seat of mockers. But his delight
is in the law of the Lord, and on his law he meditates day and night."*
- Psalm 1:1-2

Jon's steps were filled with purpose as he walked down the long front hallway
of MindShare's corporate office building. He had spent most of his morning in exhaustive and frustrating creative brainstorming sessions with other
junior advertising team members and needed his lunch break. As he passed
fellow employees, Jon noticed their eyes glancing down at the thick black
Book he carried in his hand. Their curious stares made him feel like he was
stealing something. He strode through the lobby, nodded to a smiling security
guard, and pushed the heavy glass door open into the parking lot. A group of
co-workers loitered in the hot sun, just outside the door. Without speaking,
Jon put his head down and quickened his pace towards his car.

"Where you headed, Jonny-boy?" a familiar voice called out behind him.
"A Bible study?"

"Something like that, Brant," said Jon, glancing back over his shoulder.

"Well, say hey to God for me," said Brant, prompting a few chuckles
from those standing with him.

While crass, Brant's words were the first he'd directed at Jon in months,
aside from an occasional snicker as they passed in the hallway. Jon gave a
small wave of his hand without looking back, gripping his Bible tightly. Sweat

from his palm began to wet the leather binding. Switching hands, he wiped his palm on the hip of his khakis and dug his keys from his pocket. Nearing his car, Jon could hear Brant singing in a mocking, overly dramatic tone from across the parking lot.

"*I have decided to follow Jesus!*" sang Brant. "*No turning back, no turning back!*"

The sound of laughter from Brant's lunch-mates floated across the hot asphalt.

"Let it go," Jon told himself, refusing to be distracted. "Just let it go." Opening the door of his white Mazda RX7, he let the heat escape for a moment before plopping into his maroon fabric seat. Noon on a midsummer day in Columbia, South Carolina was not the ideal time to be sitting in a parked car. He turned the engine over, rolled down the windows, and rooted for the air conditioner to provide cool relief.

Situating his Bible on his lap, Jon smiled as he ran his thumb across the shiny gold letters of his name embossed on the cover. Opening its pages, he pulled the thin black ribbon marking his place in the first chapter of James, where he had been reading early that morning over a bowl of cereal. As he began studying the text, a drop of sweat rolled off his nose and fell onto one of the Book's thin pages. "Crap," he said, quickly dabbing the page with his shirt. Blowing on the wavy spot left on the paper, Jon lifted his Bible and let it rest against his steering wheel, safe from dripping sweat as he continued reading.

After a few minutes, the air blowing from the dashboard vents turned cool and began to dry Jon's skin. He moved the Bible back onto his lap and rolled up his windows. As he worked through the first and second chapters in the Book of James, he read each verse once and then again, trying hard to contain each phrase in his memory. But the volume of words seemed to roll through his mind like marbles spilling off a tabletop. Maybe it would help if he read aloud, he thought. In the third chapter, he spoke verses thirteen through eighteen just to hear God's Word in his ears.

> Who is wise and understanding among you? Let them show it by their good life, by deeds done in the humility that comes from wisdom. But if you harbor bitter envy and selfish ambition in your hearts, do not boast about it or deny the truth. Such "wisdom" does not come down from heaven

but is earthly, unspiritual, demonic. For where you have envy and selfish ambition, there you find disorder and every evil practice. But the wisdom that comes from heaven is first of all pure; then peace-loving, considerate, submissive, full of mercy and good fruit, impartial and sincere. Peacemakers who sow in peace reap a harvest of righteousness.

Confused, Jon repeated verse 3:18, "Peacemakers who sow in peace reap a harvest of righteousness." He sat staring at the puzzling words. "What am I supposed to do with that?" he wondered. "I don't even know what that means." Jon read the verse again several more times. "A harvest of righteousness," he repeated out loud. "How can you have a harvest of righteousness?" Jon knew that through his written Word, God was trying to speak to him, to give him direction, confidence, and encouragement. He wanted to understand. But the deeper meaning of some verses often left him scratching his head. He underlined James 3:18 with a black pen, drew a star in the margin, and wrote *harvest* next to the passage. He would come back to it again.

Jon turned down the air conditioning fan on his dashboard. Having finished what he'd planned to study during his lunch break, Jon bowed his head, closed his eyes, and began to pray. "Dear God, please help me understand what I've read today and what you want me to do differently in my life. It doesn't always jump out at me right away, you know? Sometimes it takes me a while to get it, like the whole drinking thing. But you fixed that for me. And I know you want me to keep growing. You've changed me a lot over the last nine months, Lord. But it hasn't been easy sometimes. I need your help, God. My best friend – well, I guess he *used* to be my best friend – makes fun of me and doesn't want to be around me anymore. My wife is frustrated with me and doesn't understand what's happened to me. *I* don't understand what's happened to me sometimes. All I know is that you did something when you saved me. Something in me changed. You healed me and fixed things I didn't even know were broken. And you keep fixing things. I don't want to do the stuff I used to do anymore. And I care about things I didn't used to care about. Nobody really gets that. I've tried to explain it, but they just don't seem to care. Or maybe I just do a crappy job – whoops, sorry – a bad job explaining it. I feel like you're the only friend I've got right now, God. I'd be all alone if it weren't for you and my Bible. Lacey and I don't even have a church to go to, yet. We went to that one for Easter, but she won't go back. And I don't want to go there alone. I need you, God. And I hope that these times we have together reading your Word, during lunch and before work, will help me live the way you want me to. I just wish I could help the people I love and care about find what I've found in you. Please help me with that, God. I love you. Amen."

Jon looked up to see Brant's red Jeep Wrangler turning into the parking lot as people began returning from lunch. "Has it been an hour?" he wondered, checking the clock on the dashboard. His lunch break was over and he hadn't eaten. Moving the black ribbon to his place in James, Jon closed his Bible and turned off the car. "See you tonight," he said and gently laid his Bible on the floor behind the passenger seat.

seven

Unprepared

"The fear of the Lord teaches a man wisdom,
and humility comes before honor."
- Proverbs 15:33

Knowing his Sunday school class had already begun, Jon peered through the small window in the classroom door to be sure no one was praying. Coming in late was bad enough, but interrupting someone's prayer would just be rude. He could see Phillip at the front of the room still sharing news and announcements about class social events, birthdays, Bible studies, and ministry opportunities. Phillip always seemed to enjoy his time in front of the class, though Jon suspected, as did others, that his intended audience was primarily the females in the room. Jon fought off a fleeting temptation to turn around and go back home, before turning the handle slowly and pushing the door open.

Phillip stopped mid-sentence and looked Jon's way. All heads followed.

"Oh, thanks for the reminder, Jon," said Phillip. "Folks, the Single Again class begins promptly at ten o'clock. So members, please try and be on time to welcome our guests." Phillip was obviously pleased with himself as laughter spread across the room at Jon's expense.

Acknowledging the smiles and laughs, Jon waved as if he had won an award and made his way to his usual front-row chair on the far side of the room. He plopped down in his seat and set his Bible on the empty chair next to him. "The *Single Again* class," Jon grumbled to himself. He hated how the name of his Sunday school class branded its members as outcasts from happily married society. "Why don't they just make us wear armbands like the Jews in Nazi Germany, for Pete's sake," thought Jon in disgust as he crossed his right leg over his left. While his advertising influenced imagination began designing *Single Again* armband logos, his eyes drifted up aimlessly to Phillip.

"Jon, would you like to pray for us this morning?" asked Phillip.

Startled to hear his name, Jon answered without thinking. "Um, sure." He quickly tried to shake the outcast analogy from his head as he felt himself rise to his feet in front of his chair. He stood with his back to the class, unprepared for what he was about to do. He'd spent his time driving to church wrestling with his own convictions without resolution or prayer. And now he was being asked to pray publicly. His heart began to race in his chest. "You can do this," Jon told himself, remembering the times he'd done it before. He lowered his head and squeezed his hands together in front of him. His eyes closed so tightly his whole face felt wrapped around them. The room fell awkwardly quiet.

Standing before the class in the darkness of his mind, Jon suddenly felt alone. He knew the kind of prayer everyone expected to hear. But if he said those words, it would just be for show. And that was the problem, wasn't it? He didn't want to just pretend anymore. But Jon knew the next time he truly spoke with God, there was no skipping past all his thoughts from the morning. The prayer that he needed to pray, the one Jon *had* to pray before anything else, was about him and God. But he couldn't do it now, not in front of everyone. He felt trapped. He would just have to make his words sound impersonal. "Just say *we* instead of *me*." Jon took a deep breath. "Here goes...."

eight

For Show

"And when you pray, do not be like the hypocrites, for they love to pray standing in the synagogues and on the street corners to be seen by men. I tell you the truth, they have received their reward in full."

- Matthew 6:5

Phillip adjusted the white and pink Easter Bunny ears on his head as he pointed the projector's remote control at the screen in front of the classroom. He pushed a button on the remote repeatedly, but failed to advance the PowerPoint slides showing on the screen.

"Point it at the projector, not the screen," said Steve, standing in the back of the room.

Phillip pretended the remote in his hand was a gun and aimed it at the projector on the stand next to Steve. He made a noise with his mouth to simulate a gunshot and the next slide appeared on the screen. Phillip blew imaginary smoke from the barrel of his imaginary gun and continued his announcements. "Bond, James Bond," he said, raising one eyebrow. "Anyway, don't forget – as you can see from my bunny ears – Easter is next Sunday, so members make sure to be here early to greet all the visitors. You won't see most of them again until Christmas…." Phillips paused for laughter. "So please be here early to make them feel welcome. And ladies – this one's for you – one week from this coming Friday is LNO, also known as Ladies' Night Out. It's not on Good Friday, but it's still going to be a *good* Friday for you girls! Sorry guys – you're on your own. But ladies, be here at the Family

Life Center at seven o'clock and be ready to par-tay! Actually, I don't know what you girls do. You won't tell me. We think you sit around and talk about us, don't we, guys? But, anyway, I heard you won't want to miss it. And I think Carla is going to be giving her testimony. Is that right Carla? OK. Contact, the always beautiful, Miss Leanne if you have any questions about LNO."

As Jon listened, he wondered if Phillip had a secret life as a cheap night-club comic, somewhere. He was entertaining, if nothing else. Phillip finished his announcements and looked quickly around the room. He had to notice almost everyone trying to avoid eye contact with him. Jon knew that Phillip was looking for someone to pray before Steve began his lesson. He was excited about the prayer he had practiced on the drive to church – just for that purpose – and kept his eyes on Phillip.

Phillip caught Jon's eye. "Jon, would you pray for us, please?"

"Absolutely," said Jon, smiling with confidence. He stood up from his chair, placed his Bible on his seat, and turned to face the class. "Please pray with me," he began. Jon closed his eyes, bowed his head, and clasped his hands in front him. "Almighty God, we worship you and praise your name in this place. We thank you for allowing us to be in your House this morning, dear Lord. God, you know that some of us are here today for different reasons. Some of us are hurting. Some of us may feel lost and are looking for answers. Others may be here to give you thanks and praise for what you're doing in their lives. Still, others may be here just to see friends. But Father God, we pray that your Holy Spirit will convict us and remind us why you called each of us here this morning. Let us be here for you, oh Lord. We pray that we will seek your face this morning, seek your will, your direction, and your grace, oh God. Father, we pray that you will speak through Steve and his lesson. That our hearts will be open to your truth and that we will leave here different than when we came in. Help us to live our lives this week in a way that's pleasing to you, oh God. We pray these things in Jesus' Holy name. Amen."

Jon opened his eyes and smiled to himself as he turned to sit down. He placed his Bible on his lap and watched Steve take his place behind the podium.

"Jon, thank you," said Steve as he organized a stack of papers in front of him. "What a wonderful way to prepare our hearts for today's lesson. I'll be teaching today on Paul's letter to the church in Philippi. My question to you this morning is, 'What does it mean to glorify Christ?'"

As Steve began his lesson, Jon replayed his prayer in his mind. He was happy with how it sounded for the most part, but he was disappointed that he forgot to include a few themes. "Crap," Jon thought, "I forgot to include the part about glorifying Christ. That would have gone perfectly with Steve's lesson. That would have been so cool."

nine

The Question

"Hear my voice when I call, O Lord; be merciful to me and answer me."
- Psalm 27:7

As Jon opened his mouth to pray, he felt like he was being pushed over a cliff. There was no turning back. All that he'd wrestled with on his drive to church flashed quickly through his mind. Had he become a hollow shell of a Christian? A lazy Believer resting on the assurance of his salvation, but doing nothing as a result of it? Was he just wearing the Christian label? Had he abandoned his relationship with God? Still, he reminded himself to avoid making his prayer all about him. "We instead of me," he thought as he began to pray.

"Oh, dear God, we…." Jon felt his voice tremble as he spoke. He hesitated for a moment and fought against the words about to escape from his mouth. "I'm so sorry." Once said, the dam that had formed around Jon's heart – slowly and unnoticed over the years – broke. And he couldn't stop the prayer about to spill into the room. "God, I'm sorry I claim to belong to you, but never talk to you anymore. I'm sorry I don't open your Word and read what you have to say to me, like I used to. I didn't even know where my Bible was this morning, God. I'm sorry I do nothing to serve you, but act like I know you. I don't even know how it got to be like this. After all you've done for me, God…after all you've done for me…." Jon could feel tears flowing from his tightly closed eyes. They dripped off the end of his nose and landed on his hands, locked tightly together before him. "You saved me, dear Lord.

31

You saved my soul and you saved my life. You were there for me when I needed you most. I couldn't have made it without you. And I've forgotten what that means to me. Help me, dear God. I don't want to just play church anymore. I don't want to just pretend. There's got to be more than this. Please help me to see what you want from me. Help me understand why you wanted me to follow you, why you saved me in the first place. *Why am I here?"*

The question hung in the air as Jon fell silent. The sound of sniffing of noses around the room reminded him that there were thirty people listening to every word he said. His morning's private struggle had just gone public. Jon felt totally exposed and ready to sit back down. But he knew he at least had to finish what he started. "Father God, thank you for hearing this prayer. And thank you for bringing us together this morning. Please be with Steve as he leads us in our lesson. In Jesus' name we pray. Amen."

Jon sat down without lifting his head. He opened his blurry eyes, but kept them focused on his hands as he rubbed the tears into his skin. The sounds of shuffling paper, people shifting in their chairs, and a few blowing noses broke the awkward silence of the room. Jon closed his eyes again as he wiped his face with both hands. "What have I done?" he thought to himself.

Steve walked slowly to the wooden podium positioned in front of the class. He placed his Bible and his new iPad on the stand and leaned against it with both hands as he looked at Jon.

"Jon," Steve said, trying to draw Jon's attention.

Jon lifted his head slowly and looked at his teacher.

"Thank you," said Steve with sincerity in his voice.

The right corner of Jon's mouth gave a faint, quick smile as he looked back down. Feeling everyone's eyes on him again, he reached for his Bible and held it tightly with both hands between his knees as he stared at the floor.

"I want you to know that what you just heard was special," Steve told the class. "It's not often that we open ourselves to each other that way and truly pray from our hearts with all honesty and conviction. Jon, I love you, brother."

Jon felt unworthy of Steve's praise. He couldn't accept it, not this morning. Where Jon had enjoyed such comments in the past, he now wished Steve had simply ignored him. He felt the need to escape. He needed to be alone. Jon looked to his left and saw the side door to the classroom just ten feet away. He could get up and leave without walking back across the room. As he waited for the right moment to leave, Jon felt the weight of a hand rest on his right shoulder. He turned around to see a once familiar face leaning forward, offering a reassuring smile.

"Hang in there, Jonny-boy," said Brant, softly.

Jon tried to hide the shock of seeing his former friend in his Sunday school class. He nodded his appreciation and turned quickly forward. It was more than he could handle. Jon stood up, took four long strides to the door, and left the room.

ten

Alone

"Doing wrong is fun for a fool, but living wisely brings pleasure to the sensible."

- *Proverbs 10:23*

Jon sat at his desk inside the gray fabric walls of his office cubical staring at the unfinished ad layout on his computer screen. He placed his left elbow next to his keyboard and rested his chin heavily on the palm of his hand. As he moved his mouse with random direction, his eyes followed the cursor lazily around the screen. Since his last design edit over thirty minutes ago, Jon's mind had been elsewhere. A simple glance at his wife's framed picture on the corner of his desk – a black and white photograph from their wedding day – had sent him into a mental fog where all of his hopes and dreams contended with reality.

"Jonny-boy!" said Brant, leaning his head into Jon's cube.

Jon jumped backward in his chair. "Geez, Brant!"

Brant laughed and stepped into Jon's workspace. "You're too intense man! You need to relax."

"You scared the crap out of me, man," said Jon, trying to recompose himself. "I'm trying to work, here."

"Yeah, sure. I saw you sitting there, all zoned out."

"I was concentrating."

"Whatever, dude. Hey, we're all going down to Harper's for a little pre-Christmas happy hour. Shut that thing off and let's go grab a few cold ones."

"Uh…." Jon tried to think of ways to say *no* as Brant shook his car keys at him. "I don't know if I can make it."

"Very funny," said Brant. "Your little advertising thing can wait. You're coming, OK? I'll even drive us over there. And I'm not taking no for an answer this time." Brant snatched Jon's car keys off his desk and put them in his coat pocket. "Come on, man. You're going. Lacey won't care."

"It's not my wife I'm worried about," said Jon, thinking of his commitment to God.

"Good, then let's go," said Brant. "Come on, I'm thirsty."

Jon looked at Brant's eager face and wished his friend understood his reluctance. He had tried to explain several times before, but couldn't seem to hold his interest. And after ducking Brant's invitations for weeks – happy hours, tailgate parties, boys' nights out – Jon had finally run out of excuses and energy to say no. He stood up and grabbed his leather jacket off the back of his chair. "All right, let's go."

"That's my man!" Brant smiled victoriously as the two men left Jon's cube.

As he walked down the hall with Brant, Jon felt every step pushing him closer to a situation he had committed himself to avoid. Brant grabbed the back of Jon's neck. "Dude, I think half of MindShare is going," he said. "And Chris said that girl, Megan, from purchasing is gonna be there. She's got it bad for you, Jonny-boy!"

"That's another reason I shouldn't be going," said Jon, feeling a new level of stress.

"I must have missed the first one," said Brant with a grin. He opened the door leading to the parking lot and held it for Jon. "Geez, will you lighten up?" he asked as Jon walked by. "What happened to my old roommate?"

Jon stopped just outside the door and turned to face Brant. "That's what I've been trying to tell you for over a month now, Brant."

Brant's smile faded as he studied Jon's serious expression.

"I'm just not the same person I used to be," Jon said. "I'm a *dad*, for Pete's sake. And I want to be a good one. I don't want to drink anymore, and I don't want to hang out in a bar and flirt with someone other than my wife, OK? Why can't you understand that?" Jon turned his back to Brant and began walking in the direction of Brant's Jeep.

"Well, you sure as hell didn't seem to mind flirting with Megan at the Wofford game a few weeks ago! Hell, it wasn't too long ago that *you* were dragging *me* out to happy hour and bragging about how she wouldn't leave you alone every day at work!"

Jon stopped and turned around to see Brant standing right where he had left him. He felt unsure how to respond to the truth in what he was hearing. "Well, that was before I...."

"Before you what, Jon? Became Pope?"

"Ah, come on, Brant," said Jon, taking a few steps back towards him. "I'm not saying I'm perfect or anything. I just can't...it's just that everything's different now, OK? I'm a Christian. Why can't you just give me a break?"

"Because I know you, Jon! I've seen you drunk more times than I can remember. So don't expect me to believe that you're suddenly some saint! You're no different than me, so save it. Let's go." Brant walked past Jon, the keys to his Jeep in his hand.

"Brant, look," said Jon, causing Brant to stop and face him again. "I know it sounds weird and all, but I just want to try and be like what a Christian is supposed to be like. OK?" Jon immediately wished he could have said something more eloquent or profound to describe the change in his life.

"Well, good for you, Jon! But I believe in God and I still drink. Hell, Jesus drank didn't he? What's the big friggin' deal? I don't see why you have to be so *Holier than Thou* about it all of a sudden! Is this why you've been blowing me off for a month? You think you're better than me or something?"

Jon could see Brant was angry. And he became conscious of several other people walking past them in the parking lot. He looked around quickly to see who might be in earshot. Nancie from human resources passed by a short distance away and glanced at them briefly. "*Great,*" Jon thought, wary of the woman's reputation for gossip. He lowered his voice. "Look, I'm sorry I brought it up, OK? I'll go to happy hour. I'll hang out for a while. But just don't ask me to drink, OK? Can we do that?"

Brant studied Jon's face for a long awkward moment.

Jon extended his arms out by his side. "What?"

Brant pulled Jon's car keys from his coat pocket and tossed them at Jon's feet. "Don't do me any favors, pal," he said and walked away.

"Brant! Come on, man! Listen!"

"Later, dude," said Brant over his shoulder. "Go home and read your stupid Bible or something."

Jon watched Brant climb into his Jeep and drive away as he stood alone in the middle of the parking lot.

eleven

The Answer

"The prayer of a righteous man is powerful and effective."
- *James 5:16*

Jon left his Sunday school classroom and closed the door behind him. His immediate desire was to put distance between himself and the people who had just witnessed his soul-baring prayer moments before. He walked quickly down the quiet, carpeted hallway. Were it not for his pride and the windows in each passing classroom door, he would have broken into a full jog down the hall towards the exit.

"Jon!" called a male voice in a loud whisper behind him.

Jon stopped and turned around. His old friend Brant was jogging down the hall after him. It was not something Jon was happy to see, but he forced a half smile onto his face as Brant caught up with him. "Hey, Brant. I'm surprised to see you."

Brant laughed, slightly out of breath, and extended his hand to Jon. "Surprised to see me *here*, you mean," he said, shaking Jon's hand. "It's my first time in Sunday school, but I've visited the worship service a few times. I saw you there a couple weeks ago across the room. How are you, man?"

Jon wasn't sure he knew the answer. He looked back down the hall towards his classroom. "Well, I guess you heard all that a few minutes ago. Things could be better."

"Yeah, about that," said Brant. "Can we talk for a few minutes?"

Jon looked down the hall at the exit door leading to the parking lot. He didn't want to talk with anyone at the moment, particularly Brant. He just wanted to go home. "I'm sorry, I really need to be going." Jon reached out and shook Brant's hand again as he leaned towards the exit.

"Ah, come on, Jon," said Brant, moving with Jon as he backed down the hallway. "We haven't talked in years. Give me just a minute."

"It's really not a good time, Brant. I just need to —"

"One minute. I promise. That's all."

Brant was still as persistent as Jon remembered. Jon stopped before opening the door and sighed. "Just for a minute," he said, "then I have to go."

"Deal. I bet the sanctuary's empty. Want to go in there?"

"I don't think they serve beer in there, Brant, if that's what you're after."

"No problem," said Brant, unfazed by Jon's sarcasm. "That's why I always bring my own beer whenever I come to church." Brant playfully grabbed the back of Jon's neck and patted him on the back. "It's good to see you, man!" he said as they walked towards the sanctuary.

Jon couldn't say the same. "We can go in these doors over here," Jon said, pointing to the large double doors of the sanctuary. He took comfort knowing there would at least be a time limit to their conversation. The beginning of the 11:15 worship service would effectively end whatever it was Brant wanted to discuss. He could endure it until then.

Jon pulled one of the heavy doors open and led Brant down a center aisle dividing rows of black chairs. He turned into a row on his right and made his way to the fourth chair from the aisle. To ensure an empty chair remained between them, he set his Bible on the chair to his left. Brant followed and sat down, placing a new paperback Bible next to Jon's.

Jon looked at Brant's Bible curiously. "So, how have you been, Brant? It's been, what — at least fifteen years, hasn't it? Since I left MindShare?" Jon wasn't particularly interested in the answer. He just wanted to get the conversation started and over with.

"Yeah, I think so. Fifteen years and about twenty pounds ago for me," said Brant, patting his stomach.

"Well, you've still got all that hair. Be thankful for that."

Brant smiled and ran his hand through his thick dirty-blonde hair. "It's turning gray, but at least it's still there. Most of it, anyway." Brant paused for a moment and looked down at the two Bibles between them.

Already growing weary of their forced conversation, Jon sat quietly and waited for Brant to speak.

"Listen, Jon…I wanted to tell you…I'm sorry about what happened with Lacey."

Jon flinched reflexively and turned away from Brant. "Yeah, well," he managed to say.

"What I mean is…."

Jon's curiosity pulled his attention back to Brant's face.

Brant paused as he turned his eyes towards the large white cross hanging behind the main stage. He lowered his head, before looking up to find Jon's eyes. "I'm sorry for being such a bad friend to you back then," he said, a knot shooting up into his throat. "I disowned you. And I'm sorry."

Jon looked down at the Bibles between them and shifted in his seat without responding. Brant's contrition made him uncomfortable. And he wasn't sure if he wanted to discuss a friendship that died a long time ago.

"But Jon, I want you to know that you're the reason I'm here today."

"What, do I owe you money or something?" While Jon's intent was sarcasm, his tone revealed contempt. He could see there was something Brant wanted to say, and he wasn't making it easy for him.

Brant's eyes searched uncomfortably around the sanctuary. "I know it's been a long time since we were friends," he said, "and you've got a right to be short with me." Brant refocused on Jon. "But I've been through a lot myself since we were friends back then. I got married, got divorced, got married, had a kid, got divorced, lost my job. But through everything, I kept thinking of how you were back when we were at MindShare."

"Brant, you *hated* how I was when we were at MindShare."

"I know I did. And I'm sorry about that. I just didn't understand at the time."

"And you're all grown up now? Is that it?"

"Jon, please…just listen for a minute."

The pained look on Brant's face gave Jon a tinge of guilt. Brant's sincerity had taken him by surprise. It certainly wasn't the same Brant he remembered. "I'm sorry," said Jon. "Go ahead."

"Well, it's just that…I watched you and how you handled yourself back then. How you handled the crap I gave you and then how you handled everything with Lacey." Brant looked down at the floor. "I know I never said anything to you at the time. I just didn't know what to say. But then, when I went through my own stuff with Debbie and then Kim, I kept wishing I could be more like you." Brant turned his eyes to Jon. "You seemed to have it all figured out."

"Ha," scoffed Jon. "You heard me this morning, Brant. I don't have anything figured out."

"But that's why I followed you out the door, Jon. You do have it figured out. Or at least you did. I don't know what's got you off track, but you need to know you made a difference in my life. After Kim left me last year and took Jacob, I hit rock bottom, man. It was awful. I went to counseling and everything. But nothing mattered anymore. I got laid-off from my job and was drinking more than ever. I was at the end of my rope. And one night about three months ago, I was in a heap on the floor in my bedroom thinking seriously about killing myself."

"Ah, come on, Brant," said Jon, unwilling to believe what he was hearing. "You don't mean that."

"I'm serious. I was. But I remembered what you told me on your last day at MindShare."

Jon frowned as he tried to remember anything significant about that day.

"I'd heard you were leaving," said Brant, "but I hadn't spoken to you at all in, like, a year or more. But you walked into my office without saying hello or anything and shook my hand and said, 'I'm still praying for you, brother.' And then you just walked out."

The memory flashed through Jon's mind. He remembered walking to Brant's office that day, determined to let his faith shine on him one last time, whether Brant liked it or not. And he remembered praying that Brant would find salvation in Jesus Christ. He remembered caring about Brant's soul, despite the scorn and rejection he'd received from him. And Jon began to remember his relationship with God in those days. How close he felt to him every day. And now, Jon remembered what he'd really been missing. And he desperately wanted it back.

"Jon, I gave my life to Jesus that night on my bedroom floor. He was the only hope I had left. And your prayers are what gave me that hope." Brant reached out and grabbed Jon's shoulder as he smiled. "This morning, in your prayer, you asked God to tell you why you're here. If I had to answer that for him, I'd say you're here so that slobs like me could know what it really means to be a Christian. You showed me that a long time ago, Jon. And it saved my life. I just wanted you to know that."

Jon's head was spinning and his emotions were close to overflowing. On a morning filled with doubt and frustration over his faith, Jon was getting encouragement from the last person he could have imagined. "Brant, I...." Jon couldn't continue. He leaned over, rested his elbows on his knees, and let his head hang from his shoulders. He closed his watery eyes and prayed quietly. "Thank you, dear God. Thank you. Thank you for reminding me of what it used to be like with you. Thank you." It was all Jon could think to say. Feeling overwhelmed, he sat in silence. His eyes still closed, he simply tried to absorb the events of the last hour. After a moment, he took a deep breath and let it out. He leaned back in his chair and wiped the tears from his face with both hands. "Thank you, Brant. You don't know how much I needed to hear that."

"I think I do," said Brant, smiling warmly. The two sat quietly for a moment. Brant looked at his old friend and shifted forward on his chair, putting his hand on Jon's knee. "Come on, man. Let's go get that beer."

A laugh escaped from Jon's mouth. He wasn't quite sure if Brant was serious, but it didn't matter. The laugh felt good, regardless.

"Just kidding, Jonny-boy," said Brant as he rose to his feet. "Seriously, let's get you back to Sunday school."

"You go ahead," said Jon, staying put in his chair. "I need a moment to just...."

"No worries, buddy," said Brant as he moved into the aisle. "We're gonna get together sometime soon, though." Brant walked backwards up the aisle towards the door. "I stuck my phone number in your Bible while you were praying."

"Uh, OK," said Jon. "I'll call you, then. Thanks, man." As he watched Brant leave the sanctuary, he shook his head slowly, back and forth. "Holy cow. That was really Brant."

Now alone in the sanctuary, Jon turned to face the front of the room and gazed at the altar. He leaned forward, bowed his head and prayed. "Dear Heavenly Father, thank you for what you've done for Brant. That just blows me away. It really does. You're just amazing, God. And thank you for using him this morning to encourage me and remind me of who you are. I was feeling pretty useless and lost. But I guess you knew that. This isn't the first time you've put someone in my path and held them up like a mirror in front of me to show me things about myself. Sometimes I just need a whack in the head, I guess. And that's been painful sometimes, but you always know exactly what I need. Thank you for redirecting me when I need it most. I don't know why you love me enough to do that. I've drifted away from you, but you're still there for me, aren't you? Please guide me back to you, God. I want to feel close to you again, like I did before."

Jon could hear people in the sanctuary now. He opened his eyes briefly to see the worship band setting up their instruments on the stage and a few ushers filling the backs of chairs with offering envelopes. Jon closed his eyes and quickly finished his prayer. "Let's talk more when I get home. In Jesus' name, I pray. Amen."

twelve

The Game

"Then out came a woman to meet him, dressed like a prostitute and with crafty intent."
- *Proverbs 7:10*

"Here's your beer, buddy," said Brant, stepping over a cooler and handing a cold can to Jon.

"Thanks, man," said Jon. He slid the can into his favorite Gamecock-themed koozie, popped the aluminum tab, and slurped the foam from the top of the can. Jon had arrived with Brant on the State Fairgrounds parking lot just after lunchtime for the South Carolina-Wofford football game, scheduled to kick-off some six hours later. As the fall afternoon passed slowly by, they'd watched the parking lots around Williams-Brice stadium fill with decorated cars, vans, and sport utility vehicles. Now, as Jon's watch ticked past 4:30, every space was full of garnet and black-clad Gamecock alumni, students, and fans enjoying a homecoming Saturday.

Jon could hear a mix of music and sports talk radio blaring across the grass and dirt field as he surveyed the scene around him. Out of the blue October sky came an errant football, flying in his direction. Instinctively, Jon took two steps backward and trapped the ball against his body with his left arm, careful not to spill the full beer in his right hand. A young boy, wearing a garnet South Carolina jersey several sizes too big, ran towards him with his hands extended.

"Go deep," Jon said to the boy, switching his beer to his left hand and the ball to his right. The boy took off running down the open lane between rows of cars, looking over his shoulder as he watched for Jon's throw. Jon stretched his right arm behind his head and sent the football spiraling through the air, sailing it over the boy's outstretched arms and into the side of a lime green portable toilet.

"Hey!" shouted a woman from inside the port-a-john.

"Sorry!" shouted Jon, laughing at his aim.

"And that's why we lost the intramural championship our senior year," said Brant, stepping over a cooler next to Jon.

"I had a beer in my hand; give me a break. Besides, it's not easy throwing to a kid that short."

"I don't remember beer or children being on the field when you over-threw me in the end zone on the last play of the game. We would've won, been carried off the field like heroes, had all the girls clamoring for us. But no, you had to zing one ten feet over my head. I was wide open, man."

"You would've dropped it, anyway."

"That's probably true," said Brant. "Besides, I like being able to blame you." A group of girls approaching from Brant's right distracted his attention. "Hel-lo," he said, elbowing Jon.

Jon watched the girls, each carrying a red plastic cup, parade by in their black dresses, boots, and large sunglasses without acknowledging Brant's inviting grin. They continued down the row of cars to a group of college-aged boys, crowded under a tent with their fraternity flag flying on a pole overhead.

"What, are we invisible now that we've graduated?" asked Brant.

"We have jobs. We're old men," said Jon. "And one of us is married."

"That's your problem, Jonny-boy," said Brant, patting Jon on the back. "Go see if the burgers are ready, will ya? And crank-up the generator. I want to find the Clemson game on TV."

Just a year out of college, Brant had already become a master at tailgating. During the week leading up to a South Carolina football game, he'd spend hours planning and preparing for the daylong experience. Jon, on the other hand, while still wanting to enjoy the benefits of a well-planned day at the game, was unwilling to invest his own time and resources. As a trade-off, he allowed Brant to treat him as his tailgating assistant.

Jon stepped to the left side of Brant's new red Jeep Wrangler and positioned himself over a small, portable, gas-powered generator. Pulling up on the starting cord as if he were starting his lawn mower, Jon heard the generator whirl to life. "All right, try it," he called out to Brant.

Under the shade of his garnet and black canopy tent, Brant pointed a remote control at a thirty-two inch color television tucked into the back of his Jeep. Brant gave Jon a thumbs-up as the TV powered on. "Go check on the burgers before they burn-up!" said Brant.

Jon grabbed a spatula and paper plate from their folding table and walked around to the front of the Jeep. Lifting the lid from a small Hibachi grill, Jon waived away a plume of smoke from four burned hamburgers. "I think they're done!" he shouted with a laugh. He scooped them off the grill and placed them on the plate in his hand, trying to decide if they were still edible. "They look like hockey pucks," he said to himself. He dumped the burgers back onto the grill and closed the lid. "No burgers today, I guess."

Standing up in front of the Jeep, Jon looked through the windshield to get Brant's attention. A crowd had already begun to form around the TV to watch the Clemson-Wake Forest game. He walked around the Jeep behind the crowd, finding four older women – two of whom he recognized from work – sitting in Brant's beach chairs. The women propped their feet on Brant's coolers as their men huddled around the TV.

"Excuse me," said Jon, motioning for the women to lift their feet off the cooler. He dug a fresh beer from the ice, placed it in his koozie and closed the lid with his foot.

"Can you get me one, too, honey?" one of the women asked, waving her empty hand at Jon.

"Uh, sure," said Jon, thinking she didn't need another. He repeated the process anyway and handed the woman a beer.

"Haven't I seen you before?" she asked, scrunching her face as if she'd bit into a lemon.

Jon tried not to roll his eyes. "We both work at Mindshare."

"That's where I work!" she said, her eyes fixed on the beer in Jon's left hand. "Can I borrow your koozie, sweetie?"

"You mean this one?" Jon looked at his favorite koozie covering his cold beer.

"That one's fine," she said, extending her hand.

Frustrated, but unwilling to be rude to someone who may be important at his new company, Jon obliged, knowing he'd never see his koozie again.

"Thanks, sweetie!" she slurred, returning to conversation with her friends. Jon turned his back to the women as Brant appeared next him.

"You might want to slow down on those," said Brant, pointing to Jon's beer. "Or you're going to owe me some more money for beer."

"I didn't know you were counting," said Jon, taking a sip. "I guess I'm just thirsty today. It's hot out here." Jon turned around and studied the growing crowd behind Brant's Jeep. "Did you tell everyone at MindShare where we'd be tailgating today? This is almost like being at work."

"Relax, Jonny-boy. No one's going to ask you to run an ad or anything. It's a party."

"I don't run ads. I...." Jon started to explain his job when he saw Megan moving through the crowd around their coolers. She took off her sunglasses and made eye contact. Jon felt his chest tighten, as if he'd dropped over the first hill of a roller coaster.

"Hey, Jon!" said Megan, happily, as she inserted herself before him. "I was hoping I'd see you out here today."

Brant made a quick exit and returned to the crowd watching the Clemson game on TV.

"Oh, hey Megan," said Jon, trying to act surprised to see her. But with all the people from work hanging around Brant's Jeep, he suspected she would appear eventually.

"So, how's it going?" she asked, smiling up at Jon.

"Oh, it's...say, have you met my friend Brant? He's right over there. Hey, Brant!" Brant turned from the TV and looked at Jon with a quizzical look on his face. "Have you met Megan Foster?" Jon pointed at Megan. "She works down in the purchasing department. You know, down the back hallway."

"Oh, hey. How's it going," said Brant, with little interest, and turned back towards the television.

Jon didn't want to talk with Megan alone, but Brant wasn't cooperating. "He's a good friend of mine," said Jon. "He and I were roommates in school together and got jobs at the same time with MindShare when we graduated last year. He works in the IT department. Fixing things, I guess."

"Uh-huh," said Megan, watching Jon's mouth as he talked.

"You may have seen him. He's always walking around pushing one of those carts with computer stuff on it. He's a good guy. Really smart, too. About computers, I mean." Jon was rambling. His head suddenly felt light, and he wondered if he was making any sense. He watched Megan sip from her red cup as she listened. "What are you drinking, there?" he asked.

"Bourbon and Coke. My brother made it for me," she said, pointing down the row of cars. "Want some?" Megan held her cup out to Jon.

"Uh, no thanks," said Jon, pointing at his koozie-less Miller Lite can. "Beer. It's not good to mix, you know."

"So, where's your wife?" asked Megan as she set her cup on the folding table next to them.

Jon watched her peel the back off a round, garnet and white, *Beat Wofford* sticker and place it carefully on her short black dress, just above her left breast.

"I'm sorry, what?" asked Jon.

"Where's your wife, today?"

"Oh, um, she's at home with the baby," said Jon as he watched Megan reposition the sticker closer to her cleavage. "Babysitter games get pretty expensive when you have to pay a football for twelve hours."

Megan giggled and looked down at her red cup.

Jon played back what he'd just said and tried to correct himself. "I mean...*football* games are expensive. You know what I mean. Anyway, she — my wife — decided to stay home and just let me go this time. We thought about her coming and leaving me home, but the game's not on TV so that's why she stayed home, and I came with Brant." Jon took a deep breath to fill his empty lungs.

"She's pretty trusting to let you come out by yourself." Megan circled her index finger around the lip of her cup.

"Oh," said Jon, laughing uncomfortably. "She, uh, well, she knows I'm a...," Jon cleared his throat, "a Christian. So, she's got nothing to worry about, you know?" It was the first time Jon had claimed to be a Christian publicly. And he hoped it would keep Megan at bay.

"I thought Christians didn't drink," said Megan, tapping her cup against Jon's beer and smiling.

"Oh. Well," said Jon. He hadn't considered the question before and was unsure of the right response. But it didn't stop him from trying to answer on behalf of all Christianity. "I think as long as we don't do anything wrong while we're drinking, I guess, you know, it's OK."

"Anyway," said Megan, "some friends of mine and I are leaving at half-time to go back to my place for drinks. Why don't you join us? We're going to make margaritas."

Jon wiped the sweat from his forehead and upper lip. He knew he would be in trouble with Lacey for just talking to a girl as cute as Megan, much less going to her apartment for a drink. Jon tried to look disappointed. "Oh, I would, but I'm riding with Brant, you know," he said, relieved to have an excuse.

"He can come, too," she said. Megan looked up at Jon while she sipped her drink through a stirring straw. She took a step closer. "It'll be fun, I promise."

Jon could feel the toe of her black boot between his shoes as her thigh brushed against his jeans. He smelled her perfume as he tilted his beer against his mouth, taking a long drink as he stalled for an answer. He didn't want to offend Megan. He saw her almost every day at work and actually liked how she'd stop by his cube whenever she was in the advertising area. He'd wondered if she might have a crush on him, but he preferred to assume she was just being nice. Maybe it would be OK. These were people he worked with, after all. Nothing's going to happen. And Brant would be there. He would just tell Lacey he was at a MindShare party. Or maybe he just wouldn't tell her.

"So, what do you say?" Megan pressed with a smile. "Come on, say you'll go."

"I'll ask Brant and see if he wants to go," said Jon, hoping Brant would refuse.

"Cool! Tell him I want him to meet my friend Debbie." Megan smiled as she twisted back and forth.

Jon felt trapped and needed room to maneuver. "OK. But if it's a close game and all, you know, Brant's not going to want to leave at halftime. So...."

Jon was now placing his hope in the tiny school of Wofford to save him from what he knew was a bad decision.

"OK. Well...." Megan sounded disappointed with Jon's conditional answer. She glanced at the crowd under Brant's tent then looked up at Jon.

Her sparkling green eyes made Jon feel woozy. He wanted to go. He would just have to be careful, he told himself. "But you know, it'll probably be a blow-out by half-time, so I'm sure we can make it."

"Awesome!" said Megan, bouncing with her answer. She reached inside her black purse and retrieved a pen. "Here's my address." She took Jon's left hand, turned it palm-side up and wrote her address on his skin with a blue ballpoint pen. "And here's my cell phone number, too. Just in case." She added a happy face on Jon's thumb. "See you there!"

"See, ya," said Jon, with a wave of his hand as Megan turned to leave. As she walked away, Jon watched the form of her body sway underneath her tight black dress. He imagined what her apartment would be like. He wondered what her bedroom would be like. He wondered what Megan would be like.

"Jon!" shouted Brant from the crowd surrounding his Jeep.

Startled for a moment, Jon shook his head. "What?"

"What the hell are you doing? Get over here! You gotta see this! Clemson's losing to Wake Forest!"

Jon walked towards the TV as the phone in his pocket began to vibrate. He pulled it out and saw his home number appear on the screen. "Hello?" he said, holding the flip phone to his ear.

"Hey sweetie!" said Lacey. "How's the game?"

"Hey, honey," said Jon, clearing his throat. "We're all just standing around watching the Clemson game on the TV in Brant's Jeep. You're not missing anything." Jon listened to himself as he spoke and wondered if he sounded drunk.

"Brant knows how to tailgate, doesn't he?" asked Lacey.

"I'm sorry, I can't hear you very well," lied Jon, hoping to shorten the conversation. "Lots of noise out here."

"Oh, well. I won't keep you," said Lacey, sounding a bit dejected. "I just wanted to say *hey*."

"OK." Jon was ready to get off the phone.

"Oh, hang on! Your little girl wants to say *hello*."

The crowd around Brant's Jeep cheered as Wake Forest scored against Clemson. Jon put his beer down on the ground next to him and put a finger in his other ear.

"Say *hey* to Daddy," Jon heard Lacey say. "Say *hey* to Daddy."

Holly cooed into the phone.

Jon's eyes glazed over at the sound of his baby girl's voice. "Hey, sweet pea," he said, with a broken smile. "How's my girl? How's my little girl?"

"I just gave her a bath in the sink, so she's happy," said Lacey. "You guys have fun and don't talk to any cute girls! I don't trust that Brant!"

"We will. I mean – we won't." Jon shook his head at himself. "You know what I mean."

Lacey laughed. "I know. We love you! See you when you get home, OK? And go Gamecocks!"

"I love you, too," said Jon, feeling the words as they came out of his mouth. Returning the phone to his pocket, he thought of his little girl at home in his wife's arms and wished he were there with them. He looked at Megan's address and phone number written on his left hand. "What the hell am I doing?" Jon licked his right thumb and rubbed it hard against his left palm until Megan's writing became a blue mess. He leaned his head back and looked up into the clear evening sky. "I'm sorry," he said to God with a heavy sigh.

Dropping his head, Jon saw his beer waiting on the ground next to his right foot. He moved two steps backwards. Stepping forward quickly, he kicked the half-full can down the long row of cars. White foam sprayed along the ground as it rolled to a stop in the dirt.

"It's good!" Brant shouted, holding his arms in the air like an official. "You want another one, Jonny-boy?" he asked, reaching into a cooler.

"No, thanks," said Jon. "I've had enough."

Jon opened his eyes. The morning sun was just beginning to seep through the blinds covering his bedroom window.

"Jon, are you awake?" asked Lacey, laying with her back next to him in their bed. "Jon?"

Jon heard the sounds of Holly crying in her nursery down the hall. "I'm up," he said, dutifully. With his eyes still closed, he swung his legs from underneath the covers and sat up on the edge of the bed as Holly cried impatiently in her crib. He pushed himself off the edge of the bed onto the hardwood floor and stood unsteadily for a moment before letting himself sit down again.

"Jon, she's crying," said Lacey, without lifting her head from her pillow.

"I know, I know," said Jon. He rubbed his hands slowly against his face. "I'm going." Jon stood again and staggered towards the hallway. His head hurt and his eyelids felt swollen as he made his way in his boxer shorts and T-shirt to Holly's room. He found her kicking and squirming under her blanket as she cried.

"Shhhh. Daddy's here," Jon said softly, lifting her from her crib. He cradled her in his left arm, wrapped her snugly in the blanket, and hummed a random tune as he shuffled to the kitchen. Swaying gently back and forth, he opened the refrigerator and found a bottle of baby formula Lacey had already prepared. Shaking it for a moment, he removed the top and warmed it briefly in the microwave. "Are you hungry? Hmm?"

Jon walked Holly into the den and took a seat on the couch, repositioning her on his arm as he held the bottle to her mouth. Adjusting the blanket around her, Jon noticed the smeared blue ink still on the palm of his left hand and a smiley face drawn on his thumb. His strong desire to wash away the unwanted reminder of his encounter with Megan would have to wait for Holly to finish her bottle. Closing his eyes, Jon's mind drifted back to the game the night before. It troubled him to think how easily he'd been tempted. And he wondered how he could have come so close to risking everything he loves. He opened his eyes and looked down at his daughter's soft little face as she sucked contently on her bottle. Jon closed his eyes again and began to pray.

"Dear, God...I'm such an idiot. What was I thinking yesterday? You know I love my little family, God. Why would I risk losing them over the chance to hook up with some flirt from work? I thought when you saved me that I wouldn't want to do stuff like that. But I did – for a moment, anyway. Maybe it was because I was drunk. Not *maybe* – I *know* that was the problem. And if Lacey hadn't called me, I probably...I don't know what stupid thing I would have done. I hope I wouldn't have gone. But it scares the crap out of me to think about it, God. It really does. I want to be the person you want me to be, and I know it's not that guy. God, please help me. I don't ever want to be in that situation again. But I can't just make Megan or every other cute girl on the planet disappear. I know I'm going to see her at work and other places. But that shouldn't matter, should it? I've got to be who I say I am, who you want me to be."

A memory from his conversation with Megan popped into his head. "Geez…I told Megan I was a Christian last night as I stood there with a beer in my hand, half-drunk, flirting with the idea of going to her apartment. What an idiot. Great way to represent you, huh, God? I'm so sorry."

Jon looked down and shook his head. His baby daughter had finished her bottle and was asleep in his arms. As he watched her sleep, he tried to reconcile who he was at the football game with how he felt at that moment. He stroked the soft hair on Holly's head as he continued his conversation with God. "It's like I'm two different people. But this is who I want to be. I'm Holly's dad and Lacey's husband. They deserve better, for Pete's sake. Ugh…I can't believe me. It's the alcohol. I know it is. And I'm going to get myself in trouble if I keep on drinking like I was still in college every time I go out. And then what would I do? I wish it wasn't even a factor. I wish alcohol didn't even exist."

Jon tried to imagine his social life without drinking. But the two were synonymous. It had been that way since he was a freshman in college. "God, everything I do socially revolves around drinking. I don't see how I could just stop." Jon looked down at Holly. "But I'd do anything for this little girl in my arms, God. She needs me to be a good dad. And Lacey needs me to be a good husband. I love her, God. And she deserves better. But I don't see how I can be either of those things if keep acting like I'm still in college. I just don't know what to do. I feel like I'm trapped."

Jon searched his mind for answers. He opened his eyes to Holly and then looked aimlessly around the room while he thought. On the end table next to the couch sat the Bible he had bought for Lacey. The last place he'd seen it was on Lacey's nightstand, where he had left it with hopeful enthusiasm that she may read it. Jon moved Holly gently to his right arm and picked up Lacey's Bible with his left. Setting the Bible on the couch next to him, he pulled the black ribbon bookmark hanging from between its pages and flipped the Book open to the fourth chapter of Philippians. Jon wondered if Lacey had been reading this passage or if it was merely where the ribbon happened to be. Curious, he read from the top of the page.

> Finally, brothers, whatever is true, whatever is noble, whatever is right, whatever is pure, whatever is lovely, whatever is admirable – if anything is excellent or praiseworthy – think about such things.

"He's telling me to think about you, sweet pea," said Jon, smiling at Holly as she slept soundly. "He's sure not talking about me." He continued reading.

> Whatever you have learned or received or heard from me, or seen in me – put it into practice. And the God of peace will be with you. I rejoice greatly in the Lord that at last you have renewed your concern for me. Indeed, you have been concerned, but you had no opportunity to show it. I am not saying this because I am in need, for I have learned to be content whatever the circumstances. I know what it is to be in need, and I know what it is to have plenty. I have learned the secret of being content in any and every situation, whether well fed or hungry, whether living in plenty or in want. I can do everything through him who gives me strength.

"Who is this talking?" Jon wondered. He flipped to the study guide in front of the Book of Philippians, leaving the bookmark in chapter four. "The Apostle Paul," read Jon. He remembered hearing about Paul in Sunday school growing up. Thinking of a real person who lived and struggled just like him seemed to add meaning to the words he read. Jon flipped the pages back to the bookmark and read verses twelve and thirteen again.

> I have learned the secret of being content in any and every situation, whether well fed or hungry, whether living in plenty or in want. I can do everything through him who gives me strength.

"I can do everything through him," Jon said, reading the verse out loud. "*Everything?*" He considered the passage for a moment. He knew God had the power to change his heart. God proved that when Jon had accepted Jesus as his Savior a month before. He knew he was different on the inside. It just wasn't showing much on the outside, yet. Jon took a deep breath and closed his eyes. He had trusted Jesus to save him. Maybe it was time to trust him again.

"God," Jon prayed, "I believe you have the power to do anything you want. Paul said he could do anything through you. Anything. God, I don't want to keep living like I was before you came into my life. It doesn't feel right anymore. I can't live like two different people. There's only one choice and I know what it is. But I need your help, God. I'm asking you now to just take the desire to drink away from me, Lord. Just take it away. I'm weak. I've proven that. I need you to just take the desire away, altogether. I don't know how it's going to work, but I need things to be different. I need to be different. And I believe you want this for me. Please be with me God. Thank you. Amen."

Jon opened his eyes and wrapped both arms under Holly. Her brown eyes slowly opened and met his. A toothless smile crept across her little face.

"Hey little, girl," Jon beamed as a tear of joy ran down his face. "It's your daddy."

thirteen

About Nothing

"Therefore each of you must put off falsehood and speak truthfully to his neighbor, for we are all members of one body. In your anger do not sin."
- Ephesians 4:25-26

The worship service would start in fifteen minutes, but Jon was ready to go home. The morning had been eventful enough. His internal battle over his faith, his open prayer in front of his Sunday school class, and his revealing discussion with Brant had left him emotionally drained. He wanted desperately to be alone. Standing up from his seat in the rear of the sanctuary, he picked up his Bible and made his way to the center aisle. Turning towards the double doors leading to the open area between the sanctuary and education building, Jon saw Phillip entering the room. With nowhere to hide and no interest in another conversation, Jon offered a greeting without slowing down.

"Hey, Phillip."

"Oh, Jon!" said Phillip, reaching out to stop him. "Just the man I was looking for. Your friend, Brent, thought you might still be in here."

"It's Brant," corrected Jon.

"Brant. Got it. Anyway, do you have a moment?"

"Phillip, I really don't right now."

"This won't take but a minute," said Phillip. He placed his hand on Jon's back and turned to walk with him as they entered the lobby.

"Do you need an encore for my opening prayer or something?" asked Jon with a mix of sarcasm and embarrassment.

"That's actually what I was hoping to talk with you about."

"Wow. Seriously, can we do this some other time? I really—"

"Two minutes, I promise," said Phillip. "Come on, there's an open room over here."

Jon sighed and tried to contain his irritation. "Fine."

"Good man."

Phillip guided Jon into a small counseling room with a round table and four folding chairs. Jon took a seat at the table as Phillip closed the glass door.

"I'm sorry about all that in class this morning," Jon offered first, hoping it was all that needed to be said.

"No, Jon. I'm sorry I put you on the spot like that. I didn't even give you time to get settled before I just threw you out there. Please accept my apology."

"Oh, hey, Phillip, it wasn't your fault. I was just going through a lot of...soul searching, I guess, this morning. That's all. You didn't know."

"Well, still. Steve suggested I should come find you. You've always done such a good job praying for us whenever I call on you. You're the one person in the class who can just pray off the top of his head like some preacher or something."

"Oh, wow," said Jon, feeling convicted all over again for seeking glory from his rehearsed prayers. He felt the need to be honest. "Phillip, about that...you should know, I...that was all just...." Jon hesitated as he looked at Phillip's eager face. Maybe he wasn't the right person to trust with that confession, he thought. "I mean...thank you, Phillip."

"Sure, man. I just didn't want you beating yourself up over nothing." Phillip smiled as he rose from his chair.

Jon felt his blood pressure rise, slightly. With no reprieve from an already difficult morning, Jon's emotions lingered close to the surface. "What do you mean by *nothing*, Phillip?"

Phillip sat back down in his chair. "Oh, I didn't mean it like that, Jon. It's all good. I mean, we're all just there to be social and meet other single Believers, right?" Phillip winked conspicuously. "Like I always say, it's the Single *Again* class, not the Single *Forever* class. No sense in taking things too seriously, right? That's why I try and keep it light whenever I can. I mean, the ladies cry enough in small group as it is. Amen? It's like watching *Oprah* in there sometimes!" Phillip laughed at his own joke.

Jon studied Phillip without expression. In him, Jon was seeing what he feared becoming himself – a church club member instead of a Christ follower. No wonder Phillip asked someone else to pray every week. Jon looked down, shook his head, and tried to contain his contempt. "Phillip," he said, afraid of what would come out of his mouth next, "I think it would be best if I just left now." Jon began to stand up.

"Hang on, Jon," said Phillip, standing up with him. "I was just joking around, buddy. I wasn't trying to compare you to the girls or anything just because you cried in front of everybody. So, no harm, no foul, right? We're good?"

Jon's self-restraint finally crumbled. "No, we're *not* good, Phillip! Do you think this is some big *joke*? Did you hear one thing I said in class this morning? Were you listening to my prayer at all?"

"Jon, I was just—"

Jon leaned over the table towards Phillip. "You don't have one stinking clue what that was all about, do you? You think me trying to find God's direction and purpose in my life is taking things too seriously? What's wrong with you?!"

"Whoa, now. Easy, Jon." Phillip held his hands out in front of him as he looked to the door. "Let's just calm down and go out in the—"

"No, you're going to stand right here and listen to this, Phillip! You're just part of the problem around here! You and your little stand-up act every Sunday – it's all *bullshit!* The only reason you even do it is to impress the girls and everyone knows it! Did you ever stop to think that people are hurting or lost when they come in here? Did it ever occur to you – even once – that they need Jesus more than your stupid little jokes? You're supposed to be a class leader, but instead you're just some two-bit stand-up comic in the wrong place!"

"Now wait just a minute, Jon. I'm—"

"No, *you* wait, Phillip!" Jon's heart was racing and his breathing was heavy with anger. "I spent the last two years coming to this class, and this morning it hit me like a ton of bricks – you and this stupid Single Again class do nothing but make it easy to be a lazy, good for nothing, self-absorbed Christian!

Believe me, I know! I'm one of them! You and me and everybody in it, we're all here for the wrong damn reasons!"

"Jon, calm down, man," said Phillip in a low voice. "We're in *church*."

"I'm glad you finally noticed, Phillip!" Jon pushed the chair aside. "I'm wasting my time talking to you. I've got to get out of here." Jon walked out of the counseling room and headed for the church exit. He knew where he needed to go.

fourteen

The Mirror

"Then I will tell them plainly, 'I never knew you.'"
- Matthew 7:23

Jon waited anxiously in the hot August sun. Drops of sweat trickled down his ribs inside his white T-shirt as he paced back and forth outside Oscar Ray's Bar & Grill. Jenny would be there any moment, and he was quickly becoming a sweaty mess. Finding shade around the corner, Jon flapped his shirt around his torso and tried to calm his nerves. "I'm ready…I'm ready," he assured himself. He was in love with Jenny and was ready to tell her so. Since their day-trip to the Isle of Palms two days before, Jon had thought of nothing else. And in a few minutes, he would sit across a table from Jenny and tell her how he felt.

While Jon was sure of his feelings, he couldn't help being somewhat surprised by them. After meeting Jenny in May through mutual friends, he had no plans to ask her out. She was mildly cute, but nothing to get excited about, he remembered telling Brant at the time. But given the opportunity to overcome his initial lack of interest, Jon found her unlike anyone he'd ever met. She even reminded him of Amy. Jenny was genuine, sweet, and cared about people in a way that seemed new to Jon. She didn't drink alcohol or use profanity and he learned to refrain from both when he was around her. It was a welcome change from the fraternity parties, bars, and drunken girls of his first three years at school. Though they had only kissed in nearly three months of dating, Jon didn't mind. It seemed right to him, for some reason. He had even gone with her to church once and to dinner at her parent's house. And Jenny was the first girl he had ever taken home to meet his mother and father. "Being with her makes me feel like a better person," Jon remembered telling his mom.

Jon knew he enjoyed being around Jenny, but sitting next to her on the beach two days before – listening to her share her innermost thoughts about life and her faith in God – he began to feel something deeper. It was an attraction beyond his usual interest in a girl's appearance. Something inside Jenny was too beautiful for words. And now, as he waited for her to arrive for their lunch date, he wondered why it had taken him three months to see it.

Jon looked around the corner and saw Jenny walking up the sidewalk towards him. His heart began to race in his chest. "Oh, my God," he thought. "She's absolutely beautiful."

"Hey!" said Jenny, smiling as she approached. "Sorry I'm late."

"You're not late," said Jon, walking up to meet her. He gave her a hug and kissed her on the cheek. "Are you hungry?"

"Starving," she said as they moved towards the old wooden door of the restaurant. "I ran five miles this morning and haven't eaten anything since."

"Well, let me help you fix that," said Jon opening the door for her. He was surprised to see four people just inside the door, waiting for a table. Jon wasn't expecting the restaurant to be crowded for Saturday lunch. Most students wouldn't be back in town from summer break for two more weeks, but it was full nonetheless. Jon and Jenny waited at the hostess' station for several minutes before finally gaining her attention.

"Just two?" the hostess asked, looking at Jon.

Jon glanced around him. "Was I supposed to bring more?" he asked with clear sarcasm, hoping to make Jenny laugh.

The hostess ignored Jon's attempted humor. "Follow me," she said, grabbing two menus from her stand.

Jenny was trying not to laugh as they followed the hostess to their table. "I can't believe you just said that to her," she said, holding her hand over her mouth.

"She's in high school, for Pete's sake," said Jon without worrying about being heard.

"Katie will be right with you," the hostess said, leaving their menus on the table as she walked away.

"She's at least three years younger than me. Who cares?" asked Jon, smiling at himself as he sat down and picked up his menu. He looked around the crowded restaurant's wood-paneled walls, brown indoor-outdoor carpeting and backwoods shack decor. The whole interior needed a facelift. "I bet Oscar Ray's hasn't changed since it opened twenty years ago."

"I know," said Jenny, looking around the dining room. "My grandmother used to bring me here when I was little. We'd go shopping then come here for lunch. It looks exactly the same. It even smells the same."

As Jenny's eyes bounced around the restaurant, the comfortable smile on her face told Jon how much she enjoyed the memories of her grandmother. "I wouldn't change a thing," he said.

Jenny gave Jon a wink and looked down at her menu.

"My roommate from last semester, Brant, and I came in here all the time last spring."

"To eat?"

"Well, no. Not exactly," said Jon, glancing towards the barroom. "You'll meet him when he comes back to school next week. I told him all about you after we met in May, but he doesn't know we've dated all summer. He's from Orangeburg. I think they put a fence around that town and lock it during the summer. He hasn't been back to Columbia once since he left."

"What are you going to get?" asked Jenny, redirecting Jon's attention to the menu.

"Oh. I'm not sure yet," said Jon. He looked up as the waitress appeared next to their table.

"Hi, I'm Katie," said the waitress. "I'll be taking care of you guys today. Have you had time to look over the menus or do you still need a moment?"

"We can order," said Jenny. She looked at Jon and nodded her head for agreement.

"Sure, go ahead," Jon said. His choice would depend on what Jenny ordered to ensure he had enough money to cover both their lunches. Most of the money he made working part-time at the pharmacy went towards his car, a white Mazda RX7. He had promised his parents he would help make the payments when they agreed to buy it two months ago, leaving him perpetually short on cash.

"Let's see," said Jenny. "I'll have the chicken-fried steak with green beans and mashed potatoes. And sweet tea to drink."

"Chicken-fried steak. OK," said the waitress. "And for you, sir?"

"Oh, and can I have some extra cornbread, too?" asked Jenny. She looked at Jon with a smile. "I told you I was hungry."

The waitress made a note and looked at Jon as he tried to calculate the bill in his head. "I'll just have some fried mozzarella sticks," he said pointing to the appetizer section of the menu.

"And to drink?"

"Um, water's fine, thanks."

"Got it. I'll have that right out for you," Katie said and left for the kitchen.

"Fried cheese and water?" asked Jenny. "Are you on that new kindergarten diet?"

Jon laughed. "No, I'm just not that hungry," he fibbed. "Besides, I seriously doubt you'll eat all of yours."

"I wouldn't bet against me," said Jenny. She unrolled her black cloth napkin, placed it on her lap, and arranged her silverware neatly around where her plate would soon be. "So have you made up your mind about going to see Cam Parsons with me?" she asked.

Jon was afraid Jenny would raise that subject again, but didn't think she'd begin their conversation with it. "Uh, I'm not sure about that, yet," said Jon, hoping to delay his answer once again. "My parents are going, though."

"Oh, really? That's cool!"

"Yeah, they're volunteering through their church to sing in a big choir that sits behind the stage, I think."

"I think that's great!" said Jenny. "So, what about us? Are you going with me?"

Jon leaned back in his chair and crossed his arms. "I don't know, you know?" he said, struggling to give Jenny a straight answer. "I mean there must be something more fun for two college students to do on a Saturday than to go see some evangelist, right?"

"I think it would be fun. Come on, say you'll go with me."

Her persistence had left Jon little room to maneuver. She'd been asking him to go with her for a month, and he had evaded the question each time. With the evangelist's crusade coming to Columbia in just one week, it was time to give her an honest answer. He waited while the waitress placed their drinks on the table. "I kind of don't see the point," Jon said after the waitress left them. "I mean, his sermons are for people who aren't Christians to get them to become Christians, aren't they? So why would someone who's already a Christian want to go? I guess I just don't get that. Seems like a waste of time to me."

Jenny didn't respond beyond the frown she wore on her face. She looked around the restaurant while she sipped her sweet tea through a straw.

The silence felt worse to Jon than Jenny's persistence. He tried to change the subject. "Have you seen that new Nike commercial?" he asked, hoping to steer their conversation to a topic closer to his comfort level. Critiquing commercials gave Jon a chance to show off his growing knowledge of advertising, a degree in which he hoped to earn after just two more semesters.

"Um, I'm not sure," said Jenny, without making eye contact. "You mean the one with the Beatles song?"

"Yeah, isn't that awesome? I wonder how much they had to pay to use that. My professor said they'll sell a ton of shoes, though. I love the active imagery in it. It's just bam-bam-bam! One shot after another. It makes me want to go out and just do something athletic, you know?"

Jenny played with the straw in her glass. "I guess I'll have to pay more attention next time it comes on. I probably changed the channel when I heard the Beatles."

"Oh, I forgot," said Jon, remembering their ongoing debate. "You're the one girl in America who doesn't like the Beatles."

"Not a fan, sorry." Jenny regained her smile, briefly, and glanced up at Jon. "And I assure you, there are more of me than you think."

"Maybe you could be president of the Beatles' Anti-Fan Club."

"If there was one, I would be," Jenny promised. "Besides, I'd rather listen to Steve Camp or Ray Boltz or Amy Grant, any day."

"OK, you lost me," said Jon. "Who are those people?"

"They're Christian artists, silly." She smiled at Jon as if he should know better.

"Oh, right, duh. A guy in my dorm likes that stuff, believe it or not."

"Why is that so hard to believe?"

"Oh, well, you know. It's not exactly *fun* music," said Jon, making quotation marks in the air with his fingers. "I mean, it's fine for church and all, I guess, but not for hanging out. We pretty much shout him down whenever he tries to listen to it on the hall." Jon laughed to himself, thinking of the last time it happened.

"So, if we were in the car and I wanted to listen to Christian music, you'd tell me to put on something else?"

"Of course not. That's different."

"How is that different?" asked Jenny, her eyes trained on Jon's face.

"Well, you're a girl, for one thing." Jon felt a bit cornered, but he quickly saw his way out. "And you're my girl, for another."

"And it's not manly for a guy to listen to Christian music, is that what you're saying?" Jenny was apparently unmoved by Jon's appeal to their relationship.

"I hadn't thought about it like that, but I guess not. It's just not something most guys do, particularly in a college dorm with a bunch of other guys around, for Pete's sake."

Jenny sat quietly for a moment, looking around the restaurant. The burdened expression on her face was one Jon hadn't seen before. She couldn't be that upset about his taste in music. Maybe she was just hungry.

"Jon, can I ask you a question?"

"You just did," Jon replied quickly, grinning at his own joke.

"Ha-ha, very funny. I'm serious." Jenny pulled several strands of blonde hair away from her tanned face and tucked them behind her left ear. Her freckled cheeks and nose were still pink from their day at the beach.

"Of course you can. I hereby grant you one question," said Jon, waving his hand over the table. He was relieved to see a server heading towards their table carrying two plates of food.

"Chicken-fried steak, green beans, and mashed potatoes?" the man asked, looking at Jon.

"That's me," said Jenny, raising her hand. She studied her food as the server set her plate on the table.

"And a fried cheese appetizer for the gentleman." The server placed Jon's lunch in front of him. "Enjoy."

"That's a lot of food for such a little girl," joked Jon as he felt his empty stomach rumble.

Jenny rested her hands in her lap. "Are you sure you're not hungry? Seriously, you can have some of mine if you want."

"I'm fine," said Jon, picking up his fork. Despite his hunger, he knew to wait a moment before starting to eat. He watched Jenny bow her head and close her eyes. Jon remained still to avoid making noise while Jenny prayed over her food. When she looked up, he reached for his knife and cut off a piece of fried cheese. "So, what's the question?"

"OK, I want to ask you," said Jenny, "do you see yourself as a Christian?" She tilted her head slightly as she looked at Jon.

The question caught Jon off guard. Talking about Christian music or Cam Parsons was one thing, but this was the first time Jenny had directed the subject of religion squarely at him. Jon held up his index finger as he finished chewing the bite of cheese in his mouth, using his manners as an excuse while he prepared an answer. "Well, yeah, of course. I guess," he said, hoping it would satisfy her reason for asking. Once again, he tried to change the subject. "What time are you meeting your mom at the mall?"

Jenny rearranged a few green beans on her plate with her fork. "So what is it, do you think, that makes you a Christian?" she asked, ignoring Jon's diversion.

"That's two questions," said Jon, hoping to escape the subject on a technicality.

Jenny gave a brief grin and sat waiting for an answer.

Jon sighed, realizing she was not giving up. He stared at the tropical fish in the large tank behind Jenny's shoulder as he thought of possible answers. "What is it that makes me a Christian?" he asked, stalling.

"Mmhmm, I'm curious."

The question left him feeling mildly inadequate. "I don't know," he finally replied. "I mean, that's like asking, 'What makes you think you're a guy?' You know? I just am." He hoped Jenny would laugh with him over his analogy.

"So…you're a Christian, but you can't explain why you're a Christian."

The disappointment in Jenny's voice made Jon want to try again. He tried to appear more serious. "Um, I guess it's because my parents are, you know?

They took me to church growing up and all. I remember sitting in church with my mom and dad ever since I was little. I guess I've just always seen myself that way."

"But don't you think there's more to it than that, Jon?"

"More to what?"

"More to being a Christian than just saying you go to church or that you were raised that way?" Jenny seemed to know the answer to her own questions. Her eyes were serious and penetrating; her voice was filled with intention. "What about Jesus?"

Jon felt his defenses go up. "Jenny, look, if you are talking about being one of those born-again Jesus types who wear fake smiles all the time, I'm sorry – that's just not me. I don't want to be like that, OK?" Jon picked up a piece of fried cheese with his fingers and stuffed it in his mouth.

Jenny looked at Jon carefully for a moment. She lowered her eyes as she fumbled with the napkin in her lap and forced a sad smile onto her face. "I don't think you'll ever be like that, Jon," she said without looking up.

Jon could tell by Jenny's reaction that he had pushed back a little harder than he should have. And the fact that his lunch date with her was spiraling downhill was suddenly obvious. He forced the cheese in his mouth down his throat with a drink of water. "Hey, I'm sorry if that sounded ugly. Is this about the whole Cam Parsons thing? Because if it is, I'll go, OK? I promise. I'll even wear a cowboy hat in his honor." Jon looked for the hint of a smile on Jenny's face, but couldn't find one. She sat quietly across the table, scraping the white gravy off her chicken-fried steak. He hoped his offer had settled the issue and welcomed the pause in conversation. Going to the crusade wouldn't be so bad. At least he'd be with Jenny. He studied her soft features as she toyed with her food. Their conversation had distracted him from his real purpose for asking her to lunch. He had almost forgotten. But was it the right time to tell her how he felt? Given the holes he kept digging himself into ever since they sat down, maybe it was the perfect time. A smile grew across his face as he thought of the words to say. And he was sure she'd be happy to hear them.

"Jenny," he said, breaking the silence. "I've been doing a lot of thinking and—"

"Jon, I don't think we should see each other anymore."

Jon's mouth hung open. The remnants of a smile still pushed against his cheeks. "I'm sorry – what?" he asked, almost laughing. "You don't what?"

Jenny set her fork down on the side of her plate. "I don't think it's God's will for us to be together."

Jon studied the stoic expression on Jenny's face, trying to make sense of what he was hearing. The words he had wanted to say, just seconds ago, still floated through his head. "Jenny, what are you talking about?"

"I'm sorry, Jon, but that's how I feel. I can't see you anymore."

"That's it? *I'm sorry, Jon?*" he asked in a slightly raised voice. Jon's face flushed with embarrassment and confusion. He looked around the restaurant at people eating and tried to gather himself. Leaning over his plate, he lowered his voice. "Jenny, what's wrong? Talk to me."

Jenny tried to avoid eye contact. "I think it would be better if we didn't talk about it, Jon."

Jon leaned back in his chair and stared at Jenny in disbelief. Her words replayed in his head. "Look, Jenny, you tell me all of a sudden that God doesn't want you to be with me. I think one of the two of you owes me some kind of explanation!"

"Jon, please," said Jenny. "I just…."

Jon waited for Jenny to finish her sentence, but nothing else came. Trying to calm himself, he took a deep breath and let it out. If she really felt that way, he realized arguing with her wasn't going to help. "Jenny," he said in a softer voice. He slid his open right hand across the table. Jenny kept her hands in her lap. "Hey, I'm sorry if I didn't take what you were asking seriously. But it's not worth breaking-up over, is it? Whatever's going on, we can work it out. Just give me a chance." Jon pulled his hand back. "Isn't that the Christian thing to do?" he asked, hoping to use her faith to his advantage.

Jenny straightened in her chair and looked directly at Jon. "The *Christian* thing to do is to be obedient to God, Jon. And I don't think he wants me to be with someone who doesn't share my faith." Jenny seemed startled by her own words. She paused for a moment, her eyes darting around Jon's face.

Jon shrunk back in his chair. He knew Jenny was strong in her faith. It was one of the things he loved about her. But now, that very faith seemed to be the reason he couldn't be with her. It seemed like a cruel joke. And he couldn't hide the hurt on his face.

"Jon, look, I've struggled with this over the last month or so. I really have. I've prayed and prayed about it. I've even talked to my mom about it."

"You talked to your *mom* about it?" asked Jon, adding embarrassment to the hurt he was feeling. He looked away from Jenny and was about to concede defeat.

"Jon, listen to me. I have...I have feelings for you. I do."

Jon's head turned quickly back towards Jenny. Her eyes softened as he searched for a glimmer of hope.

"I know this hurts, Jon. It hurts me, too. But I have to do what God leads me to do and what his Word says. I'm sorry."

Above everything else, Jon heard Jenny say she had feelings for him. He couldn't lose her now. If his faith was the issue, he could fix that. "Jenny, I can change. I'll go to church. I'll go to your Bible study with you. I'll go to see Cam Parsons. I'll do whatever you want, OK?"

Jenny looked at Jon calmly, unmoved by his offer. "Jon, I'm glad to hear that you would do all that. I really am. But I'm not the reason you should want to do those things. That has to be between you and God. I'm sorry. I'll still pray for you, and I hope one day you'll understand." Jenny looked to the floor around both sides of her chair. "I need to go," she said. Finding her purse hanging on the back of her chair, she hooked it with her thumb and put it on her shoulder.

As Jenny prepared to leave, Jon's head swam in a pool of confusion.

"I'm sorry, Jon," she said, looking into his glazed eyes.

Jon knew he had only one thing left to say. "Jenny, I'm in love with you."

Jenny froze in her chair.

Jon looked into her wide-open green eyes and leaned instinctively across the small wooden table. He drew himself close to her face and closed his eyes. She let him kiss her softly on her lips. Jon's head spun as he opened his eyes and sank back to his seat, hoping he had just changed everything. He watched Jenny push her chair away from the table and place her napkin next to her plate. She stood up and walked quickly, her head down, through the maze of tables and out the front door.

Jon covered his face with his hands and tried to understand what had just happened.

"Are you still working on your mozzarella sticks or can I take this?" asked the waitress.

Jon pulled his hands from his face, exasperated with the woman's timing. He looked at the back of Jenny's empty chair. "I'm through," he said.

The waitress picked up his plate. "Is she coming back, hon?" she asked, pointing to Jenny's plate of uneaten food.

"No, she's not."

The waitress tore Jon's check from her pad and placed it on the table. "They'll take this up front or at the bar whenever you're ready, sweetie."

Jon looked around the restaurant at people enjoying their lunches – laughing and talking – clueless to what had just happened to him. But he felt no rush to leave. When he walked out the door, the world would look very different than it did just an hour ago. And he wasn't ready to face it.

Jon closed his eyes. As he played back his conversation with Jenny, his pain turned slowly to anger. Jenny did what she believed God wanted her to do. He could respect that at some level, even if he disagreed with it. It was God who had taken sides against him. "I guess I'm not good enough to date a real Christian, huh, God?" Jon said in mocking prayer. He threw his napkin onto the table. "Screw it." He was ready to leave.

Jon rose from his table and walked slowly into the barroom to pay his check. A familiar face behind the bar greeted him as he approached the dark wood counter.

"Hey, man," said the bartender with a smile. "Haven't seen you or your buddy in here in a while."

"Yeah, um…summer. You know." Jon slid the tab and his last fifteen dollars across the bar. "I'm sure we'll be back when school starts."

The bartender counted Jon's change and placed it on the bar in front of him. "Seventy-two cents. Come back and see us, man."

Jon nodded and stuffed the coins in his pocket without worrying about a tip. He made his way out the door and walked slowly down the sidewalk to his car, parked a half block down the street. Coming to his RX7, he looked down at the rear bumper and stared at the burnt-orange *Cam Parsons Crusade* sticker Jenny had placed there before their trip to the beach. Wedging his fingernail under a corner of the sticker, he pulled it off in one ripping motion, rolled it into a tight ball, and tossed it in the gutter.

fifteen

Sanctuary

"The Lord came and stood there, calling as at the other times, 'Samuel! Samuel!' Then Samuel said, 'Speak, for your servant is listening.'"
- *1 Samuel 3:10*

Jon stepped into the garden tub in his master bathroom and lowered himself slowly into the clear hot water. A sense of relief consumed him as the heat surrounded his body. The sound of the water moving in the tub echoed around the room as he shifted his weight to get comfortable. As he became still, the room grew quiet. He could hear birds chirping in his yard and an occasional car pass by his house. Elvis was outside and Jon hoped he would want to stay there for a while.

It had been an emotional Sunday morning. Jon had beaten himself up on the way to church for ignoring his faith, confessed as much in front of everyone in his Sunday school class, and then received encouragement from the most improbable source imaginable. He had topped it off by losing his temper with Phillip. But now, Jon was exactly where he needed to be. He sighed deeply, closed his eyes, and prayed.

"Dear Heavenly Father, it seems like it's been a long time since I've sat here in this tub and talked to you. I guess that's because it *has* been a long time. This used to be where we talked every morning after breakfast. I miss that. I don't know when that stopped." Jon tested his memory. "Maybe it stopped when I started going to the gym before work a few years ago, instead of spending time with you. I told myself I'd find other time to pray and stuff,

71

but I guess that didn't happen, did it? Maybe that's when I started drifting away from you, started pretending to be your follower instead of being one. I guess I just wanted to stay in shape in case I met someone."

Jon laughed and shook his head. "Like *that's* going to happen. It's just that, Holly's been after me to date more since I moved mom out to the nursing home. That's why I started going to the singles Sunday school class in the first place. I don't know…it probably goes back further than just the last couple of years. I don't know when I stopped caring about you and seeking you. At some point everything just kind of got comfortable. I mean, my career is good, the house is good, Holly's doing fine…everything's good. It's been that way for years. I guess, maybe…that's why I stopped needing you. I hate to say that. You were there for me in the tough times, but I think I've put you on a shelf when things are good. I'm sorry, God. I'm sorry for neglecting you."

Jon let his thoughts settle for a moment. It was hard to offer a specific apology for something that happened so gradually over the years, one little compromise at a time.

"I just ask that you forgive me, God. Please restore my relationship with you. I want to feel you in my life again. And I'm sorry about how I talked to Phillip today. I don't know if all of what I said was wrong, but I know how I said it was. I just lost my temper with him. Plain and simple. I just…I cussed in your House, too. Ugh. I can't believe I did that. I'm so sorry, God. And I know I need to apologize to Phillip, too. Please forgive me for all this, God. What a morning, huh?"

As Jon let his body soak in the hot water, he began to enjoy a sense of comfort as he trusted in God's grace. He felt renewed, even excited about his faith. His mind drifted to his conversation with Brant in the sanctuary. "God, I'm so thankful that you reminded me this morning of the time when you were all I had. Those first few years after I was saved, I leaned on you so hard. And you were there for me. You helped me through it all. But I never knew that you used me to make a difference with Brant. That just blows my mind. He said my prayers gave him hope and brought him to you. That's just amazing to me. It humbles me to know that you heard my prayers for him and used me as part of your will to save him. I've never felt like I was much of a witness for you. That's always been a problem for me. But maybe you've used me in ways I don't even know about."

Jon waved his hands slowly to stir the water around him. He thought about how God, the Creator of the Universe, had used him to help bring someone into an eternal relationship with him. It gave him a sense of purpose and fulfillment. It all started to make sense. "God, I asked you this morning to tell me why you saved me. What was the purpose for my faith? And I think you gave me the answer. Maybe that's the reason — to bring others to you. You're probably going, '*Duh, Jon,*' right now, aren't you? I know your Word says that we should witness to others, but how many Believers really do what we're supposed to do with that, you know? I guess that's what I was on Phillip about. Everything we do at church just seems so self-serving sometimes — like it exists to serve us instead of us serving you. I don't know why I didn't see that before. It feels like I'm just part of some big comfortable club. I know there should be more to following you than that."

Jon began to consider the responsibility he had just grasped. It was easy to be critical of other Believers for not sharing their faith. But what about him? He suddenly felt pressured by his own words.

"I'd like to be able to reach people, God. But I just don't know how being a witness for you fits with everything else in my life, right now. I mean, I've been raising Holly and taking care of mom. And dad, too, before he passed away. I go to work, go to the gym, go to church, pay bills, take care of the house and the yard. It's hard to see how I could have time to be doing anything more. Plus, I see the same people every day. I bet between work and church and the gym, I probably interact with the same nine or ten, maybe twelve, people every week. My world has gotten pretty small. I don't know how I could make much of a difference for you right now, even if I tried. I mean, how could I? Work takes up most of my time. And it's not like I have a choice about that. There's the house and the car to pay for. And Holly's in college. All that's expensive. I would love to reach people for you — people like Brant — but I'm kind of trapped in the life I'm in, right now."

As Jon rambled on in prayer, an uneasy feeling of guilt began to replace the joy he had experienced just moments ago. He knew he was making excuses to God. Everything he said was true, but they were excuses, nonetheless. If he was going to make a difference for Christ, something had to change. He sighed and let his body slide deeper into the hot water. "God, what do you want me to do?" he asked, looking up at the ceiling. "How can I serve you?"

Jon stopped talking and tried to stop thinking. In the stillness, he closed his eyes and just listened. He could feel his heart beat calmly in his chest. The water around him rose and fell slightly, in rhythm with his shallow breathing. After a morning of doubt and turmoil, Jon found peace in the moment. And waited.

"Go quickly," Jon heard a voice say inside his head.

Jon's eyes popped open as he held himself motionless in the water. "Was that you, God?" he asked fearfully, looking up at the ceiling. He waited for something else, anything. But nothing came. "Go quickly," Jon repeated, out loud. "Go quickly and do what?" He pushed himself upright, spilling water onto the tile floor, and reached for the towel hanging above his head. He dried his hands and picked up his iPhone from the bench next to the tub. Opening his Bible app, he quickly searched for the words *go quickly*. At the top of the results, he read Matthew 28:7, "Then go quickly and tell his disciples: 'He has risen from the dead and is going ahead of you into Galilee. There you will see him.' Now I have told you."

A chill ran through Jon's body as he sat in the tub of hot water. Could God be talking to him? For several minutes, Jon stared blankly at the wall before him. He knew what the verse meant. He remembered hearing it that first Easter after becoming a Christian, almost twenty years ago, when he took Lacey to church with him for the first time. He sat next to his young wife, hoping she was listening to the story of Jesus' resurrection. But now, it seemed God was speaking the same verse directly to him. And the angel's message to the women at the tomb was the same message for him: Don't wait to share the Good News of Jesus with those who desperately need to hear it. He couldn't ignore the sense of urgency in the verse. *Do it now.*

Jon struggled to comprehend what was happening. He had asked God an open-ended question and had his answer. And he understood what he believed God was telling him to do. But now, an unforeseen decision hovered like the humid air over his bath. Jon could move forward in faith and see where God would lead him. Or he could get out of the tub and try to forget the morning had ever happened. One path was unknown. The other was terribly familiar. And he had reason to fear both.

"God, if my faith is ever going to mean anything...." Jon looked down and saw his face reflected in the water. His wrinkled brow, searching eyes and firm jaw told him where his heart was. "I can't go backwards. But....." Jon thought about the obstacles – the excuses – that kept him from devoting his time and energy to reaching others for Christ. His work, his bills, his house. "How God? You're going to have to show me. I want to be yours. I want to serve you. I think you want that. But, just show me how."

The water had begun to cool. Jon reached forward and turned the brass handle above his feet. A wide sheet of hot clear water poured from the water-fall faucet, surrounding his body in warmth. He splashed the sweat from his face and leaned against the side of the tub, crossing his legs before him. His excuses recycled through his mind. Work...bills...his house. Suddenly, Jon felt the weight of those seemingly insurmountable burdens vanish. He turned off the water. "I could ask for an unpaid leave of absence from work," Jon thought, assessing the possibility. "I could do that. It's company policy. I could ask for six months. And then I'd be free to go wherever God leads me and be a witness for Christ." Jon could feel his heart thump strongly in his chest. "My vacation time could cover some of it. And I can take a loan from my 401k to keep things paid for." His mind was racing. "Holly could live here while I'm gone and take care of Elvis. She'd do that for me, I think. It's her dog, anyway. And she could look after Mom, too."

In a matter of minutes, Jon's excuses had been replaced with resolve and purpose. What had seemed unthinkable now seemed obvious. He looked up at the ceiling as he prayed once again. "Dear God, this all sounds crazy. It *is* crazy...it is. But I feel you leading me. I heard your voice. I know it was you, God. And I read your Word. I know it was you. I'd never come up with this on my own in a million years. It sounds insane, but...." Jon's face dripped with sweat as his body began to tremble. He took a deep breath and prepared himself for what he was about to say.

"Lord God, I have no idea what you have planned for me, but I commit myself to you, right here and now in this bathtub, to be a witness for you. To share the Good News of Jesus Christ with people who need to hear it. I feel like you're calling me to do that, Lord. But you know that's not my strong suit. You and I both know that. I've failed at it. So, you must have some reason for calling me that I can't see. Oh, God...I'm excited and scared to death, all at the same time. I pray that you'll show me what you want me to do and guide me in your path. Just use me, dear Lord. Use me to reach others for Jesus, so that you can save them like you saved me. I *know* that's what you want me to do. Please teach me to be your servant and a witness for you, Lord. I pray this in Jesus' Holy and precious name. Amen."

Jon slowly opened his eyes and drifted into a stupor, gazing at the bathroom wallpaper. His life had just changed while taking a bath. It almost seemed funny. His job, his relationships, his priorities, his future…he had put them in God's hands. And when he climbed out of the tub, he'd be stepping into a life he didn't know. But he knew he would be OK.

Leaning back against the slanted end of the tub, Jon held his breath, closed his eyes, and slid his whole body under water. Finding each side of the tub with his hands, he lifted himself up again and rose to his feet, pushing his wet hair away from his face. Warm water ran off his skin and splashed loudly into the full tub. Reaching for his towel, Jon saw himself in the large mirror hanging over the bathroom sinks. He shook his head and smiled at his reflection. "Well…you asked."

sixteen

The Lunch Girl

"See, I am setting before you today a blessing and a curse"

- Deuteronomy 11:26

Jon sat at the bar in Oscar Ray's, smiling his way through a daydream. In his mind, he was back on the golf course earlier in the afternoon. He imagined the feel of his careful backswing, winding his driver behind his head so far he could see the copper-colored titanium club-head out of the corner of his left eye. At the apex of his backswing, his body unleashed all its stored energy, rotating his hips and torso while his arms swung the club in a perfect circle, touching nothing but the small white ball resting on the tee before him. When he turned his head and found his ball high in the blue sky, he knew. His arms lifted into the air in triumph.

"Earth to Jon," said Brant, over the noise in the bar.

"Huh?" said Jon, his mind jolted back to the present.

Brant held up his empty beer bottle in front of Jon. "I said, 'Are you ready?' I need another one."

Jon looked down the crowded bar at the only bartender working. "By the time you get that guy's attention, I will be." Jon set his beer down on the bar and held his index finger and thumb an inch apart in front of Brant's face. "I was *this* close to making eagle today."

Brant stretched his arms wide across the bar. "No, you were *this* close. And you ended up with a bogey. You choked."

"Still, did you see that tee shot?" Jon swept his hand across the bar. "All the way across the water, right onto the green! I can't believe I cut that corner. It must have been three hundred yards, at least!"

"For the last time: Yes, I saw it. I also saw the other hundred and fifty swings you took today. Including the ten it took you to get out of the woods on that par three. I don't hear you talking about those, do I?"

"Like I said, all it takes is one good swing, and I'm good for the day. I can say I had a putt for an eagle. Can you say that? Who cares about the other hundred strokes?"

"Hundred and fifty," said Brant.

"Fine. A hundred and fifty. Who cares?"

"Well, when we're playing for money against two old guys who play every day, I do."

"So, we lost a few bucks. It was worth it, wasn't it? What an awesome day."

"Yeah," said Brant, peeling the label off his empty beer bottle. "Awesome."

"I just hope Dr. Feldman's in a forgiving mood tomorrow," said Jon. "What are we going to tell him?"

"We'll just tell him the truth," said Brant.

"What? That we skipped our exam to go play golf? Are you insane?"

"It's a religion class, isn't it?" asked Brant. "I bet he'll appreciate our honesty."

Jon shook his head and laughed. "This is what happens when you drink all day."

"Look, we'll tell him it was my idea," said Brant. "He likes me better than you, anyway."

"Brant, it *was* your idea. And no, he doesn't."

"He does, too." Brant waved his hand to get the bartender's attention.

"No, he doesn't." Jon sipped his beer and watched the bartender serving drinks at the other end of the bar. "That guy doesn't see you."

"He will," said Brant, extending his arm across the bar.

"Oh, so get this," said Jon. "I met this girl when we were in Charleston last weekend for that Kappa Delta party."

"And you didn't tell your roommate? What gives, man?"

"No, that's just it. There wasn't anything to tell. She was a friend of Keller's girlfriend, what's-her-name. Anyway, she just walked up as I was talking to them, and they introduced us."

"So what? You slept with her, is that it? Big news." Brant extended his arm further across the bar and waved two fingers at the bartender. "I know that guy sees me."

"No, I didn't sleep with her," said Jon, unsure if he had Brant's attention. "I forgot about her two minutes after we met."

Brant waved a five-dollar bill in the air over the bar. "So, why are we talking about her now?"

"Because she called me yesterday out of nowhere and asked me to lunch. She got our number from Keller."

Brant lifted himself off his barstool and leaned over the bar on his elbows to make himself more visible to the bartender. "Lunch?" he asked, looking back at Jon. "Who cares about lunch?"

"Exactly! But I was like, 'Uh, sure, OK.' I didn't know what else to say." Jon took a long swig from his beer, trying to catch up with Brant.

The bartender had finally acknowledged Brant's presence and set a pair of cold Miller Lite bottles in front of them on the dark wooden bar. Brant tilted his new beer between his lips for several seconds, set it back on the bar, and burped. "You're such a wuss," he said, wiping his mouth with his sleeve. "What's this lunch girl like, anyway? Hey, maybe she likes nooners." Brant laughed and took another drink.

"Does your mind always go there? Anyway, I seriously doubt it. What's-her-face – Keller's girlfriend – introduced her as a friend from church."

"Church?! Maybe she wants to save you, Jonny-boy!"

"Yeah, like I need that. No, my point is that it's not fair. If I wanted to go out with her, I would have asked her. That's how it's supposed to work, right? She's not even that cute. I mean, she's OK. But now I have to buy lunch for someone I don't give a rip about seeing. Besides, the semester's almost over. It's too late to start dating anyone before summer break, anyway."

"Well, what's so bad about her? Does she only have one leg or something?"

"That's your standard? As long as they have two legs you're good. Is that it?"

"Well, that and a—"

"I'm closing out," said the bartender. "You guys want another round?"

"Nah, we're good," said Jon, holding up his full beer.

"We'll take two more," said Brant, before turning back to Jon. "Look, I don't see what the big deal is. If you don't want to go out with her, just stand her up. Leave her hanging and she'll leave you alone."

"Yeah, I thought about that. But then I'd hear about it from Keller's girlfriend. And she does have a lot of good-looking friends, you know. I don't want her to think I'm a jerk or something."

"For the record, you *are* a jerk," said Brant, tilting his beer to his mouth.

"Oh, thanks."

"But so am I. So that makes it OK." Brant finished his beer in one long swig and set the empty bottle loudly on the bar as the bartender brought two more. "And her name's Kim, you dolt."

"Who?" asked Jon, distracted with the thought of his lunch date.

"Keller's girlfriend! Jesus, pay attention!"

"Whatever," said Jon. He held his beer up to his lips as he stared past the rows of half empty liquor bottles on glass shelves behind the bar. "She does seem nice, though."

"Who? Kim? Yeah, I guess. A little whiny, for my taste. I don't know how Keller puts up with that crap."

"No, you idiot – Jenny," said Jon. "The lunch girl's name is Jenny."

seventeen

Amends

"For this reason I remind you to fan into flame the gift of God, which is in you through the laying on of my hands. For God did not give us a spirit of timidity, but a spirit of power, of love and of self-discipline."
- *2 Timothy 1:6-7*

Jon sat on a padded bench outside a small counseling room – the same room in which he had yelled at Phillip three days earlier – watching people mill about in the common area between the church's education wing and the sanctuary. Most carried Bibles. Some seemed to be waiting for someone or something. Others passed through the area with purposeful direction. Jon wondered if the Wednesday night Bible study he attended six months earlier was still meeting regularly upstairs. He thought of the men in the group and the struggles they had shared openly. Jon had shared nothing. And he began to regret not taking a more active role in the study and in the men's lives. Maybe he would try again someday. Looking to his right, Jon saw Steve approaching with Phillip following close behind. He rose to his feet and prepared to greet them.

"Hey, Jon," said Steve, reaching out to shake Jon's hand.

"Hey, guys," said Jon, glancing at Phillip.

Phillip remained a few feet behind Steve without acknowledging Jon's greeting.

"This room's open," said Steve, pointing to the counseling room behind Jon. "You want to just go in here?"

"Sure," said Jon. "That works."

Steve pulled the glass door open and stepped back, waiting for Jon and Phillip to enter. Jon paused, deferring to Phillip, but stepped ahead when Phillip failed to move forward. Steve ushered Phillip into the room and let the door swing closed behind them.

"Thanks for meeting me here on a Wednesday night," said Jon as the three men chose their seats around the small table.

"Sure thing, Jon," said Steve. "We were already here for a department leaders' meeting, so this worked out fine."

Jon watched Phillip attempt to get comfortable in his chair. Phillip's eyes stayed focused on the table as he crossed his arms over his chest and his legs under the table. The serious expression on Phillip's face was in stark contrast to his usual jovial demeanor.

"What's on your mind, Jon?" asked Steve.

"Well, first of all, I wanted to apologize to Phillip. I don't know if he told you, but—"

"He did," said Steve, interrupting with a polite smile.

"Oh. Well," said Jon. He turned his focus directly towards Phillip and offered the apology he had prepared on the way to their meeting. "Phillip, I'm sorry for the harsh things I said to you Sunday. How I spoke to you was wrong. If I have issues or problems with our class or your leadership, that wasn't the way for me to express them. I lost my temper with you, and I'm sorry. I hope you can forgive me."

Phillip looked at Jon and then down at the table. He pushed himself upright in his chair, but said nothing. Jon looked at Steve and raised his eyebrows, hoping for some support.

"Was there anything else, Jon?" asked Steve, appearing ready to leave.

Jon had hoped for a better reaction from both men. But his apology was only half of the reason Jon wanted to meet with the two leaders of his Sunday school class. "Actually, there is something I was hoping to get your thoughts on."

"OK, shoot," said Steve, relaxing again in his chair.

Phillip continued to avoid eye contact with Jon.

"Well, for the past few days I've been doing a lot of praying and thinking about what God wants me to do as a Christian. Obviously, you heard some of that in class this past Sunday."

Phillip huffed subtly, still looking down at the table.

Steve leaned forward. "Actually, I was going to call you this week if you hadn't called me first. Are you all right, Jon? I've been praying for you."

"I appreciate that, Steve. Really. But I'm fine. It's just that, I've made a decision to – I mean – I believe God is leading me, or calling me, to share Christ with people. You know, to be a witness for him."

"Hey, that's great, Jon!" said Steve, shaking Jon's hand across the table. "You know, we need people to help with our Tuesday night outreach. Why don't you come next week and we can go see some recent visitors? You can ride with me."

"Oh, wow. Thanks, Steve. But that's not really what I have in mind. I think God wants me to make a bigger commitment than that. I'm actually planning to take a leave of absence from work and just go wherever He leads me and share the Gospel with people."

Steve smiled in a way that made Jon feel silly. Phillip sat up straight in his chair. His eyes were now on Jon.

"Wow, that's huge," said Steve, but with much less energy than before.

"Yeah, it's kind of scary," said Jon. The drop in Steve's enthusiasm left him puzzled. "But I feel like it's what God is calling me to do."

Steve's expression became serious as he leaned forward. "Jon, I think it's great that you feel called to be a witness for Christ. But understand, your first responsibility is to your church. We have people here every Sunday that need to hear what Christ can do in their lives. You can make an impact right here."

"I appreciate that, Steve," said Jon. "But that's just not what I feel like God is leading me to do, right now. I was just hoping to get some advice from you on how to reach people. You know, what to say to folks when you witness or how to share your testimony. Things like that."

Phillip let out a laugh. "You're ready to take time off from work to be an evangelist, but you don't even know what to say to people? It doesn't sound to me like you've thought this through, Jon. You sure it's God leading you to do this? Maybe you're just feeling guilty."

Steve slid his hand across the table towards Phillip and smiled politely at Jon. Phillip took the cue and leaned back in his chair, folding his arms across his chest. Despite his apology, Jon could see Phillip was still sore.

"Phillip has a point, Jon," said Steve. "We train our full-time missionaries thoroughly before sending them out into the field. A calling is just the first step. Maybe you should consider taking some classes at the local seminary. They offer night courses for people who work during the day. They even have online courses. You wouldn't have to take time off from work, and you could take one or two classes this spring. Then, when you've got a better handle on how you can serve in some way, we could talk again. Maybe Phillip can put you in touch with Earl."

"Earl?" asked Jon, guessing he should know the person to whom Steve was referring.

"Earl Rogers, our minister of evangelism," said Phillip with a sigh. "You don't even know who that is, do you?"

"What difference does that make, Phillip?" asked Jon. He was starting to feel irritated with Phillip all over again. And Phillip's unwillingness to forgive was beginning to undo Jon's regret over yelling at him on Sunday.

"Guys, let's keep this friendly, OK?" asked Steve. "Phillip, Jon's already apologized."

"So what, Steve?" Phillip argued. "I had to listen to him in this room Sunday, now he's going to listen to me." Phillip turned towards Jon. "Jon, do you know how long I've served as the director of our class?"

Jon sat quietly out of respect for Steve and let Phillip have his say.

"Five years," said Phillip, answering his own question. "Way before you came along. And I was social director for two years before that. Steve, here, has been teaching in this church for ten years. But you come in here like you're Cam Parsons or something and expect us to hand you the keys to the church, just because you prayed for a couple of days?"

"I'm not asking for anything from the church, Phillip," said Jon. "I just wanted some advice, that's all. And to apologize to you, which I've already done."

"Well, you can keep your apology, Jon," said Phillip. "You made yourself perfectly clear, Sunday."

"Phillip," said Steve, motioning again for Phillip to stop.

"That's OK, Steve," said Jon, preparing himself to leave. "This was obviously a mistake."

Steve mustered a smile that made Jon stay in his chair, at least momentarily. "Jon, I think what Phillip is trying to say is that sometimes we need to put the needs of the church first. He and I've both served here for a while now and feel used by God every week. But if you're really looking to go somewhere to spread the Gospel, we have a mission trip coming this spring to Brazil. Maybe you should consider going on that as a first step. Then over time, who knows where God may lead you."

Jon was feeling resistance from the one person he thought would be excited for him. He respected Steve, even though he had little interaction with him beyond listening to his lessons on Sunday mornings. Phillip's reaction he could at least understand. But Jon had hoped for more encouragement from Steve. "Steve, I respect what you're saying," said Jon. "But I've got to do this *now*. Matthew 28:7 tells us to *go quickly* and share the Gospel. I really believe that's what God's wanting me to do."

"Jon, in my experience," said Steve, "the best way to evangelize is through relationships, not walking up to strangers and trying to sell them Jesus in a brief conversation and then leaving them to fend for themselves. If you feel a sense of urgency to reach others for Christ, start with the people you already know, the people around you in your life. You don't have to go anywhere to do that. Start a Bible study at your work or – I bet there are people who sit beside you in Sunday school every week who need someone to reach out to them personally. I can only do so much teaching a lesson, but you could make a real difference right where you are."

Jon weighed Steve's advice against what he was sure God was telling him to do. There was nothing wrong with what Steve was saying. In fact, Jon almost wished it were the direction God had placed on his heart. It would certainly be less disruptive. But it just didn't fit for some reason. "Steve, I don't know why I'm being pulled in this specific direction right now, but I am. What you're saying makes sense, but I can't change what God's calling me to do. And it's not that I have anything against serving in the church. What you and Phillip do is important, and I'm glad you're here."

"Yeah, the church needs two-bit comics, doesn't it, Jon?" asked Phillip, glaring at Jon.

Jon could see the hurt still showing on Phillip's face. His words had cut him deeper than he realized. "Phillip, I know I hurt you. I can see that and I'm very sorry. I wish I hadn't said what I did. I really do. I was more angry at myself than anything. And what I said to you was sinful. I've asked God to forgive me, and all I can do is ask the same of you. But I understand if that's difficult. I was a complete jerk to you Sunday."

Phillip sat with his eyes down for a long moment.

Jon extended his hand across the table. "Please, brother."

Phillip slowly looked up at Jon. The anger in his eyes had faded. He stretched his hand to Jon's, grabbing it firmly. "OK."

"Thanks, man," said Jon, feeling the relief forgiveness brings as the two shook hands.

"I guess I *could* use some new material, huh?" said Phillip as a smile crept slowly across his face.

Steve jostled Phillip's shoulder. "Hey, I couldn't ask for a better opening act. Don't change a thing."

With the tension gone from the room, Jon felt it would be a good time to end their meeting on a positive note. "I should let you guys go. Steve, I really appreciate your thoughts on everything. But I need to do this the way I feel led to. Maybe if you guys could just keep me in your prayers, I'd appreciate it."

"Why don't we start that right now?" Steve suggested. "Can I pray for you?"

"Yeah, that would be awesome," said Jon.

As Steve leaned forward and closed his eyes, Jon and Phillip followed suit. Jon felt Steve's hand take hold of his forearm as he began to pray.

"Dear Heavenly Father" said Steve, "we thank you for softening Jon's heart towards you, Lord. We thank you for speaking to him and placing a call for service on his life. You tell us in John 12:26 that you honor the one who serves you. We ask that you honor Jon's desire to serve you and let your Holy Spirit lead him and guide him in your path. Give him strength, encouragement, and direction from your Word. Let him know that you're with him, dear Lord, even when things get tough. When he's facing rejection or persecution for his faith, comfort him. And let him rest in the assurance that, in all things, you work for the good of those who love you and who have been called according to your purpose. Almighty God, we pray that Jon will be an instrument of your glory and that others will see your Son, Jesus, in his efforts to spread your message of salvation. And we ask that you keep him safe until your work in him is done, Father. We pray these things in Jesus' Holy name. Amen."

"Amen," said Jon, humbled by Steve's heart-felt prayer. "Thanks, man. That's exactly what I needed."

Steve shook Jon's hand as the three rose from the table. "Give me a call before you leave," he said. "I'll give you a good book I have on how to share your faith."

"Awesome," said Jon. "I definitely will."

"And when you get back," said Phillip, reaching out to shake Jon's hand, "let's schedule a time for you to share with the class how God's been using you."

Jon paused to be sure Phillip wasn't going to add a punch line.

"Seriously," Phillip added, with a smile.

eighteen

The Line

"I saw some naive young men, and one in particular who lacked common sense."

- *Proverbs 7:7*

It was the first Friday night since fall semester classes began, and Oscar Ray's barroom was filled with its usual eclectic crowd. Preppy college students drank pitchers of draft beer next to older, bohemian-looking ex-hippies swilling heavy glasses of dark lager. A group of professional men and women, still in business attire, enjoyed mixed drinks and loud conversation next to Jon while he twisted on his barstool and waited for Brant's response to his news. His friend's mouth still hung open in surprise.

"The *lunch* girl?" Brant shouted above the crowd and music.

"Yep," said Jon, crossing his arms before him on the bar.

"You dated the lunch girl all summer?" A huge smile grew across Brant's face. "The one you didn't want to go out with?"

"That's the one," said Jon, reaching for his beer.

Brant sat poised on the edge of his barstool. "And *she* dumped *you?*"

"Yep," said Jon, taking a drink.

Brant roared with laughter as he struggled to maintain his balance on his stool. "Oh, man! You sat right here three months ago and bitched and moaned about how you had to go to lunch with that girl!"

"Thanks for reminding me." Jon watched Brant enjoy himself at his expense.

"Why did—" Brant stopped briefly to catch his breath. "Why did she break-up with you?"

"She said it was because I wasn't Christian enough, basically." Jon braced himself for another round of Brant's laughter.

"Well, you did fail that religion class last year. Dude, maybe she found out!"

"I'm serious, man. She said that dating me wasn't what God wanted her to do. Or it wasn't God's will or some crap like that." Jon was hoping to see some measure of understanding, compassion, or insight from his friend and roommate.

"Man," said Brant, shaking his head. "Christian girls suck." He took a long drink from his beer and burped into his sleeve. "None for me, thanks. I'll stick with normal chicks."

"Well, that's the last time I get sucked into all that. That's for damn sure." Jon drank from his beer and set it on the bar loudly, sending white foam up the neck of the bottle. "I don't need some bitch telling me whether I'm a Christian or not."

"Damn straight. That F in religion speaks for itself." Brant laughed again, enjoying his own joke.

"Um, we both failed that class, remember? Thanks to you and your stupid idea to play golf instead of taking our exam. And then you had to actually tell Dr. Feldman that's why we missed it!" Jon realized he had lost Brant's attention in the middle of his rant, his friend's gaze now focused over Jon's right shoulder.

"Dude, forget about all that," said Brant. "The love of your life just sat down on the barstool right next to you." Brant nodded his head for Jon to look to his right. "I'll give you twenty bucks if you talk to her."

Jon didn't bother to look. "You don't have twenty bucks."

"Well, do it anyway, so I can meet her friend." Brant nudged Jon's elbow. "Go on, man. I promise you're gonna like this."

"Brant, I just broke up with somebody."

"No, she broke up with you. Get over it and talk to this girl."

"You just want to see me get shot down so you can laugh your ass off again."

"Exactly. Now, turn around and say something. Hurry up."

Jon knew Brant wouldn't leave him alone until he at least tried. He turned to his right without looking first and said, "Hi."

Slender and tanned with long dark hair, she turned her head towards Jon. The brown skin of her bare shoulders glistened as she leaned her elbows on the bar. Jon's eyes dilated.

"Hi, yourself," she said, smiling with smooth red lips and perfect white teeth. Her light brown eyes moved around Jon's face as he struggled for something else to say.

"Can I buy you a beer?" Jon asked by default.

She lifted a full bottle of Michelob Light close to her mouth. "Sorry," she said, taking a sip.

"Ah." Jon began to turn back towards Brant in defeat.

"But I'll tell you what," she said. "If you can keep my interest long enough for me to finish this one, you're welcome to buy me the next one."

Jon smiled cautiously. "I think I can do that," he said. But as he looked down at the beer in front of him, he began to have second thoughts. Only three weeks before, he sat in the same restaurant with Jenny, desperately confessing his love for her. And he had spent every day since then in various forms of moody depression. Was he ready to chase after someone else so soon?

"So?" she asked, raising an eyebrow at Jon. "You're supposed to entertain me, not just stare at your beer."

"Oh, I'm sorry," said Jon, shaking the thoughts of Jenny from his head. "I, um…."

"Oh, I love this song," she said, pointing her finger upwards as the music played over the noise of the bar.

"*Suspicious Minds*?" asked Jon. "It's OK, but it's not Elvis' best song." Jon attempted to regain some bravado by appearing smug in his opinion.

"What do you mean it's not his best song? It's my favorite Elvis song!"

"What?" asked Jon, laughing. "We might have a problem, then."

"I think we might." She lifted her beer to her lips, took a slow drink from the bottle and set it down gently on the bar. "Well then, what do *you* think is Elvis' best song?"

"That's easy," said Jon. "*Always on My Mind*."

A laugh escaped from her mouth as she rolled her eyes away from Jon. "The Willy Nelson song?" she asked, shaking her head. "You're out of your mind."

"That may be true," said Jon, hoping to hear her laugh again. "But it's still his best song. And Elvis sang it first, not Willie Nelson."

"You cannot be serious!" she said, pushing Jon's elbow off the edge of the bar. "I've never even heard him sing it, so how can it be his best song?"

"Because, he recorded it after Priscilla left him back in the early Seventies." Jon hoped the only bit of Elvis trivia he knew would impress her. "So it's got meaning behind it, unlike ninety-nine percent of his other songs, like *Hound Dog* or *Blue Suede Shoes*, for Pete's sake. What's that all about?"

"Did you ever stop to think that Priscilla left him because she was suspicious of all his catting around with other women? And that's why he recorded *Suspicious Minds* in 1969?"

Jon bowed his head in submission. "Nicely done."

"See? I win." She took a long drink from her beer and then held the bottle in front of her at eye level. "Over half-way there. What else you got?"

Jon studied her face as the two exchanged long looks. She was gorgeous. And he was beginning to believe she might actually be interested. But the butterflies in Jon's chest still told him it might be happening too fast. And he couldn't take a chance on repeating the ordeal he just went through with Jenny. One battle with God was enough. He decided to clear the air upfront. "OK, let me ask you something," he said. "Are you a Christian?"

"Wow," she said, laughing. "That's a new one."

"A new what?"

"Pick-up line."

"No, seriously, I want to know. Do you believe in God?"

She lifted her bottle to her mouth and poured beer past her red lips. Looking at her near empty brown bottle, she shook her head. "And you were doing so good, Slick. Are you sure you don't want to try a different line than that?"

Jon didn't intend his question to be a pick-up line, but he played along, nevertheless. "Nope, this is the line."

"That's the line? Do I believe in God?"

"That's it." Jon smiled and waited for her response.

"Wow. OK. How about this," she said, leaning in closer to Jon's face. "I believe in cold beer, Elvis Presley, and warm beds. Does that answer your question?"

Jon grinned broadly. "Yes, it does." He held up his beer in front of her. "I'm Jon."

She tapped her bottle against his. "Lacey," she said, with a smile. "It's nice to meet you, Jon."

As Jon stared into Lacey's beautiful brown eyes, Brant and the crowd of people around them seemed to slowly disappear.

"You can buy me that beer now, Jon."

nineteen

The Wrong Way

"The tongue of the wise makes knowledge appealing,
but the mouth of a fool belches out foolishness."
- *Proverbs 15:2*

Jon sat comfortably in the leather recliner in his den, a blanket over his legs, reading his Bible. He moved his head slightly up and down, trying to find the best angle to see the small text through his seldom used, bifocal reading glasses. He had purchased the glasses shortly after turning forty, but rarely gave in to wearing them. Able to get by with an occasional squint of his eyes, he resisted adjusting his self-image to someone who wore glasses. But when studying his Bible for any length of time, he found them most helpful. And while the Bible app on his iPhone was much easier to see, with its large fonts and bright screen, Jon still preferred the soft feel of his Bible's worn leather cover resting heavily in his hands. It had aged with him over the years like a good friend.

"I'm home!" announced Holly as she entered the house from the garage.

"Hey, sweet pea," said Jon, getting up from his recliner.

"Oh, hey, Daddy. I didn't see you in there."

Jon set his Bible on the end table and took off his glasses. "How's my college girl?"

"Starving," she said, setting her purse on the kitchen table. "And my car's running a little rough. Can you look at it?"

Jon smiled and gave his daughter a hug. "You didn't let the oil run out of my old 4Runner again, did you?"

"No, Dad," huffed Holly. "Can we eat something before we talk about whatever it is you wanted to talk to me about? I didn't have time to eat lunch between classes today and I'm dying."

"Sure," said Jon. He walked into the kitchen and opened his empty refrigerator. A half full gallon of milk and a protein shake sat alone on separate shelves. "Well, unless you want to eat a bowl of cereal, we're going to have to go somewhere."

"What, no turkey sandwiches?" asked Holly, poking fun at her dad.

"Sorry. I'm fresh out."

"How you don't get sick of eating cereal and turkey sandwiches every day, I'll never understand."

"Hey, I mix it up every now and then. Just yesterday, I put mayonnaise *and* mustard on my sandwich for lunch."

"You see? I go away to college for one year and you go wild."

They both laughed as Jon glanced around the kitchen for his keys. "So, where do you want to go?"

Holly looked thoughtful for a moment. "Some place good."

Jon found his keys in a bowl on the kitchen counter. "Oh, somewhere good. That's an idea."

"Very funny. Can we go to Moe's? I feel like a burrito. Where's Elvis?"

"He's outside somewhere. I'm surprised he didn't come running when he heard your 4Runner. You can say *hey* to him when we get back."

Jon held the restaurant's glass door open for Holly and heard the familiar greeting.

"Welcome to Moe's!" shouted two teenagers in red T-shirts behind the serving counter.

Looking around the restaurant, Jon saw only two people waiting in line before them and most of the tables empty. He was thankful it wasn't *Kids Eat Free Day*, which effectively turned the restaurant into a noisy kindergarten cafeteria. They would be able to have a peaceful conversation, and he could tell Holly about his plans.

As they walked towards the counter, Holly suddenly stopped and turned in the other direction. "Can you just get me an Art Vandalay with black beans and a drink? I'm gonna go to the restroom."

"Sure thing, honey," said Jon as he stepped up to order.

"What can I get for you today, sir?" asked the boy behind the counter.

"An Art Vandalay with black beans and a Jon Coctostan with chicken," said Jon. "No beans on the JC, but I'll have some rice and mushrooms on it instead. And that's for here."

"Yes, sir. Coming right up," said the boy, reaching for two flour tortilla shells. "We need to give your JC its own name on the menu so you can just order it that way every time."

Jon laughed. "That's a sure sign I eat here too much. But let me know if you think of a good name for it."

"Yes, sir," said the boy as he busily prepared Jon's order.

Jon drifted down the counter to the cashier, paid for their meals and waited a moment for their food to be ready. Holly reappeared from the restroom and waved at her father as she chose a booth for them along the far wall of the dining room.

"Here you go, sir," said the girl at the cash register with a polite smile. She slid a tray with two plastic baskets, overflowing with corn chips, towards him. "Have a good night."

"Thanks. You, too." Jon made his way to the drink machine, filled their cups with iced tea and then carefully maneuvered around empty tables and chairs across the dining room to their booth. He unloaded their food onto the table as Holly cut her eyes towards the cashier.

"Oh, I hate that girl," said Holly.

Jon sat down across from his daughter. "Who? The one at the cash register?"

"Yes. Don't look over there!"

"Why?" he asked, without looking. "What's wrong with her?"

"She's the worst. That's why I didn't want to wait in line with you. She was in my eleventh grade English class."

"Wow, what did she do to you?"

"Nothing, really. But she was just always so...." Holly made a sour face. "You know?"

"No, I really don't," said Jon, laughing. He looked over at the girl behind the register. She saw him looking and smiled, before turning away. "She seems nice enough to me."

"Well, anyway…," said Holly, dropping the subject and picking up her burrito.

"Can we say a quick blessing?" asked Jon.

"Oh, sorry." Holly put down her food. "Go ahead."

The two bowed their heads over their food as Jon prayed, "Father God, we just thank you for this time together and ask you to bless this food to our bodies, in Jesus' name. Amen."

Jon took a bite of his quesadilla and thought about how best to approach Holly with his news. He wasn't sure how she'd react to his leaving or how she'd feel about living at home while he was gone. He hoped she'd be supportive, but decided to ease slowly into the subject, nevertheless.

Holly picked up her burrito. "So, what is it that you wanted to talk with me about, Dad?"

His daughter's curiosity trumped Jon's plan to ease into the discussion. "Oh," he said with his mouth full of food. He chewed slowly and took a sip of his tea while he thought of the best way to answer. "I want to talk with you about…kind of a big decision I've made. And how it's going to affect you."

"OK, that sounds pretty scary," said Holly, raising her dark eyebrows at her father.

Jon immediately wished he had chosen his words differently. He was talking with his daughter, not his staff at work, he reminded himself. "I'm sorry. Let me try again. What I meant to say is…I'm going to be doing something over the next few months, and I need your help to do it. But it may be a little inconvenient for you. Does that sound any better?"

"Not much. What is it, for heaven's sake?"

Jon took a deep breath and looked into his daughter's eyes. "I'm going to ask for a leave of absence from work for six months."

"Six months? Are you sick? Do you have cancer? What's wrong?" Holly's wide eyes gazed anxiously at her father.

"No, I'm not sick. And I don't have cancer. I promise."

Holly let herself fall back against the padded cushion of the booth. "Geez, Dad. You scared me."

"I'm sorry, honey. But I'm fine, really."

"OK, so let me guess…you're going to build that big deck and Jacuzzi on the back of the house that you've been talking about forever."

"Oh, gosh, no," said Jon. "And I wouldn't need six months to do that, anyway. At least I hope not." He wondered briefly if Holly's guess was a reflection of his priorities over the last few years.

"Well, what is it then?"

Jon gathered his courage. "I'm going to be traveling around the country and sharing the Gospel with people. You know…being a witness for Christ."

Holly stared blankly at her father for a moment as she held her burrito over her basket of chips. "You mean like, trying to save people?"

Jon nodded. "Yeah, like trying to save people."

Holly dropped her burrito back into the plastic serving basket, bouncing corn chips and salt onto the table. "You're just going to leave your job and me and everything for six months to do that? Are you serious?"

"Holly, it's just for a short time," said Jon, trying to soften the impact.

"It's half a year, Dad! Is this some sort of middle-aged crisis thing or something? Why don't you just buy a red convertible like most men your age do?"

"Ouch. Thanks for that. But no, it's not a midlife crisis. I promise."

"Dad, you're always telling me to be responsible and make good decisions and here you are…just going off and…I don't even know what you want me to say."

"Holly, just let me explain, OK?"

"Well, can you start with how it's going to *inconvenience* me?" Holly crossed her arms and glared at her father. "You said you need my help. How can I help you travel around saving people? I'm in school, Dad."

"I know," said Jon. Already off balance from his daughter's strong reaction, he knew she wasn't going to like his answer. "I, um…I need you to move home and stay in the house while I'm gone and look after Elvis."

"What?! I have a roommate and friends in my dorm, Dad! I'm in a sorority! I can't just leave them in the middle of the semester! How can you ask me to do that?"

Jon looked around the restaurant to see if anyone was taking notice of their discussion. The girl at the cash register smiled in their direction. "Maybe this wasn't the best place to talk about this."

Holly scowled at her father. "I don't care who's listening."

"Well, I guess I do," said Jon. "Let's just talk about it when we get home."

"Fine!"

The two sat in uncomfortable silence for several minutes as they ate their dinner, trying to avoid eye contact with each other. Jon struggled to think of conversation starters to help lighten the mood. Unable to come up with anything new, he went for an old standby. "You know, this is kind of like that *Seinfeld* episode where George and Jerry go and meet Elaine's father and—"

"Not now, Dad."

twenty

Dear Jon

*"Gently instruct those who oppose the truth. Perhaps God will
change those people's hearts, and they will learn the truth."*
- *2 Timothy 2:25 NLT*

March 22ⁿᵈ

Dear Jonny,

    *You are such a mess! I can't believe you jumped out of a moving car! I didn't realize I
needed to be praying for you to wait until a car stops before you get out. Haha! The people
behind your friend's convertible must have thought you were crazy! I hate that you'll be in
a cast for a while. I'm just happy you didn't break more than your wrist! At least it's not
summer, yet. I know you would hate to have a cast on your arm at the beach. Are you
coming down with your folks the same week in June this year?*

    *I was on the beach yesterday, believe it or not. First time this year! It was the warmest
day in March I can remember. I thought about you. My friend Donna — you know, the
one in the black bikini last 4ᵗʰ of July? She and I spent the whole day laughing at some
Canadians swimming in that cold water! They were totally in! I don't know how they do
that. I let it wash up on my feet once and it felt like ice!*

    *Oh, my gosh! I need to tell you — they tore down King's Funland!!! It's all gone!
Everything! They must have done it a few months ago. They're building two beach houses
there now. I'm so sad! Oh well, I guess you'll never get to beat me in Skee-Ball!*

Can you believe we'll be seniors next year!! That gives me one more year to talk you out of going to Carolina. Clemson is so much nicer, and you wouldn't have to worry about your football team losing every Saturday after Thanksgiving!

Did you read the book I sent you? He is such an inspiration. I see him every once in a while around Pawleys. You can't miss him with that black patch over his eye and his missing arm. His faith got him through all that mess in Vietnam. My dad had him come speak to our church last year, and two people accepted Christ afterwards! Are you making it to church on Sundays with your folks? When you come down this summer, you need to go with us to Surfside Community Church before my dad retires. You've only heard him preach once, and that was five years ago. And that silly bird stole the show! So promise you'll go with me, OK?

I'd better go. We're heading back to church for Sunday evening worship in a few minutes. Write me! And no more jumping out of cars!!

Love,

Amy

P.S. Thanks for the picture! I want one of you smiling, though!

twenty one

What About Me?

"Fathers, do not exasperate your children; instead, bring them up in the training and instruction of the Lord."

- Ephesians 6:4

Jon's stomach felt uncomfortably full as he sat down next to Holly on the couch in their den. He had eaten every one of the tortilla chips that came with his Moe's quesadilla purely to fill the awkward silence that dominated their dinner. His first attempt to share his news with his daughter had been a disaster. But now, back home, he was ready to try once again to explain the reason for his trip. "Just hear me out for a few minutes, OK, sweetie?"

"Fine, Dad. Whatever." Holly turned away from her father and looked out the French doors leading onto the patio and back yard.

Jon sighed as he watched his daughter avoid eye contact with him. She reminded him of her mother sometimes – passionate and stubborn. Or maybe she was just more like him than he was willing to admit. "Look, I know this is hard to understand," he said. "I don't understand it myself, sometimes. But I realized lately that I've just been coasting along in my faith for quite a while now. And it really bothered me. I felt like my faith wasn't worth anything to anybody, even me. So I started praying about it. And I know it sounds crazy, but I honestly feel like God is leading me to do this."

Holly shook her head back and forth as she stared into the back yard.

"Holly, please look at me."

Holly turned towards her father. Jon realized why she'd been hiding her face from him. As she blinked, her eyes flooded her cheeks with tears. He gently led a few long strands of hair away from her soft wet skin and tucked them behind her ear. "Honey, please understand," he said. "I need to know I can make a difference for Christ. I just can't keep going through the motions. I need to follow where God leads me and do my best to be a witness for him, to share my faith and reach people. It means a lot to me to do this." He watched Holly keep her eyes down as he spoke and wondered if he was making any sense. "I'm sorry if I'm not doing a good job of explaining all this. But I hope you can understand."

Holly fought back her emotions as tears streamed down her face. "But, Dad, what about *me*?"

Jon placed his hand on hers. "You'll be fine here, sweetie. Besides, you're so busy with school and your sorority, you won't even know I'm gone. And I'll leave enough money in your account so you won't have to worry about anything. And I won't be out of touch at all, I promise."

Holly wiped the tears from her cheeks. "I'm not talking about money, Dad. I mean…what about me?"

"I'm sorry, sweetie," said Jon, feeling confused. "I guess I'm not following you. I honestly didn't think you'd be this upset about it."

Holly turned fully towards her father on the couch. "I'll tell you why I'm upset" she said, her tone becoming emphatic. "You say you're going all over God knows where telling people about Jesus, right?"

"That's right," said Jon, unsure where her question was leading.

"But you've never even done that with *me!* You're going to talk to people you don't even know about Jesus, but you won't talk to me?" Holly shook her head and looked away.

Jon was staggered by the truth in what he was hearing. "Holly, I…."

"Why would you put strangers ahead of me, Daddy?" Holly's soft voice trembled as she spoke. "I'm your daughter. I've been right here. Don't I matter as much as some…anybody off the street?" Holly wiped her face with both hands and then opened the purse on her lap. "I need a tissue." She rose from the couch and walked to the hall bathroom.

Jon struggled for words to say. "Holly," he called after her as he stood up from the couch. "I just thought that…I mean, I just assumed that you were…that you were already…."

Holly walked back from the bathroom, wiping her nose with a tissue. "What, Dad? A Christian?" she asked, meeting her father in the kitchen.

"Well…yeah."

"Sure, but…I went to church growing up because you took me. And my friends were there. That's about it. The stuff you're talking about – God leading you and witnessing and being called and all that – I just don't understand. I can't relate to it." Holly blew her nose into the tissue. "What does that say about me?"

Jon was afraid to answer. He leaned against the kitchen counter and listened to his daughter.

"I mean, I believe in God and all, but that doesn't lead me to do anything like what you're talking about. I don't pray or read the Bible like you do. I don't get it, Dad. I just don't get it."

"But honey, when you asked to be baptized, I thought you said—"

"I was ten, Dad. And Mary Beth Roberts was getting baptized the same day, remember? You know I used to do everything she did when I was little."

"Yeah, I do remember that," said Jon, staring at the floor as he thought of Holly as a ten-year-old, playing upstairs with her friend.

Holly shook her head as she tossed a tissue into the trashcan under the kitchen sink. "Never mind, OK? Just forget it. I'm sorry. I'll help you out any way I can, all right? I don't mind living here for a few months. I'll just make it work." Holly took two steps towards the den before turning back towards the hall bathroom. She then stopped and turned around again. "I don't know what I'm doing," she said, clearly flustered. She turned her head away from Jon, put her right hand over her eyes and began to cry.

Jon moved towards her. "Wait a minute, honey," he said, reaching out to take his daughter's left hand from her hip. "You aren't the one that should be apologizing." Jon shook his head at himself. "I can't believe I've made the same mistake with you as my parents made with me. I should have known better."

Holly lowered her hand from her face and looked at her father. "What did Nana and Papa do wrong with you?"

Jon sighed. "It's not that they did anything wrong, necessarily. It's just that…I think they assumed that I was a Christian just because they took me to church growing up. And then I just assumed the same thing about myself.

They never really talked with me about it. I fooled myself for a long time until I finally accepted Christ right after you were born."

Holly thought for a moment. "But I think of myself as a Christian. I mean, I try and be good and all. I guess I just don't understand the whole faith part."

"Well," said Jon, trying to gather his thoughts to help her understand. The last person with whom he expected to be sharing his faith was his own daughter. But it seemed his calling to be a witness for Christ was beginning right in front of him in his own home. And he didn't feel prepared to handle it. He searched his mind for a starting point and went with the first thing that came to his mind. "Sweetie, let me ask you something."

"OK."

"Do you think of yourself as a sinner?" The question felt cold and impersonal coming out of Jon's mouth. It certainly didn't feel like something he would be asking his daughter.

"I know the answer is *yes*, Dad. I've been to church, remember?"

"Well, I know. That's why this is kind of difficult for me. I know you've heard this stuff before and it's hard for me to know where to start explaining it." Jon felt like he was talking with Lacey all over again. And the feeling scared him.

"Why did you ask me about sin, then?" asked Holly.

"I don't know. To be honest, no father likes to think of his daughter as a sinner. But it just came to me."

"Well, I hate to break this to you, Dad, but I'm not perfect."

"I know. But since we're on the subject, I guess I would have to ask if you've ever done anything about it."

"About what?"

"About your sins." Jon still wished she had none.

"My sins? What do you mean? I may not be perfect, but I'm not a bad person, either, Daddy. You know that."

"Of course you're not. But do you think you're good enough to get into heaven?"

"I don't know. Maybe. I just assumed…wait, is this the kind of thing you plan to do with people on your trip?"

"I hope so," said Jon, smiling cautiously. "I obviously need some practice."

"Well, can we just skip to the part where you tell me what I need to do?"

"Really? You just want me to skip to the end?" He hadn't thought that far ahead, yet.

Holly nodded.

Jon tried to stall for time while his brain caught up with the situation. "You mean…you want to know how you can have real faith and know that you're saved?"

Holly pressed her lips together as she stared into her father's eyes. "Mmhmm," she said.

Jon felt a wave of anxiety flash through his body as he fully realized the opportunity before him. "God, help me," he prayed quickly in his head. "Don't let me screw this up like before." He took a deep breath and reached for Holly's hand. "OK, honey, here's what you have to do. First, recognize that God loves you. And he wants to have a relationship with you that's as real as what you and I have here right now. Do you want that?"

Holly leaned against the kitchen center island in front of her father. "I do, but…that scares me a little. I mean, I'm not going to want to drop out of school and go be a foreign missionary or something, am I?"

Jon laughed and squeezed her hand. "One step at a time, OK? And it's all right to be a little scared. That tells me you understand this is a big deal, because it is. And I can't say how God will change you, but I know that he will. So, are you sure you're ready for it?"

Holly paused for a moment, looking down at her feet, and then nodded. "I'm sure."

"OK, well, I guess the reason I asked you about sin before is because that's what separates us from a relationship with God. Have you ever had a friend that lied to you or said something bad about you?"

"Yeah, Mary Beth Roberts."

"Really? I wondered what ever happened with you two. What did she say?"

"I don't want to go into it."

"Were you guys ever friends after that?"

"No. She sucks."

"OK, well, when we do stuff that's offensive to God – when we sin – it hurts our relationship with him, just like what happened with you and Mary Beth. Except, we're the ones that suck, not him."

"OK. So…I just have to not sin. Is that what you're saying?"

"Of course not."

"So what, then?"

"Look, the answer is really amazingly simple. Are you ready?"

"Just hit me with it, please."

"You just need to surrender."

"Surrender? To God, you mean?"

"Yep."

"But what does that even mean, Dad? I mean, seriously."

"I *am* serious. Surrendering means you've realized that no matter how hard you try, you're never going to be good enough to earn that relationship with God."

"So, am I supposed to be feeling better or worse right about now?"

"Just stick with me," said Jon, offering a smile. "I'm new at this, remember?"

"OK, sorry. Go ahead."

"I was just going to say that it's not about what you can do. It's about what God's already done for you. You need to accept the gift that he's offered you through Jesus. You know that God sent Jesus to die on the Cross for our sins, right?"

"Of course, I do. That's church 101."

"Right. So he took the punishment in our place. And it's a gift we don't deserve. But if we accept it and believe in our hearts that Jesus died and rose again for us, then we have a way to restore that relationship with God, forever."

"But I guess this is what I don't get. I mean, I already believe all that stuff, Dad. So, why don't I have what you have?"

"I thought you believed, already, sweetie. I guess that's why I never said anything more to you. But the question is, have you ever acted on your belief?"

"Acted on it? What do you mean? How would I act on it?"

"OK, let me ask you – if Mary Beth told you she wanted to be friends again, what would you say?"

"I'd say, *Step-off, bitch!* Oops, sorry. That was unfiltered."

"It's OK," said Jon, grinning. "So, what would Mary Beth have to do for you to accept her as a friend again?"

Holly thought for a moment. "Well, she would have to apologize for a whole bunch of stuff, for starters."

"You mean, she would have to admit that she's done things that were wrong, things that hurt you, and say she was sorry?"

"Absolutely."

"OK. So, have you ever admitted to God that you've done things that were wrong, things that hurt him, and that you're sorry?"

Holly paused and looked at her father. "No," she said, softly.

"That's the first thing you need to do then, honey. And taking that step is where faith comes in. You need to trust God. That he's already made a way to forgive all that you've done wrong and restore your relationship with him through faith in what Jesus did for you on the Cross. It's more than just believing in your mind that Jesus is God's Son. You have to trust him to do what he came to do. That's acting on your belief. Understand?"

Holly nodded her head as she looked down at the floor. "I understand," she said. "So, what do I do?"

"Well, I can lead you in a prayer right now if you want. We can settle this forever. And I promise God won't tell you to step-off."

Holly laughed softly as she wiped a tear from her eye. "OK, Daddy."

Jon reached out and held both her hands. "Just repeat this after me and mean it in your heart, OK, sweetie?"

"OK." Holly closed her eyes and bowed her head as Jon led her in prayer.

"Dear Heavenly Father, I know that I'm a sinner. I know that I've fallen short of what you want me to be. I'm sorry for my sins, God. Please forgive me. I thank you for offering your Son, Jesus, to die on the Cross as punishment for my sins. It's something I don't deserve, but I accept it as your gift of grace and mercy and love for me. And I ask you, Jesus, to come into my life right now and be my risen Lord and my Savior. Thank you for saving me and forgiving me and loving me. It's in your Holy name I pray. Amen."

Holly bounced onto her toes and wrapped her arms around her father's neck, hugging him tightly. "Thank you, Daddy. I love you."

"You mean everything to me, Holly," said Jon, embracing his daughter. "I love you, too. And I'm sorry it took me this long to talk with you about all this."

"It's OK," she said, sniffing her running nose as she stepped back and fumbled with the remnants of her tissue. "And don't worry about everything here. I'll take care of the house and Elvis, OK? I'll look in on Nana, too."

"OK, sweet pea. Thank you. I knew I could count on you."

"Hang on just a sec," said Holly. She left the kitchen and disappeared into the hall bathroom, closing the door behind her.

Jon turned around and placed both hands on the kitchen counter, letting his head hang from his shoulders. Closing his eyes to pray, his mind instead took him to a memory of a small dark bedroom eighteen years earlier. He remembered holding his baby daughter in his arms as he sat on the floor, crying. And he remembered a prayer for God's help in raising her and for her salvation. And a hope that he wouldn't be alone. Jon opened his eyes and watched a tear fall onto the kitchen counter in between his hands. Lifting his eyes to the ceiling, he prayed, "Thank you, dear God. Thank you for answering that prayer. Thank you for saving my precious little girl. You've always been here with me. It's a promise kept. Thank you, dear Lord. Thank you."

twenty two

Independence Day

"You are altogether beautiful, my darling, and there is no blemish in you."
- Song of Songs 4:7

Warm remnants of another small wave washed sand from underneath Jon's feet, sinking his heels a few inches more. Splashing about beneath him, a small black Labrador Retriever puppy chased the thin red leash extending to Jon's right hand. Jon's eyes followed the Pawleys Island shoreline north as it curved eastward into the ocean. He wondered if his puppy could walk with him the half mile to the north end or if he'd be carrying him most of the way there and back. Maybe a shorter walk, south to the pier, would be better. It was the first time Jon had ever been to the beach without his parents, and he was free to roam as he pleased. And though he needed their permission to drive the two and a half hours from Columbia, the small taste of freedom fed his excitement about starting college the next month. It was the perfect way to celebrate a Fourth of July.

Looking towards the pier, Jon could see the crowd already filling the beach. And once the annual parade along the three-mile-long island road ended around eleven o'clock, even more vacationers and locals would be pouring over the dunes. Jon had beaten the rush by arriving shortly after nine. He'd set-up his umbrella and chair close to the water, hopeful that the tide was going out. The year before, high tide came just after noon and pressed the holiday crowd close together against the dunes. He spent the entire day with his parents sitting two feet from a large, loud family from Kentucky.

But he already knew this year would be better. As he watched his puppy play in the ankle-deep water, his chair was now some twenty yards behind him. And the tide was still inching out, leaving plenty of room for everyone.

"I was wondering if I'd see you out here today," Jon heard a voice behind him say.

He turned to see Amy, her tanned face happily anticipating his reaction. A feeling of relief pushed the air from Jon's lungs and a large smile across his face. Hope that he might see her had fought against fear that he may not. But there she was. "It's the Fourth of July," he said, pulling back on the leash to control his pup. "Where else would I be?" Jon hugged Amy with his free arm, sliding his hand over the arch of her bare back as he felt her arms wrap around his neck.

Amy took a step back, her blue eyes beaming at Jon from underneath an orange visor. "I'm so glad you came!" she said. "I just got your letter two days ago. I thought I'd find you further up the beach in front of where King's used to be. That's your usual spot."

"Nowhere to park up there," said Jon, trying to keep his puppy from scratching Amy's legs.

"Is that your puppy?!" Amy leaned forward, placed her hands on her knees, and exchanged looks with the tiny, black, wagging fur ball.

"Yep," said Jon, proudly.

A blob of white wave foam distracted the pup's attention from Amy. He dropped his chin onto the wet sand and pointed his tail towards the sky, growling as he watched the bubbles dance on the sand with the breeze. He recoiled and barked fiercely, before hiding behind Jon's legs.

"Get it boy!" said Jon, slightly embarrassed by the dog's fear of foam.

Amy knelt down on the sand. "Oh, my gosh! He's so cute! What's his name?"

"This is Jo-Jo." Jon pulled the pup in front of him. "He's the surprise I mentioned in my letter. I got him last week as a late graduation present from my parents." Jon knelt next to Amy. "Actually, I think I bugged 'em about wanting a puppy for so long, they finally just gave in."

"Hey, Jo-Jo!" said Amy. She scooped the wet puppy into her arms, cradling him on his back like an infant. "You're just a baby! Yes, you are!" Jo-Jo arched his back and squirmed as she tickled his soft, pink belly. "Ouch! He's got my hair."

Jon pulled the dog's short black muzzle away from Amy's blonde ponytail and reset him in her arms. Jo-Jo licked her face before twisting to get free. She set him gently on the sand and stood up with Jon as they watched the pup bounce back and forth to avoid the lapping waves.

"He's got puppy breath," said Amy, brushing the sand off her knees.

"I like puppy breath," said Jon, smiling at Amy. "So, how's it going? I missed seeing you when I was down here last month with my parents."

"I know. I went with my folks to my uncle's cabin in the mountains outside of Asheville."

"The mountains? In June?" asked Jon, holding his arms out to his surroundings. "Why in the world would anyone leave the beach in the summer to go to the mountains?"

"I guess my folks just wanted to do something different," said Amy, trying to get Jo-Jo to play with an oyster shell. "My dad says you can only look at the ocean for so long before it gets boring."

"Wow," said Jon, unable to relate. "And he thinks the mountains are exciting? They just sit there. The beach is so much better. I mean – come on – this is like heaven!"

Amy laughed as she glanced around her. "I know. But it's different when you live here. Sometimes it feels good to get away from all the tourists and stuff. Present company excluded." She poked Jon in the ribs.

"Hey, I'm not a tourist," he said, pretending to be insulted.

"Oh, that's right – you're from here." Amy winked at Jon. "I forgot."

"Are you ever going to let me forget about that?" he asked while Jo-Jo chased a ghost crab around his feet.

"Nope. I'll remind you even when we're old and in our forties. By the way," said Amy, pausing as she glanced around the beach, "where's your surfboard?"

"Very funny. I was twelve, remember? And I was trying to impress you." Jon looked at Amy out of the corner of his eye, hoping for a reaction.

"And how'd that work out for you?" she asked, letting her sly grin break into a smile.

Jon took a step back and kicked water in Amy's direction as she ran away laughing. A safe distance from the water, she slowed and turned back towards Jon.

"Want to sit for a few minutes?" he called to her, pointing towards his beach chair halfway to the dunes. "I want to put Jo-Jo under the umbrella for a little while before the parade comes around. He needs some fresh water."

"Sure," said Amy, turning to walk with him. "Did you come down with your folks?"

"Nah, they had some church barbeque thing to go to," said Jon, carrying his puppy under his arm. "So, Jo-Jo and I just hopped in the car early this morning and came down for the day. Kind of a last hurrah before school starts next month." Jon offered Amy his chair and sat on the sand under his umbrella with Jo-Jo resting in his lap. He pulled a thermos from his beach bag and poured a small puddle into the palm of his hand. Jo-Jo's tongue tickled Jon's skin as he lapped the cool water.

Amy adjusted the angle of her chair and aligned it to face the sun's warm rays. "So, are you still going to Carolina?" she asked, once properly situated.

Jon smiled proudly and nodded. "Yep. I can't wait."

"I don't know how you can go to a school with a chicken for a mascot."

"It's a Gamecock and it beats wearing day-glow orange for four years," countered Jon, wishing he had a better insult for Amy's school of choice.

"Let's see if you still say that after we beat you again in November," teased Amy, grinning underneath her orange Clemson visor.

"Yeah, yeah," said Jon in surrender. He knew this would be the last time he'd see Amy for at least a year, and he didn't want to spend their time talking about college football. He looked out at the ocean and tried to think of something else to say.

Amy leaned forward and patted her hand lightly on Jon's forearm. "You should spend the night at our house and go to the Chapel with us in the morning. My dad's preaching."

"He is? I thought your dad was going to retire or something."

"He did last month. But he still volunteers to preach at the Pawleys Island Chapel when they need someone. You should stay and go with us. It's my favorite place to worship."

"Oh, I would. But I've got Jo-Jo. And I promised my parents I'd be back late this afternoon."

Amy's eyes studied Jon for a moment. "I'm going to get you back into church with me one of these days, Jonny Smoak."

Other than Jon's father, Amy was the only person he knew who still called him Jonny. But he liked hearing her say it. "I go to church," he said. His conscience kicked at him to be more honest. "Whenever my parents make me, I mean."

"You'd better get yourself in a church when you get to college, Jonny. How else are you going to meet a girl like me there?"

Amy's smile left Jon light-headed. "Well, you could solve that problem for me if you'd just go to a real university." Jon snatched the visor off Amy's head and dangled it over Jo-Jo's open mouth.

Amy laughed and struggled to reach Jon's hand from the beach chair. "Give me that!"

Jon relented and handed the visor back to Amy. He watched her carefully place it back on her head and adjust her blonde ponytail. "Think you'll have time to write, every now and then, once you get up to Clemson?" he asked.

"I will if you promise to go to church when you get to school."

"I promise," said Jon, looking into Amy's clear blue eyes.

The two sat quietly for a moment watching the waves wash over the sand. It had been twelve months since Jon had last seen Amy. And almost every day since then, he'd thought of her and looked forward to the very moment in which he now found himself. Sitting on the sand next to her, he wished time would just slow down and let him enjoy the feeling. But every passing second felt like priceless treasure slipping through his fingers. And he knew it would soon be gone.

Amy leaned forward and reached for Jon's hand, giving it a squeeze. "I'd better head back down the beach. I promised to watch the parade with my folks." She rose to her feet and patted Jon's puppy on the head. "Bye, Jo-Jo. You be a good boy."

Jon moved Jo-Jo off his lap and stood up to give Amy a hug. "I'm glad I got to see you," he said, wrapping both arms around her.

"Me, too. Be safe driving back home, OK?"

"I will." Jon's heart sank as he watched Amy turn to leave.

"Bye," she said, smiling back over her shoulder.

"Bye." Jon pulled on his puppy's leash as it strained to go with her. "Stay here, Jo-Jo." They both watched Amy make her way towards the water through a maze of children digging holes and watchful parents sitting in beach chairs. "See you later!" Jon called out, trying to make her turn around one more time.

Amy looked back at Jon without slowing. "Church!" she hollered, pointing towards him with a smile.

"OK. I promise!" Jon waved goodbye. He sat down in his chair and watched Amy's slender figure grow smaller and smaller as she walked south along the shoreline. Even when she neared the pier, he could still make out her shape and familiar walk.

A feeling of emptiness swallowed Jon as he sat alone on the crowded beach. Amy had been a part of his summers since he was twelve. The two had traded letters often during each school year since. And now, as he watched her walk out of sight down the beach, he could feel his childhood slipping away.

The sound of a fire engine siren rang from behind the rows of beach houses, signaling the arrival of the annual Fourth of July parade. Jon watched the beach begin to empty as people scurried towards the dunes to watch the line of patriotic homemade floats and decorated cars and trucks work their way up Atlantic Avenue. Noticing the excitement, Jo-Jo rose to his feet and tugged lightly against the leash in Jon's hand. Jon scooped the puppy onto his lap and dug his heels into the moist sand. "Let's sit this one out, Jo-Jo," he said, casting an empty gaze towards the ocean. "I don't feel much like celebrating."

twenty three

Count The Cost

"Jesus replied, 'No one who puts a hand to the plow and looks back is fit for service in the kingdom of God.'"
- *Luke 9:62*

While Amanda read Jon's leave request, he sat comfortably in one of the large fabric-covered guest chairs Crescent-Tango vice presidents were allowed to purchase from an interior designer at company expense. The chairs, artwork, and most of the other pieces in her office were nicer than what could be found in Jon's home. Even so, he preferred the simplicity of his own office down the hall and his collection of Holly's elementary school artwork on his walls. But the one thing in Amanda's office Jon did envy sat on the credenza behind her high-back leather chair. He watched the brightly colored exotic fish swim slowly around the large salt-water aquarium. His favorite – a plump, Green Mandarin he had given the name George – hovered next to the glass, enduring the unfortunate fate of a lifetime floating captive in Amanda's office. The fish's frog-like red eyes seemed to be staring directly at Jon. *Take me with you*, he imagined George thinking.

Amanda looked up at Jon from across her mahogany desk. "Are you sure you want to do this, Jon?"

Jon crossed his legs. "I'm sure, Amanda. It's what I'm called to do."

"What you're *called* to do?"

"That's right. It's just for six months. Then I'll be back. Andrew and Lauren should be able to handle things while I'm gone. I hope you can understand, Amanda."

A smirk began to show on Amanda's face. "Oh, I understand, all right, Jon," she said, rising up from her chair. "I understand, perfectly."

"Good," Jon said, cautiously. As he watched his boss step from behind her desk, Jon felt uncomfortably aware of her appearance. Not too much older than him, Amanda was an attractive single woman who dressed in a way that overtly accentuated her assets, often to the point of distraction. And as she adjusted the short skirt on her hips, Jon knew to keep his attention above her neckline.

"You know, when I was growing up in Maryland," she said, moving slowly around the corner of her desk, "I guess I was in middle school. My parents took me to church with them all the time."

"Really?" asked Jon, immediately wishing he had tempered the surprise in his voice.

"Don't look so shocked, Jon. I'm not the church type, is that it?"

"No, it's not that at all, Amanda. I just didn't—"

"Oh, save it," she said. Amanda sat down in the guest chair next to Jon and crossed her bare legs. "I remember, on Wednesday nights my parents would take me to church, and we'd eat supper in the gym. It was always something cheap, like hot dogs or spaghetti. And then, while the adults listened to the pastor teach a Bible lesson, they would have kids in the youth department get on the phones and call a list of people who had visited the church. They had us read from a script. We'd say nice things about the church and why they should come back, etc. No one's going to hang up on a kid, right? And then we were supposed to ask them if they knew Jesus."

"I didn't realize you were a Christian, Amanda," said Jon, hoping against his better judgment. "So you do understand, then."

"You didn't let me finish. Do you know what the youth pastor was doing while we were on the phones?"

Jon began to feel slightly alarmed. He hadn't anticipated a personal reaction from Amanda, just an explanation of company policy about leave of absence requests and, hopefully, her approval. "No, what?"

"He was molesting my best friend in his office."

"Oh, my gosh, Amanda. That's horrible."

"It didn't come out until I was in high school. It was a big deal – news stories, everything. And it made me realize what a scam church was. Even my parents said so. They never went back after that."

Jon uncrossed his legs and placed both feet on the floor, pushing himself into a more upright position. "Amanda, listen, I'm sorry you had a bad experience with church growing up, but—"

"But, nothing! Jon, I swore when I was sixteen that I was never going to be taken advantage of by *anyone*. And now look at me." Amanda waved her hand to lead Jon's eyes around her large office. "I'm VP of Business Development for the fastest growing ad agency in the Southeast. And how many women do you see around me at my level, Jon?"

Jon thought it best not to answer.

Amanda's eyes stared intensely at Jon. "Not many, do you?"

"You've done well, Amanda. And I appreciate the opportunity and support you've given me here."

Amanda repositioned herself in her chair. Turning towards Jon, she recrossed her legs while holding the hem of her short skirt on top of her thigh. Her expression softened slightly. "Jon, you're my best creative director," she said, smoothing the tone of her voice. "You're at the top of my succession plan. Why would you want to throw your career away for some stupid religious field trip? I always thought you were smarter than that. Was I wrong?"

Jon had watched Amanda close business deals with her cornering questions many times before. He knew to ignore them. "Amanda, I respect your opinion and what you've done with your career. And I assure you, I'm not trying to throw away mine. I've got almost ten years invested here. I'm just requesting a six-month unpaid leave of absence. It's not a vacation. I've talked to Matt in Human Resources, and he said I just need your approval. Can I get that from you?"

Amanda stared unblinking at Jon, her thinly plucked eyebrows slowly pushing downward. He could see the wheels turning in her head. Whatever was coming next, Jon knew it wasn't going to be good. But as he waited for her response, a peaceful calm washed over him.

"I'll tell you what, Jon," said Amanda, her voice tinged with controlled anger. "I'll approve your leave of absence if only to keep those hacks in HR off my back."

Jon knew there was more coming.

Amanda leaned towards Jon in her chair. "But let me tell you this – I refuse to hold your job for you. I don't care what Matt says. So if you do have the nerve to come back to Crescent-Tango after your little Jesus trip, you'll be emptying trashcans, if I have anything to do with it. So, I'll ask you one last time. Do you really want to do this?"

"Absolutely," said Jon, without hesitation.

Amanda stood up and leaned over the front of her desk. She spun Jon's request form around and signed it. "Here's your damn approval," she said, whipping the form to Jon. "Now, get out of my office!"

"Thank you, Amanda," said Jon as he got up to leave.

Amanda walked around to her side of the desk. "And shut the goddamn door on your way out!"

Jon heard her mumble something under her breath as she enabled the speaker on her phone and dialed a number on the keypad. He walked towards the door and closed it behind him as he left. Just outside her office, Jon paused as he heard Matt's voice on Amanda's speakerphone.

"Hey, Amanda."

"Don't *hey* me, Matt! What the hell are you trying to do to me?!"

Jon smiled to himself as he walked down the hall to his office. "Here we go, Lord."

twenty four

Buzz Kill

"Do not suppose that I have come to bring peace to the earth.
I did not come to bring peace, but a sword. For I have come
to turn 'a man against his father, a daughter against her
mother, a daughter-in-law against her mother-in-law – a man's
enemies will be the members of his own household.'"
- *Matthew 10:34-36*

"Could you please lighten up tonight?" asked Lacey, fluffing her long brown hair with her fingers in front of the bathroom mirror. "This party's important to me, and I don't want you being a buzz-kill." She glanced at Jon's reflection as she adjusted her short black dress around her bust line.

Jon stood behind her in his undershirt and jeans, brushing his teeth. "I'm not a buzz-kill," he said, trying to keep toothpaste from spilling from his mouth.

"You didn't used to be," said Lacey, leaving the bathroom. "And when are we going to get a house with more than one bathroom?" she asked as she walked down the hall to their bedroom.

Jon sighed as he took the toothbrush out of his mouth and spit into the pedestal sink. He rinsed his mouth out with water, wiped his face off with the hand towel, and walked slowly to the bedroom to find Lacey. He could hear her bumping around inside their closet.

"Why does it bother you so much that I don't drink anymore?" asked Jon through the closet door. "I'd think you'd be happy to have a husband you don't have to worry about that way."

Lacey opened the closet door. "One drink is not going to kill you, Jon."

"That's fine, but it's just not who I am anymore, OK?" Jon waited for her response as he watched her slip a mismatched pair of black shoes on her feet. "Lacey, it's important to me that you—"

"Which one looks the best?" she asked, looking down at her feet. She lifted her right foot behind her for a moment, returned it loudly to the hardwood floor and then repeated the process with her left.

"I like the one on your right foot," said Jon, pointing to the black open-toed pump.

Lacey kicked off the pump and replaced it with a black dress sandal matching the one on her left foot.

"Why did you even ask me?" he asked, shaking his head as he left for the bathroom.

Looking in the mirror over the bathroom sink, Jon saw a scowl on his face as he ran styling gel through his damp dark brown hair. He knew Lacey's attitude was about more than whether or not he drank at parties. It was about his new faith. He had tried talking with her about it several times before – he'd even bought her a Bible – but the discussions never went the way he hoped. Maybe it was time to try again. Jon closed his eyes for a moment to gather his courage once more. "Please let me do this right, this time," he prayed as he walked back down the hall towards the bedroom. "Honey?"

"I'm in here," replied Lacey, from the opposite direction. "Are you ready?"

Jon walked the hallway towards the den, glancing in Holly's room on the way to make sure she was sleeping. Entering the den, he found Lacey sitting on the edge of the couch touching-up her fingernails with red nail polish.

"Why aren't you dressed?" she asked. "We need to be leaving soon. I told Brittany's mom we'd pick her up at seven."

Jon sat down next to her on the couch. "Lacey, I want to talk to you for a minute, and I need you to listen to me, OK?"

"Fine, but can you make it quick? You need to go get her." Lacey twisted the top onto her bottle of nail polish, set it on the coffee table, and looked expectantly at Jon.

"The babysitter can wait a few minutes; this is important," said Jon, reaching for Lacey's hand.

"Don't touch me! My nails are wet!"

"Sorry! I'm sorry," said Jon, trying to contain his quickly growing frustration. He felt tempted to just retreat to the bedroom and finish dressing for the party. Maybe it wasn't the best time, after all.

"What's *so* important that it can't wait?" asked Lacey, waving her hands quickly in front of her to dry her nails.

Jon took a deep breath and exhaled. "Look, I know you've struggled with some of the changes in my life since I accepted Christ last year." Watching Lacey roll her eyes, he hesitated for a moment and gathered the resolve he needed to continue. "And I know you don't like the fact that I don't drink anymore."

"I don't like the fact that you're no fun anymore, Jon. That's the problem," said Lacey. "I don't see why it's such a big deal to have a drink with friends. It doesn't mean you're not a Christian if you drink. Mark drinks. Courtney drinks. Thompson drinks. They're all Christians. They go to church every week. But no – you have to be all *Holier than Thou* about it."

"First of all, the people at this party tonight are not my friends, they're *your* friends. *My* friends ditched me when I stopped drinking. But that's beside the point."

"No, Jon. That *is* the point. You don't care about your friends anymore. You don't care about me anymore. All you care about is that Bible of yours, Holly, and that stupid dog."

Jon shook his head in disagreement, but let Lacey vent.

"Honestly, Jon, I just don't know what to do with you anymore. You're not the same man I married."

"Exactly! I'm *not* the same man you married. That's what I've been trying to make you see. God's changed me, Lacey. And I can't do anything about that; I won't."

"Well, I've got news, buster. If you don't get your nose out of that Bible and start paying more attention to me, I'm out of here!"

"What?! Oh, come on! Give me a break! I shouldn't have to choose between you and God, Lacey. That's ridiculous!"

"Well, it sure looks that way to me, Jon! I want things back to the way they were. Back when you were normal!"

"Normal?! What's normal, Lacey? Getting drunk at these stupid parties like we're back in college? That sure seems normal enough for you!"

"No one's saying you have to get drunk, Jon!" Lacey rose from the couch and stomped into the kitchen. "You're being such an ass right now!"

"If normal means living without God in my life," shouted Jon from the den, "I'm not going back to that, Lacey! I know what that's like, and I won't do it! End of story!"

Jon found himself alone in the den. Dropping his head into his hands, he realized he had done it again. Every time he had tried to talk with Lacey about his faith, he'd just made things worse. He closed his eyes and took a deep breath to reset himself. Leaving the couch, he walked into the kitchen and found Lacey emptying items out of a small black purse on the counter and stuffing them angrily into another small black purse.

"And when are you going to make me a new key to the front door?" she asked, holding her keys out to Jon. "I can't even get in the house half the time with this one."

"I'm sorry. I'll do it tomorrow."

Lacey threw her keys into her purse. "You've said that how many times now, Jon?"

Jon chose not to answer. He stood beside her for a moment, hoping her emotions would fade. He didn't want to talk about house keys. He wanted to talk about faith. "Look," he said, in a softer voice, "I just don't see why we can't do this together."

Lacey stopped fumbling with her purse and looked at Jon. "Do what together, Jon?!"

Jon studied her eyes for a moment. They appeared cold and intimidating. He tried to swallow, but his mouth was dry. His mind raced to put the right words together. "The whole faith thing," he said, feebly.

"The what?"

Jon closed his eyes briefly and shook his head. "That's not what I wanted to say. I meant – I want us to start going to church together. I want you to have the same peace and joy I've found in my relationship with Christ."

"*Peace and joy*? Is that what you call this? We're arguing, Jon, in case you haven't noticed."

Jon tried to apologize, "Lacey, I'm—"

Lacey put up her hand. "Don't even start that with me again, Jon. I'm happy that you've found God or whatever. That's fine." She walked past him and opened her purse on the kitchen table. "But we should be having *fun* while we're young! That's all I'm saying."

"I'm not against fun, sweetie. I'm not," said Jon, following behind her. "I just find fun in different things than I used to."

"Well, if you want to act like some old man while you're still in your twenties, that's your choice. But don't expect me to be happy about it." Lacey pulled a tube of dark red lipstick from her purse. "And don't *sweetie* me in the middle of an argument. I'm mad at you right now."

"Fair enough," said Jon, trying to offer a smile.

"Look, Jon, I know you mean well," Lacey said, walking to the wall mirror next to the table. "I've read some of the Bible you gave me. And that church we went to for Easter wasn't bad. But I'm just not ready for all that. I've got plenty of time to worry about being religious later." She smoothed lipstick onto her lips and smacked them together as she looked at her reflection. "But right now," she said, returning the lipstick to her purse, "I'm ready to go to a party. And I plan on having a good time."

"Lacey, I didn't mean to start a fight with all this."

"Well, you did anyway, didn't you? Look, I tell you what – you stay here tonight with Holly and your Bible and Jo-Jo. That's what you want to do, anyway. And I'll go to the party by myself." She paused to check her hair in the mirror. "I'll have a better time without dragging you around all night, anyway."

"Lacey, I want to go, OK? Just give me a minute to get ready."

"No, Jon! You don't get it – I don't want you to go. Call Brittany right now and tell her we don't need her. Her number's on the wall next to the phone." She picked up her purse from the kitchen table and walked towards the front door.

"Lacey, please," said Jon, following her.

"I'll just tell everyone Holly's sick or something," she said, opening the door. "Have fun alone, Jon." Lacey walked out the door and closed it behind her.

Jon gave her a moment to come back inside, confident she was just trying to make a point. But the sound of her car door closing and the engine
starting pushed him quickly through the door and out onto the front stoop.
"Lacey!" he shouted. He watched her car pull away from the curb and speed
up the street.

Jon stepped back inside, closed the door and plopped down heavily on
the couch. "What a disaster," he said out loud. Jo-Jo crept slowly into the den
and pushed the top of his head against Jon's leg. "You don't like us arguing,
do you, boy?" he said, scratching behind his dog's ears. "And she doesn't
really think you're stupid." Jon leaned back and looked around his den. On
the fireplace mantel and on tables and shelves around the room sat framed
pictures of Lacey and her girlfriends, posing together at recent parties. He
noticed how he wasn't in any of them. He imagined the same frames filled
with pictures of him with his wife and baby daughter, smiling together as
a family. "How can I make that happen?" he wondered. He moved off the
couch and onto his knees. Lowering his head, Jon began to pray.

"Almighty God, I suck at this. Are you sure you want me to follow you?
I don't know what I'm doing. When I talk with Lacey about you I just cause
arguments. And at work they just laugh at me. Brant doesn't even speak to
me anymore. I love it when it's just you and me, God, but when I get around
other people…it's just not easy for me. I can't seem to say or do the right
things with anybody. I want to help Lacey find what I've found in you, but I
think I'm just making things worse. Please help me, God. Help me to share
my faith with her. Please give me the words to say, Lord, because I screw it
up every time. I'm sorry, God."

twenty five

Mom

"Honor your father and your mother, as the
Lord your God has commanded you"
- Deuteronomy 5:16

The elevator doors closed. And though the second floor button glowed brightly, Jon pushed it again to be sure he was moving. He could easily walk up the two flights of stairs faster than the nursing home elevator could travel one floor, but he was in no hurry. It was Saturday afternoon and he had nowhere else to be. When the doors finally opened to the second floor residence hall, two white-haired women, each leaning over aluminum-frame walkers with tennis balls covering the back glides, blocked Jon's exit.

"Good afternoon, ladies," said Jon with a smile as he took a step back and held the doors open.

"Hello," both ladies said as they made their way into the elevator.

"That's Ella Smoak's boy," said one of the women to the other, as if Jon couldn't hear.

"I know that," said the other, smiling at Jon.

Jon slid by them and let go of the elevator doors. "Y'all have a good day," he said, stepping into the hallway.

"He sure is easy on the eyes," Jon heard one of the old women say as the doors clanged shut.

Jon smiled to himself as he headed down the hall. Passing an open apartment door, he saw an elderly woman relaxing in a recliner watching

125

television. Pink bedroom slippers hung off the toes of her white feet, which poked from underneath a crocheted throw blanket. "Hello, Ms. Lilly," he said, slowing in front of her door. The woman waved absently without shifting her focus from the TV. Pleased that he at least got a reaction this time, Jon continued towards the nurses' station. His favorite nurse, a tall Jamaican woman with long rope twist hair, rounded the corner from the other direction and stopped at the station.

"How is she today, Angelique?" asked Jon as he approached.

"Hey, Mr. Smoak," said the nurse. "She's had a good day. She got a little fussy this afternoon when she couldn't remember how to work her TV remote, but she was fine after that."

"Is she eating OK?" asked Jon, pausing for a moment at the desk.

"That you don't have to worry about, Mr. Smoak. She eats just about everything we bring to her. She had a chicken salad sandwich, some fruit, and a bowl of ice cream about an hour ago."

"Well, I appreciate you looking after her."

"She's one of my favorites. You know that."

Jon smiled at the nurse and continued on his way through a common area filled with orange couches, a large screen television, tables, and chairs. A plump elderly man, wearing red suspenders over a white T-shirt, sat asleep on the couch facing the TV. "Hey, Mr. Meetze," said Jon. The man's eyes opened briefly as Jon passed by and turned left into another hallway.

Seeing his mother's door open, he entered the small apartment to find her asleep in her chair in front of a college football game on television. Jon took advantage of his unnoticed arrival to browse the assorted family relics, preserved from his parents' former home, decorating her small living space. Framed pictures from family vacations and sittings at Olan Mills, seemingly random brass and porcelain knickknacks, and their large ornately framed family portrait, which had hung proudly over his parents' mantel for years, but now hung askew on the wall behind his mother's chair. Taken by a professional photographer in front of the dunes on Pawleys the summer before Jon began high school, the picture had become an iconic reminder of his youth and love for the beach.

Jon placed two fingers under the left corner of the portrait and lifted slightly. As he leaned back to see if he had leveled the picture, he found himself gazing into his own smiling fourteen-year-old eyes. He remembered kneeling on the sand next to his father, facing the ocean as he watched the photographer – a cranky old woman from Georgetown – race against the setting sun and incoming tide. He could still hear her raspy voice barking instructions for their poses as each successive wave inched closer to her heels. As Jon studied his youthful face, he felt as though he were staring at a stranger. "What was going on in that head of yours?" he mumbled to himself.

Jon's eyes dropped to a small narrow table pushed against the wall underneath the portrait. Next to a brass lamp, sat the cheap, battery-powered, glass and brass clock he remembered giving his father for a birthday present some thirty years earlier. At five minutes after two on some forgotten day since then, the clock's hands had permanently stopped moving. As Jon wondered why it remained among this last small vestige of his family's life together, his mother began to stir in her chair.

"Hey, Mom," said Jon over the noise of the game on her TV.

She lifted her head and smiled, as if she hadn't been asleep. "Hey there, Son. It's so good to see you. What a nice surprise."

Jon kissed his mother on her cheek. "I told you I'd be out after lunch, silly."

"Oh, I know that. I was just kidding. How are you, Son?"

"I'm fine," said Jon, looking at the football game on the TV screen. "Duke and Virginia. Who are you pulling for, Mom?"

His mother squinted her eyes at the screen. "I can't see who's playing."

"It's Duke and Virginia, Mom."

She waved her hand in front of her like she was shooing away a fly. "Move my glasses and that stuff off the rocking chair, Son, so you can sit down. And turn the TV down a little, so we can talk."

Jon picked up the newspaper, reading glasses, and a box of tissues from the rocking chair and placed them a few feet away on the counter by the sink. Taking the TV remote from her lap, he turned down the volume so they could hear each other and took a seat in the chair.

"How was your day, Mom?"

"Fine, fine. I think they're trying to starve me here, though. I haven't eaten a thing all day."

Jon smiled, knowing better. "Would you like something now? I could ask Angelique to get you something."

"No, I'm fine. What did you do today, Son?" It was her usual conversation starter.

"Oh, just a few things around the house. Nothing exciting." Jon began to feel slightly anxious about the purpose for his visit and turned his attention back to the game on TV. "Looks like Duke's about to score. You like Duke, don't you, Mom?"

"Only if they're playing basketball. Then I'd be more interested."

"Um, look, Mom, there's something I came to talk to you about."

His mother smiled, her eyes suddenly beaming as she turned to Jon. "Did I ever tell you about the time your father took me to a South Carolina basketball game and locked his keys in the car with the engine still running?"

Jon pretended to hear the story for the first time. "Did he really? What happened?"

"Well, he...I was...." Her voice faded as her eyes searched the room in confusion.

"Did he forget to turn the car off, Mom?" asked Jon, trying to prompt her to finish her favorite story. She continued to look around the room. "Mom?"

"I put my glasses somewhere this morning and now I don't know where they are."

"I'm sorry, Mom, I put them on the counter just a minute ago." Jon retrieved them for her. "Here you go."

"Oh, I don't need them. Just put them here on the table next to the phone in case Jon calls."

Jon smiled to himself as he set her glasses on the end table and returned to the rocking chair. "I'm right here, Mom."

"Hey, Son, it's so good to see you." His mother smiled and patted the back of Jon's hand. "What did you do today?"

Jon tried to make his answer sound different than before. "Oh, let's see...I worked in the yard and cleaned up around the house. Just a regular Saturday, I guess." He inched forward in the rocker. "Mom, I need to talk with you about something."

"And how's Lacey and my favorite grand-dog, Jo-Jo?"

Jon looked at the old picture of Lacey, Jo-Jo, and himself on the table next to his mother. "Um, they're fine, Mom. They're fine."

"Well, you need to bring them with you next time you come. The residents love when people bring dogs to visit, you know."

"I will, Mom." Jon took his mother's hand gently in his. "Mom, I'm going to be going away for a little while."

"How's Holly doing in school? What grade is she in now?"

"Holly's in college now, Mom. She's at USC." Jon began to feel slightly frustrated. "Mom, did you hear me? I said, 'I'm going to be going away for a while.'"

"Well, I might take a nap soon, so don't be gone long."

"No, Mom. I mean I'm going on a trip. For about six months."

His mother looked at him, but didn't respond. It seemed she'd heard him and was now trying to process the news.

"It's just for five or six months. Holly's going to look after you while I'm gone. And I'm still going to call you every day, OK?"

His mother sat quietly looking at the television.

"Mom, do you understand? I'm going on a trip for a while."

She turned her face towards her son. "Where will you be going? Do you need money?"

"No. Mom, listen," said Jon, placing his other hand on hers. "It's something I need to do for God."

His mother's eyes moved slowly around his face. "What do you mean, Son?"

Jon leaned forward in the rocking chair. "Mom, I realized lately that I've been just coasting in my faith. Just going through the motions of being a Christian. It's become meaningless to me. And I can't accept that. I need to find out what it's like to really do what the Bible tells us to do. So, I'm taking some time off from work, and I'm just going to travel and look for opportunities to share Christ with people. It's just something I feel God's calling me to do." Jon studied her aged face and blue eyes, trying to discern what she was thinking. "Do you understand, Mom?"

His mother nodded and squeezed Jon's hand. "You're such a good boy, Jon. You remind me so much of your father. He'd be so proud of you. You know, he went on a mission trip, once. To Russia. I think you were in college at the time."

"I remember him going on that, yes ma'am."

"Oh, he was so excited about the Lord when he came back home. He got to tell the whole church about it in one of our services. I was so proud of him."

"I wish I could have been there for that," said Jon. He looked down at his mother's hand and rubbed his thumb across her age-spotted skin as he thought of his father. A memory from his childhood – walking on the beach with his dad, looking for sharks' teeth and sharing stories – played warmly in his mind. His vision blurred with tears. "I still miss him, Mom."

"I do, too," she said, squeezing his hand. "Look at me, Son."

Jon sensed a new resolve in his mother's voice as he looked up into her face. Her eyes seemed more clear and lucid than he had seen in over a year.

"Jon, you do what you need to do, and don't worry about me," she said. "They take good care of me here. You just remember that I'm praying for you every day. Just like I always do."

Jon got on one knee beside his mother's chair and wrapped his arms around her. "Thank you, Mom. I love you." Tears dripped off his face and fell on the back of her pink nightgown.

"I love you, too, Son. Now, you go make God proud of you."

"Yes, ma'am."

twenty six

The Cowboy Preacher

"Therefore, if he is in Christ, he is a new creation;
the old has gone, the new has come!"
- 2 Corinthians 5:17

From his place on the couch in the den, Jon could hear the sound of pots and pans clanging, cabinet doors closing, and utensils being shuffled in drawers. The loud whirling of a mixer added to the noise coming from the kitchen. Pointing the remote at the television, Jon turned up the volume. While he was hungry from raking leaves and pine straw in the yard all afternoon, he didn't want to hear all the noise that went into making his Saturday dinner. "What are you making in there?" he asked, loudly.

The sound of the mixer stopped. "Did you say something?" asked Lacey from the kitchen.

"I said, 'What are you making?'"

Lacey leaned her head around the doorway of the den. "That asparagus, chicken, noodle stuff my mom made after we brought Holly home from the hospital last month. And a few other things."

"Oh," said Jon, with little interest as he looked at the TV. He hoped Lacey didn't notice his dog sleeping on the other end of the couch near his feet.

Lacey disappeared back into the kitchen. "Is that OK?" she called out. "Because it's gonna be a little while."

"That's fine. Take your time." Jon adjusted the blanket to cover his cold feet and looked at his dog. "I think I'd rather eat your food, Jo-Jo."

"What?" asked Lacey.

"I said, 'That's fine!'" He pointed the remote control at their nineteen-inch television on the table across the room and changed the channel. He wasn't looking for anything specific to watch, just cycling through stations one at a time while he relaxed on the couch. Trying to get more comfortable, Jon pushed his feet against his black Labrador Retriever. "Move, Jo-Jo. Give me some room."

Lacey leaned back around the doorway and looked at Jon. "And what is that dog doing on the couch?"

"He's sleeping," said Jon, without taking his eyes off the TV.

Lacey stepped into the den. "I don't want him on our furniture, Jon. He stinks."

Jon continued flipping channels. "I'll give him a bath later."

"Are you going to bathe the couch, too? Get him off. And please turn that TV down. You'll wake up Holly."

"*I'll* wake her up? You're like a demolition crew in there."

"I'm trying to make us supper, Jon. Now, get the dog off the couch." Lacey snapped her fingers and pointed at the floor. "Now."

Jon pushed the mute button on the TV remote and sighed. "Hop down, Jo-Jo." He gently pushed his feet against Jo-Jo's back, moving him toward the edge of the couch as Lacey returned to the kitchen. The dog's long legs lazily reached for the floor as he slid off the cushion. His eyes slowly opened as he found himself standing up, leaning against the couch. Jo-Jo looked at Jon then sulked away to the middle of the den, plopping onto the rug in a tight ball of protest.

Jon stretched his legs across the warm cushion where Jo-Jo had been and resettled himself under the blanket. He had stopped changing channels while pushing Jo-Jo onto the floor and now tried to assess what he was seeing on the TV screen. The seats of a small baseball stadium were full of people, all sitting quietly and looking towards the field. The view on the screen changed to a tall, older man standing behind a wooden podium. He was speaking from a large stage in center field positioned just behind a University of Texas Longhorn logo painted on the artificial grass surface, but Jon couldn't hear what he was saying. "What's with the sound?" He looked at the remote and realized he had pushed the mute button. "Oh, duh," he said, pushing the button again. The twang of a Texas accent filled Jon's ears as the man addressed the crowd.

"And out of all the other things you could be doing tonight, you're here with us. And we're thankful that you are. You know, it's tough to compete with Longhorn football any Saturday. But like I told my beautiful wife, Martha, A&M fans in Austin need Jesus, too." The crowd erupted in a loud ovation as the man stepped back from the podium and smiled.

"Ah, Cam Parsons, *The Cowboy Preacher*," Jon said to himself in a fake Texas accent. "Yee-haw." He remembered when the old evangelist had brought his crusade to Columbia almost three years before. "That seems like forever ago," he thought. Since that time, he had met and married Lacey, graduated from college, started his first job, and had just welcomed his daughter, Holly, into the world. And here was Cam Parsons, once again, still going strong. "When's this old fossil going to retire, for Pete's sake?" wondered Jon as he took in the scene.

Covering the infield – from the backstop to second base – sat rows and rows of folding chairs filled with quiet, attentive people of all generations. The seats of the stadium were full, as well. "I just don't get it," thought Jon. "Is there nothing better for these people to be doing in Austin on a Saturday?"

The famous preacher looked at the crowd before him through thin, round, wire-framed glasses. A mix of thinning blonde and gray hair gave way to thick sideburns on either side of his tanned, aging face. His white dress shirt and bolo tie, underneath a tan sport coat with brown suede yokes, fit perfectly with the southwestern attire of his audience. On the stage behind him sat important looking people, including several men in suits sporting cowboy hats. "Texas," laughed Jon, shaking his head. As the preacher continued speaking, he gripped the lectern with both hands. His arms were straight and his feet spread apart, one positioned behind the other, as if he were bracing himself against a strong wind.

As Jon pointed the remote at the TV, his thumb poised to change the channel, he found himself lingering curiously on the spectacle before him. "Maybe just for grins," he said to Jo-Jo and lowered the remote. Jo-Jo had finished pouting and was now stretched out on the floor against the couch. Jon's fingers scratched behind Jo-Jo's soft ears as he listened to the preacher's message.

A recent major study on religion in America found that eighty-six percent of the population call themselves Christian. Eighty-six percent. I find that to be an amazing figure. Compare that to the results of several other surveys, which report that only about twenty-five percent of the population attends church on a regular basis. Eighty-six percent say they're Christian, but only twenty-five percent attend church. That means only thirty percent of those who say they are Christian actually go to church. Let me say that again. Only thirty percent of those people who say they are Christian go to church. What do you make of that?

Jon smiled to himself. "I guess that means we're in the seventy percent, eh, Jo-Jo?"

Even more revealing is the concern among those conducting these studies that many people participating in the surveys are not truthful in their responses. One such study sampled a county population in Ohio and compared actual church attendance with the results of their survey of the same county. In other words, they compared the percent of people who actually went to church with the percent who *said* they go to church in their survey. The difference? Thirty-six percent of the population in the county *said* they attend church regularly. But only twenty percent actually did. How about that? People lied about how often they go to church. You would never do that would you?

"Of course, not – I never go," said Jon, enjoying his dialogue with the Texas preacher.

I think it's safe to say that all people who claim to be Christians are not really Christians. All people who claim to be Christians don't follow Christ. They may have religion in their lives to some degree, but they don't have Jesus.

Suddenly, Jon wasn't so amused. He was a Christian and he didn't need some hayseed evangelist telling him otherwise. He picked up the remote and pointed it at the TV as he heard the preacher say, "But some would say, 'Well, Cameron, I can be a Christian without going to church.'"

"Damn straight," agreed Jon. He gave the preacher a reprieve and lowered the remote control.

> They say, "I worship God in my own way, through nature or meditation or exercise." Well, friend, that and a quarter will get you a cup of coffee. I just showed my age, didn't I? Coffee is a little more than a quarter these days, isn't it? But my point is that those things will get you nowhere. The Bible tells us if you are in fellowship with Christ, you'll want to be around other Believers. First John chapter one, verse seven tells us, "But if we walk in the light, as he is in the light, we have fellowship with one another, and the blood of Jesus, his Son, purifies us from all sin." Simply put, Believers want to be around other Believers.

"I'm not sure I even know any other Christians, besides Mom and Dad," Jon admitted to himself. "If I do, I don't know it."

> God's people are drawn to each other. Through our shared faith we strengthen each other "as iron sharpens iron," Proverbs 27 tells us. Moreover, we are commanded to meet together. Paul tells us in the tenth chapter of the Book of Hebrews, "And let us consider how we may spur one another on toward love and good deeds. Let us not give up meeting together, as some are in the habit of doing, but let us encourage one another." So, where does that leave us when we hear statistics like this? Can you be a Christian without going to church?

Jon wasn't as quick to answer this time. He was now frowning at the television, his arms crossed in front of him.

The preacher continued, "OK, let me turn that around. Does going to church make you a Christian?"

Jon wanted to answer, "Yes," given his upbringing, but the question left him arguing with himself. He felt he could be a Christian without going to church, but he also thought going to church is what makes you a Christian. He felt trapped between his own answers.

"Why are you watching that?" asked Lacey, suddenly appearing in the den with a mixing bowl in her arm.

Startled by the intrusion, Jon tried to appear uninterested. "Oh, um…I'm just flipping channels."

Jo-Jo raised his head off the floor and looked at Jon and then at Lacey.

"Whatever," she said and returned to the kitchen.

Jo-Jo flopped onto his side as Jon turned his attention back to the TV. As Cam Parsons continued, the camera showed the face of a young girl sitting in the crowd. She appeared to be in her early to mid-twenties, Jon guessed. About his age. She sat motionless, her unblinking green eyes fixed on the old man speaking from the middle of the field. The small freckles scattered across her nose and cheeks reminded him of Jenny. And his focus on the preacher's message grew stronger.

> We said earlier that of the people who call themselves Christian in this country, only thirty percent attend church regularly. So of those thirty percent, how many would you say are born-again Christians? All of them? Half of them? It's best to say we're not sure, are we?

Jon considered the question. "Half of them probably," he thought. But he wondered which half he fell into and if it really mattered.

> You might ask, "What does it mean to be born again, any-way?" That's what Nicodemus asked. In the Gospel of John, when Nicodemus came to Jesus in secret with questions in his heart, Jesus told him "no one can see the kingdom of God unless they are born again." You must be born again if you want to spend eternity in heaven with God. It means from

the moment you place your faith in Jesus Christ and confess that he is your Lord and Savior – that he is the way, the truth, and the life who saves you by his grace from the eternal consequence of your sins – you are a new creation. Look around you here in this wonderful baseball stadium. There are eight to ten thousand people here tonight. How many people in this stadium would you say are born again Christians? What about the person seated next to you? What about you?

"What about me?" Jon wondered.

So that begs another question: Why are you here tonight? What brought you here tonight? And don't say a car or a bus. Or why are you watching on television tonight?

Jon felt a chill run down his spine. He had no idea why he was watching. He had actively avoided going to see the evangelist when he came to Columbia – to the point of losing Jenny in the process – but now he was watching Cam Parsons in his own house, by his own choice. And he didn't know why.

What is it that you're hoping to hear? What is it that you're hoping to see? When Jesus was preaching the Sermon on the Mount, Matthew and Luke both tell us that he asked a similar question. Speaking to those who had followed John the Baptist, and there were many, Jesus asked, "What did you go out into the desert to see? A reed swayed by the wind? If not, what did you go out to see? A man dressed in fine clothes? No, those who wear fine clothes are in kings' palaces. Then what did you go out to see?" Jesus was saying, what was your motivation? Why did you go through all the trouble to go see this man? So, I'm asking you the same question tonight. Why are you here? If that question makes you uncomfortable or if you're simply not sure why you're here, then I'm glad you are. Because, this message is for you.

Cam Parsons looked into the television camera. Whether he did so intentionally or by chance, Jon felt the preacher's eyes penetrate him. His words were becoming personal. Jon pulled his knees up close to his chest and wrapped his arms around them.

> Tonight, we're going to look at several more passages from the greatest sermon ever preached, Jesus' Sermon on the Mount. If you have a Bible, turn with me to the Gospel of Matthew, the first book in the New Testament.

Jon realized he had no idea where his Bible was. His parents had given him one when he went through Confirmation in seventh grade, but he hadn't seen it in years.

> The seventh chapter of Matthew, verses twenty-one through twenty-three. This is our text for this evening. Jesus was speaking to the crowd and he said, "Not everyone who says to me, 'Lord, Lord,' will enter the kingdom of heaven, but only he who does the will of my Father who is in heaven. Many will say to me on that day, 'Lord, Lord, did we not prophesy in your name, and in your name drive out demons and perform many miracles?' Then I will tell them plainly, 'I never knew you. Away from me, you evildoers!'"

Jon felt confused by what he was hearing. He had never heard these verses before. If he had, he didn't remember.

> If you look at the ministry of Jesus, it becomes clear that he was not simply seeking to grow a large fan base. He drove a hard message. He wasn't telling folks things they wanted to hear. In fact, many of his followers had their hopes in a messiah who would overthrow the occupying Romans and establish a Jewish kingdom. They were following him for the wrong reasons and would soon be disappointed and disillusioned when he was crucified. Jesus didn't make it easy to follow him. In fact, he turned many people away.

"Why would he do that?" Jon wondered. "If someone wants to be a follower, why would he say no?"

> In the Gospel of Mark, the second book in the New Testament, we're told the story of a young man who wanted eternal life. In the tenth chapter, beginning in verse seventeen, Mark tells us, "As Jesus started on his way, a man ran up to him and fell on his knees before him. 'Good teacher,' he asked, 'what must I do to inherit eternal life?' 'Why do you call me good?' Jesus answered. 'No one is good – except God alone. You know the commandments: Do not murder, do not commit adultery, do not steal, do not give false testimony, do not defraud, honor your father and mother.' 'Teacher,' he declared, 'all these I have kept since I was a boy.' Jesus looked at him and loved him. 'One thing you lack,' he said. 'Go, sell everything you have and give to the poor, and you will have treasure in heaven. Then come, follow me.'"

"Oh, come on," said Jon. "Who would do that?"

> "At this the man's face fell. He went away sad, because he had great wealth." Here was a successful, young man who claimed to be morally upright. I believe he was a good person, by most standards. I believe he respected God and was probably well known and admired in his community. Why wouldn't Jesus just welcome this young man into his fold? Hadn't he earned it through his goodness and respect for God's moral code? The answer is that – despite his grand appearances – Jesus knew this man's heart. Jesus said in Luke chapter sixteen, verse fifteen, "You are the ones who justify yourselves in the eyes of men, but God knows your hearts." The young man claimed to have kept all the laws and maybe he even believed that about himself. If he did, he was fooling himself. And Jesus knew better. He knew, for starters, the young man had broken the very

first commandment, "you shall have no other gods before me." This man's wealth was his god, whether he realized it or not. It occupied a place in his heart above God. But you'll notice, after he claimed to have kept all the laws, the Bible tells us Jesus looked at him and loved him. Why is that? Jesus knew that what he was claiming wasn't true. So why did Jesus look at him with love? It reminds me of a time when I was a young boy growing up in Shallowater, Texas. I had brought home a report card that I was less than proud of. And I was afraid to show it to my father. When he got home from work that day, I said nothing about it and went to bed early, right after supper. That must have tipped him off that something was wrong. The next day, when he got home from work, he asked me if I had received my report card. I had the chance to be honest, but I lied and said, "No, sir." I remember him kneeling down before me so he could look me in the eyes. He smiled as he held me by my shoulders and said, "Cam, I know you've had your report card for two days now. Now go and bring it to me." He knew. I don't know how he knew, but he knew. Despite that, he gave me a chance to be honest, to live up to what he expected of me. But I chose to lie. I was so ashamed. I was more ashamed of my lie than I was of my grades. And yes, I was punished for both. The rich young man in our story told Jesus he had kept all the commandments. I believe when Jesus looked at him with love and told him to sell all he had and give to the poor, he was giving him a chance – just as my father did with me – to do the right thing, to be the man God wanted him to be. What I find beautiful in this story is that Jesus didn't simply point out this young man's sin and call him a liar. He gave him an opportunity to demonstrate his love for God, to overcome his sin and be forgiven. He had a chance to choose God. Instead, he chose the lie. How sad. Understand that Jesus didn't have anything against wealth. But he knew the young man loved his wealth more than he loved God.

> Jesus said in Matthew chapter six, "You cannot serve both God and money." Love of money was the problem for this young man. And it kept him from following Jesus. Let me ask you — What do you love? If you were in this story, what would Jesus say to you? Is there something that you're clinging to that's keeping you from a relationship with God? Is there something or someone you're putting before your love for God? For this man, it was his wealth. What is it for you?

Jon didn't know how to answer. He hadn't really thought about what it means to love God. He had never given God much thought at all, except when he was angry with him occasionally when things didn't go his way. The preacher's question left Jon wondering. What was he missing?

> Maybe you love being admired or being liked by your friends or respected for your work. Or maybe yours is the same struggle this young man had. You love money or possessions. The Bible tells us he had an opportunity to make a choice. But when he left his encounter with Jesus, he went away sad. He had an opportunity to be rejoicing for all eternity. But instead, he went away sad. In a few minutes, I'm going to give you the same opportunity this young man had. You'll have a choice. How will you feel when you leave here tonight?

Jon felt the sermon leading him down a path he didn't intend to follow when he sat down on the couch with Jo-Jo. If he continued watching, he would have a decision to make. He placed his hand back on the remote and let his thumb find the button to change the channel. Still, he kept watching.

> If we look at Jesus' Sermon on the Mount, surely many people were moved by his message. Matthew 7:28-29 tell us, "When Jesus had finished saying these things, the crowds were amazed at his teaching, because he taught as one who had authority, and not as their teachers of the law."

This was the sermon to beat all sermons! Here was the Son of God preaching truth straight at them! They had never heard anything like this, not even from John the Baptist. So, as you would expect, the Bible tells us the crowds followed him down from the mountainside. Matthew picks it up there in chapter eight, verse eighteen and tells us, "Then a teacher of the law came to him and said, 'Teacher, I will follow you wherever you go.' Jesus replied, 'Foxes have holes and birds of the air have nests, but the Son of Man has no place to lay his head.'" Now, this man was a teacher of the law – God's law! He knew the Scriptures backwards and forwards. He had heard the words of Jesus in his Sermon on the Mount and he was sold! He said, "Jesus, I'll follow you wherever you go!" What an impact this man could have for Jesus in his ministry. He was one of the most respected men in his community and in the Synagogue. But Jesus knew his heart. This man was probably in a very comfortable position. Maybe he enjoyed his stature in the community. Maybe he liked being admired for his knowledge. So Jesus was telling this teacher, "Look, following me will cost you something you love." It will cost you the comfort you enjoy. Jesus was saying, "Which do you love more?" The Bible doesn't tell us this man's response, but again, like the rich young man before, he had to make a choice. What would you have done if you were this man?

"I'm not sure," Jon thought to himself. He let the remote fall from his hand onto the cushion as he continued watching.

Years ago, when I was pastoring a small church in West Texas, I was asked to preach at a revival for a church in another town about seventy miles away. The revival was on a Sunday night, but I wanted to attend the church's Sunday morning service, so I could get a feel for the people there.

I made arrangements for my associate pastor to preach for me at my church, and I drove over to the other town early that Sunday morning. During the worship service, I sat in a pew towards the back of the church next to a man in his mid-thirties, I'd say. He was a rugged man. I could tell by his hands that he worked hard for a living. We worshiped together, this man and me. And after the service was over, I asked him how long he'd been a member. "Oh, I'm not a member," he said. So, I asked him how long he'd been visiting. "About five years," he said. That seemed like a long time to just be a visitor. So I said, "Can I ask why you haven't joined?" The man looked at me and said, "It don't cost nothing just to visit."

Jon laughed. But he could see himself doing the same thing.

Like the young man before in our story, this man liked the idea of belonging to Jesus, but he wasn't willing to suffer the cost. It's tragic, really. In the next few verses, Matthew gives us one more example. "Another disciple said to him, 'Lord, first let me go and bury my father.' But Jesus told him, 'Follow me, and let the dead bury their own dead.'" Notice that Matthew said this man was already a disciple. He had already been following Jesus around the countryside, listening and learning. Maybe even helping out in some way. Others knew him as a disciple of Jesus. Still, as we see in this passage, he had not yet committed himself to Jesus. But now, perhaps after being moved by Jesus' preaching in the Sermon on the Mount, he realized he had to take the next step. Maybe you're like this man. You go to church. Maybe you're always on the front pew every Sunday morning. Or maybe you're even a deacon or an usher. You serve on committees or maybe even teach Sunday school. Anyone who knows you would say you're a Christian.

Jon wondered what people would say about him. Would anyone say he's a Christian? He always thought he was. Had he been fooling himself his whole life? Had he been fooling anyone else?

> You may be seen that way by others, but have you really committed yourself to following Jesus?

"No," Jon answered, honestly.

> This man was ready to do that. He wanted to commit. But he said to Jesus, "Can it be a little later? Can I just wait until my father passes away? Then I'm all yours, Jesus." This man obviously loved his father. And that's good, right? But Jesus was asking him to make a choice – Who do you love more? Me or your father? That's tough, isn't it? Some of you have tough choices to make tonight. Who do you love more than God? Is it your wife or your husband? Is it your children? Maybe it's a boyfriend or girlfriend. Maybe it's the person sitting next to you. Jesus said in Matthew chapter ten, "Anyone who loves his father or mother more than me is not worthy of me; anyone who loves his son or daughter more than me is not worthy of me; and anyone who does not take up his cross and follow me is not worthy of me. Whoever finds his life will lose it, and whoever loses his life for my sake will find it." Who do you love more than God? We don't know what either of these men decided. But they each had a choice to make. I know some of you might be sitting there listening to this saying, "Cam, I'm already a Christian. I've made my choice. Where do you come off questioning my faith?"

A few minutes earlier, Jon certainly felt that way. But his arrogance, fueled by ignorance, had been stripped away.

> It's not me that's questioning your faith, friend. It's Jesus. Remember our text for this evening? Jesus said, "Not

everyone who says to me, 'Lord, Lord,' will enter the kingdom of heaven, but only he who does the will of my Father who is in heaven. Many will say to me on that day, 'Lord, Lord, did we not prophesy in your name, and in your name drive out demons and perform many miracles?' Then I will tell them plainly, 'I never knew you.'" This, to me, is the scariest verse in all of Scripture. Imagine living your whole life, thinking of yourself as a Christian, going to church, helping old ladies cross the street, maybe even going on a mission trip here and there. Then one day you die. And we'll all do this one day regardless of what we believe now – one day you'll stand before Jesus. But instead of hearing Jesus say, "Well done, good and faithful servant," you hear, "Sorry, I never knew you." Friends, hear me now when I say this: In that day that Jesus speaks of, it won't matter whether you sat in church every Sunday. Or served on the church finance committee. Or listened to Christian radio stations. It won't matter if you had a Christian fish on your car. Or even told others about Jesus. Jesus isn't interested in your Christian resume. He's after your heart. And if you can't give him that, he's already told you what he's going to say to you – "I never knew you." Tonight, many of you have a choice to make. I believe you know who you are. The Holy Spirit is working in you right now, tugging on your heart.

Jon felt his heart begin to beat faster in his chest.

But you say, "Cam, I already believe in God and Jesus. Isn't that enough?" The Book of James says, "You believe that there is one God. Good! Even the demons believe that – and shudder." Friends, belief is not the same as faith. Each of the men in our Scriptures tonight had belief. That wasn't the problem. Jesus wanted more. He wanted their hearts. He wanted their trust. Understand this: Faith comes when you act on your belief, when you put your trust in the

One who can save you. You must step beyond belief and trust your heart and your life to Jesus. Dear friends, please don't fool yourselves. Don't just listen to what I'm saying here tonight and say, "Gee, honey. That was a good sermon. Let's go eat." If you feel something pulling on your heart tonight, I beg you to act on it. Your eternal life may depend on what you decide this very evening. James 1:22 says, "Do not merely listen to the word, and so deceive yourselves. Do what it says." And what does Jesus say we are to do? He says, "Come to me... come to me, all you who are weary and burdened, and I will give you rest." Jesus died for you. He took the Cross for your sins. And he rose again for you so that by faith you might have a place with him in eternity. He wants you to come to him tonight. The three men in our story had their opportunity. This is yours. It's time to make a choice. Jesus said, "I stand at the door and knock. If anyone hears my voice and opens the door, I will come in." Jesus is knocking on the door of your heart, right now. The choice is yours. Will you open the door? If you want to say yes to Jesus tonight, to give your heart and life to him in faith, to be sure he knows you as his own – I'm going to ask that you come forward from wherever you are in this stadium. Come and stand here before this stage. You come right now. But you ask, "Cam, why do I have to come forward? Can't I just sit where I am?" Jesus himself said in the tenth chapter of Matthew, "Whoever acknowledges me before others, I will also acknowledge before my Father in heaven. But whoever disowns me before others, I will disown before my Father in heaven." Jesus wants you to acknowledge him publicly. All those he called to follow him in Scripture, he called publicly. And that's what you need to do tonight. You say, "But I don't even know what to do when I get down there." Don't worry about that. I'm going to lead you in a prayer in just a moment and we'll settle this for all eternity. Second Corinthians six, verse two says, "I tell you, now is the time of God's favor, now is the day of salvation." You come now as the choir sings.

The choir behind Cam Parsons began to sing a song Jon had heard before in church with his parents.

> *Just as I am, without one plea,*
> *but that thy blood was shed for me,*
> *and that thou bidst me come to thee,*
> *O Lamb of God, I come, I come.*
> *Just as I am, and waiting not,*
> *to rid my soul of one dark blot,*
> *to thee whose blood can cleanse each spot,*
> *O Lamb of God, I come, I come.*

As Jon watched hundreds of people make their way onto the baseball field, tears flowed down his face. He wished he were one of them. With the choir humming the song's melody softly in the background, Cam Parsons turned to the television camera. A wave of anticipation flushed over Jon's body. He straightened himself on the couch.

"As the people here in Austin make their decisions," said the preacher, "this is your opportunity. If you've never made a decision to follow Jesus, to trust him to save you from your sins, you can do that right now."

Jon was trembling. He held his breath for what was to come next.

"If you'd like to accept Jesus as your Lord and Savior, if you'd like to make that choice tonight, wherever you are, would you pray this after me?"

A feeling of fear began to grip Jon. He watched and listened as the preacher prayed.

> Dear God, I've made my choice tonight. And I choose to
> follow Jesus. I admit that I'm a sinner, Lord. But I know that
> you love me, anyway. I know that, because you gave your
> Son to die for me on the Cross, so I could be forgiven and
> made righteous in your sight. I'm sorry for my sins, Lord.
> And I ask you now to forgive me. I choose to accept Jesus
> into my heart and make him my risen Lord and Savior from
> this moment on. It's in his name I pray. Amen.

Cam Parsons, smiling broadly, looked into the camera.

> If you just prayed that prayer with me and meant it in your
> heart, then on the authority of God's Word, you now belong
> to Jesus. Second Corinthians five seventeen tells us that if
> anyone is in Christ, "he is a new creation□ the old has gone,
> the new has come." Welcome to the family of God.

Jon felt his emotions overtake him as he threw off the blanket, stepped over Jo-Jo and hurried down the hallway. Just past Holly's nursery, he turned quickly into the bathroom and shut the door. Falling on his knees, he buried his face in the blue bath rug. Flashing rapidly through his mind came memories of things he had done, words he had said and people he had hurt. On and on, memories of sin in his life flowed like a cruel slide show. He'd never felt remorse for any of them. But now his heart was breaking over all of them. For the first time in his life, Jon saw himself the way God saw him – as a sinner. And it hurt.

"I'm sorry. I'm sorry. I'm so sorry," Jon sobbed into the rug. "Jesus, please forgive me. Please forgive me. Oh, God, I'm so sorry. I didn't know."

Jon let the tears flow as his mind began to empty. His forehead still pressed against the rug, a peace came over him as his breathing slowed. "Thank you, dear God. Thank you, Lord Jesus. Thank you for dying for me. Thank you for saving me. I want to accept you now, Jesus, as my Lord and Savior. I love you. Amen."

Jon reached for the bathroom counter with his right hand and pulled himself up to his knees. His bewildered face stared back at him in the mirror over the sink as he stood to his feet. His eyes were swollen and his cheeks were wet. On his forehead was a red spot from pressing hard against the rug. He looked like he had been in a fight. After splashing cool water on his face, he dried it with the hand towel and studied himself in the mirror. He felt different and unsure what would happen next. But he knew his life had just changed. "I think I understand now, Jenny," Jon said into the mirror. "I think I understand."

twenty seven

The Note

"Reflect on what I am saying, for the Lord
will give you insight into all this."
- 2 Timothy 2:7

Jon stood in his boxer shorts, looking around his bedroom floor at the mess he'd created. Stacks of shirts, jeans, underwear, sweaters, and socks waited to be sorted through. "I'll do this tomorrow," he told himself. He moved a suitcase, gym bag, and a pile of shoes off his bed and arranged his pillows against the headboard so he could sit upright against them. Sliding his legs under the covers, he lifted his Bible from the nightstand and placed it on his lap. He could hear the click of his dog's toenails on the hardwood floor in the hallway as Elvis approached his closed bedroom door. The dog whimpered and scratched at the door. Knowing the fun Elvis would have with his clothes on the floor, Jon had intentionally kept him out while he decided what to take and what to leave behind.

"No, Elvis. Go lay down, boy."

The whimpering stopped and the sound of toenails clicking away from his door faded into silence.

Jon sighed and looked around his room. In three days, he would be leaving the comforts of his home to go wherever God led him to share the Gospel. With his Bible on his lap, he closed his eyes and prayed. "Dear God, this is freaking me out a little. I'm packing for a trip, and I don't even know where I'm going. Shouldn't I know by now? I've been waiting for you to show me or put something on my heart or…maybe Phillip was right. Maybe I haven't thought this through. I mean, who knows what kind of stuff is waiting for me out there. This is such a stretch for me, God. But I guess that's what it's all about, isn't it? Leaving my comfort zone, right? Lacey would think I've gone crazy or something. Maybe I have; I don't know. God, please just encourage me with your Word right now. I need you to take away all these feelings of doubt and fear and…I just need the same conviction I had for this trip when you first placed it on my heart, Lord. Just strengthen my resolve and let me know you're with me on this. Please, God. Amen."

Jon positioned his reading glasses on the middle of his nose and settled into his bed. Feeling for his bookmark in the Book of Colossians, Jon saw the tip of a white, church offering envelope peeking out from the top of his Bible. He opened the Book to where the envelope was placed, finding it tucked in the middle of Second Timothy. Flipping the envelope over, he saw a handwritten phone number and note.

Hey, brother! Give me a call sometime! – Brant.

"Brant," Jon said to himself, remembering their conversation in the church sanctuary almost three weeks ago. "He's probably thinking I blew him off, by now." Looking down at his open Bible, Jon read the first few verses of chapter two in Second Timothy. "You then, my son, be strong in the grace that is in Christ Jesus. And the things you have heard me say in the presence of many witnesses entrust to reliable men who will also be qualified to teach others. Endure hardship with us like a good soldier of Christ Jesus."

"Are you kidding me?" Jon said out loud. He felt God speaking through the words Paul wrote to Timothy – the very encouragement he had asked for in prayer only a minute before. Could God really be answering his prayers that quickly? He looked in his hand at the note Brant left in his Bible. Maybe it was just a coincidence. Brant had probably just randomly placed the envelope in its pages. "But it was *exactly* what I needed to hear, right now," thought Jon, countering his own doubts. "Out of this entire Book, I was led to these verses, right here." He read the passage in Second Timothy again and on through verse seven. "Reflect on what I am saying, for the Lord will give you insight into all this."

Jon laughed, shook his head and prayed. "OK, God, you win. I'm sorry I doubted you. I pray for something, then you deliver, and I try and write it off as coincidence. I guess it's just kind of scary to think that you, the Creator of the Universe, are sitting there listening to me. Actually, you knew three weeks ago I'd need this verse tonight when you had Brant leave his note for me, didn't you? It's all more than I can comprehend sometimes. But it tells me that what I'm preparing to do is important to you for some reason, Lord. It tells me you want me to press ahead and be a good soldier for you, hardships and all. And it also tells me I need to stay in your Word. Father God, thank you for loving me and encouraging me when I need it most. I love you, Lord. Amen."

Jon looked at the envelope in his hand. "I should give Brant a call and let him know what's going on." He reached for the phone on the far side of the nightstand and dialed Brant's number. Brant answered on the second ring.

"Hello," said Brant.

"Brant, hey – it's me, Jon."

"Jonny-boy! You found my number!"

"Yeah, man. You know, you could have just handed it to me there in the church. You might have heard from me a little sooner."

"Nah, I wanted to make sure you were still reading your Bible. And it took you over two weeks to find it. That's not a good sign, man."

"Believe me, I've been reading. Anyway, how are you?"

"I'm good," said Brant. "Things are good. I'm divorced, unemployed, with no furniture. But I'm good. How are *you* man? Where you been?"

"Oh, I've been around…you know."

"I was hoping to see you at church or Sunday school the last couple of weeks, but you've been missing."

"Yeah, I know. Sorry about that. I haven't been to church since you and I talked a few weeks ago."

"Why? Is everything all right? I didn't say anything wrong, did I? Did I scare you off or something?"

"No, Brant. Gosh no. What you shared with me was huge. It was a big encouragement to me."

"Oh. Well, I'm glad to hear that. So, what's up, then? Are you sick or something?"

"No, actually – and I should have thought to call you about this sooner – um, I've been getting ready to go on a little trip."

"Like a work trip? Is your boss sending you somewhere?"

Jon laughed. "I guess you could say that."

"Cool, where are you going?"

"Actually, it's not really a work trip. I'm taking six months off – a leave of absence – to go on kind of a journey."

"A journey?" asked Brant. "You make it sound like *Homeward Bound* or something."

"No, it's not like *Homeward Bound*. This is something that's come out of some prayer time with God. I'm going to be traveling around wherever he leads me and just sharing the Gospel."

"Wow," said Brant. "You're going all Jack Kerouac on me, man."

"Yeah, I guess I am. But I'm not sure the reference fits exactly."

"And your work is OK with all this? You said it's a leave of absence?"

"Well, they're not too thrilled. Actually, my boss was pretty ticked-off."

"So…I don't understand," said Brant, beginning to sound concerned. "Did they fire you or something?"

"No, like I said, it's a leave of absence. It's unpaid, but I'm still employed there and all, technically. They approved it, but I'm not really guaranteed my job when I get back."

"Hmph," grunted Brant.

"To be honest, my boss told me I'd be taking out the trash if I did come back."

"Sounds to me like you got fired, dude."

"I didn't get fired. I can still go back there, if I want to. But honestly, I may look for something else, anyway."

"Jon, I've got to say – as your friend – I'm not sure you're doing the right thing here, man."

"OK, why not?" asked Jon, honestly curious for Brant's opinion.

"Well, look at yourself. You've got a great job, right? What do you do now, anyway?"

Jon laughed at Brant's blind compliment. "I'm Creative Director for an ad agency here in town."

"Creative Director. OK, I don't really know what that is, but I'm sure it's a good job, right?"

"Yeah, sure. It's a good job."

"And I'm sure you probably live in a nice house, right?"

"Yeah, I guess you could say that."

"Jon! You're successful, man! Why would you just walk away from all that? Do you know how hard it is to find work nowadays? I can't find crap out here. And who knows what it's going to be like six months from now! What are you thinking?"

"Brant, I promise you, I've thought of all that."

"And you still want to go off and leave your job? I think you're nuts man."

"Brant, can I just explain for a moment?"

"I'm sorry. Sure, go ahead, buddy. I'm sorry."

"It's all right. But do you remember what you told me in the sanctuary at church three weeks ago?"

"Of course, I do."

"You told me how God used me to help you come to him, to be saved in Christ, right?"

"Absolutely."

"And you said that maybe God's purpose for me was to show others what it really means to be a Christian, right?"

"I said that, sure. But I didn't mean for you to go off the deep end and quit your job. Geez, Jon."

"Well, it doesn't matter what *you* meant, Brant. It matters what God meant. And I think he wanted me to see that bringing others to Jesus is the reason for my faith. It's our purpose as Believers. So I started praying about it and telling God all the reasons why I couldn't do that, even if I wanted to. There was my job, the house, my daughter, even my dog. And all of a sudden he just took all those excuses away from me. I believe he spoke to me, Brant. And he told me to just stop whining and go. I need to do this. You'll just have to trust me."

Brant was silent on the other end of the phone.

"You still there, man?" asked Jon.

"Yeah, I'm here. I'm just trying to absorb all that, Jon. I'm not sure what to say, you know? I feel like I did this to you."

Jon laughed. "I promise, it was God who did this to me. Don't worry; it's gonna be cool. It's already helped me talk to my daughter, Holly, about her faith. So that alone makes everything else worth it before I even start. Anyway, I'll tell you all about it when I get back, OK?"

"Hey!" said Brant, suddenly excited. "Let me take you out to dinner Friday night. It'll be like a going away dinner. What do you say?"

"That actually sounds great, Brant. But only if you let me buy. I'm the one with a job remember?"

"Not anymore, you're not," said Brant with a laugh.

"All right, point taken. We'll go Dutch, then. How 'bout that?"

"Perfect. How about Ray's at 7:00?"

"Oscar Ray's?" asked Jon, chuckling. "I haven't been there in years."

"Neither have I," said Brant. "Let's go see if they remember us."

"God, I hope not."

Brant laughed into the phone. "Don't worry, brother, I won't blow your cover. See you Friday."

"All right. See you then." Jon hung up the phone and looked up at the ceiling. "God? Is there one person out there, besides my mom, who thinks this is a good idea?"

twenty eight

Not Alone

*"You have allowed me to suffer much hardship, but you will restore
me to life again and lift me up from the depths of the earth."*
- Psalm 71:20

Jon tossed the decorative pillows on the floor beside his bed and pulled back the comforter. With Lacey gone to the party and no interest in watching television, he decided to just relax and read his Bible. It was only ten minutes after eight o'clock, but he felt tired. His failed attempt at sharing his faith with his wife had left him replaying their argument in his mind for the last hour, wishing he could somehow change it. And the thought that she would rather go to a party by herself than "drag him around all night" continually echoed in his head. He needed to turn his brain off and just read. "I need to check on Holly, first," he said to himself.

Jon walked down the hall to Holly's bedroom with Jo-Jo following close behind. As he slowly pushed her door open, light from the hallway spilled into the small room. On her dresser sat the baby monitor, still surrounded by presents from her first birthday party a week before. He slid the monitor closer to the crib, moving several of her presents onto the floor to make room. "Good night, sweetheart," he said softly, stroking her silky brown hair. "You look just like your mama."

As Jon watched Holly sleeping, his regret over missing the party with Lacey faded. He knew she might want to continue their argument when she got home, particularly if she'd been drinking. But for the moment, he was just happy to be home with his daughter. Leaning into the crib, he kissed Holly on the cheek and pulled the soft pink blanket over her chest. "Stop kicking this off, little girl," he whispered.

Returning to his bedroom, Jon changed into his favorite pajama bottoms and climbed into bed. Jo-Jo curled up on the floor beside him. As he reached for his Bible on the nightstand, he hesitated. Jon knew he was reaching for the very source of conflict between Lacey and him. Her voice played in his head, warning him to get his nose out of his Bible and pay her more attention. His hand hovered over the black leather-bound Book. "Maybe I should take a little break from it," he thought. "Maybe I've been pressing too hard. If I eased up, maybe she'd come around." He moved his hand over the Michael Crichton novel Lacey had given him for Christmas and picked it up. "Just for tonight," he said in compromise with his conscience. Jon read until he fell asleep.

The sounds of the doorbell and Jo-Jo barking woke Jon abruptly. He sat-up, swung his feet out of bed, and looked at his alarm clock. "Two forty-five?" He looked to his left and realized Lacey wasn't beside him in the bed. "What the heck is she still doing out at 2:45 in the morning?" Jon muttered. The doorbell rang again as he shuffled towards the hallway. "It's that dang key, again. I'm sure I'll hear about that," he thought as he entered the den. Jo-Jo danced by the front door, anxious to see Lacey. "Hang on, Jo-Jo," he said, crossing the entrance hall rug. Jon pulled on his dog's collar as he opened the door. Two uniformed state troopers and a third man dressed in a sport coat and tie stood before him on the front stoop. Jo-Jo barked once for good measure, still under Jon's restraint. "Hush, Jo-Jo. Yes, officers?" Jon tried to see around the men as he looked for Lacey's car. He was not going to be happy if she got a DUI.

"Good evening, sir. I'm Sergeant Wilder with the South Carolina Highway Patrol and this is Corporal Glass and Chaplain Phil Evans."

Jon tried to remain calm as fear entered his body. "What's the problem officer?"

"Are you related in any way to Ms. Lacey Andrews Smoak?" the trooper asked formally.

Jon's stomach dropped. "I'm her husband, Jon Smoak." His heart began to race in his chest. "Is Lacey in trouble?"

The trooper removed the wide brimmed hat from his head. "I'm sorry to inform you, Mr. Smoak, that your wife was in an automobile accident earlier this evening. She died while paramedics were trying to revive her. I'm very sorry."

Jon felt the air go out of his lungs as he let go of Jo-Jo's collar and staggered backwards, his heel catching the edge of the entrance hall rug. The corporal tried to catch Jon's arm as he stumbled, but missed, leaving Jon to land on his backside.

The chaplain rushed through the door and knelt beside Jon. "Mr. Smoak, are you all right?"

Jon sat motionless on the rug as cool air began to fill the house through the open front door.

"Mr. Smoak?" asked the chaplain.

"How?" asked Jon, softly.

The corporal knelt beside the chaplain. "She ran off the road about two miles from here, Mr. Smoak. Her car hit a tree."

Jon stared blankly toward the open door as he replayed memories from just a few hours before. Lacey trying on shoes in her closet, fixing her hair in the hallway mirror, driving away from the house…alone. "It's my fault," whispered Jon.

"It wasn't your fault, Mr. Smoak," said the corporal. "It was an accident. We think she fell asleep and her car left the road."

"I was supposed to be with her," said Jon, softly, to no one. "I was supposed to…." He leaned forward onto his knees and elbows and pressed the top of his head against the rug. Blood rushed to his face as every muscle in his body contracted. His fingernails dug tightly into the palms of his hands. "Oh, God!!" he cried.

The chaplain placed his hand on Jon's back as he sobbed heavily, his body convulsing as he struggled to breath.

"Mr. Smoak, is there anyone here with you, sir?" Sergeant Wilder asked.

Beginning to feel dizzy, Jon rolled onto his side and rested on one elbow before letting himself collapse onto his back. He closed his eyes and fought his body's desire to throw-up. "She can't be…." Jon couldn't finish the sentence. "She can't be."

"Jon," said the chaplain. "Can I call anyone for you? A family member?"

Jon's breathing began to slow. "God, why couldn't I save her?" he whispered.

"I'm sorry, sir?" asked Sergeant Wilder.

"Why?" asked Jon, looking past the three men leaning over him to the ceiling above.

"I think he's going into shock, Sergeant," said the chaplain.

The sound of Holly crying came from down the hall, amplified by the baby monitor in Jon's bedroom. Jon sat up quickly, wiped his face off with his hand, and struggled to his feet, staggering sideways into Corporal Glass. The trooper caught Jon in his arms and helped him regain his balance.

"Excuse me," said Jon, pushing himself away and drifting quickly toward the hallway.

"Mr. Smoak, can I help you?" asked the chaplain, calling after Jon.

Jon steadied himself, sliding his right hand along the wall as he made his way down the hall and into Holly's room. In the faint glow of a night-light, he saw her standing in the crib holding the side rail as she cried. Jon walked across the hardwood floor, put his hands underneath her arms, and lifted his daughter onto his chest. Her cries stopped as she laid her wet face on his shoulder and wrapped her arms around his neck. Jon closed his eyes and swayed back and forth, holding her gently with both arms as he cried. "Oh, God please help me," he sobbed. "This can't be happening; it just can't. It can't." His legs began to weaken as he held Holly close against his chest. He slowly knelt to the rug beside the crib as Holly stirred in his arms. "Shhh, shhh…it's gonna be all right," he whispered. "We're gonna be all right." The words felt like a lie.

The chaplain entered the room, lowered himself to the floor beside Jon, and placed his hand on his shoulder. Jon rocked Holly gently as he cried.

"Jon, is there someone I can call for you?" asked the chaplain. "Someone who can come be with you?"

Jon tried to gather himself. He sniffed and wiped his nose with his hand. "My dad. Will you call my dad for me?"

"Absolutely. But first, would you mind if I asked about your faith?"

"What do you mean?" asked Jon, his head beginning to clear.

"Are you of any particular faith or denomination? Is there a pastor I can call for you?"

"Um, I'm a Christian, but we don't have a church or anything, yet." Realizing he said "we," Jon flinched in pain.

"Was your wife a Believer, as well?"

Jon felt afraid to answer the question. "Um, I don't…I mean, I tried…." Jon struggled with his doubts. "I'm not sure."

"Well, would you mind if I prayed here with you now?" asked Chaplain Evans.

"OK," said Jon. As he closed his eyes, Jon realized he had never prayed with anyone before. He felt comforted even before the chaplain began to speak.

"Almighty God," said Chaplain Evans, "please comfort this young man, Jon Smoak. We don't know why these horrible things happen, Father. But in our pain, we turn to you and trust that you love us. And we trust that your Word can comfort us in times of doubt and fear and sorrow. You are the Father of compassion and the God of all comfort, who comforts us in all our troubles. Dear Lord, I just lift up this young man, this young father and the little girl he holds in his arms. Please shepherd them. Guide them through this difficult time and give them strength to face tomorrow. Help him to raise this little girl, that she may know you and experience salvation in the name of Jesus. It's in his name we pray. Amen."

Jon wept uncontrollably. He leaned against the chaplain who steadied him, embracing him with one arm around his shoulders as Jon cradled Holly close to his chest. "I can't do this alone," said Jon.

"You're not alone, son. Just hold on to your faith. Jesus said, 'Surely I am with you always, to the very end of the age.' He'll always be with you. He promised us that. And he always keeps his promises. Just stay in his Word and he'll give you the strength and direction you need to raise your little girl. You can count on that."

Jon straightened himself on his knees and adjusted Holly in his arms. "Thank you, sir," he said, wiping his face on his arm. "I'll try my best."

twenty nine

The Test

"For God has something better in mind for you."
- *Hebrews 11:40*

After sorting through his clothes for two hours and talking on the phone with Brant, Jon was finally ready for bed. But Elvis wasn't. As Jon walked through the den turning off lights, his dog stood whining at the back door. His dark, expressive eyes turned towards Jon politely asking to go outside. Letting Elvis out would slow Jon's efforts to get in bed, but it was better than finding a mess in the morning or being awakened in the middle of the night. He opened the door and watched Elvis disappear into the darkness of the backyard.

To pass the time while he waited for his dog to scratch on the door, Jon sat down at his kitchen table to play a game of solitaire on his laptop. Opening his MacBook, he found the web browser still open on Facebook, the site he last visited that morning while eating his bowl of Honey Bunches of Oats. A red notification icon appeared at the top of the page. "Wow, I actually have a friend request," Jon said to himself with low expectations. "Let me guess – another person I don't remember from high school." He slid his finger across the trackpad, moving his cursor over the icon, and read the name. "Amy Cribb-Martin? No way! That's awesome!" He accepted the request and opened Amy's profile. His wide eyes darted quickly around her photos. Jon tried to reconcile his memories of Amy with the changes time had brought to her still pretty face. "Wow...she looks great," he said, shaking his head.

Seeing that she was online, Jon moved his cursor over Amy's name. He could opened a chat session and talk with her, instantly. But after so many years, what would he say? And what would be the point, anyway? He'd probably just feel worse after hearing how perfect her life has been compared to his. As his finger hovered above the track pad, his mind frozen with indecision, a chat notification appeared on his screen from Amy. Jon's heart jumped in his chest.

Amy:	Hey stranger!	9:25
Jon:	Hey there! Thanks for sending me a friend request!	9:25
Amy:	np! It's nice to see you joining the rest of the world.	9:26
Jon:	I know, right? I got on fb when my daughter Holly left for college last year.	9:26
Amy:	Wow, do you really have kids in college??	9:28
Jon:	Yep! Just the one. Seems like yesterday we were that age.	9:28
Amy:	It was yesterday.	9:28
Jon:	Haha, I wish. So, how are you?	9:29
Amy:	I'm good. Just adjusting to the whole single mom thing. It keeps me hopping.	9:31
Jon:	Uh-oh. What happened?	9:31
Amy:	Let's just say life didn't turn out exactly as I thought it would.	9:32

Jon:	Does it ever? ☺	9:32
Amy:	No.	9:32
Jon:	Well, I'm sorry.	9:33
Amy:	Yeah, me too.	9:34
Jon:	What about your ex? He's not around to help you with the kids?	9:35
Amy:	My ex-husband is an "ex" at a lot of things. ☺	9:37
Jon:	When did all that happen?	9:37
Amy:	He left the ministry a few years ago and things went downhill from there.	9:39
Jon:	He was in the ministry??	9:40
Jon:	Was he a preacher?	9:41
Amy:	No, not a preacher. He started out as a worship leader in a church on Johns Island. He's a very talented musician. Great voice, lots of charisma on stage. But then we moved to Hilton Head so he could take the same job at a bigger church in Bluffton.	9:43
Jon:	What happened there?	9:44

Amy:	There's a lot of $$ flowing around down there. He got involved with some people who wanted to market him in Nashville. So he left the church (and me!) and moved up there. He's living with his "agent." At least that's what he calls her. ☺	9:48
Jon:	I'm so sorry. How long were y'all married?	9:49
Amy:	16 years.	9:49
Jon:	But you're back in Pawleys now?	9:50
Amy:	Litchfield, actually. I moved the kids back here after the divorce to be close to family. I need all the help I can get. ☺	9:50
Jon:	I saw your kids in your pictures. How old are they?	9:51
Amy:	Sorry, I had to go upstairs for a minute. Dillon is 12 and Mattie is 10.	10:01
Jon:	They're both cute! They look like you.	10:03
Amy:	I know. Poor kids.	10:03
Jon:	Haha. That was meant to be a compliment.	10:04
Amy:	OK, I'll take it.	10:04
Jon:	My daughter got lucky. She got her mom's looks.	10:05

Amy:	She's beautiful! Where is her mom? I don't see any pics of her and your relationship status is blank. You like being mysterious? ☺	10:05
Jon:	Well, she died when Holly was little.	10:07
Amy:	Oh no, I'm so sorry, Jonny. I didn't know.	10:07
Jon:	It's OK. It happened a long time ago.	10:08
Amy:	Did she get sick?	10:09
Jon:	No, she died in a car accident.	10:10
Amy:	Oh how awful. Were you with her when it happened?	10:12
Jon:	No, I was at home with Holly. She went to a party and ran off the road on her way home. She fell asleep.	10:15
Amy:	Has it just been you and your daughter ever since?	10:16
Jon:	Yep. So I can relate to the single parent thing.	10:16
Amy:	That must have been horrible. I'm so sorry that happened.	10:17
Jon:	One sec.	10:18
Amy:	OK	10:18
Jon:	OK, I'm back. My dog was outside barking at something.	10:22

| Amy: | So, I have to ask – Have you been in a relationship since you lost your wife? | 10:22 |

| Amy: | You still there? | 10:25 |

| Jon: | Yep, sorry. | 10:26 |

| Jon: | I really haven't seen anyone beyond just a date or two. The first few years after it happened I was so busy with Holly and work, I really just wasn't interested in seeing anyone. Plus, the year before the accident, I had accepted Christ and was saved, so my life was just turned upside down in a lot of ways. I couldn't see adding someone new on top of everything else. And then my dad had a stroke a few years later and my mom had early-onset dementia, so I moved them in with me when Holly was in fourth grade. I guess I just never had the time for anybody. | 10:28 |

| Amy: | Wait, you were saved? That's awesome!!! I remember praying for you a long time ago when we were kids! | 10:29 |

| Jon: | Well, it took a while, but God finally got through to me. ☺ | 10:29 |

| Amy: | That makes me so happy! ☺☺ | 10:29 |

| Jon: | Well, I think God used you to help get my attention early on. You were always after me about church and stuff in your letters or whenever I'd see you on the beach. | 10:31 |

Amy: Preacher's daughter. It was my job. ☺   10:32

Jon: You were good at it! I remember the last time I saw you. It was the 4th of July on the beach and you invited me to stay over and go to church with you at the Chapel on Pawleys the next day. I think your dad was going to be preaching.   10:33

Amy: That's right!! I remember! And you had that cute little puppy with you!   10:33

Jon: Jo-Jo!   10:33

Amy: Yes! Is that who was barking a few minutes ago?   10:34

Jon: No, Jo-Jo passed away about 10 years ago. That was my daughter's dog barking.   10:34

Amy: Oh, duh. That was like 20 years ago wasn't it?   10:35

Jon: Yep. 25 actually.   10:36

Amy: Ouch. Are we that old??   10:36

Jon: I'm afraid so. And for the record – I wish I had stayed that night and gone to church with you. ☺   10:37

Amy: Well how bout I give you another chance?   10:38

Jon: Haha!   10:38

Amy: I'm serious! Next time you're down here you can buy me dinner and I'll take you to church with me. Deal?   10:39

Jon:	How can I say no? ☺	10:39
Amy:	You can't! And we don't allow birds in our sanctuary, so you don't have to worry.	10:40
Jon:	I almost forgot about that! My poor dad! In that case I accept!	10:40
Amy:	Yay!!	10:40
Jon:	Wow, it only took me 30 years to finally get a date with you.	10:41
Amy:	I don't remember you ever asking!	10:41
Jon:	You've got a point!	10:41
Amy:	But I'll only go if you promise to stop quoting years to me. You're going to get me depressed. ☺	10:43
Jon:	OK, sorry!	10:43
Amy:	All righty then! When can you come down?	10:44
Jon:	Well, it may be a little while. I'm taking a 6 month leave of absence from work.	10:46
Amy:	Why? Are you sick?	10:46
Jon:	Well that depends who you ask. ☺	10:46
Amy:	Very funny. What are you going to be doing?	10:47

Jon:	I know this sounds weird, but I feel like God is calling me to be a witness for Christ.	10:49
Amy:	We're all supposed to do that, silly.	10:49
Jon:	I know, but that's my point. How many people really do it?? I reached a point where I was just coasting along in my faith and just doing the normal church thing. But God's calling me to do more than that.	10:51
Amy:	So are you going on a mission trip or something?	10:52
Jon:	I guess you could say that. I'm just going to travel around the country wherever God leads me and share Christ with anyone I can.	10:54
Amy:	Wow! Is this something through your church?	10:54
Jon:	nope. It's something apart from church. They weren't that supportive of my plans at first.	10:55
Amy:	What do you mean?	10:55
Jon:	I didn't mean that to sound bad. But they just wanted to plug me into the normal roles they have there. Calling visitors, outreach, etc.	10:57
Amy:	You wouldn't want to just start with that and grow into evangelism later?	10:58
Jon:	Well, that's kind of what my Sunday school teacher said. But I feel like God has spoken to me in prayer about this and I want to know what it's like to really follow Jesus. You know? Just do what his Word tells us to do, free from all the restraints we put on ourselves.	11:00

Amy:	I'm proud of you, Jonny. I really am. That's awesome. When do you leave?	11:02
Jon:	Thanks, Amy. That means a lot to me. I'm leaving Saturday.	11:02
Amy:	Well, I'll have to start praying for you again, so look out!! God's going to be all over you!	11:04
Jon:	Thanks! I'll need it!	11:04
Amy:	So, whenever you get back, you call me, OK? We'll have our date. ☺	11:06
Jon:	I will! And I'll look forward to it!	11:06
Amy:	Just think – If you had only been a Clemson fan, who knows what might have happened between us. ☺	11:08
Jon:	Ha! God made me a Gamecock. Nothing I could do about that. ☺	11:09
Amy:	You may be a Gamecock, but you're certainly no chicken. ☺ It takes a lot of courage to do what you're doing. Be strong in your faith and know that I'll be praying for you.	11:11
Jon:	Thank you! I'll see you in 6 months and tell you all about it over dinner.	11:11
Amy:	You have to take me somewhere nice for making me wait.	11:12
Jon:	You pick the place.	11:12

Amy:	Franks!	11:12

Jon:	How did I know you were going to say that?!	11:13

Amy:	And make sure you bring cash or a credit card. I don't think you can fit enough dimes in your pocket to cover the tab. ☺	11:15

Jon:	I'm so glad I made such a lasting first impression on you! That was 31 years ago, you know.	11:15

Amy:	No counting years, remember? And yes, you did. ☺	11:16

Jon:	Well, I had to try. You were awfully cute.	11:16

Amy:	Just pretend I still am and we'll be fine. ☺	11:17

Jon:	That won't be hard to do. ☺	11:17

Amy:	You're sweet. And I'm tired. I'm going to get ready for bed.	11:19

Jon:	OK, goodnight. I enjoyed talking with you!	11:19

Amy:	Me too! Be safe and I'll see you in 6 months! ☺	11:20

As Jon closed his MacBook, he heard Elvis scratching to come in. He walked to the door and pulled it open. Elvis burst into the den and ran straight for Jon's bedroom. "Good idea," he said, closing the door. He turned off the lights and checked the doors before making his way in the dark to his room. Elvis was already curled-up on the floor beside the bed. Jon stepped over his dog and climbed into bed, pulling the covers up to his chin. Taking a deep breath, he closed his eyes and smiled as he thought about his conversation with Amy. He imagined what it would be like to sit across a table from her at Franks, to finally spend time with her after so many years. And he allowed himself to wonder…if there could be a chance for something more. But he would have to wait six months to find out. Six months. He opened his eyes and stared at the dark ceiling. He began to pray.

"Dear God, what am I doing? Do you really want me to do this? Do you really want me to leave everything for six months? I think I know the answer to that, God, but…I've been alone for so long. Everything I've done…it's been for either Holly or my parents. But now Amy is all of a sudden back in my life out of nowhere. And she wants to see me. I finally have someone I can be excited about. And it's just for me, you know? After all I've been through…can't I have this? Can't I just see where it would go?"

Jon paused to think about the challenge of changing his plans. What would he say to Brant, Amanda, and even Amy? How could he go back against his word now? What would everyone think? He knew the answer to that question, too. "I've already told everyone what I'm doing. Amy even said how proud she was of me. If I didn't go now, my faith would be a joke. But just because I've already told everyone is no reason to go through with it. It's just not fair, God. It's not. You know it's not. Isn't there some other way? What if I were to just go see Amy for one date and then go on my trip?"

Jon waited for any sign or feeling that his negotiation with God would change his direction. He closed his eyes and waited. He played back his question in his mind. And an honest answer came to him. "If I saw her it would change everything, wouldn't it? I probably wouldn't go at all." Jon sighed deeply and let his lungs slowly fill again.

"Please God…please help me. I know what you want me to do, but you're going to have to help me do it. I can't do this out of empty obligation. It's just that…when you called me to leave everything, I didn't know Amy would be in the picture. But now she is and…."

Jon opened his eyes and sat-up in bed. His mind was suddenly clear on what was happening. "God? Did you put her in touch with me to test my resolve? You did, didn't you?" He crossed his arms around his knees and squeezed them against his chest as he bounced his forehead against them.

"OK, I get it…daggum it. I get it. And my answer is still *yes*. I'll go on this journey with you. I'll follow you wherever you lead me, and I'll be your witness to whomever you put in my path. I put my trust in you, Lord. But can you just keep me on Amy's mind until I get back? If it's your will, Lord, I'd love to have that dinner with her. But we have some business to take care of first, don't we?" Jon let his body fall back onto the bed like a dropped rope. "Thank you, Lord. Goodnight."

thirty

Farther Along

"'For my thoughts are not your thoughts, neither are your ways my ways,' declares the Lord."
- Isaiah 55:8

Jon walked with his parents along the sun-bleached asphalt road, passing in and out of shadows cast by the oaks and wax myrtles still blocking the mid-morning sun. The slapping sound of his flip-flops echoed through the still air, bouncing off the beach houses lining Myrtle Avenue. Without a supporting breeze, several egrets and blue herons settled for a muddy stroll in the salt marsh to his right. Jon didn't mind the walk to church. And according to his mother, they were still a few minutes away.

He had seen the Pawleys Island Chapel many times before, but had never been inside. Whenever his family arrived each year for their vacation, his father liked to drive the length of the island just to see what had changed from their last visit. And when they'd pass the small, white, wood-frame chapel, resting on the side of the road between the north and south causeways, Jon always wondered what kept the old building from falling into the marsh.

Jon shuffled a few steps to catch up with his parents. "How come that paper on the fridge at the beach house showed a different preacher every Sunday?" he asked. "That's not like our church. We have the same preacher every week."

"That's because it's not a real church," Jon's mother answered. "It's just a chapel. It doesn't have a regular congregation like ours does. Pastors from local churches take turns preaching there on Sunday mornings in the summertime so people on vacation, like us, can have a place to worship."

"Is that why I can wear flip-flops and a T-shirt and shorts without getting in trouble?" asked Jon.

"That's why, honey," said Jon's mother with a smile.

"Why do we have to walk there?" asked Jon. "They don't let people drive?"

Jon's father laughed briefly and covered his mouth with his hand as he cleared his throat.

"No one's making us walk, honey," said his mother, glancing to her left at Jon's father. "It's so beautiful out this morning, I just thought it would be nice for us to walk to church as a family. *Right*, honey?"

Jon's father kept his smile and raised both hands. "I didn't say anything."

They had left their rented beach house on the north end of Pawleys at 9:45, giving them fifteen minutes to reach the chapel on foot for the ten o'clock service. As they rounded a curve on Myrtle Avenue, Jon could see long lines of cars parked on both sides of the road leading to and away from the chapel. A crowd stood outside the front doors, waiting to go in.

"Goodness gracious," said Jon's mother. "I hope we can get a seat." She lifted a finger towards Jon's father. "Don't say it."

"I wasn't going to say, 'I told you so,'" said his father, laughing. "But I told you so."

Jon was suddenly filled with optimism for his morning. "If we can't get in, can we go back to the house and go out on the beach?"

"We'll see," said his father as they walked in the middle of the road past the parked cars.

Arriving at the chapel, Jon followed his parents up the wooden steps and through the open double doors as the line waiting to enter moved slowly forward. Several smiling men greeted them as they stepped into the small building. Jon's father pulled him ahead and placed his large hands on his shoulders. He felt his father guiding him around people blocking the red-carpeted center aisle as they looked for open seats. Sitting on either side of the aisle beneath whirling ceiling fans, families of all generations sat dressed in comfortable summer attire sharing smiles as they talked. Several women waved paper fans glued to Popsicle sticks in front of their faces. As Jon moved closer to the front, he began to wonder where they would sit. The chapel appeared to be full.

A man wearing regular Sunday church clothes – a blue sport coat, white dress shirt, red tie, khaki pants and dress shoes – stood in front of the pulpit. Looking at Jon, the man smiled and waved them forward, pointing three fingers to his left. Jon looked towards the front of the chapel and saw two rows of chairs lining the right-side wall facing inward behind the pulpit. On the front row, three empty chairs waited, one of which sat adjacent to the large sliding glass doors that comprised the back wall of the church. His father pushed him ahead towards the empty seats.

Jon happily took his place next to the glass and immediately began studying the green marsh spreading out towards the mainland. Low tide in the creek behind the island exposed the dark brown mud around the base of the tall cordgrass. He watched the soft, wet ground pulsate with movement as tiny fiddler crabs swarmed about in unison. Not far from his seat in the chapel, a blue heron grazed slowly around the grass, searching for breakfast with his long orange beak. And above the thick mesh of live oak trees rising from the mainland side of the marsh, a clear, blue, summer sky called for Jon to come out and play. Jon hooked his fingers on the edge of the sliding glass door and pushed it open slightly. A light breeze blew warm, heavy air against his face.

Taking his eyes off the marsh, Jon turned his attention forward. Directly across the chapel next to the piano, the girl from King's Funland sat staring at him. She wore a sly, subtle smile and an orange sundress. Jon's stomach tingled with nerves as he quickly threw his gaze back out the window. *"Great,"* he thought, "just my luck." He refocused his eyes on the heron as he struggled to remember the girl's name, though he knew it couldn't really matter. He had blown his only chance to talk with her.

The man in the sport coat took his place behind the pulpit. "Good morning," he said above the many conversations happening around the room.

The people responded with a loud and scattered, "Good morning," and then became silent.

"My name is Alden Cribb," said the man. "I'm the Senior Pastor at Surfside Community Church just up the road, and I have the honor of delivering your message to you this morning. Surfside is just about fifteen miles up

Highway 17 for those folks from out of town. Which is everyone, I assume."
The people in the chapel laughed politely at the preacher's humor. "It's always
such a blessing to be here on Pawleys Island, in this beautiful setting, to
preach God's Word to folks who are so relaxed and ready to laugh at all of
my jokes." The people laughed again. "My family is also here with me this
morning. Over there at the piano is my beautiful wife, Sarah. And seated in
the chair next to her, against the wall, is my twelve-year-old daughter, Amy."

"*Amy*," Jon said to himself, trying not to look in her direction.

Jon's father elbowed him and leaned over to his left ear. "Isn't that the girl
from the arcade yesterday?" he whispered.

"*Shhh*," said Jon. He looked across the chapel at Amy, who was now
watching her father as he spoke from the pulpit. Jon studied her tanned,
pretty face and wished he hadn't made such a fool of himself at King's. "Why
do I have to be such an idiot?" he wondered.

"Let's begin our time together in prayer," said the preacher, bowing his
head to pray. "Oh, great and merciful Father, we thank you for bringing us
together this morning on this beautiful island to worship you. Some folks in
this humble little chapel have traveled a good ways to be here this week, to
relax and enjoy the wonder of your creation. Lord, we pray that our short
time together this morning will be glorifying to your Son, Jesus, who died on
the Cross for our sins, so that we may know you and live with you in all eternity. Many things we don't understand, Lord, but we do know that you love
us. And that is what draws us here this morning. We thank you and praise
your Holy name. And it's in Jesus' name we pray. Amen."

With his eyes closed during the prayer, Jon had begun to realize that the
girl he lied to in the arcade the day before was the daughter of a preacher. He
opened his eyes with a heavy sigh and wondered if it could get any worse.
Turning his attention back to the safety of the marsh, Jon heard the fluttering
of a bird's wings over his head. He looked up to see a small brown bird cir-
cling inside the chapel close to the ceiling. It came to rest on top of a framed
portrait of Jesus hanging over the piano. The crowd in the chapel laughed
and murmured over the unintentional visitor.

"I see we have one of God's smaller creatures joining us this morning,"
said the preacher as everyone laughed again. "Let's see if he'll sing along with
us. Please stand and open your songbook to hymn number twenty-three.

We'll sing one of my favorite old hymns as my wife leads us on the piano. Sarah?"

Amy's mom began to play the piano as Jon's father flipped through the small brown songbook. Finding the hymn, he held it low enough for Jon to read the words as the people began to sing.

> Tempted and tried, we're oft made to wonder
> Why it should be thus all the day long;
> While there are others living about us,
> Never molested, though in the wrong.
> Farther along we'll know more about it,
> Farther along we'll understand why.

The bird hopped off the painting of Jesus and flew quickly around the chapel two times before taking its perch again on the wooden picture frame. Jon watched the bird breath heavily as the people continued to sing.

> Cheer up, my brother, live in the sunshine,
> We'll understand it all by and by.
> Often I wonder why I must journey
> Over a road so rugged and steep;
> While there are others living in comfort,
> While with the lost I labor and weep.

The bird took flight again, making the same circles around the chapel close to the ceiling before landing back on Jesus. Jon's father leaned down to Jon's ear and whispered, "If that bird flies around again, he's going to have a bowel movement."

Jon looked up curiously at his father. "How do you know that?"

"I'm older than you." His father winked at Jon, smiled, and continued singing.

> Farther along we'll know more about it,
> Farther along we'll understand why;
> Cheer up, my brother, live in the sunshine,
> We'll understand it all by and by.

Jon looked over at Amy to see if she was paying attention to the bird. He noticed she wasn't holding a hymnal as she sang along with the music. But her eyes did catch his before he could look away. He quickly found the hymnal in his father's hand.

Tempted and tried, how often we question
Why we must suffer year after year,
Being accused by those of our loved ones,
Even though we've walked in God's holy fear.

Jon looked at the painting of Jesus again just in time to see the bird leap into the air. It beat its wings furiously as it circled above the people's heads, flying closer to the sliding glass door with each pass as Jon sang along with his father.

Often when death has taken our loved ones,
Leaving our home so lonely and so drear,
Then do we wonder why others prosper,
Living so wicked year after year.

The bird circled once more and then flew low, directly towards Jon. Jon's father ducked as the bird flew just over his head, veering away from the sliding glass door at the last moment, barely avoiding a collision. The exhausted bird found his perch again on top of the painting above the piano. Jon felt a nudge on his shoulder and looked up at his father. White bird droppings hung off the end of his father's nose as he cast a knowing smile down at Jon. Jon burst into laughter, quickly covering his mouth to contain himself. His eyes found Amy across the chapel. One of her hands covered her mouth while the other pressed against her shaking stomach. She removed her hand from her face to reveal a large smile and waved discreetly at Jon.

"Hi," mouthed Amy.

Jon quickly forgot about the bird and waved back. "Hi," he whispered, silently. Her surprise greeting made his head feel light.

Amy tried to continue singing without laughing as she glanced back and forth between Jon and her father.

Farther along we'll know more about it,
Farther along we'll understand why.

"Meet me on the beach later," Amy mouthed deliberately at Jon, motioning with her eyes and head in the direction of the beach.

It took Jon a second to process his lip reading, but he understood the invitation. "OK," he mouthed, holding his thumb and index finger at his waist in an O shape.

"By the pier," Amy added silently.

Jon nodded his understanding as his heart pounded in his chest. He smiled in disbelief and looked out the sliding glass door as the people around him sang. He had made a new friend in spite of his own worst efforts. He wondered how that could have happened as he watched the blue heron fly away.

Then will our toiling seem to be nothing,
When we shall pass the heavenly gate.
Farther along we'll know more about it,
Farther along we'll understand why;
Cheer up, my brother, live in the sunshine,
We'll understand it all by and by.

thirty one

Just Two

*"Two are better than one, because they have a good return for
their work: If one falls down, his friend can help him up."*
- Ecclesiastes 4:9-10

Standing in Oscar Ray's again with Brant was something Jon never saw coming. Yet, there they were waiting for a table in the same place they had spent
so many misguided hours more than twenty years before. As Brant read fly-
ers on the wall promoting local musicians and drink specials, Jon struggled to
define his attitude towards his old friend. Any fondness he felt for his days as
Brant's college roommate was tempered by the memories of rejection following his decision to accept Christ. But now, after Brant's own recent encounter
with Jesus, his friend seemed…different. Still very much Brant, but different.

"Just two?" asked the hostess, grabbing two dinner menus from the stack
on top of her stand.

"Yep, just us," said Jon.

"OK, follow me," she said as she turned to walk into the dining area.

"You're not going to make her feel like crap for saying *just two* this time?"
asked Brant as they followed the young hostess to their table.

"I stopped doing that a long time ago when I realized I was the only one
who thought it was funny."

"Hey, I always laughed," said Brant, pulling his chair from the table.

"Your server will be right with you," the hostess said, leaving the menus
on the table.

"Yeah, but you just laughed to make sure the hostess noticed you," said Jon, taking his seat.

"Well, it worked that one time, if I remember right," said Brant with a grin.

"I thought this was my going away dinner. Are you going to reminisce about your bar conquests all night?"

"No, of course not," said Brant. "I'm a changed man, remember?"

"Oh, that's right. I forgot," said Jon, rolling his eyes.

"Sorry, I guess it's just the atmosphere," said Brant, glancing around the restaurant. "Seems like old times, doesn't it?"

Jon noticed the fish tank behind Brant's shoulder. He had the same view the last time he had lunch with Jenny, all those years ago. "Yeah, I guess it does," he said, dropping his eyes to his menu. "So, you said in your text earlier you had something important to talk with me about."

"Oh, yeah," said Brant. "Well—"

"Good evening, gentlemen," said a young waiter appearing at their table. "My name's Stewart and I'll be taking care of you tonight. Can I start you off with a couple drinks from the bar or an appetizer? Maybe some fried mozzarella or stuffed jalapeño poppers?"

"Drinks and fried cheese!" said Brant. "Son, when we were your age, we would have been all over that." Brant laughed and looked at Jon for agreement.

Jon grinned and looked down at his menu, not wanting to encourage Brant.

"But I'll just have a sweet tea," said Brant.

"Un-sweet tea for me, thanks," said Jon, looking up at their young waiter. He wondered if the boy might know Holly from school.

"Great! I'll have those right out for you," said Stewart as he left to check on another table.

"Un-sweet?" asked Brant. "What's up with that? Are you a Yankee now or something?"

"No. Just trying to watch the calories, you know? I'm not twenty years old anymore. Besides, there's no point in going to the gym if you're just going to drink sugar water all the time."

"I think you had it right to start with – there's no point in going to the gym." Brant patted his round stomach proudly.

"So, anyway," said Jon, waving his hand in a circle to reengage Brant in their conversation. "What did you want to talk with me about?"

"Oh, right," said Brant, looking serious. He straightened himself in his chair, putting his elbows on the table. "Jon, I've been giving this a lot of thought since you called me Tuesday and told me about your decision to leave for six months and go around and witness to people and all that."

"And you still think it's a bad idea, right?"

"No, it's not that. I only said that because you're walking away from a great job. I mean, I'm out of work and I'd kill to have a good job like that. It just kind of shocked me to hear what you're doing, I guess. And from what you told me, it doesn't sound like your company's too thrilled about it, either."

"My boss isn't thrilled. That's for sure. I'm not sure about anyone else, there. They didn't throw me a going away party. Let's put it like that. A few people were pretty nice about it, though. But I think most folks may have just been confused or unsure what to say. I'm not sure which."

"Well, you've got to admit," said Brant, "it sounds pretty crazy to most people."

"I'm sure it does. So, if you want to try and talk me out of it again, you wouldn't be alone; I promise."

"No, that's not it at all," said Brant, scratching the back of his head. "Actually, I—"

"Have you gentlemen made a decision?" asked Stewart, reappearing at their table with their drinks. He looked back and forth at Brant and Jon. "Who wants to go first?"

"You go ahead, Jon," said Brant, now giving the menu more serious attention.

"Sure, I can go. I'll have the shrimp and grits with collard greens."

"Excellent choice," said Stewart. "And you, sir?"

"Uh, yeah," said Brant, still scanning the menu. "I'll take the chicken-fried steak with – sides, sides, where are the sides – ah, mashed potatoes and gravy."

"You get one more side with that, sir," said the waiter, his pen poised over his notepad.

"Oh, uh…macaroni and cheese, then."

"Fantastic. I'll put those in for you right away." Stewart took their menus and left for the kitchen.

"Still trying to avoid anything green, I see," said Jon.

"Still trying to be my mom, I see," said Brant, looking around the restaurant. "This place really hasn't changed much since we were in college, has it?"

"I don't think it's changed since it opened." Jon experienced a brief sense of déjà vu, but dismissed it just as quickly. "We could have gone somewhere else, you know. Columbia does have other restaurants these days."

"I know," said Brant, still looking around. "I just thought it would be fun for the two of us to come back here. Considering how much we've both changed since college and all."

"Speaking of that, how are you doing in your new faith, man? You said you accepted Christ just a few months ago. Is there anything I can do to help you?"

"Oh, well that's actually what I wanted to talk with you about," said Brant, leaning forward. "I've given this a lot of thought since you told me you were leaving and—"

"I think we've already covered this ground, haven't we?" asked Jon, smirking.

"Shut up and let me talk, will you? Here's the thing – I want to go with you."

"You what?" Jon had never even remotely considered the possibility of anyone going with him. It was *his* calling. And even if he'd wanted company for the trip, Brant's name would not have come to mind.

"I want to go with you," repeated Brant.

Jon sat looking at Brant, still unable to process what he was hearing.

"Hello?" asked Brant, waving at Jon. "Earth to Jon."

"You want to go with me."

"Yep. What do you think?" Brant raised his eyebrows as he smiled.

Jon crossed his arms, leaned forward, and rested his elbows on the table. "Brant, please tell me what you're thinking, because I don't have a clue."

"Well, after we got off the phone the other night, I started thinking about how you said God helped you see a way past all the reasons why you couldn't do something bold for him. Holly and your job and everything. You said you were praying and all of a sudden, your path seemed clear. Right?"

"That's about the gist of it, yeah. But I didn't say anything about you coming with me. How did you come up with that?"

"Well, I felt like I should pray for you after we talked. I'm still not very good at praying, yet. I never know what to say. And then my mind wanders and I end up talking to myself."

"Your point?"

"Oh, but anyway, I did ask God to be with you and when I did, I realized that I have nothing holding me back, either." A smile began to grow across Brant's face. "I mean, I have no job. I'm living off a nice severance package. Kim's got Jacob and everything else I own – or used to own. I live in an apartment on a month-to-month lease. And I have no pets. I'm your man, bro!" Brant stretched his arms out wide, hitting a waitress on the hip as she passed by. "Sorry!"

Jon rubbed his eyes with both hands, trying to think of ways to discourage Brant's naive enthusiasm. "Brant, first of all, I'm not looking for anyone to go with me, OK? And second, I don't think you know what you're asking or have any concept of what this is going to be like."

"Sure I do. We're gonna road trip around the country for Jesus, right? I get it! Yeah, baby!" Brant clapped his hands together once for effect.

Jon dropped his head in embarrassment as he felt people around them looking their way.

Brant quickly put his hands in his lap and looked around the restaurant. "Sorry. I just think it sounds cool."

"Brant, listen to me. It's not going to be some joy ride, OK? It's going to be hard work. I don't know where I'm going to go, much less where I'll stay. And I hate to spoil your idea of fun, but most folks aren't going to fall all over themselves thanking me for sharing the Gospel with them. It ticks a lot of people off. It's offensive. It may be one rejection after another."

"So?"

"*So?!*" repeated Jon.

"Jon, I know you've been a Christian a lot longer than me. Heck, I've only been to church a few times since I was saved. But I've got to tell you – you're looking at this all wrong, man."

"Oh, *really*?" Jon became conscious of his blood flowing faster through his veins. He told himself to keep calm, but knew he was right. He had followed God's leading. And he didn't need Brant, of all people, to tell him he was wrong. "Well, please tell me what I'm missing, Reverend Morris."

"Jon, look at the opportunity we have here. We're both free to serve God in a really cool way, and there's no reason why it can't be fun! No offense, man, but you seem to be all burdened by it. All I'm saying is, let's just – the two of us, I mean – let's just let go and enjoy it! Let's rock this thing for Jesus, man!"

Jon sighed and looked at his friend's excited face. "Rock this thing for Jesus? Did you really just say that?"

"Yeah, man. Let's do it!"

"You think it's that simple? We're just going to go have a good time and share Christ with people. That's how you see it?"

"Well sure, Jonny-boy. It's that simple."

Jon thought of a quick, sure way to prove Brant wrong. "OK, let's see how simple you think it is," he said, looking around the restaurant. He saw their waiter pass through the dining room on his way to the kitchen. "All right, when our waiter brings us our food, why don't you share Christ with him? He seems like a sharp kid. Witness to him and see what he says."

"Stewart?" asked Brant.

"Who's Stewart?"

"You said our waiter, Stewart."

"You know him?"

"No, I don't know him, you dolt. He told us his name when he walked up."

"Oh. I guess I missed that."

"You still suck at names don't you? You know, you're going to have to work on that if we're going to reach people for Christ."

"Are you going to do it or not?"

"What will you give me if I do it?"

"It's not a bet, Brant."

"Well, let's make it one, then," said Brant, confidently. "Come on, you were never shy about betting on the golf course. What'll you give me?"

"All right," said Jon, considering his options. "You can ride shotgun in my car for the next six months." It was a bold wager, but Jon had no doubts he would still be riding alone.

"And an Oreo brownie sundae for dessert," said Brant, upping the ante.

"Fine, whatever you want."

"And if I don't do it. I'll buy your dinner tonight."

"Deal," said Jon. He smiled and straightened in his chair anticipating Brant's failure and a free dinner. "And we're in luck. Here he comes with our food."

"You forgot his name already, didn't you?" asked Brant as Stewart approached their table.

"Whatever. You're on, buddy."

thirty two

The Gift

*"Husbands, love your wives, just as Christ loved
the church and gave himself up for her."*
- *Ephesians 5:25*

Jon guided his RX7 to a stop along the curb in front of their rented, one-story, brick house. He could feel his heart beating in his chest as he thought of his plans to talk with Lacey. Two days had passed since he decided to accept Jesus Christ as his Savior following the Cam Parsons crusade on television. And he still hadn't told his wife he was now a Christian. Jon had spent those two days trying to separate the reality of his decision from the emotion he experienced when he made it. But he knew there was no turning back.

Despite his excitement over his new faith, the changes Jon knew it would bring scared him. In the eighteen months since their wedding, Lacey had never once brought up religion. And neither had he. But that was all about to change. Jon reached into the Christian bookstore shopping bag sitting on the passenger seat and pulled out a new, black, leather-bound Bible. The Book felt heavy and limp in his hands as he ran his thumb against the gold edges of its pages. On the cover's bottom right corner, shiny gold letters spelled out his name, *Jon M. Smoak*. Jon's first Bible, which he received after going through Confirmation in seventh grade, remained unread somewhere in his parents' house. But this Bible seemed different, almost magical. And it suddenly felt like the most important thing he had ever owned.

Sliding his hand back into the bag, he removed a second Bible with *Lacey A. Smoak* embossed on the cover. Jon's hands shook with anticipation as he held his gift for Lacey. His entire Monday at work had been consumed with thoughts of his now imminent discussion with her. Sitting at his desk, he had daydreamed about giving her the Bible and telling her about how he had been saved Saturday night. He imagined kneeling on their bedroom floor with Lacey, watching tears flow down her face as she prayed to accept Jesus as her Lord and Savior. He held his wife's new Bible against his chest and bowed his head to pray. "Dear God, please let this be a new start for Lacey and me. I have no idea what to say to her. I just know that I love my wife, and I want her to know you. Please help me explain all this. Thank you. Amen."

Jon opened his eyes and hoped his prayer was enough. He turned into the yard and parked next to the house. His car was just small enough to fit between the neighbor's wooden privacy fence and the brick stairs leading up to the kitchen door. He entered the house and placed his keys and Bible on the counter just inside the door, leaving Lacey's Bible in the bag. The house was quiet. "Hello," he called out.

"Shhh! We're in here," Jon heard Lacey say in a whispering voice. He found her on the den couch in her pajamas with Holly, who was wrapped in a blanket asleep on Lacey's lap.

"Hey, sweetie," said Jon softly as he sat down gently next to her. "Already in your pajamas?"

"Hey." Lacey let Jon kiss her on the cheek. "I never changed out of them."

"I'm jealous. How's our little girl?"

"Fine now," said Lacey with a sigh. "She's been fussy all day. She just finally went to sleep a few minutes ago. How was work?"

"Long. But I had lunch with Brant and some of the guys at that burger place over on Rosewood. So that was fun."

Lacey looked down at the white bag next to Jon's feet. "What's in there?"

"Oh, I picked something up for you on the way home. It's a surprise."

"Shhh, not so loud," Lacey said softly, looking at Holly. "You're going to wake her."

"Sorry," whispered Jon. "Here, I'll take her so you can look at your present." Jon lifted Holly from Lacey's lap and positioned her in his arms.

"Be careful," said Lacey as she watched Jon closely. "Hold her head."

"She's fine," Jon assured her, cradling Holly in his left arm. "You just relax."

Lacey let her head fall back against the couch. "Oh, my god. I'm so exhausted. What did you get me?"

"OK, close your eyes," said Jon, reaching down for the bag.

"They *are* closed. It's getting them open again that's gonna be the problem."

Jon lifted the bag from the floor and placed it on her lap. "OK, open your eyes."

"I don't want to," she said with a faint smile. "This feels too good."

"Come on," prodded Jon. "I got this for you."

Lacey opened her eyes and reached her hand inside the bag. "What did you...." Lacey pulled the gift from the bag. "A Bible? You got me a *Bible*?"

"It's a study Bible," said Jon, smiling broadly. "I got one, too. Except mine's black."

Lacey turned the burgundy leather Bible over and fanned the gold-gilded pages with her thumb. "How much were these?"

"Um, yours was seventy-five and mine was seventy," said Jon, nervously. "Yours has extra stuff in it, though. Look." Jon flipped open Lacey's Bible on her lap and tried to find the color-coded maps in the back of the Book.

"You spent a hundred and fifty dollars on Bibles? Are you crazy? What the hell were you thinking, Jon? We can't afford that!"

Jon's heart sank. Holly began to stir in his arms at the sound of her mother's raised voice. "Um, I'll go put her down," Jon said getting up. "Maybe she'll stay in her crib for a while so we can talk. I'll be right back."

Lacey's reaction had caught Jon off-guard, and he needed a moment to gather himself. With Holly in his arms, he left the den and walked down the hall to her bedroom. Leaning over her crib, Jon placed her gently on her back and pulled the small blanket over her pink footie pajamas. Holly stretched her arms over her head and yawned silently before falling limp again.

Jon stood at Holly's crib for a moment watching his daughter. He dreaded going back to the den. What he thought would be a wonderful surprise had landed him in hot water, instead. With no ideas for what to say, he turned and left Holly's room. He walked slowly down the hall and back into the den to find the couch empty. Jo-Jo was nosing Lacey's Bible on the coffee table. "Get away from that," he said and called out for Lacey. "Honey?"

"I'm in the kitchen," said Lacey with clear agitation in her voice.

Jon passed through the den and breakfast area into the kitchen. Lacey stood at the sink washing plastic baby bottles.

"Hey," said Jon. He watched her scrubbing and rinsing the bottles as she ignored his presence. "I was hoping you'd like what I bought you. I thought we could study together."

"*Study*? Have you lost your mind?" asked Lacey, tossing a bottle into the sink and turning to face Jon. "You're taking them back."

"Um, I can't take them back," said Jon, bracing himself for the next wave of anger from Lacey. "I had our names engraved on each of them."

"Jesus, Jon! Are you stupid or something?"

Jon felt a touch of anger flash through his body. "Uh, I don't think you should say 'Jesus' like that. And, no, I'm not stupid!"

"Why did you think I needed a Bible, then? Did I ask you for one? No, I didn't. But you go out and blow seventy-five bucks of our money, anyway! Did you even remember to get the diapers I asked you to?"

"It was supposed to be a gift, you idiot!"

Lacey threw her dishtowel onto the counter next to the sink. "Oh, so now I'm an idiot, just because I care about having enough money to pay our bills! We have a baby, Jon! Hello!"

Jon suddenly realized his hopes for the evening were disintegrating before his eyes. He and Lacey were both angry, and he had just called his wife an idiot. How could he talk with her about his faith now? "OK, I'm sorry," he said. "I didn't mean that. I honestly thought you'd be happy about it."

"Well, Jon, you were wrong, weren't you? As usual. Where are the diapers?"

"Um, I'll go to the store when we finish talking."

"Ugh! We are finished talking, Jon!" Lacey stomped out of the kitchen and down the hallway.

Jon dropped his head and leaned his hip against the kitchen counter. Hearing their bedroom door slam, he turned to see Jo-Jo curled into a tight ball and hiding under the kitchen table. "I screwed that up pretty bad, didn't I, boy?" Jon knew he needed to follow Lacey and talk with her. He just lacked confidence in his ability to do so without making things worse. But he pushed himself away from the kitchen counter and turned to go, anyway. "Wish me luck, Jo-Jo."

Jon walked quietly down the hall. He opened the bedroom door to find Lacey sitting on the floor next to the bed crying with a box of tissues resting on her lap. He moved slowly across the room and sat down next to her without speaking.

"You want to know what I did all day?" she asked in-between sobs. "While you were at work doing whatever it is you do and yucking it up at lunch with Brant, do you know what I was doing?"

Jon knew she wasn't looking for him to answer and remained quiet.

"I was here listening to Holly cry," she said, her voice shaking with emotion. "She cried all day, Jon. I couldn't get her to stop. I tried everything. I called my mom. I called your mom. I even called the doctor's office. They were no help. Then you walk in here five minutes after she finally goes to sleep and get to put her in her crib like you're some big hero." Lacey blew her nose into a tissue and threw it at the wall in front of them.

Jon placed his hand on Lacey's knee, but she quickly knocked it away with a swat of her tissue box.

"And after all that, all I want to do is relax. But, no. You have to come in with your stupid Bibles and – what's that all about, anyway? Why did you buy us Bibles?"

Jon wasn't ready for the sudden change in Lacey's thinking. "Huh?" he asked.

"Why did you buy us Bibles? Where did that come from?" Lacey blew her nose into a tissue and glared into Jon's eyes.

"I, um…." Jon was unsure where to begin discussing his new faith. Or if he should even try, given her reaction to the Bibles. But he remembered his prayer in the car before he came inside and how he'd imagined his conversation with Lacey unfolding. Maybe this was the opportunity for which he had hoped.

"You what, Jon?"

Jon decided to start from the beginning. "Do you remember when you came in the den Saturday, and I was watching that Cam Parson's thing on TV?"

"That Texas preacher guy? Yeah, so? What, did he convert you or something?" Lacey laughed, slightly.

Jon didn't like the implication that he had needed to be *converted* to Christianity. But he knew it was true, nonetheless. "Well, yeah. I guess you could say it like that."

"Oh great! Now you're going to go all Jesus Freak on me, is that it?"

"No! I mean…all I know is that something happened to me Saturday night. And it was real. I know I'm a Christian now."

"Jon, you already *were* a Christian! You told me you were raised going to church all the time. We even got married in your parents' church, for Christ's sake!"

"That doesn't mean anything, Lacey. Look, I'm not saying I didn't think of myself as a Christian before. I did. I know that. But I was wrong. Whatever Cam Parsons said Saturday made me realize that I've just been kidding myself. I needed to be forgiven and accept Jesus as my Savior. And that's what I did. And I want you to do that, too."

"Fine, I accept Jesus as my Savior. Are we all done, now?"

"Lacey, don't joke about things like that. This is important."

"Jon, I don't know what's gotten into you about all this, but I just don't have time to worry about it now, OK? Give me a break." Lacey got up off the floor, picked up her tissues, and walked to their only bathroom down the hall.

Jon sat on the floor wondering what else he could say to help her understand. After a moment, he rose and followed Lacey to the bathroom. He stood quietly in the open doorframe watching her lean towards the small mirror over the sink and dab a cotton ball beneath her eyes.

"Jon, I get that you think something happened with you," she said, looking in the mirror. "I knew something was up the last couple of days. I could tell. But don't expect me to just jump right in with you, OK? I'm not like that."

Hearing the calmer tone in Lacey's voice filled Jon with relief. It wasn't the response he had hoped for, but at least their argument seemed to be over. He decided not to push the issue any further. "OK. I understand." He leaned against the door as he watched Lacey brush her long brown hair. She was beautiful, even when she was upset. He wanted to pull her close and wrap his arms around her, but he was unsure if he'd be welcome.

"Thank you for my Bible," said Lacey. She cut her eyes at him briefly in the mirror and forced a slight smile onto her face.

"You're welcome," said Jon, starting to move towards her.

"Now, will you please go get some diapers?"

"Absolutely," said Jon. He kissed her quickly on the cheek and left the bathroom, crossing the hallway into the kitchen. Jo-Jo was still curled-up under the breakfast table. "Come on, Jo-Jo. It's all safe, now. Let's go for a ride." Jo-Jo scrambled to his feet under the table, knocking over a chair in the process. Jon righted the chair and looked around for his keys. Seeing them on the kitchen counter next to his new Bible, he reached for both of them as he opened the side door. Jo-Jo scooted past him, leapt off the stoop, and bounced expectantly by Jon's car door. Jon squeezed the Bible in his left hand and pressed it firmly against the side of his chest. Though he had yet to read a word from its pages, just holding the Book gave him a feeling of comfort. "I guess it's just you and me for now," he said to his Bible and closed the door behind him.

thirty three

The Bet

*"Always be prepared to give an answer to everyone who asks
you to give the reason for the hope that you have."*
- 1 Peter 3:15

Jon smiled confidently as their waiter approached the table. He was certain Brant would either chicken-out of their bet altogether or fail miserably in his attempt at witnessing to the young man. Either way, Jon knew God's plan for his trip would remain unchanged. He would be riding alone.

"OK, I've got chicken-fried steak for you," said Stewart, placing the plate in front of Jon.

"I had the shrimp and grits," said Jon. "That's his."

"Oh. That's right," said Stewart, showing signs of embarrassment in his face. "I'm sorry about that." The young waiter appeared flustered, more than should be expected from such a small mistake. "Here you go," he said, setting the correct plates down in front of Brant and Jon. "And I'm sorry that took so long. I got held up in the back for a few minutes. Can I get you gentlemen anything else right now?" Stewart stood up straight and tried to regain his confident demeanor.

"Um, my friend, here," said Jon, nodding to Brant, "has something he'd like to talk with you about. Isn't that right, Brant?"

"Why, yes I do," said Brant, looking up at Stewart. "Do you have a minute?"

"Um," said Stewart, hesitating. "If there's a problem, I'd be happy to get my manager. Again, I'm sorry the food took so long. It was my fault. I just got held up in the kitchen by someone."

"Don't worry about it," said Brant. "We didn't even notice. Can you sit for a minute?"

"Oh, I'm not allowed to sit down with customers," said Stewart, looking around the restaurant.

"That's OK," said Brant. "I just want to ask you something."

"Yes, sir?" asked Stewart, his eyebrows raised with interest.

"My friend and I are both Christians," said Brant, glancing at Jon for affirmation. "And we're getting ready to go on a trip to share Jesus with as many people as we can over the next six months. And we were just talking about what a sharp young man you are. You seem like a pretty smart guy."

"Oh, thank you, sir," said Stewart, his eyes darting between Brant and Jon.

"And we were just wondering if you had ever accepted Jesus Christ as your Savior," said Brant.

Stewart's face flushed with color and his mouth dropped open. He swung his head around and watched a petite young waitress pass through the dining room. Her eyes flashed briefly at him as she stopped at a table near the front door. "Did *she* tell you to say that?" asked Stewart as he pointed at the waitress.

"Who? Her?" asked Brant, looking at the girl.

"Yes, sir," said Stewart, growing visibly anxious. "Did she come out here and tell you to ask me that?"

"Son, we've never talked to her, I promise," said Brant. "Why do you think she has anything to do with us?"

"Because she's why I was held up in the kitchen. She's been telling me about her relationship with Jesus all night and how I need to be saved."

Jon's eyes widened as he leaned back in his chair. He realized there was more happening than just his silly bet with Brant. God might really be using them to reach this young man. "Stewart," said Jon, "we're just doing what Christians are supposed to do. We're just trying to share the Good News. And I'm sure that girl is just doing the same thing. The three of us aren't ganging up on you, I promise. But it seems to me like God is really trying to get your attention tonight."

Stewart looked over at the waitress again as she waited on another table. As her customers looked over their menus, she glanced at Stewart briefly and smiled.

"Is she your girlfriend?" asked Brant.

"Kinda," said Stewart, still watching the girl. "I mean, no. Not really, I guess. We've been out a couple times. She wants me to go to church with her."

Jon's mind flashed back to his conversation with Jenny at the very same table twenty-two years earlier. Suddenly, he knew what Stewart needed to hear. "Stewart, when I was about your age, I was in the same situation that you're in now. Can I share some advice with you?"

"Sure," said Stewart, his eyes fixed on Jon.

"Listen to what she has to say. Don't be afraid to listen. And think seriously about what she's telling you. Accepting what Jesus did for you on the Cross will change your life in the best way possible. You'll never regret it. But here's the thing: You've got to do it for you. Not for her. It's between you and God. Do you understand?"

"Yes, sir. I think so," said Stewart, lowering his eyes to the floor. "I should go back to work now. I, um…I really appreciate what y'all are doing. And I'll think about what you said. I'm glad you sat in my section." Stewart smiled, timidly, and left their table.

Jon's eyes followed Stewart as he walked back to the kitchen and disappeared through the swinging double doors. He turned and looked across the table at Brant.

"So, when do we leave?" asked Brant, grinning broadly.

Jon looked back towards the kitchen. "Tomorrow," he heard himself say. "We leave tomorrow."

"Cool. Can I have my Oreo brownie sundae, now?"

Part II

Smoak And Fire

*"They saw what seemed to be tongues of fire that
separated and came to rest on each of them."*

- Acts 2:3

thirty four

Sidekick

"Can two people walk together without agreeing on the direction?"
- Amos 3:3 NLT

Jon reached for the clock, turned off the alarm, and looked at the time. Five o'clock in the morning. He let his arm flop across his body and yawned slowly as he lay on his back in the darkness. It was all about to begin. Seconds ago he was in deep, peaceful sleep. Now, anxiety began to fill his body even as he lay comfortably underneath his covers. He turned on the lamp next to his bed, sat-up, and rubbed his eyes as they adjusted from the darkness. Elvis continued snoring under Jon's bed, his hindquarters and tail protruding from underneath the dust ruffle. Jon lifted his Bible from the nightstand onto his lap. The Book felt heavy on his legs as he opened its pages to his place in the tenth chapter of Romans. He read the chapter slowly, hoping every word would find a permanent resting place in his mind and heart. After finishing the chapter, Jon closed his eyes in prayer.

"Dear God, Heavenly Father, I'm scared to death. I know this is what you have planned for me, what you want me to do, but I feel so...unprepared and unqualified to do what you're asking. I don't even know where I'm supposed to go or who I'm supposed to talk to. Please provide me some direction, Lord. I mean, I'm leaving in a few hours, and I don't even have a plan or destination in mind. Shouldn't I know? Shouldn't I know where I'm going? I've been waiting for you to tell me or show me or something. And Brant...where do I even start? It's been years since he and I were friends, and

I'm not sure I even know much about him anymore. But now he's going with me. How did that happen? I know I should have prayed about it first before I agreed to it. I just hope taking him isn't a mistake. I'm scared I won't have the energy to manage him and all that you're calling me to do. He can just be so...*Brant* sometimes. You know?"

Jon sat in silence for a moment. He moved the Bible from his lap and rolled over onto his stomach. Dropping his head into his hands, he continued his prayer. "Oh God, what have I done? This was going to be hard enough for me as it was, and now I've made it even more complicated. I could just not go pick him up. I could just leave without him. But I gave him my word last night that he could go with me. God, please help me. I need your strength and your patience and your wisdom. I don't want to fail you, God. I know that I need you. Please help me. Guide me in your path, and help me to see the opportunities you put in front of me to share your Gospel. And help me disciple Brant, dear God. Give me patience. Use me to help him mature as a Believer. It wasn't part of my plan to do that, so I'll just have to trust that it was part of yours. I hope I'm up for all this, Lord. Please help me. In Jesus' name I pray. Amen."

Jon tossed the last of his travel bags into the trunk of his car and closed the lid. He'd told Brant to expect him at his apartment by eight thirty. But as Jon double-checked the to-do list on his iPhone, he saw that it was almost nine. Holly knelt a few feet away on the driveway petting Elvis. "I'm late," he said.

"Did you remember to take the charger for your iPhone?" asked Holly.

"Got it. Thanks for reminding me, though. I think that's everything."

"What about your Bible?" Holly grinned at her dad.

"Very funny," said Jon, walking over to give his daughter a hug. "I'll be back for Christmas, OK?"

"I was going to ask you about that. That's just a little over two months from now, you know. What about Thanksgiving?"

"I'm not sure about that yet. I guess it all depends on where we are. But don't worry. We've got plenty of time to talk about all that."

"Lisa said I could go home with her to Manning for Thanksgiving if you're not here. She said I could even bring Elvis."

"That's nice of her. I'm glad you ended up with a roommate you like this year. I hope you guys can stay friends even though you've moved out."

"Oh, we will. I'll still hang out there during the day in between classes and stuff. Oh, and I think I got a part-time job!"

"That's awesome, honey! Where?"

"Well, this boy I met in my law class works at a coffee shop near campus and I go in there all the time with Lisa and he was working when we went in there Tuesday – no – Wednesday night and he asked me if I wanted a job there and I said I did and then the owner came out and she was like, 'When can you work?' and I was like, 'Anytime, really,' so she had me fill-out an application and told me to come back today so after you leave I'm going to go down there and talk to her about it. He's really nice." Holly smiled.

"Who's nice?" asked Jon, trying to keep up.

"Brighton."

"I must have missed that part. Who's Brighton?"

"Oh, he's the boy I know from class. He's the one who asked me if I wanted a job."

"Oh, *I see*," said Jon, letting a grin grow across his face.

Holly gave him a playful shove. "It's not like that, Dad."

"Uh-huh."

"Stop!" said Holly, laughing. "He's just this really nice guy, that's all. And he sings in a band."

"OK, that's it," said Jon, pretending to be serious. "I'm not going."

"Oh, whatever!" Holly turned her dad's shoulders and pushed him towards his car. "Just *leave*, already!"

Jon leaned back against Holly's efforts to push him along. "OK, but no boys named Brighton over at the house while I'm gone."

"Fine, I'll go over to his house."

"I'm not going!" said Jon, turning around.

"Just *go*, already! God's waiting on you."

"All right," said Jon, realizing it really was time to go. "But I think it's Brant that's waiting on me. He's probably wondering where I am right now."

Jon hugged his daughter tightly and kissed her on the cheek. "Bye, sweetie. I love you."

"Bye, Daddy. I love you, too. And I'm proud of you."

Jon turned slowly into the apartment complex parking lot. Several letters from the entrance sign were missing, but his GPS navigation system confirmed he had arrived at Greengate Apartments. Maneuvering his car around potholes in the uneven patchwork-asphalt pavement, he looked for Brant's building number as he leaned forward over the steering wheel. Jon began to feel slightly uncomfortable as he drove slowly past the aging, wood-siding apartments. Clothes hung on lines stretched between rusting, metal poles behind the units. Trash and cigarette butts littered the grounds and parking lot. "Good Lord," he said to himself. "Why in the world does he live *here*?"

Spotting the number 42 on the building straight-ahead, Jon eased his car towards an open parking space, steering around an empty beer bottle and the broken remains of what looked like a laptop computer. "Guess they dropped that during the getaway last night," Jon said to himself as he rolled to a stop. He got out of his car, locked it behind him, and climbed the stairs to the second floor walkway. Two white trash bags, packed full and tied at the top, leaned against the railing outside of apartment C. Jon knocked on the door.

"Jonny-boy!" Jon heard from inside the apartment.

The door swung open and Brant welcomed his friend with a smile and energetic handshake. "Come in the house, man!" said Brant, pulling Jon through the doorway. "I was beginning to think you left without me."

"I'm sorry about that. It took a little longer to get all my stuff together than I thought it would."

"No worries, brother," said Brant as he punched Jon on the shoulder. "I had fun last night at dinner."

Jon looked around the empty apartment. "Yeah, it was good."

Brant walked into his kitchen and opened the refrigerator. "So, do you think Stewart is gonna get saved?"

"Our waiter?" asked Jon, realizing he hadn't thought about it since they left the restaurant. "I have no idea, Brant. I guess that's between him and God at this point. We need to pray for him, though."

"Maybe that cute waitress will stay after him about it," said Brant, walking back into the den. "Let's go back in there when we get back and see what happened."

"We can." Jon stood awkwardly in the middle of the room, unsure what to do with himself. "We can definitely do that."

"Give me just a minute," said Brant. "I'm almost ready. Grab a seat." He left Jon alone in the den as he disappeared into his bedroom. "I'd offer you something to drink, but I don't have anything," shouted Brant from his room.

"I'm fine," said Jon, looking down at his only seating option. A small flat panel television sat on the floor against the wall in front of a foldout beach chair. "I just had a Diet Mountain Dew on the way over here."

"Some things don't change, do they?" asked Brant, chuckling in his bedroom.

Jon looked at the opened family-size bag of barbeque potato chips on the floor next to the chair. "No, they don't," he said. He could hear Brant zipping up his luggage in his bedroom. "Brant, if it weren't for the TV and your bag of chips here, I wouldn't think anyone lived here."

"I told you I didn't have any furniture," answered Brant from his bedroom. "At least I don't have to worry about anything getting stolen."

Jon looked out the window at his car below. "Speaking of that, I almost ran-over a laptop in the parking lot out there coming in. What's up with that?"

"I'm not surprised," said Brant, sticking his head out of his bedroom. "Apartments get broken into around here all the time. I guess it's hard to carry a stolen TV and a laptop at the same time." He smiled at his joke and disappeared again into his room.

"You know," said Jon through the bare white wall, "if you found an apartment in a nicer neighborhood, maybe you wouldn't have to worry about stuff like that."

"Well, it was either this or move in with my folks in Orangeburg. I chose poverty."

Jon tried to be a little more compassionate. "Well, it's not so bad. That is a pretty nice…twelve inch TV," he said, giving in to sarcasm instead. "I didn't think they made them that small."

Brant walked into the den. "Like I said, no self-respecting thief is ever going to risk prison time to steal that TV." He tossed a large gym bag and a backpack onto the middle of the den floor. "So, where are we headed first?"

Jon felt like he should know the answer to Brant's question. Since God had called him so clearly to embark on this trip, he'd hoped for equally clear direction on where to go. But the lack of an answer to his prayers weighed heavily on him. "I'm still not sure, believe it or not," he said, jingling the keys in his hand. "I've been praying about it, but I haven't decided for sure. I do think we need to stay to the south, given the weather and all. It'll be getting cold soon."

"I think we should head for Charleston first," said Brant, clapping his hands. "Maybe we can save some pretty ladies in the Holy City!"

Jon shook his head. Brant's frivolous attitude struck a nerve. "OK, let's get one thing straight, right from the start. This is not some spring break trip. We're not in college anymore, and this is not about meeting girls or having fun."

"Wow! Look everyone," said Brant, pointing at Jon, "it's Mr. Buzz-kill!"

"I'm not a…." Jon stopped himself midsentence. Brant's choice of words stabbed an old wound. A memory from Jon's last argument with Lacey the night she died forced its way up from the depths of his mind. He turned around, walked to the window, and looked through the blinds at the parking lot below. "Brant, if we're going to do this together, we need to be on the same page, OK?"

Brant paused a moment before answering. "OK."

"I'm fine with heading to Charleston first. But anywhere we go, we have to have the right motivation." Jon turned back to face Brant. "And we should pray about it first."

"I agree. And I'm sorry if I…I was just joking around."

"I know. But why don't we pray right now before we head out?"

"Good idea!"

"Cool," said Jon, feeling somewhat relieved. He knelt on one knee in the middle of the den with Brant. Jon placed his hand on Brant's wrist and began to pray out loud. "Dear Heavenly Father, we seek your face and your direction as we set out to serve you and share your Gospel with those who need to hear it. We do this in obedience to you and love for you. Our hearts are filled with gratitude for what your Son, Jesus, did for us on the Cross, Lord. We pray that you'll lead us and show us opportunities to bring others to salvation in him. Guide us as we make decisions on where to go and who to share your Truth with, God. We pray these things in Jesus' name. Amen."

"Amen!" said Brant.

Jon rose to his feet with Brant and shook his hand. "Are you ready?" he asked, feeling slightly less burdened.

Brant lifted his bags from the floor. "Let's roll!"

Jon opened the apartment door. "All right, we'll toss your stuff in the car and then we can figure out everything else once we get going."

"Can we get something to eat first?" asked Brant as they moved outside the apartment. "I'm starving."

Jon had already eaten and was ready to get on the road. "Um, sure, man," he said as he watched Brant lock the door. "How about a bagel to go or something?"

"A bagel? How about some pancakes or a sausage, egg, and cheese biscuit with some hash browns and a large coffee?"

"Wow, OK," laughed Jon as they walked towards the stairs. "But we might be eating at different restaurants for the next six months."

"A bagel," said Brant, shaking his head as he slapped Jon's back. "Man-up, Jonny-boy! You could stand to gain a few pounds, anyway."

"Yeah, yeah," said Jon.

The two walked down the stairs from Brant's apartment and into the parking lot. Jon led them towards his car and pointed his key fob at his white BMW 535. The interior lights illuminated as the doors unlocked.

"We're going in that?" asked Brant, slowing as they walked towards Jon's car.

"Is there a problem with that?" asked Jon sarcastically as he pointed his remote to open his trunk.

"Well, yeah. Maybe." Brant stood holding his bags as he stared at the car.

"What's wrong with it?" asked Jon as he rearranged his luggage in the trunk to make room for Brant's bags. "Not your favorite color or something?"

"It's just not what I had in mind, I guess."

Jon turned and looked at Brant. "Wait, you're serious?"

"Kind of, yeah."

"Well, I'm sorry I don't have anything nicer for you, Brant. I'll try and upgrade before our next trip."

"No, that's not what I'm saying. It's a nice car, Jon."

"Well, I'm so glad you think so. Now hand me your bags and I'll toss them in the trunk."

"But don't you think it's a little *too* nice for what we're going to be doing?"

"It's just a car, Brant."

Brant held on to his bags. "Yeah, but can you imagine us pulling up to a homeless shelter in this? What does that say about us?"

"It says we found the homeless shelter because I have a navigation system. Come on, let's go."

"I'm serious, Jon. I just don't think this will help us reach people. It might even make it harder."

Jon closed the trunk. "OK, make up your mind, Brant. A minute ago you wanted to use Jesus to pick-up girls in Charleston. Now you're worried my car is too nice for us to witness to a homeless person?"

"OK, I was out of line on the girl thing. But still, think about it, Jon."

Though it pained him to admit it, Jon could see some legitimacy in Brant's point, however small. And in spite of his desire to drive his own car, Jon offered an alternative just to avoid further discussion. "All right, we'll take your car, then." Jon looked around the parking lot. "Where is it?"

"It's right next to you," said Brant, pointing to the twenty-two-year-old red Jeep Wrangler parked next to Jon's car.

"That's yours? That looks like the same Jeep you bought when you graduated from college."

"That *is* the same Jeep I bought when I graduated from college. It's a classic!"

"That's one word for it." Jon stepped back to get a better look at the rusting Jeep. "You've driven this thing ever since we were at MindShare together?"

"Yep," said Brant. He set his bags on the ground and walked around his Jeep, inspecting it as if he were a potential buyer. "It's old, I know. It leaks oil everywhere and doesn't start about half the time. Plus, the top leaks like crazy in the rain. But I'd never get rid of it. It's still my baby."

"And you want us to take *this*?"

"Well, sure. It'll be great!" said Brant, pounding his hand on the hood.

Jon leaned against the rear of his car. "Brant, we can't take that. We'd spend half our time stranded and hitching rides."

"Well, that wouldn't be such a bad thing, would it?"

"No, of course not. I love car trouble and hitch-hiking."

"Wait a minute – that's an idea!" said Brant, becoming excited. "Listen, what if we just hitched everywhere?"

"Why on earth would we do that?" Jon turned around, stretched his arms out towards his car. "*Hello?*"

"Jon, I love your ride, OK? Seriously. It's nice. But think about this for a minute. If we drive everywhere, we're going to spend most of our time just talking with each other, right?"

"I suppose," said Jon, trying to determine how he felt about that fact.

"Well, what if we hitched everywhere and let God decide who picks us up? Then we share Christ with them! It'll be awesome!" Brant's face beamed with enthusiasm.

Jon dropped his shoulders and looked into the morning sky. They hadn't even left the parking lot and already he felt Brant trying to take control of his trip. It was classic Brant. "Brant," Jon sighed, "I know you like to control everything, but this is a little more involved than tailgating for a football game. This is *my* calling, not yours. You're just along for the ride, remember? Mr. Oreo Brownie Sundae."

"I'm *not* just along for the ride, Jon. I'm in this thing, too. I'm committed. So don't act like you're the…Lone Ranger, and I'm Tonto or something."

Jon took a deep breath to control his growing frustration. He forced a smile onto his face and tried to respond in keeping with Brant's analogy. "I was thinking more like Batman and Robin."

"Oh, so I'm supposed to be the Boy Wonder? I don't think so. I want to reach people for Christ, just like you do, Jon. So don't give me any of this *useless sidekick* crap."

"OK, look, why don't we just say we're like the Super Friends then?" offered Jon. "Equal members of the Justice League. You know, like the cartoon when we were kids. How's that?"

Brant nodded his head in thoughtful agreement. "I can live with that. I'll be Spiderman," he said, pretending to shoot a spider web from his wrist at Jon.

"Spiderman wasn't in the Justice League."

"Yes, he was! With the Hulk and Captain America and all those other guys."

"Those were The Avengers. Totally different." Jon opened his trunk again. "And Spiderman wasn't in The Avengers, either."

"Who was he with then?"

Jon shrugged his shoulders and reached for Brant's luggage. "He just did his own thing, I guess."

"Well, who was in the Justice League?"

Jon placed Brant's bags in his trunk and closed the lid. "That was Superman, Batman, and Aquaman."

Brant laughed. "Speaking of useless," he said, walking around to the passenger side of Jon's car.

Jon walked to his door and looked across the roof at Brant. "Yeah, no kidding. I mean, how many underwater emergencies are there, right?"

Brant laughed and folded his arms on the top of the car as he leaned his body against it.

"Anyway, what were we talking about?" asked Jon, opening the driver's side door.

"Um…," said Brant, his eyes drifting up in thought.

"Whatever," said Jon, grinning to himself. "Hop in. Let's go get you some breakfast."

"Sweet! I call dibs on the iPod," said Brant, plopping into the passenger seat.

"Of course you do."

thirty five

Wrath

"Therefore, since we are surrounded by such a great cloud of witnesses,
let us throw off everything that hinders and the sin that so easily
entangles. And let us run with perseverance the race marked out for us."

- *Hebrews 12:1*

Saturday morning traffic on I-26 was light. On any weekday morning, both eastbound lanes would be filled with eighteen-wheelers hauling goods down to the ports in Charleston. And the rolling hills from Columbia to Orangeburg would make maintaining a constant speed impossible. The big trucks would struggle to pull their full loads up the long inclines, then speed like runaway trains down the other side. Driving around them was usually a white-knuckle experience Jon never enjoyed. And the ever-present risk of a speeding ticket only added to the stress. But this morning, Jon could relax. Only a few trucks rolled along the highway, and the drivers in his immediate vicinity were all behaving themselves for the moment. He settled into his leather seat and set his cruise control to seventy-two. "You think that sausage biscuit will hold you until we get to Charleston?" he asked Brant with intended sarcasm.

"It might." Brant leaned his left elbow against the center console as he scrolled through songs and playlists from Jon's iPod, displayed on the dashboard screen. "Where do you want to eat lunch when we get down there?"

"Brant, our goal isn't to just go from one restaurant to another, you know. We have other things to do and plan for than just where we're going to eat."

"Hey, 'survival is the first order of business' – James T. Kirk in *Star Trek II: The Wrath of Khan*. Look it up." Brant squinted his eyes to focus on the song titles listed on the display.

"First of all, you're not Captain of the Enterprise. And, secondly, we're not stranded in some man-made underground cavern on a distant planet with Ricardo Montalban chasing after us. Are you going to play some music or just read the playlists on my iPod?"

"What's Shoegaze?" asked Brant. "What kind of music is that?" Brant selected a song from the playlist, and the piano melody of *Mesmerise*, by Chapterhouse, filled the car. He turned up the volume and bobbed his head. "Not bad."

Jon turned down the volume from the controls on his steering wheel. "Just put on some worship music. There's a playlist called *Worship*. Just hit that. And we need to talk about what we're going to do when we get to Charleston. I want to witness to some people today."

"I'm game," said Brant, turning the volume up slightly without changing the song. "So, how do you see us doing that, by the way? Just stopping random people on the street and asking them if they know Jesus?"

"Well, that's one way, I guess," said Jon, talking over the music. "I thought about that, but if people are on their way somewhere, they might not want to stop to talk, you know? But I think if we find folks just sitting around, like in Marion Square or on the Battery, we might be able to have a conversation with them. What do you think?"

"That makes sense," said Brant, looking out the window. "It's a beautiful day, so folks should be out and about. What do you think we should say when we walk up?"

"Honestly, I think I'll just have to make it up as it comes to me. I don't want it to sound like some canned sales pitch, you know?" Jon switched into a TV pitchman voice. "And if you accept Jesus Christ as your Lord and Savior in the next fifteen minutes, we'll send you this free pocket organizer! Just pay shipping and handling."

"You're pretty good at that," laughed Brant.

"I am in advertising, you know. Seriously, I'm sure we'll get more comfortable the more we do it."

"Yeah, too bad for the first couple of guinea pigs. Maybe they won't be too hard on us."

"I wouldn't count on it being easy, Brant."

Brant ignored Jon's warning and continued playing with the iPod. "I've never even heard of half of these bands on here. You need to get some real music, man."

Jon sighed and glanced at Brant. "Real music, huh? You probably still think *Play That Funky Music White-boy* is the ultimate party song."

"You know it! Ladies love that song, are you kidding me?" Brant began to sing while pumping his hands up and down. "And they were dancin' and signin' and movin' to the...something."

"You don't even know the words!"

"Play that funky music, white-boy!" sang Brant, loudly. "Play that funky music, right!"

Jon laughed. "That's horrible."

"Lay down the buggy and—"

"OK, stop!" begged Jon. "Or I'm pulling the car over and putting you out."

Brant stopped singing and dropped his hands back onto his lap. "I bet you'd do it, too, wouldn't you?"

"You're darn right. My dad did that to me when I was like five or something. So don't think I wouldn't."

"Your dad dumped you out of the car when you were five years old?"

"Yes, he did."

"Well, that explains a lot," said Brant. "Poor kid. Probably scarred you for life. What were you doing to get tossed out? You don't have any brothers or sisters to annoy."

"I don't remember. Probably whining about something. But I do remember watching our old, dark green, Chevy station wagon drive away while I stood there crying on the curb."

"What the heck, man! What happened?"

"He drove around the block and came back, obviously. My mom was not happy with him; I remember that."

"Man," said Brant, shaking his head. "I remember your dad. I always thought he was a good guy. I can't imagine him doing that."

"He was a great guy. He just always had a way of teaching me stuff so I'd remember it."

Brant laughed. "You obviously didn't forget that. I bet you never acted up in the car again."

"No, I didn't. As a matter of fact, one time we were…oh geez, check-out this billboard." Jon pointed up at a large black and yellow sign for an adult book and video store. "Why don't they just say, *'Ruin your life! Next exit!'*? At least that would be honest advertising."

Brant looked up at the sign, but didn't comment. Their conversation died as Brant stared straight ahead down the road. Realizing his attempt at humor had failed, Jon turned up the volume on the stereo and wondered what he had said to change Brant's demeanor.

Brant turned off the stereo. "Take this exit," he said, pointing to the approaching exit ramp.

"Why? You have to go to the bathroom again?"

"Just take this exit, Jon!"

Jon swerved onto the exit ramp and let the car coast up the hill to the stop sign. "All right, now what?" he asked, looking around the intersection. To the left, Jon saw nothing but a two-lane road disappearing into a pine forest. Down the road to his right was the adult bookstore advertised on the billboard.

"Take a right," said Brant.

Jon kept his foot firmly on the brake. "The only thing over there is that adult bookstore, Brant."

"That's where we're going."

"The heck we are! I'm not—"

"You said you wanted to witness to somebody today, Jon. Here's our chance."

Jon sighed and looked down the road toward the store. Against his better judgment, he let the car move slowly forward as he made a right turn. "We are not going in there, Brant."

Brant stared through the windshield at the store ahead. "Just stay in the car, then. Let me handle it."

Brant's serious expression began to worry Jon. "Handle what? What are you going to do?"

"Just turn in here," said Brant, pointing to the store parking lot entrance. "Park over there."

Jon parked a safe distance from the building and turned off the car. "What are you going to do, Brant?"

Brant opened the car door and lifted himself out. "I'm going to save some people," he said as he closed the door.

"Brant," Jon called after him, unsure what to do next. He released his seat belt and opened his door, but remained in the driver's seat as he watched Brant stride purposefully towards the entrance of the store.

Brant reached the front door, but turned to face the parking lot rather than go inside. He folded his arms across his chest, looking more like a bouncer at a nightclub than a witness for Christ. Seeing a young man in his twenties approaching the store entrance, Brant held up his hands. Jon could hear him from the car.

"Don't go in there, brother," said Brant to the young man.

"Why? What's going on?"

"You don't need this." Brant pointed towards the man's car. "Just go home."

The young man stopped and looked around. His eyes landed on Jon as he sat watching from his car. The man turned quickly and retreated to his car.

"You need Jesus!" shouted Brant. He pointed at Jon, smiled, and gave him a thumbs-up gesture.

Jon watched the man get in his car and speed way across the gravel parking lot and up the road. Jon got out of his car and closed the door. He walked slowly towards Brant as he looked around the parking lot. Several cars and two eighteen-wheel trucks were parked randomly across the large unpaved lot. As he neared the store entrance, a thin, bearded man in a plain white T-shirt exited the building carrying a small white bag. Brant turned to face him.

"Hey man, you don't need that," said Brant, pointing to the bag in the man's hand. "Take that stuff back in there and leave it. You don't need it."

"Go to hell," said the man as he maneuvered around Brant and past Jon.

"That's where you're going, man!" shouted Brant as the man walked away. "Jesus can save you from that! Come back and talk to me about it. Leave that filth here!"

The man planted his foot and turned quickly back towards the store. Without speaking, he walked by Brant and Jon and re-entered through the front door.

Brant smiled at Jon. "You see, Jonny-boy? Just doing God's work!"

Jon cast a worried eye at the store entrance and wondered what was going on inside. "I don't know about this, Brant."

The tinted glass door swung open as the man reemerged from the store with a tall, bald, heavyset friend in tow. Dark green tattoos covered the large man's arms from his wrists to the short sleeves of his black T-shirt. White letters across his chest spelled *Got beer?* And beneath a silver nose ring, an overgrown mustache obscured his upper lip as he spoke. "What's the damn problem out here?" the man asked.

"These two faggots are out here pushing Jesus to your customers," the thin man said. He pointed at Brant. "That's the one who told me I was going to hell."

The large man stepped closer to Brant. Jon took a step back while Brant held his ground.

"I'll give you five seconds to get off my property before I kick your ass or have you thrown in jail or both," said the man.

Brant leaned inches from the man's face. "You're the one who ought to be locked up, you scumbag."

The man pushed Brant hard, sending him backward several feet. Brant recovered quickly and rushed forward, his hands clinched into fists. Jon dove and tackled Brant around the waist and tumbled to the ground with him. The thin man ran away towards a parked eighteen-wheeler as the large man grabbed the back of Jon's shirt, lifted him to his feet, and spun him around. The man's fist struck Jon's left temple, sending him quickly back to the ground. Jon rolled onto his back in time to see Brant leap onto the man from the side, tackling him around his neck. Both fell to the concrete slab in front of the store entrance.

"Brant!" shouted Jon as he scrambled to his feet. He ran towards Brant, who struggled to maintain control of the enraged man underneath him. Jon pulled Brant away with both hands as Brant swung his fist wildly at the man's bald head, missing by inches.

"Come on!" yelled Jon as he pulled Brant with him into the parking lot.

Brant resisted and stumbled as Jon tugged on his arm, but finally submitted. The two began running full speed towards Jon's car.

"I'm calling the cops on you assholes!" shouted the man behind them.

Jon and Brant jumped into the car and closed the doors. The man jogged slowly towards them, shouting obscenities as Jon started the engine and backed quickly out of the parking lot. His rear tires kicked up gravel and dust all around them as he accelerated in reverse. Looking over his right shoulder, Jon steered the car backwards onto the main road in the direction from which they came without slowing down. Back on the asphalt pavement, he spun the steering wheel to the left sending the rear of the car onto the grassy shoulder. The front of the car slid around to the right, the tires screeching against the pavement as Jon shifted into drive and pressed hard on the accelerator. The rear wheels spun in the grass before finding forward traction, sending them down the on-ramp and back onto the interstate.

Jon exhaled the tension from his chest and looked incredulously at Brant. "What the heck, Brant! What was *that*?"

Still breathing heavily, Brant looked out the passenger side window without responding.

"I don't know what you're thinking," barked Jon, "but that is *not* how we're going to win people for Christ! Geez, man! We could have been arrested! You want to tell me what that was all about?"

Jon waited for a response as Brant continued to stare out the window. He grew impatient. "*Hello?*"

Turning his face forward, Brant took a deep breath and exhaled. "You know that laptop you saw in the parking lot outside my apartment?"

"Yeah, what about it?" Jon snapped.

"That was mine," said Brant, lowering his head.

Jon glanced over at Brant, unsure of the connection. "I'm not following."

Brant paused for a long moment before continuing. "I've been...um...I've been struggling with stuff on the Internet for a long time."

Jon felt his heart sink. "Pornography, you mean?"

"Yeah," Brant said softly, still looking down.

Jon gripped his steering wheel tightly, unsure how to respond.

"When I was saved a few months ago," said Brant, "I thought I was free from it. I felt clean and new. You know what I mean?"

"Yeah, I know."

"It was awesome. And I stayed away from looking at anything for weeks. But it got tougher every time I was online. And then this past Sunday night I was surfing around, wasting time and before I knew it, I was neck deep in it again."

Jon lifted his foot off the gas without thinking. He was growing uncomfortable with his friend's confession. Brant was a spiritual infant, having only been in the faith a few months. Maybe he just wasn't ready for what they were about to do. Maybe he should turn the car around and take Brant home.

"I cried out to Jesus to forgive me," said Brant. "It was horrible having to go back to him again like that after he had saved me and forgiven me. I wanted to be free from that stuff so bad. And then you called me on Tuesday and told me about your trip."

"Uh-huh," said Jon, wondering when the next exit would appear so he could turn around.

"And after we hung up," said Brant, "I started thinking about what you were doing, just leaving everything. And going with you seemed like a way to escape, you know? To just serve Jesus and do all the right things a Christian is supposed to do and not worry about anything else. To be free."

They rode in silence for a moment.

Jon thought about how Brant described his reason for going on the trip. And while his friend reached his decision through a totally different experience, they appeared to share the same desire: To simply do what a Christian is supposed to do. To be free from everything that kept that from happening. "I guess that explains your enthusiasm in Oscar Ray's last night," said Jon.

"Yeah. I was excited about it. But then when I got home last night, I went online and was searching for stuff about how to share your faith. And I clicked on this site that really bashed Christians about being intolerant and arrogant and hypocrites and stuff. And it had these banner ads with nude women in them. And I just...."

Jon rubbed his hand over his mouth, unsure what he was going to hear next.

"I just clicked on it. But at the same time I clicked on it, I closed my eyes. And I just sat there with my eyes closed not wanting to see what was on the screen. I could feel this war going on in my head and my body, you know?

So I just started praying with my eyes closed. All I could say was, *God help me.* Over and over again. *Jesus help me.*"

Jon took his eyes off the road to look at his friend. He saw tears rolling down Brant's face.

"And then, I don't know how this happened – because it's not something I thought about doing – but I just closed the laptop and ran to my door and threw it off the balcony, out into the parking lot." Brant laughed once, awkwardly, and sniffed his running nose. "I don't ever want to see that stuff again."

"So that's why you wanted to turn those guys away from the bookstore," said Jon.

"Yeah, I mean…I wanted them to know they don't have to live like that." Brant looked at Jon. "They don't. Jesus can save them from all that."

Jon let his foot press down on the accelerator and set the cruise control again to seventy-two. "I'm sure God loves your motivation, man," he said, smiling warmly at Brant. "We just need to work on your approach." Jon reached across the center console and punched Brant's thigh.

"Ouch. Yeah, sorry about that," said Brant, laughing at himself. "At least I didn't hit that guy."

"You swung and missed! I think that still counts."

"But I didn't connect!"

"Only because I pulled you off him. You still meant to hit him."

"OK, whatever. I'm guilty," Brant conceded. "You're not going to make me get out of the car like your dad did, are you?"

Jon laughed. "No, not this time."

Brant slid his hands under the front of his shirt and used it to dry his face. "By the way, that was some impressive Jim Rockford driving back there."

"The backwards, hide-my-license-plate getaway, you mean?" asked Jon. "I think James Garner would be proud."

"No kidding. Do you practice that or something?"

"Nah, but you're really showing our age making *Rockford Files* references."

"I loved that show," said Brant, a smile coming back to his face. "Best TV show theme song ever!"

"No way! The theme song for *Simon & Simon* ruled!"

"*Simon & Simon?*" asked Brant. "You have the worst taste in music."

"*Me?*" asked Jon, laughing. "You're the one who used to listen to Ratt before you went out on dates!"

"That was just during my mullet phase. Anyway, *Simon & Simon* was an all right show, I guess."

"Come on! It was awesome!" said Jon. "Two brothers solving crimes. A yuppie and a cowboy. I watched it every Thursday, right after *Magnum, P.I.*"

"Hey, maybe they'll make a TV show about us one day," said Brant. "Two guys saving the world for Jesus."

"Well, if they do, we won't tell them about the time you punched the porno store owner."

"That's a whole episode right there! And I didn't hit him."

"Yeah, yeah," said Jon, waving his hand dismissively. "Hey look, we're almost to I-95. We'll be in Charleston in about forty-five minutes."

"Cool, where do you want to eat?" asked Brant.

thirty six

Overthrow

"Even the wind and the waves obey him!'"
- Mark 4:41

It had been two months since Jon made the short drive to Charleston with Holly for their annual back-to-school shopping day on King Street. The father-daughter day trips had been a tradition since she was a little girl and had developed into a fairly consistent routine: Stroll through the shops along King Street, laugh at the tourist trade in the City Market, and finish with dinner at the Boulevard Diner in Mt. Pleasant. The fact that his college-age daughter would still spend a summer Saturday with her dad walking around Charleston meant something to Jon. And though he knew the bags Holly stuffed into his trunk from Urban Outfitters, Banana Republic, and Copper Penny might have something to do with her motivation, he treasured their time together, nonetheless. And now, even though it was Brant who walked with him along lower King Street, Jon felt glad to be back in the Holy City's familiar surroundings. The narrow, slate-tiled sidewalks. The faint smell of horse manure in the heavy salt air. Historic buildings giving home to retail stores, restaurants, and antique shops. But something about the city felt different since his last trip with Holly. And as he maneuvered around wandering tourists, local shoppers, and college students, Jon began to realize the difference was in him. He wasn't looking for clothes, shoes, or additions to his home décor. He was looking for people who needed Jesus. And it made the old city seem new.

"Let's head on over to Marion Square," said Jon, pointing ahead of them.

"Can we eat first?" asked Brant. "There's a Moe's up there on the corner."

Jon stepped aside to make room for two uniformed Citadel cadets passing in the opposite direction. "We're in Charleston, Brant. We can at least eat somewhere we can't find anywhere else."

"Food's food, man. Doesn't matter where you eat it."

"Spoken like a true connoisseur."

"Thank you."

Jon stopped himself from further debating lunch options with Brant. He felt anxious to begin the task to which God had called him. "Why don't we see if we can talk to somebody before we eat?"

"I witness better on a full stomach," said Brant.

Jon laughed. "Like you would know."

"Hey, I'm just saying," said Brant. He leaned down to pet a small Pit Bull puppy on a leash while its owner stood talking on a cell phone.

"Brant, I'll make a deal with you." Jon stepped off the curb to navigate around a bicycle locked to a parking meter. "I'll buy you lunch at Moe's if you promise not to use that cliché again."

"What cliché? 'I'm just saying'?"

"Yes. I hate that," said Jon, hopping back on the sidewalk. "It's what people say when they have nothing to say. It's totally meaningless."

"Geez, Jon. Any more rules I should know about?" asked Brant, looking through the open double-doors of Urban Outfitters.

"I'll let you know as we go," said Jon, only partially joking. "Come on, let's cross the street."

Jon and Brant crossed to the east side of the street, stopping at the corner of Calhoun and King. Before the traffic light turned green, they trotted over the brick crosswalk to the southwest corner of Marion Square. The open grassy area, covering a full city block, had once been used as a parade ground for Citadel cadets, but had long since been turned into a park.

Brant pointed to a round pool of water supplying a fountain on the corner. "Hey, we can use that if we need to baptize anybody," he joked.

"That's what it's for," said Jon.

"Are you serious?" asked Brant, looking back at the fountain.

"No, I'm not. Come on."

As they walked onto the expanse of grass, trees, and monuments, Jon's eyes scanned the square for opportunities. College of Charleston students dotted the brown grass, lying in the sun, listening to iPods, reading books, and throwing Frisbees.

"What exactly are we looking for?" asked Brant.

"Lost sheep," answered Jon.

"Heads up!" someone shouted. A Frisbee flew inches over Brant's head and landed on the grass next to two girls lying on beach towels, just a few feet away. Jon turned and saw a shirtless boy across the square waving his arm over his head.

"Nice throw, dude!" shouted Brant.

"Sorry! The wind got it!" the boy called back, pointing to the blue sky above.

One of the girls sat up and flipped the Frisbee to Jon. The boy's throwing partner trotter over and held up his hands. Jon tossed him the disc.

"Thanks!" the boy said as he turned to throw to his friend.

Jon glanced back at the girl on the towel.

The slender attractive blonde, wearing a mismatched black and green bikini, leaned back on her elbows and looked up at Jon. "Sorry, I thought that was yours," she said, placing a pair of large sunglasses on her face.

"No problem," replied Jon. The boy's overthrow had presented an opportunity. He stepped closer. "Do you mind if we talk with you for a minute?"

Without responding, the girl glanced at her friend, a modest-looking brunet wearing a sorority T-shirt and gym shorts, reclining on a towel next to her. The brunet pushed herself into a sitting position. She crossed her legs and looked at Jon.

"We're not selling anything, I promise," said Jon. "Just a few questions. Won't take but a couple of minutes."

"How many questions?" asked the blonde. "I'm trying to relax."

"How about two?" asked Jon, without knowing what they would be.

"OK, two questions," she said, straightening her sunglasses. "That's it."

"Perfect." Jon offered a handshake. "I'm Jon and this is my friend Brant."

"Tiffany," said the girl, reaching across her body to shake Jon's hand.

Her friend gave them a brief wave of her hand. "I'm Megan."

"Oh, I used to know a Megan," said Jon, trying to make conversation as he crouched down beside them.

"Great," said Megan, with little interest as she looked across the square.

"Nice to meet you, ladies," said Brant, still standing.

Tiffany chuckled at Brant's greeting and turned to Jon. "So, what do you want to ask us?"

"Oh, well, you see," said Jon, looking at his reflection in her sunglasses, "We're are going around talking with people about Jesus today, and we were just wondering what experience you've had with him and what your thoughts are about faith."

"Seriously?" asked Tiffany.

"Yeah, seriously," said Jon.

"Well," said Tiffany, "we're both Christians, so…."

Jon paused at her response. He wasn't sure if she was being dismissive or understanding.

"Excellent!" exclaimed Brant, filling the momentary silence and taking a seat on the grass. "So, do you girls ever go out and witness to folks like we're doing?"

Jon's mouth hung open in bewilderment as he looked at Brant.

Tiffany seemed equally surprised by Brant's question, smiling nervously before she answered. "Um, well…I used to when I was younger in youth groups and stuff. But I really haven't been to church since I got to college."

"What do you think is holding you back?" asked Brant.

"From what?" she asked. "Going to church or witnessing to people?"

"Witnessing," said Brant. "You just said you did it when you were younger. Why not here at school?"

Jon's mind was far behind Brant's blunt line of questioning and was struggling to catch up. Nothing about the discussion was going as he had envisioned.

"Um, I don't know, really," said Tiffany. A crease formed between her eyebrows as she spoke. "I haven't really thought about it. People are just different here, I guess. Not really approachable, you know?"

"Kind of like you were a second ago, you mean?" asked Brant, smiling.

Tiffany laughed. "Well, yeah, I guess so. I admit I didn't want to be bothered. It's a nice day out."

"Well, thanks for letting us talk with you," said Jon. He stood up, ready to call it a mistake and move on. "We'll let you get back to your relaxing."

"No, I'm kind of intrigued, now," said Tiffany. "What made you guys want to do what you're doing?"

Brant, still seated on the grass, looked up at Jon, deferring the answer to him. Jon knelt again beside the girls. He was surprised by the sudden interest from Tiffany, but he'd rather be sharing his story with someone who wasn't already a Believer. Nevertheless, he answered her question. "Well, I just reached a point where the only thing I was doing in my faith was just going to church."

Megan grinned slightly and raised her hand. "That's me," she said.

Megan's honesty made Jon smile. "I just needed to know what it was like to really do what the Bible – what Jesus – tells us to do. Not just go through the motions or pretend to be something we're not. We're supposed to share the Good News of Jesus Christ. So that's what we're out doing."

Megan looked down without comment. Tiffany remained silent, reclining on her elbows. The lull in the conversation made Jon feel slightly uncomfortable. Unable to read Tiffany's expression through her large sunglasses, Jon assumed he was done and began to stand up. "I guess we've used up our two questions, so…."

"We'll grant you one more," said Tiffany with a smile.

"Oh. Well, thank you," said Jon, settling onto his knees once again. He decided he might as well make the most of the conversation and push the topic to a deeper level. "All right, let me ask you the same question I wrestled with recently. What do you think it means to be a Christian?"

Tiffany turned her head towards Megan and then back to Jon. "Well, I guess it means that you believe in Jesus," she said. "That's kind of obvious. What part of that did you wrestle with?"

Before Jon could answer, Brant blurted out, "When did you accept Jesus as your Lord and Savior?"

Jon gave Brant a quizzical look. The question sounded like one an attorney would ask a hostile witness. Brant shrugged his shoulders at Jon and looked back at Tiffany, her expression still shielded by her sunglasses. She didn't respond to Brant, and Jon had forgotten Tiffany's question.

Megan spoke softly, "My parents say I was saved when I was four."

"That's awesome, Megan," said Jon. "So you've been a Believer a long time."

"But that's just what your *parents* say," said Brant. "What do *you* say?"

"I'm sorry?" asked Megan, looking at Brant.

"You said your parents say that's when you were saved," said Brant. "But what do you say?"

"Brant," said Jon, trying to stop his friend. He had shut down Tiffany and now he was about to do the same with Megan. Jon wished Brant would just be quiet and let him handle the discussion.

"I'm not sure what you mean," said Megan, looking confused. "Are you saying my parents made that up?"

Jon sighed and tried to soften Brant's question. "I think what Brant's asking is if you've ever made a decision as an adult to follow Jesus."

"Exactly," said Brant. "That's what I'm saying."

"But I thought once you were saved, you're always saved," said Tiffany coming to Megan's defense.

"That's true," agreed Jon. "The Bible says—"

"Yeah, but come on," said Brant. "I'm not saying your parents are lying or anything, but if you were too young to remember making the decision, maybe you weren't even the one making it. Maybe that's why there's nothing more to your faith than just going to church with your parents."

"I think your time's up," said Tiffany, sitting up on her towel.

"I'm sorry," said Jon. "He's a new Believer. He's just a little—"

"No, wait," said Megan. "What exactly are you saying? That I'm not a Christian?"

"I don't know," said Brant. "Are you?"

Jon held up his hand. "Brant, that's enough."

"I just want to know if she has a relationship with Jesus, Jon. That's all."

"A relationship?" asked Megan, ignoring Jon and Tiffany's efforts to end their debate.

"Yeah," said Brant. "How is he a part of your life? How has he changed you?"

Jon looked at Megan's face and began to see doubt. Her eyes seemed troubled as she looked across the square. The fact that she was still engaging

Brant, despite his bluntness, made him wonder if she was seeking answers or just defending herself.

Megan turned her eyes back to Brant. "I told you I go to church with my parents," she answered. "Doesn't that count for anything?"

"Again with your parents," said Brant. "What about Jesus?"

"I thought evangelists are supposed to be nice and all," Tiffany said to Jon. "Your friend's kind of a—"

"Hang on, Tiff," said Megan. "What *about* Jesus? What do you mean?"

"Well, do you think he sees you as a Christian just because you go to church?" asked Brant.

"How am I supposed to know what Jesus thinks about me?" asked Megan. "He's like…in heaven. But I mean, most of my friends don't even go to church. At least I go. I don't know what more you want me to do."

Jon felt the need to insert himself in the conversation with Megan. "I'm glad you go to church with your folks," he said, "but sitting in church doesn't make you a Christian, Megan. I was raised going to church, too. But I didn't become a Christian until I was twenty-four watching Cam Parsons on TV."

"I've heard of him," said Tiffany.

"He was a big deal for a lot of years," said Jon. "And listening to him helped me make a decision to accept God's forgiveness through what Jesus did on the Cross. He died for my sins. And he wants me to know him and have a relationship with God. He wants that for you, too."

"We don't really talk about that stuff at my parents' church," said Megan.

"What the heck do you talk about, then?" asked Brant.

"It's a lot of rituals…ceremony, kneeling, responsive reading kind of stuff."

"You need to be talking about Jesus," said Brant.

"Megan, forget about your church for a minute," said Jon. "The question you need to answer is, 'Do you know Jesus?'"

"I don't know. How would I know that?"

A verse Jon had tried to memorize early that morning as he read in bed came to his mind. "Well, the Bible says in the tenth chapter of Romans that, 'if you declare with your mouth, *Jesus is Lord* and believe in your heart that God raised him from the dead, you'll be saved. It's with your heart that you believe and are justified and it's with your mouth that you profess your faith and are saved.' Megan, if you've ever done that, you wouldn't have to wonder what Jesus thinks about you. You'd know. You'd belong to him. It's God's promise of salvation. And he always keeps his promises."

"Megan, that's what I did three months ago," added Brant. "I was totally lost and just…well, I won't go into all of it. But I reached the point where I had nowhere else to turn. I cried out to God to save me. I asked Jesus to forgive me and to come into my life. I accepted who he is and what he did for me on the Cross. And it changed everything. He saved my life, literally."

Megan's eyes were wide as she listened.

"So," said Jon, "I guess we're back to Brant's original question. Have you ever made a decision to trust Jesus as your Lord and Savior?"

Megan looked at her friend Tiffany. "I don't think I have," said Megan. "All I know is what my parents told me."

Tiffany remained silent.

"Megan, this is about you and Jesus," said Brant. "Not your parents. You need your own faith."

"Megan," said Jon, "we can help you settle any doubt you have right now. It starts with admitting you're a sinner and recognizing that you need forgiveness through faith in Christ."

"Yeah. And Jon can lead you in a prayer right now to do that," said Brant. He cut his eyes quickly to Jon, who gave him a subtle nod of agreement.

Megan turned towards Jon, her eyebrows raised as her eyes searched his.

"Would you like to do that, Megan?" asked Jon.

"I don't know," she said, turning to look at her friend. Tiffany remained quiet behind her sunglasses.

Jon felt he had run out of things to say to Megan and decided to leave the rest up to God. He waited for her response.

Brant repositioned himself on his knees and looked at Megan. "Megan, I promise you, you'll never regret it."

Megan looked into Brant's eyes for a long moment. "OK," she said.

Tiffany removed her sunglasses and made eye contact with Jon. "Me, too."

"Really? Are you sure?" asked Jon, feeling a wave of excitement flush through him.

"I'm sure," said Tiffany.

"Tiff, you don't have to just for my sake," said Megan. "This is something I think I need to do."

"It's not for you, I promise," said Tiffany. "It's for me. I need to settle a few things."

"OK," said Megan, looking back at Jon.

"Cool," said Jon. "Then I'm going to lead you both in a prayer, and I want you just to pray along with me and mean what you say in your hearts, OK?"

"We're ready," said Megan, looking at Tiffany, who smiled back at her friend.

Jon could feel his heart pounding in his chest as he reached for Tiffany's hand and placed his other on Megan's shoulder. He felt the weight of Brant's hand resting on his back. "Just pray this with me," said Jon, bowing his head. "Almighty God, I come to you now and admit that I need you to save me. Going to church can't save me. Being good can't save me. Only you can save me, Lord. I admit that I'm a sinner. And I ask for your forgiveness. I need your grace and mercy, dear Lord. I accept the sacrifice you made for me in your Son, Jesus. I believe he died on the Cross for my sins and that he rose again. Please forgive me Father and restore me to you. Make me new, Lord. Jesus, I ask you now to come into my life, fill me with your Holy Spirit and be my risen Savior from this day forward. In your name I pray. Amen."

Jon opened his eyes to see Megan wiping tears from her face. Tiffany leaned toward her friend and hugged her around the neck.

"That's it," said Jon, watching the two friends embrace. "You belong to Jesus and nothing can take that away from you." He looked at Brant and received a thunderous high-five that stung the skin on his hand.

"Yeah, brother!" said Brant.

Tiffany and Megan began to recompose themselves.

"Thank you," said Megan, wiping her face with her hands.

"Yeah, thank you, so much," said Tiffany, searching for her sunglasses on her towel. "I'm sorry I wasn't that welcoming to you at first."

"That's OK," said Jon. "You two need to find a church down here that teaches the Bible and can help you grow in your faith. And you need to take the next step and be baptized."

"Hey, we can do that right now!" said Brant. "In the fountain!" He pointed to the corner of the square as the girls laughed.

"Yeah, right," said Tiffany.

"Oh, come on!" said Brant. "You're already in your bathing suit. And I'll do it with you."

"You haven't been baptized yet, Brant?" asked Jon.

Brant rose to his feet. "Nope, you're going to do it for me, right now."

"I can't baptize people."

"Why not? Is that one of your rules?"

"No, it's just that…." Jon tried to think of a reason for his hesitancy.

"Come on, man, let's do it!" urged Brant, clapping his hands.

Jon laughed and shook his head. "All right. Why not, right?"

"Yes!" said Brant, pumping his fist.

Jon stood and looked at the girls. "Are y'all in?"

"Seriously?" asked Tiffany. "You're really going to baptize him in that fountain?"

Brant held out his hand to Tiffany. "Come on, Tiffany, let's show Jesus we're serious about this thing."

Tiffany looked at Megan.

"I will, if you will," said Megan.

"What if someone sees us?" asked Tiffany, glancing around her.

"That's kind of the point," said Jon with a slight smirk.

"Come on, Tiffany," said Brant. "Megan and I are in."

Tiffany put up her hands in submission. "OK, OK," she said. "I can't believe I'm saying this, but I'm in."

Brant raised his arms over his head. "That's it! Let's do it!" Turning to Jon with a broad smile as they set off for the fountain, he whispered discretely, "See, Jonny-boy? Two for two. I told you this would be easy."

Jon was too amazed in the moment to argue. He walked towards the fountain praising God in silent prayer. "Almighty, God, thank you for using us to reach these two girls. It's amazing to see you work in people's lives like this. And to actually be doing what you called me to do. It feels so awesome, God. Thank you for letting me serve you like this. Please just watch over Tiffany and Megan and be with us as we go on. Thank you, dear Lord. In Jesus' name, amen."

Megan and Tiffany walked arm in arm carrying their towels with them. Brant ran the last ten yards and jumped onto the edge of the fountain and kicked off his flip-flops. Jon took a seat on the concrete bench molded into the side of the fountain, took off his shoes and socks, and stuffed his wallet and keys into his shoes. After rolling up his jeans to his knees, he climbed onto the edge of the round fountain.

"Who's first?" asked Jon.

"I'll go first," said Megan.

"All right, Megan!" cheered Brant, clapping his hands loudly.

People passing by on the sidewalk began to take notice as Megan climbed onto the edge of the fountain pool. Several more turned to watch as they waited to cross King or Calhoun Streets. Jon stepped into the cold, two-foot deep pool and offered his hand to Megan. She took his hand and placed her bare foot carefully into the water. Jon realized he would have to get on his knees to baptize Megan, defeating any benefit of rolling up his jeans.

"Are you ready?" asked Jon.

"Yep," said Megan with a nervous smile.

Jon knelt down into the water as Megan joined him on her knees.

"Oh, my gosh!" she said. "That's cold."

"I should have mentioned – I'm going to dunk you. No sprinkling."

"Dunk away," said Megan.

Jon readied himself beside her. "Just hold your nose with one hand, and hold onto my right arm with the other, OK?"

"OK."

"What's your last name, by the way?"

"Saylor," said Megan, staring straight ahead.

"OK. Megan Saylor, have you accepted Jesus Christ as your Lord and Savior?"

"I have." Megan pinched her nose with her fingers.

"Then as a public profession of your faith, I baptize you in the name of the Father, Son, and Holy Spirit." Jon lowered Megan backwards into the water and lifted her quickly back to her knees. She threw her arms around Jon's neck for a brief hug as several people watching on the street clapped and cheered.

"Thank you," said Megan. Brant stepped into the pool and helped Megan to her feet and out of the fountain.

"I'm next," said Tiffany. She reached for Brant's hand to pull her up as Megan stepped down.

"Awesome," said Brant as he pulled her up on the edge of the fountain pool.

"Come on in, Tiffany," said Jon, offering his hand.

Tiffany stepped into the pool, her foot slipping briefly on the smooth round stones that paved the bottom.

"Careful!" said Jon as he pulled her closer to him. "You saw how we did it?"

"Yep," said Tiffany, cheerfully.

"Tiffany!!" shouted several girls exiting a Starbucks directly across King Street. "*Woooooo!!*"

Jon looked at Tiffany to gauge her reaction.

"Don't mind them," she said. "Go ahead."

"OK. Tell me your last name."

"It's Bassett. And Tiffany's not my real name. It's Susan. People just call me Tiffany because...never mind."

"OK. Can I call you Susan, then?"

"Yes, please."

Jon placed his hand on her back while she stared straight ahead at her friends watching from across the street. "Are you ready, Susan?" he asked.

"I'm ready."

"OK, Susan Bassett, who's your Lord and Savior?"

"Jesus Christ," she said with a smile.

"Then as a public profession of your faith—"

"Go, Tiffany!" shouted a girl from the mix of people passing in front of the Francis Marion Hotel.

Tiffany smiled towards her friend across the street.

"As a public profession of your faith," Jon continued, "I baptize you, my sister in Christ, in the name of the Father, Son, and Holy Spirit." As Jon lowered Susan into the pool of cold water, his knees slipped from underneath him. With Susan pulling on his arm, Jon fell directly on top of her in the water totally submerging both of them. He rolled quickly off her and pushed her up into a sitting position. Susan sat laughing as she pulled wet hair from her face and wiped water from her eyes. The crowd, now growing larger around the fountain, cheered and laughed with applause.

"She baptized *you*, Jon!" Brant laughed as he helped Susan from the fountain.

Jon got back to his knees and wiped off his face with his hands. "Well, you're next!" he said.

"I'm ready!" said Brant as he stepped into the water and knelt eagerly next to Jon.

Jon looked at his old friend and thought briefly about what they were doing. "This is pretty crazy, isn't it?"

"I told you this trip would be fun," said Brant, holding his hands up in front of him.

Jon grabbed Brant's wrist and placed his other hand behind his back for support. "Brant Morris, my old friend, who's your Lord and Savior?"

"Jesus Christ!" Brant shouted loud enough for everyone within a block radius to hear. He raised his fist in the air as Megan, Susan, and several in the crowd around them cheered.

Jon took a second to enjoy his friend's enthusiasm. Trying to suppress his laughter, he continued, "Then, my brother in Christ, it's my honor to baptize you in the name of the Father, Son, and Holy Spirit." Jon steadied himself with one foot beside Brant as he lowered him into the water.

Brant sat-up on his own, shook the water from his hair, and shouted, "*Who's next?*"

thirty seven

Not So Easy

"If the world hates you, keep in mind that it hated me first."
- John 15:18

The cool breeze from Charleston Harbor was exactly what Jon needed. Walking with Brant along the wide pier extending into the mouth of the Cooper River, Jon could feel his clothes beginning to dry as the midday autumn sun cast their shadows before them. The city's waterfront park offered a less conspicuous place for two men in wet clothes to air-dry than the shopping districts of King Street and the City Market. Along the long wood and concrete pier, couples and families strolled by while others sat on benches and swings under covered colonnades. The thought of baptizing Megan, Susan, and Brant seemed surreal, even though Jon had just climbed out of the Marion Square fountain less than thirty minutes before. "Not to complain," he said, "but is there anything worse than walking around Charleston in wet clothes?"

"Yeah," said Brant, pulling his wet shirt away from his stomach, "being *hungry* and walking around Charleston in wet clothes. What happened to Moe's?"

"Well, we couldn't walk in Moe's soaking wet."

"That's why we should have eaten first, then gone witnessing."

"I think it worked out pretty good, don't you?"

"Yeah, it did," said Brant. "That was cool. Maybe we should just wear bathing suits when we go witnessing in case we need to baptize someone."

"It's almost November. I think you mean *wet suits*. That water was cold."

Reaching the end of the long T-shaped pier, Jon leaned his forearms on the thick metal rail guarding the salt water below. Brant plopped onto a bench next to him as they both took in the scene around them. To their left, the two massive concrete towers of the Ravenel Bridge rose from the broad, ancient Cooper River. Across the water, the retired USS Yorktown sat moored in pluff mud at Patriot's Point Naval & Maritime Museum. And in the hazy distance to their right, Fort Sumter lay like a ghost on the horizon.

"This is nice out here," Jon said, enjoying the majestic blend of God's creation and man's work.

"Yeah," agreed Brant. "Let's just hang-out here for a while."

"I thought you were hungry," said Jon, his own stomach beginning to feel a little empty.

"I'm always hungry, but this feels good to just sit here," said Brant, gazing across the harbor.

Jon toyed with the idea of just relaxing in the sun and salty breeze, but his conscience reminded him of their purpose for being there. "It does feel good, but we have work to do, you know. We didn't come down here just to be tourists."

Brant closed his eyes and lifted his face into the breeze. "We just saved two people, Jon. It's not like we're goofing off or anything."

"First of all, *we* didn't save two people, *God* did. I just don't want us to lose our focus and miss another opportunity, that's all."

Brant held his face in repose, squinting one eye open at Jon. "I'm just saying, once our clothes are dry, maybe we could talk to some folks out here on the pier. That's all."

"We can do that," said Jon, his point made. He turned around and leaned his back against the black railing. Seeing the old buildings overlooking the harbor, he remembered walking past the historic Vendue Inn just across the street from the waterfront park and realized they had no plan for where to stay the night. The thought of being able to shower and change clothes was suddenly too tempting to ignore. "But first," Jon said, pushing himself away from the railing, "I'm going to walk over to the Vendue Inn over there and see what their rates are like. We need a place to stay tonight."

"The Vendue? Dude, I'm not exactly in your tax bracket, remember?"

Jon laughed. "You may be unemployed, but soon you'll be the only one of us getting a paycheck."

"It's a severance check, Jon," said Brant, staying seated on the bench. "Those run out, you know."

"Don't worry about it," said Jon. "I'll cover us tonight. It's off-season so maybe we can get a deal. Just hang out here for a few minutes. I'll be right back, then we'll find somebody to talk to." Jon knew the Vendue Inn wouldn't be their cheapest option, but his love for historic settings and the hotel's close proximity fed his curiosity.

Jon walked the length of the pier back towards the hotel. Passing the large splash fountain marking the entrance to the waterfront park, he remembered seeing children escape the August heat, laughing and screaming as they played underneath the spouts of water arching into the fountain's round granite center. But today, despite warm temperatures, the water fell quietly on the pink stone. Half a city block past the fountain, he approached the yellow, stucco exterior of the three-story Vendue Inn. Between two palmetto trees shooting up from the sidewalk, a navy blue awning provided shade for a young, uniformed doorman standing in front of the hotel's stained wood and glass double doors. "OK, that's a bad sign," he thought, equating a doorman with an overly expensive hotel. Or maybe the boy was just a bellhop on a smoke break.

The young man greeted Jon with a smile and pulled open the door. "Welcome to the Vendue Inn," he said, professionally.

"Doorman," thought Jon as he stepped into what looked like the formal entrance hall of an antebellum home. A crystal chandelier hung over dark hardwood floors, Oriental rugs, and antique furniture. Fine oil paintings hung on wallpapered walls below thick, white crown molding. Just inside the door to the left, a small sitting room contained two burgundy leather chairs in front of a mahogany desk with ball and claw legs. Behind the desk, a young hotel clerk typed on a computer keyboard while balancing a phone on his right shoulder. Jon stepped towards the room's threshold without fully entering. He leaned against one of the two white columns framing the entrance to the room and waited patiently for the phone conversation to end.

The clerk acknowledged Jon as he hung up the phone. "May I help you?" The young man's eyes moved briefly down to Jon's damp jeans then back up to his face.

"Yes, I was wondering if you had anything available," said Jon, trying to sound more polished than his appearance.

"I'll be happy to check," said the clerk, typing on his keyboard. "When would you be arriving?"

"Well, now, I guess," said Jon. He felt the need to explain. "We're, um—"

"And how many in your party?" asked the clerk without taking his eyes off his computer screen.

"Just two." Jon smiled to himself, remembering his old joke.

"Would you like one room or two?"

"One room would be fine. But two beds, preferably."

"And how many nights would you be with us?"

"Just tonight."

The clerk glanced up at Jon and then studied his computer screen. "We have our Historical Themed Two Queen Junior for $485 per night or our Traditional Queen for $355." The clerk looked blankly at Jon and waited for a response.

Jon felt his pride feeding his temptation to book one of the rooms. If he were traveling on business, he could easily expense one night's stay at a nice hotel. In the last year alone, he had stayed at some of the finest hotels in Chicago, New York, and Atlanta. He had grown fond of that kind of luxury away from home. But the thought of spending five hundred dollars of his own money was enough to squelch his desire. He would have to pass. He looked for a graceful way to end his inquiry without appearing cheap. "The Traditional Queen – does that have just the one bed or two?"

"One queen bed, sir," said the clerk, looking back at his computer screen.

Jon made a face and rubbed his chin as if he was trying to decide between the two options. "Let me get back with you on that. Thanks for checking." With a slight wave of his hand, Jon turned to leave.

"Have a nice day, sir," said the clerk.

Jon pushed open the front door of the inn, stepped down the two stairs and onto the sidewalk. Frustrated with himself, he walked up the street back towards the waterfront park. He felt as though he had flirted with a beautiful, sophisticated woman only to find her out of his league. And while he told himself he had no reason to be embarrassed, he was. He tried to reset his mind to simpler accommodations as he passed the splash fountain on his way back to the pier. "We'll just have to find a Hampton Inn or something across the river in West Ashley," he thought and put the issue to rest.

Once again on the pier, Jon walked by a young couple resting comfortably in one of the family-sized wooden swings hanging in the shade under a colonnade. He realized he'd never seen one of swings empty and wondered how long he would have to wait to have a turn. He had never seen anyone in the act of leaving one of the swings or sitting down on an empty one. The swings just always seemed to be occupied.

Approaching the midpoint of the pier, Jon looked ahead to where he had left Brant only to see an empty bench. "Great, where is he?" Jon said out loud. He kept walking, his eyes scanning the breadth of the pier. "I bet he went to eat somewhere without me." Jon stopped and turned back towards the shore, only to see Brant sitting alone in a swing just a few feet to his right. "Brant!" said Jon in surprise. "How did you score one of the swings?"

Brant looked at Jon grimly without responding.

"Did you toss some little old lady into the marsh to get this thing or what?" Jon joked, trying to get a laugh. Brant's failure to offer a witty reply told him something was wrong. As Jon sat down on the swing, it was obvious Brant's mood had changed while he was gone. He assumed it had something to do with his flirtation with the Vendue Inn. "You were right about the Vendue. Five hundred a night. We'll just find something cheap across the river later."

Brant leaned forward, his weight shifting to his hands as he gripped the edge of the wooden bench swing. "I screwed up big time," he said, staring straight ahead at the harbor.

Jon felt slightly alarmed. "What did you do?"

Brant shook his head, quietly.

"You left your wallet at the fountain," guessed Jon.

"*No*," answered Brant, appearing annoyed at the guess.

"Well, I was only gone fifteen minutes. What could've happened?"

Brant turned his head and looked at Jon. "I tried to witness to two people sitting on this swing. A man and a woman from Ohio."

Surprised and slightly relieved, Jon was impressed at his friend's initiative. "That's great, Brant. How did it go?"

"No, it's *not* great," said Brant, shaking his head. "It sucked. I suck."

"Whoa, slow down. What happened? What did you say?"

Brant took a deep breath and exhaled. "Well, I started thinking about how things went with Megan and Tiffany. Or Susan, whatever. You know, how we both kind of worked on them together. And I just got the urge to try it on my own. No offense."

"No problem here. Did they not want to talk to you or something?"

"Oh, they talked, all right. That's the problem. I just had nothing to say back to them."

"Oh," said Jon, now understanding Brant's mood.

"Yeah. I walked up, all cheerful and stuff and asked where they were from and if I could talk to them for a minute, like you did with Tiffany. And the guy says, 'About what?' And I said, 'I was wondering if you knew Jesus as your Lord and Savior.'"

"Just like that?" asked Jon.

"Yeah. And he laughs and says, 'You don't believe in that horse crap, do you?' Except he didn't say *crap*."

"Ouch. What did you say?"

"I said, 'Of course I do.' I told him how I was depressed and drinking and divorced and out of work and all. And how Jesus saved me and gave me a new life."

"That's awesome, Brant. But I'm guessing he didn't buy it."

"No, he didn't. He told me that his mother died of cancer when he was twelve, and he lost his only daughter to leukemia when she was eight, and his first wife committed suicide six months later. He said there is no God, but if there is one, he's a…. Well, I'm not going to repeat what he said. But I think you get the idea."

Jon tried to absorb all that the man must have gone through. He certainly understood what it feels like to lose someone. "Man…that's a tough one," he said, trying to think of how he would have responded. "Where did it go from there?"

"Well, I told him not to talk about my God that way, you know? It offended me. And he said I was the one bothering them, anyway. And that I should shut the hell up and leave them alone. So I told them…."

Jon braced himself. "You told them what?"

"I told them they were both going to hell unless they accepted Jesus."

"Oh, gosh, Brant." Jon closed his eyes and dropped his head as he imagined their reaction. "I'm guessing they didn't like that too much."

"No, they didn't. He said I was basically telling him that his mom and daughter and wife all went to hell because they weren't Christians. And I'm like, 'Well, yeah.'"

"You didn't say *that* did you?"

"No. But I wanted to. It's true, isn't it?"

Jon pushed his hips against the back of the swing. "Well, yeah. Technically. But...."

"I mean, shouldn't we warn people about that if we believe it's true?"

"Sure, but we can't assume someone we've never even met went to hell, Brant. That's between them and God. We don't know what's in someone's heart."

"Well, anyway, I didn't know what to say. I just stood there. So he called me an SOB, and something else I didn't catch, and they left. And then his wife, or whatever, flipped me off as they walked away."

Jon was speechless. He stared out at the salt water and again wondered what he'd gotten himself into by accepting Brant's self-invitation for his trip.

"Anyhow," added Brant, "that's how I got the swing."

Jon dropped his head and tried not to laugh. "I'll have to remember that next time I want to free up one of these. I'll just have you witness to whoever's sitting on it."

"Well, what was I supposed to say to all that? What would you have said?"

While he didn't want to admit it, Jon realized he didn't know how he would have responded. "Brant, it wouldn't be fair for me to sit here and second guess you. You were the one having to think on your feet. I think this is gonna be hard sometimes. And I promise this won't be the last time we get shot down like that. That's what I was trying to tell you in Oscar Ray's last night. And I'm sure my turn's coming, too. It scares me to think about it."

"You didn't seem scared or nervous when we talked to Tiffany and Megan."

Jon thought for a moment about how he felt when he talked to the girls. "I guess that's because I was just letting God lead me. I had prayed about it ahead of time and just had a peace about it." He pushed his foot against the wood plank beneath him and let go. The swing moved forward gently and back again on its own. "But I think the other thing that helps is reading my Bible and knowing some Scripture verses."

"You mean like memorizing stuff?"

"Yep. Like the verse from Romans I used with Megan a little while ago. I just read that this morning, and it came right to me when I needed it. I think it made all the difference."

"I'm not big on memorizing stuff like that."

"Brant, I stink at remembering the chapter and verse numbers. I usually just try to remember the words and the meaning behind them. The numbers always mess me up. But some I do know by heart. There's power in God's Word that goes way beyond anything we can say on our own."

"My Bible's three inches thick, Jon. How am I supposed to know what to memorize out of all that?"

"I'm not saying you have to memorize the whole Bible, Brant. I tell you what — I'll write down some verses for you to look up and memorize tonight when we get settled in a hotel. That may give you some confidence the next time we talk to people. And I've been reading a book Steve gave me on how to share your faith. You can borrow that, too."

"That would be awesome," said Brant, pushing off with his foot to keep the swing moving. "But can I ask you something?"

"Sure."

"What worked for you?"

"What do you mean?"

"I mean, when you were saved, what was it that made you want to accept Jesus?"

"Oh, wow," said Jon, pushing his eyebrows up on his forehead. Jon felt his mind trying to reach back twenty years into the past. "I um...I haven't thought about that in a long time."

"Did someone witness to you like what we're doing? Or did you hear a preacher say something?"

"Actually, I accepted Christ watching Cam Parsons on TV."

"Oh, that's right. Duh. Didn't he die last year?"

"Yes, he did," said Jon. "I wonder if there'll ever be another evangelist like him."

"Well, what was it that he said in his sermon that made a difference to you?"

Jon laughed at himself. "Honestly, I don't remember. I wish I knew. It's just…I remember being sucked into his message as I sat there watching on the couch, you know? And before I knew what was happening, I was on the floor of my bathroom crying my eyes out, asking God to forgive me. It was a painful experience. It was the first time in my life I saw myself as a sinner who needed to be saved. It hurt to think of myself that way. It just broke me. So, I asked Jesus to save me and accepted what he did for me on the Cross."

"Wow," said Brant, looking ahead at the harbor.

"Yeah." Jon remembered how he felt when he picked himself up off the bathroom floor. "But it was tough being alone like that. I would have given anything to be on that baseball field where Cam Parsons was preaching that night, walking forward with all those other people. That would have been awesome."

"Where was he preaching?" asked Brant.

"That I do remember. He was in Austin, Texas. I remember laughing at all the old men wearing cowboy hats and the big Longhorn logo on the field."

Brant sat up straight on the swing. "I've got an idea," he said.

"Uh-oh," said Jon, stopping the swing with his foot. "Your last idea got us in a fight outside an adult bookstore."

"No, wait, just listen. This is good. You're gonna like this."

"All right," said Jon, still skeptical.

"We don't have a plan for where we're going after this, right?" asked Brant.

"Well, I've been…um, we might…I mean…."

"That's what I thought," said Brant. "OK, so how about we head to Austin and find that baseball field?"

Jon had good reason to guard himself against Brant's ideas, but this one made him think. He'd always wondered what it would have been like to be on that field, responding to God's call to salvation with hundreds of people around him. Brant continued selling his idea while Jon rolled it around in his head.

"We witness to folks along the way, and we seal the deal by getting you on that baseball field! What do you think?"

"Sold!" Jon said, impulsively. A renewed sense of excitement and purpose flushed through his body.

"Sweet!" said Brant, rubbing his hands together.

"That's an awesome idea, Brant. I mean…it really is. Thank you. I feel like we have our direction, now."

"Heck," said Brant, "and after that, we can head to California if you want. God knows they need Jesus out there."

Jon hopped off the swing. "Brant, let's get something to eat. I'm starving."

"That's my line," joked Brant as he rose to his feet.

"You're beginning to rub off on me."

thirty eight

Speed Reading

"I have hidden your word in my heart that I might not sin against you."
- *Psalm 119:11*

Jon huffed with impatience as he stood with Brant in a Circle K convenience store outside of Yemassee. The line to the cash register snaked into the aisle past the salty snacks and motor oil as a man in white painter's work clothes pondered his choice of lottery game tickets with the cashier. Jon's thirst couldn't wait any longer. Twisting open the green plastic bottle, he poured a mouthful of Diet Mountain Dew past his lips and felt its cold effervesce slide all the way down to his stomach. "Oh, man, that's good," he said with renewed patience.

"That's stealing, you know," said Brant. "You haven't paid for that."

"The state of South Carolina taking this guy's money for a lottery ticket – that's stealing. I'm just borrowing a sip of Dew before I pay for it."

Brant lifted his index finger away from the cup of black coffee in his hand and pointed at Jon's drink. "I don't see how you can drink that stuff in the morning."

"I don't see how you can drink coffee any time. It's nasty."

"You wouldn't understand," said Brant, raising his right eyebrow. "You're just not as sophisticated as I am."

"Wow – pretentious *and* delusional. Nice combination, Brant."

"Thank you, Jon."

After waiting several more minutes, the two finally took their turn with the cashier. Jon paid for his half-empty bottle of soda and Brant's coffee, as well, if only to speed up the process of getting out of the store.

"Can I drive?" asked Brant as they made their way into the parking lot towards Jon's car.

"Absolutely not," said Jon, instinctively. No one had ever driven his car, but him. And the thought of Brant behind the wheel made him immediately uncomfortable. On the other hand, riding in the passenger seat would allow the opportunity to quiz Brant on the Scripture verses he had encouraged him to memorize. Jon tried his best to fend off his discomfort in the interest of Brant's spiritual growth. "I tell you what," he said, "if you let me quiz you on those verses I gave you, I'll let you drive."

"Bring it, man!" Brant held out his hand and wiggled his fingers as they approached the car. "Keys?"

Jon had to stop himself from walking to the driver's side out of habit. "Oh, right. Here you go," he said, tossing his key fob to Brant. "Be careful."

"You had to say that, didn't you?"

"I've got more where that came from. Let's go." Jon settled into the passenger seat and tried to acclimate himself to the view from the right side of the car. "I've never sat on this side before."

"Well, get used to it," said Brant, taking stock of the driving controls and dashboard. "I might not want to give you the key thing back. This is nice. What are all these buttons on the steering wheel? And what is this do-hicky?" Brant toyed with the round control knob on the center console.

"That's the iDrive control. Don't worry about that." Jon pushed Brant's hand off the control knob and pointed at the buttons on the steering wheel. "Those are for the radio, and those are for the cruise control. That's all you need to know. Just start the car and let's go. I want to get to Savannah before lunch."

"Yes, sir," Brant said with a crisp salute. He pushed the ignition button next to the steering column and waited in vain for the engine to turn over.

"You have to press your foot on the brake while you push it," said Jon.

Brant followed Jon's instruction, this time feeling the engine's rumble. "Nice," he said. He pulled slowly away from the gas pump and exited the convenience store lot back onto Highway 17.

Jon peered nervously over the hood as the car moved under Brant's control. "You're going to get on I-95 South, right up here," said Jon, pointing to the large green sign.

"I can read, Jon."

"I know. I'm just navigating."

Brant shook his head as he turned left onto the onramp. "Why don't you make yourself really useful and take a nap or something?"

"Very funny," said Jon. "Now, this car's a lot quicker than your Jeep so—" He felt his body press into his leather seat as Brant accelerated quickly onto the Interstate and merged into traffic.

"Man! I could get a ticket so easy driving this thing," said Brant. He smiled as he studied the dashboard indicators. "It just floats down the road. I got up to 80 just now and didn't even realize it." Brant adjusted his seat, moving it further away from the steering wheel and reclining it slightly.

Watching his driver's seat move to a different position left Jon feeling slightly violated. "Why don't you just set the cruise control to 70 and not worry about your speed?"

"Cruise control takes all the fun out of driving. I might as well be sitting where you are if I did that."

"Well, just watch how fast you go along through here," said Jon. "I-95 is a race track and cops love to camp out in those trees in the median."

"Yes, Dad," said Brant, enjoying himself.

Jon ignored the sarcasm as he reached behind his seat and found his Bible. "So, anyway, are you ready for your quiz?"

"Sure. Fire away," said Brant with a wave of his hand. "But I should warn you – I didn't get to do much studying last night. I fell asleep pretty quick, once I hit the bed."

Jon opened the Bible on his lap. "Making excuses in advance, I see."

"Hey, I'm just saying."

"I thought we had a deal about that phrase, remember?"

"Oh, sorry. You need to make a list of all your rules so I can keep track."

"Don't tempt me," said Jon. He flipped through the pages of his Bible looking for one of the verses he gave Brant the day before. "Let's see…." He wanted to start with a verse Brant should remember easily. "OK, here's your first one – Romans 10:9."

"Romans 10:9," repeated Brant.

"You know that one?"

"I think so. Give me a minute." Brant looked serious as he changed lanes to pass a slower car. "How about a hint to get started?"

"It has to do with God," said Jon, dryly.

Brant cut his eyes at Jon and smirked.

"OK, here's a hint," said Jon. "You heard me say this verse to Megan and Susan."

"Well, it's not like I was sitting there taking notes or anything, Jon. I was focused on what they were saying, not you."

Jon sat waiting. He could tell Brant was stalling.

"Give me the first word or something," said Brant.

Jon looked down at the verse in his Bible and smiled, knowing the first word would offer very little help. "If."

"If?" asked Brant.

"If."

Brant scratched the back of his head. "That's not much to go on."

"All right. 'If *you*,'" said Jon, adding the next word in the verse.

"If I what?"

"No, *you*. That's the second word. 'If you.'"

"Oh, right. Got it." Brant twisted his grip on the leather wrapped steering wheel as he thought out loud. "If you…um."

"For Pete's sake. It starts, 'If you,' then a word that starts with a D."

"If you don't accept Jesus."

"No."

"If you don't…."

Jon shook his head. "It's not *don't*."

"If you decide?"

"It's *declare*," said Jon. "Did you even read these last night?"

"I did!" claimed Brant. "But I told you I'm not good at memorizing stuff."

Jon closed his Bible. "Fine. Whatever, man. I knew you wouldn't take this seriously."

"No, come on, Jon. I can get this."

"Well, then *try* to remember. Geez."

"I am, I promise. Now, where were we?"

Jon opened his Bible again with a sigh. "Romans 10:9. If you declare."

"Right. If you declare…OK, wait. I've got it. 'If you declare that Jesus is Lord!'"

Jon was momentarily encouraged and offered a slight correction. "With your mouth," he said.

"What do you mean? I just said it with my mouth."

Jon conjured up his best expression of parental disapproval and turned his face towards Brant.

"OK, that was a joke," said Brant, backpedaling, "but I know this one. I promise."

"OK, then. Stop messing around and just tell me the verse."

Brant appeared serious for a moment. "If you declare that Jesus is Lord with your mouth."

"No," said Jon, growing impatient with the exercise. "It says, 'If you declare with your mouth, Jesus is Lord.'"

Brant shrugged his shoulders as he changed lanes to pass a pick-up truck. "Same difference."

"No, it's *not* the same difference. This is Scripture, it matters."

"All right, all right. Sorry." Brant readied himself to try again. "If you declare with your mouth that Jesus is Lord…you'll be saved?"

"Close, but you left out something important in the middle there. How fast are you driving?"

"Don't worry about it. I left something out?"

Jon leaned to his left to see the speedometer. "*Eighty-five?*"

"Just let me drive. What did I leave out?"

Jon tried to momentarily suppress his concern for Brant's driving and refocus on what he omitted from the verse. "OK, what is it that you have to believe?" he asked.

"That Jesus is the Son of God," answered Brant, firmly.

"No."

"Yes, you do."

"OK, of course you need to believe that," conceded Jon, "but that's not what this verse says."

"Well, it should."

"Brant, we're not trying to rewrite the Bible. We're just trying to memorize what it says."

"OK, OK. It doesn't say he's the Son of God."

Jon was beginning to feel exasperated. "He *is* the Son of God, Brant. You know that. But that's not what this specific verse is telling us to believe. Come on, this should be easy."

"Well, of course it's easy for you. You're sitting there looking at it. Plus, I'm trying to drive and look out for cops hiding in trees."

"Use the cruise control!"

"Nope," replied Brant, with a grin.

Jon took a deep breath and sighed. "Look, you can hold the book on me later, if you want. Just finish this verse and I'll give you an easier one next time. John 3:16 or something."

"Everybody knows that one," said Brant.

"Fine, but do this one first. Romans 10:9. Come on. Do you know it or not?"

"I know it, I know it."

"Fine. Then what is it?"

Brant straightened himself in his seat. "How does it start again?"

"If you!"

"That's right. Sorry. If you don't—"

"*Declare!*"

"I mean declare," said Brant. "If you declare with your mouth that Jesus is Lord and…."

Jon waited hopefully for a moment before offering help. "*Believe*," he finally prompted.

"And believe that he…."

Jon waved his hand for Brant to continue. "That God…."

"Oh, yeah – that God raised him from the dead!" said Brant, sounding proud of himself.

"Bingo! Now finish it…please."

"That's not it?"

"That was just the part you left out," said Jon. "How does it end?"

"Oh, right."

"Start from the beginning and give me the whole thing."

"Why?"

"Because I seriously doubt that someone you're witnessing to is going to help you piece it together like I'm doing! You need to know the whole thing."

"OK, calm down," said Brant waving his hand at Jon. "I'll start from the beginning…If you declare with your mouth that Jesus is Lord—"

"Leave out *that*," said Jon, looking down at the text.

"You just said to do the whole thing."

"No, the word *that*. Leave it out; it's not in there. Just say, 'declare with your mouth,' and go on from there."

"I get points taken off for saying *that*?"

"It matters."

"How can *that* possibly matter?"

"You need to memorize Scripture as it's written, Brant."

"Jon, I seriously doubt someone is going to reject Christ because I include a stray relative pronoun."

"A relative pronoun?" asked Jon, looking at Brant. He felt mild surprise over his friend's knowledge of grammar beyond nouns, verbs and adjectives.

Brant shrugged his shoulders. "I spent some time as a substitute English teacher after I got laid off."

"Oh. Well, *Professor* Morris, would you please tell me what Romans 10:9 says? Or just shoot me. Either one would be fine with me, at this point."

"OK," said Brant. "If you declare with your mouth, *Jesus is Lord*, and believe in your heart that God raised him from the dead, you will be saved."

Jon read along as Brant quoted the verse, word for word. He turned his head quickly and saw a smirk hiding on Brant's face. "You knew that the whole time, didn't you?"

"Yep," answered Brant, letting his smirk grow into a full smile across his face.

"You are such a…." Jon looked out the passenger window and shook his head in disgust for letting himself get duped. In the side-view mirror, he saw a silver Dodge Charger following close behind. "I assume you know that's a state trooper on your bumper."

"Are you *serious*?" said Brant, looking into his rearview mirror.

"Who now has his lights on," added Jon.

"Oh, man! You've got to be kidding me! I can't afford a ticket!"

"How fast were you going?"

"I have no idea. I wasn't paying attention. I was too busy messing with you."

"Two words," said Jon, feeling a slight sense of vindication. "Cruise control."

Brant applied the brakes and eased the car over onto the emergency lane. The car tires rumbled loudly as they rolled across the ribbed pavement. Brant brought the car to a stop, leaving the right side of the car on the grass. He fumbled through his wallet to find his license as Jon pulled the registration and insurance card from his glove compartment. Jon looked behind the car to see a tall, muscular, South Carolina state trooper approaching from the driver's side. His gray wide-brimmed hat angled towards his dark sunglasses. His right hand rested on the holstered gun at his waist. Brant rolled down his window.

"License and registration, please," stated the trooper without pleasantries.

"Morning officer," smiled Brant. "I'm sorry if I was speeding. This is my friend's car and I'm just not used to driving it, yet."

"License and registration, please," repeated the trooper.

"Oh, sorry. Here you go, sir."

The trooper examined Brant's driver's license. "Do you know how fast you were driving, Mr. Morris?"

"Honestly, I don't. You see, we were trying to memorize Scripture, and I guess I just took my eyes off the speedometer."

The trooper removed his sunglasses and leaned over, peering into the car. Jon could see his cleanly shaven face, brown eyes and the sides of his military-style crew cut as he looked around the cabin.

"You were memorizing Bible verses while exceeding the posted speed limit by twelve miles per hour?" asked the trooper.

Brant smiled, nervously. "Yes, sir. I guess it sounds kind of bad when you put it like that."

The trooper looked across the driving compartment at Jon. "Are you two in the ministry?"

"No, sir," answered Jon. "Not officially. We're just traveling around, trying to witness to as many people as we can over the next six months."

"Are you a Christian, officer?" asked Brant.

The trooper placed his sunglasses back on his face and stood straight. "I'll be back in a moment. Please remain in your vehicle."

Jon gave Brant a quick punch in the arm with the back of his left hand. "Are you crazy?! You don't ask a highway patrolman if he's a Christian!"

"Why not? He's probably going to give me a ticket, anyway. How could it hurt?"

"Well, if he's an atheist I doubt he's going to cut you any slack, now."

"Oh, well," said Brant. "It just seemed like a natural thing to ask, given the circumstances."

After waiting together in silence for a few minutes, Jon turned to see the trooper walking back towards the car, a light blue slip of paper in his right hand. As the trooper arrived again at the driver's side window, Jon couldn't see his face, but heard his stern voice.

"Mr. Morris, I clocked you traveling 82 in a 70 mile per hour zone. But I'm going to let you off with a warning this morning. Just slow down and focus on the road."

"Thank you, officer. I really appreciate that."

"And Mr. Morris, a word of advice, if I may." The trooper leaned down, showing his face in the window.

"Yes, sir?" responded Brant.

"There's more to being a witness for Christ than quoting Scripture. You need to be an example. And obeying the law falls into that category. Do you understand?"

"Yes, sir," said Brant. "Thank you, sir."

"Have a good day," said the trooper as he stepped away from the car.

Brant exhaled and let his head fall back against the headrest. He rolled his head to the right and looked at Jon. "You want to drive? I think I've had enough fun for a little while."

"Gladly," said Jon.

thirty nine

Not Helping

"For if you forgive other people when they sin against you, your heavenly Father will also forgive you. But if you do not forgive others their sins, your Father will not forgive your sins."

- Matthew 6:14-15

"What is that smell?" asked Brant, holding his hand over his nose.

"There must be a paper mill around here somewhere," answered Jon as they walked under the ancient shade trees lining the sidewalk of Savannah's East Bay Street. "Reminds me of Georgetown, where my mom grew up. I bet half the town worked at the paper mill. She always used to say it smells like money."

"Smells like a full diaper to me."

"It's that rotten egg, sulfur smell," said Jon, unbothered by the odor. "You'll get used to it."

"Great, we go from a city that smells like horse crap to one that smells like rotten eggs," complained Brant. "What's next? A visit to the landfill?"

"Savannah's a nice town, Brant. Or at least I heard it is."

Brant looked around him at Savannah's picturesque historic district as they walked. "It definitely *looks* nice. It's like a beauty queen with a body odor problem."

Jon laughed, but he knew Brant would continue a running commentary on the paper mill smell if he didn't offer a distraction. "You want to get something to eat?"

"Now you're talking. What do you have in mind?"

"I don't know," said Jon. "Let's ask this guy up here. He looks like a local." A few yards up the sidewalk, a dapper elderly man wearing a tan fedora leaned over a small white and brown Springer Spaniel. He scratched behind the dog's ears as it drank water from the paper cup he held in his hand. Jon cleared his throat as he approached. "Excuse me, sir. Can you recommend a good place to grab some lunch around here?"

"What do you think *that* is?" asked the man, pointing to a black and gold sign hanging from the awning above Jon's head. "B. Matthews. Best lunch around. If you don't mind the wait."

"Oh, wow," said Jon. "Thank you, sir."

"That was easy," said Brant. "Let's eat."

Glancing across the street, Jon saw a small group of people sitting under large oak trees in a grassy park. Several hand painted poster-board signs leaned against them as they sat cross-legged on the grass. "What's going on over there?" Jon asked the man.

"Oh, that's some of those folks left over from that Occupy thing, I guess."

"Not much of a protest," said Brant.

"They tried to set-up camp there in Emmet Park back in September, but mostly they just waved signs at traffic along East Bay and jawed at some folks. Didn't amount to much. I'm not really clear on what they're so dang mad about." The old man and his dog turned to walk away.

As Jon stared at the group across the street, he realized he'd forgotten his manners. "Thank you, sir!"

The man waved his hand casually without turning around.

"Brant, what do you say we go over there and talk to those people for a few minutes?"

"I knew it," said Brant. "You wouldn't want to wait until after we eat would you?"

Jon stepped off the curb, glancing both ways before walking across East Bay Street.

"I guess that's a *no*," said Brant as he followed behind Jon.

Walking under the large trees, Jon approached a young man in his late teens or early twenties sitting on the ground. A yellow poster displaying the neatly printed words *WAKE UP!* leaned against his knees. "How's it going?" asked Jon.

The young man kept his eyes on passing traffic in the street. "Just fighting the good fight, man," he replied.

Jon recognized the reference to 1 Timothy 6:12. "Are you guys Christians?" he asked.

The young protester looked up at Jon, appearing startled by his question. "What? Hell no, man. Where'd you get that from?"

"What you just said was a reference to a verse in the Bible," Jon explained.

"Words are public domain, man. I can say what I want. Don't oppress me."

Brant let out a small chuckle as he stood next to Jon.

Jon reassured the young man. "I'm not going to oppress you, I promise. I just want to ask you a question."

"It's a free country, dude. Or at least it will be when we get through with it."

Jon smiled. "That's good to know. So, I just want to know what you think about religion. Do you have any beliefs about God? You know, if he exists or who he is?"

"Who wants to know?" asked the young man.

"Well…I do," said Jon, unsure how else to answer.

The young man glared up at Brant. "Who's he?"

"Just a friend. So, tell me…what do you believe?"

The young protester studied Jon for a moment. "What I believe or you believe doesn't matter, man. Reality is what it is. Believing in God doesn't change the fact that big corporations in this country murder and oppress millions of people every day."

"Big companies kill millions of people every day?" asked Brant, failing in his attempt to look serious.

"Don't be ignorant, man. Look it up. It's all there."

"Seems like we would have heard something about that," said Brant, nudging Jon's elbow.

Jon could see Brant was toying with the young man.

"They don't want you to know," said the protester. "You've got to find out for yourself, man. The media isn't going to tell you. They're all in on it.

The government's not going to tell you. Where do you think all their money comes from?"

"All whose money?" asked Jon, trying to follow the young man's rant.

"The government's money!" shouted the protester.

"Um, I'm gonna say taxes," said Brant.

The man shook his yellow sign in front of him and shouted, "Wall Street! Wake up, man! Every time you buy something from a big corporation you're just feeding the beast! But it's all gonna come crashing down. You'll see."

"All right, so, what do you think needs to happen?" asked Jon.

"That's easy, man. No laws, no companies, no personal property, no cops, no government drones killing people, no NSA. We're gonna bring it all down, man."

"How, exactly, are you going to do all that?" asked Brant, rubbing his chin. "Just curious."

"We're doin' it right here, man! This is it! We're gonna bring it all down! Yeah!" He waved his arms in the air and received a few claps of support from nearby protesters.

"This protest, you mean?" asked Brant, looking at the scene around him. "There's only, like, twelve of you."

"This is just the start, man. We got people everywhere. You'll see."

Jon made eye contact with Brant long enough to give him a frown and a subtle shake of the head, hoping to discourage his interest in amusing himself at the boy's expense. "So you think people's lives will be better off after you bring down the government and big corporations?" asked Jon.

"I don't give a shit about people's lives, man. All I care about is justice. Those corporate bastards are gonna get what's coming to them."

"What about religion?" asked Jon. "How do you see people of faith fitting in with everything?"

"They can all go to hell, too. I don't care. The church is all in on it. They oppress and kill as many people as anyone else, man. It's just another big corporation." The sound of a horn from a passing car prompted the boy to raise his sign over his head. "Yeah!" he said, turning back toward Jon. "See? We represent the people, man."

"That was one car," said Brant. "How do you know they weren't honking at a squirrel or something?"

Jon looked at Brant in frustration. "Brant, do you mind?" He turned back to the young protestor. "Have you ever been to church?"

"Me?" asked the boy.

"Yeah," said Jon. "Did you ever go to church growing up?"

"Yeah, man, I went. My parents made me go all the time when I lived with them."

"Why did you stop going?" asked Jon.

"Because I flew that coop, man."

Jon began to wonder just how old the young man was. "You ran away from home?" he asked.

"I didn't run from nothing, man. My dad ditched my mom for some piece of ass at work and I said, 'I'm out of here.' Never looked back, man. I'm free from all that shit."

"How old were you when all that happened?" asked Jon.

The boy appeared distracted in thought for a moment. "Huh?" he asked.

"How old were you when you left home?" repeated Jon.

"I ain't got no home, man. Any place you call home is just a self-made prison."

"So, where do you live?" asked Jon, out of real concern. "Do you own a car or anything?"

"Possession is theft, man. I don't own nothing and nothing owns me."

"Wow," said Brant. "You should write bumper stickers."

The young man's face lit up. "Dude, I could so do that!"

"Be careful," said Brant, "you might accidentally make some money."

The young man appeared lost in thought for a moment. "Nah, I'd give the stickers away, man. Art belongs to no one."

"Wow. See, there's another one," said Brant, rubbing his hand over his mouth to hide his smile.

Jon tried to redirect the discussion back to the young man. "So, were you and your dad close?"

"What?" asked the boy, looking up at Jon. A touch of anger appeared in his eyes.

"Your dad – were you and him close before he left your mom?"

"Man, what is it with you? Where do you get off asking me all this shit? What are you? Some spy for Fox News or something?"

"No, I promise I'm not a spy. I'm a Christian and I want to talk with you about Jesus and God's love for you."

The young man laughed. "God don't love nobody, man. That's obvious."

"You don't think God loves you?" asked Jon.

"I know he doesn't. Look at me. Do you think my life would look like this if God loved me?"

The boy's question was the opening for which Jon was hoping. "So, you're not happy with your life?"

The boy straightened his arms behind him and leaned back. "Happy people don't raise hell, man. You gotta be angry if you want to change the world."

"So you *want* to be angry?" asked Jon.

"It's who I am, man. I've got lots to be angry about. And so do you. You just don't know it, 'cause you and your pal here got your heads up your asses. You're being screwed by the one percent, and you're all happy about it."

"That's not why I'm happy," said Jon with a smile. "Jesus said in the Bible that if you come to him, he'll take away your burdens and give you rest. He's the source of joy in my life. Doesn't that sound better than being angry?"

"My burden is bringing down the capitalist assholes that run this country. It's my right to be angry! Why don't you go spread your peace, love, and joy somewhere else, man?"

"All right," said Jon, though not ready to give up. "But let me ask you one last thing and then I'll leave you alone."

"Ask anything you want, man. I got nothing to hide."

Jon crouched down in front of the young man, their eyes now on the same level. "If your dad walked up right now, what would you want to say to him?"

"My dad, again? What's with you and my dad, man?"

"You said you had nothing to hide. If he walked up right now and was standing right here and you could say anything you wanted, what would it be?"

The young man mustered a crooked smile. "Man, you're just trying to mess with me. I know what you're doing."

"I'm not messing with you," said Jon. "I'm just wondering what you would say."

The young man looked at Jon and leaned forward, crossing his legs, Indian style. "All right, I'd say...." He paused for a moment and looked around the park as he considered his answer. His eyes fell on a man and a middle school-aged boy, happily tossing a baseball back and forth near a monument on the other side of the grass field. As he stared at the man playing with his son, the young protester's eyes narrowed. His face began to quiver with emotion.

Jon felt his heart ache in his chest as he studied the boy's grimaced expression. "Son...what's your name?"

The boy dropped his head as a tear fell onto his yellow poster. "David."

"David, I know what your dad did hurt you," said Jon, placing his hand on the boy's shoulder. "But all this protesting isn't going to take that hurt away. What your dad did had nothing to do with you. It was his—"

"It had *everything* to do with me!" David pushed Jon's hand off his shoulder. "He left me! Don't you get that? He didn't give a shit about me! All he cared about was his stupid job and his stupid Porsche! And then he screws some bitch and takes off! I hate that bastard! I *hate* him!"

"David, I'm sorry," said Jon, looking into the boy's hurting eyes.

David dropped his gaze and wrapped his arms around his knees in front of his chest. He rocked slowly, back and forth. "That's what I'd say to him...I hate you."

"David, I know what your dad did was wrong," said Jon. "But here's the truth: You need to forgive him."

"*What?*" asked David, recoiling from Jon.

"You need to forgive him," Jon repeated. Looking to his left and right, Jon became aware that his conversation with David was beginning to draw attention and stares from the other protesters around them.

"My dad don't deserve my forgiveness, man!" shouted David.

"Maybe not," said Jon. "But you don't deserve to be bitter and angry. You're letting what he did control your life. Can't you see that? And as long as you hold onto your anger towards him, you're just living in your own self-made prison, to use your words. You think you're free, David, but you're not. You're a slave to the past. But I'm telling you – you don't have to be."

David studied Jon for a moment. The anger appeared to leave his face. "I'm no one's slave, man," he said, quietly.

Jon could see doubt in the boy's eyes. "Yes you are, David. You're a slave to your own bitterness and hurt. But you can be free from all that. *Truly free.* And I can show you how to do that, right now."

"Don't listen to this guy, David."

Jon turned to see a bearded man, ten to fifteen years older than David, standing behind him.

"He's just trying to confuse you," the man said. "He's one of them."

Jon turned back to face David, ignoring the older protester. "David, don't let what your dad did control who you are. He's gonna have to answer to God for his life no matter what you do. But you can live your own life and be free from the hurt he caused you. Let me tell you how."

"Why do you care?" asked David. "You don't even know me."

"I care because God cares." Jon felt a sense of urgency knowing David's friend hovered behind him. "I know God loves you."

"But how can you know that?" asked David.

"Because his love is the reason I'm here talking to you, now. He wants you to know him, David. And he wants you to know he loves you enough to let his Son, Jesus, die on a cross for you."

"I don't believe that, man," said David, shaking his head. "There's no way."

"It's true, David," said Jon. "Jesus died for you. And he wants you to come to him and know the peace only he can give you. You can have that, right now."

David looked down at the ground and then back up at Jon. "But what if I—"

"Why don't you leave the kid alone, man?" said the bearded man, interrupting. "He doesn't want what you're selling."

"Take a hike, pal," said Brant, stepping in front of the man.

"I've got a right to be here, man," said the older protester. "You can't make me go anywhere."

David looked up at Brant and the protester. Jon could see the boy's attention beginning to slip away.

Brant stepped closer to the man. "If you were this kid's friend, you'd shut up and let him listen."

The protester became animated, waving his arms in the air and sticking out his chest towards Brant. "You can't shut me up, man! No one can shut us up! We speak for the people!" Several people around them clapped their hands in support.

"Yeah, all ten of you," scoffed Brant.

Jon was losing control of the discussion with David. He looked up at Brant. "Brant, I've got this, OK? You're not helping."

The bearded protester moved beside David and pointed at Jon and Brant. "These guys are just a couple of Jesus freaks, bro. Don't listen to them."

"David, listen to me," pleaded Jon. "You can change your life today, right now. You don't have to be angry anymore. The Bible says when you accept the sacrifice God made for you in Jesus, you become a new creation. You get to start over. It's a new life. Don't you want that, David?"

David looked back and forth between his fellow protester and Jon.

The older man knelt beside David and looked at Jon. "He already said *no*, man. Why don't you just beat it?"

"David, Jesus said 'I am the way, the truth and the life.' He's the answer. You can accept him as your Lord and Savior right now and be healed from all the anger and hurt and bitterness."

The older protester patted David's shoulder. "Come on Dave, some of us are heading over to Starbucks for coffee. Leave your sign here and tell these losers to blow."

David looked at Jon with a renewed grin. "Sorry, man," he said as he began to stand to his feet. "I'm fine the way I am." He left his sign on the ground and walked away, laughing with three other protesters. The older man wrapped his arm around David's shoulder.

"Brant!" said Jon as he stood up and wheeled around to face him. "Did you have to start arguing with that guy?!"

"I was trying to help, Jon."

"Well, next time don't!" Jon's heart raced in his chest. He paced aimlessly in front of Brant as he watched David cross the street with his friends. "These kids are all about solidarity, Brant! You mouthing off just gave him a reason to stick with his friend!"

"Oh, so you're blaming me for him not accepting Christ?"

"Yeah, I am!"

"Oh, that's nice, Jon. Real nice." Brant mumbled something else under his breath, turned his back to Jon and walked away towards the street.

Jon stood alone for a moment to collect himself and let his anger fade. He tilted his head backward and gazed up at the clear blue sky through the tiny leaves of the massive live oak trees. "God, I'm sorry we blew that. I know Brant was trying to help, but…this would be a lot easier if I was by myself." Jon lowered his eyes and watched his friend cross the street and enter B. Matthews. He took a deep breath and tried to imagine Brant looking out the window of a Columbia-bound Greyhound bus. As he turned to follow Brant to the restaurant, his right foot slipped on a sign left behind by the Starbucks-bound, anti-corporate protesters. Large black letters on a white poster read, *Stick Together and FIGHT!*

"Very funny." Jon kicked the sign and walked on across the street.

forty

Mary's Prayer

"I will show him how much he must suffer for my name."
- Acts 9:16

Jon wandered around uncomfortably outside the car as Brant pumped gas. His suspicion that Brant's eyes were following him behind his dark Ray-Ban sunglasses only added to his aggravation. The two men hadn't spoken beyond necessity for much of the past week. Being momentarily free from the awkward silence inside the car was a welcome relief, but the tension remained. As Jon watched the steady flow of cars passing on the sunny Florida highway, he longed to be on his own. He imagined driving alone in his car, talking to God, worshipping through music from his iPod, and looking for opportunities to share the Gospel. He had carried the same vision joyfully in his mind until the moment he agreed to take Brant with him. Then everything changed. And after several frustrating, unfruitful days in Savannah, Jon was sure he had made a mistake in bringing him along. He turned his attention back to the gas pump to find Brant staring at him.

"I'm sorry, OK?" said Brant, leaning against the car as he filled Jon's tank. "I'm sorry about the kid in the park. Is that what you wanted to hear?"

Jon stopped his pacing and looked at Brant over the top of the car. "Brant, the whole week in Savannah was a complete disaster."

Brant removed his sunglasses and tossed them on top of the gas pump. His eyes glared at Jon. "I just said I was sorry, Jon. What else do you want me to do?"

"I want you to...." Jon censored his thoughts of Brant taking a bus home. Though Brant offered an apology, Jon wasn't in a forgiving mood. "Let's just drop it, OK?"

Brant returned the gas hose to the pump. "Do you want a receipt?"

"No. Just get in," said Jon, dropping himself into the car behind the wheel.

They resettled themselves in their seats as Jon started the car.

"I can drive, you know," said Brant, in a conciliatory tone. "If you don't feel like it."

"Absolutely, not. You drive like a maniac."

"Oh, come on. You're just saying that because I almost got a ticket."

"That's *exactly* why I'm saying it!" Jon shook his head at Brant's nonsensical reasoning and eased the car across the two eastbound lanes of the divided highway and into the center median.

"I'm just offering to give you a break from driving, that's all," said Brant.

Jon ignored Brant's offer as he turned left and accelerated quickly to match the speed of oncoming traffic.

"I'm surprised you didn't want to stop in Jacksonville," said Brant. "It was on the way."

Jon debated whether to give in to Brant's attempt at normal conversation or just ignore him. A short, terse response seemed a good compromise. "We're going to Tallahassee," he said.

"I know, but why not both? We've got plenty of time."

"Brant...." Jon paused briefly and tried to let his irritation fade. "I don't *know* why, OK? How about...just because?" It was an honest answer. The campus of Florida State University had come to Jon's mind in prayer the night before as he sought God's direction. And while he was entirely uncertain if God was leading him to Tallahassee, Jon felt a sense of urgency to get there.

Brant sighed and looked out the window. "Whatever, dude," he said. With a sudden, quick motion, he put his hands on top of his head. "Oh, crap!"

"What's wrong?" asked Jon.

"I left my sunglasses back at the gas station."

Jon's annoyance returned immediately. "I'm not turning around," he said without lifting his foot off the accelerator. "They're probably gone by now, anyway."

"Oh, come on, man! We were just there! Turn around. Those were expensive!"

Jon clinched his jaws and lifted his foot off the gas without comment. He turned around at the next paved section of the median and drove the short distance back to the gas station. He watched Brant happily retrieve his sunglasses from the gas pump and plop back into the car.

"Thanks," said Brant, beaming like a kid with a new toy.

The genuine smile on Brant's face softened Jon's mood, slightly. "Can we go now?" he asked, with sarcastic drama.

"By all means," said Brant, placing his sunglasses back on his face.

For the second time in five minutes, Jon began the process of turning left across the divided highway. Glancing to his right, he saw a gray, brown, and white hound dog trotting across the eastbound side of the road. "That looks like a German Shorthaired Pointer," he said. "Who would let a nice dog like that just wander near a busy highway?"

"He's gonna get hit, if he doesn't watch out," said Brant.

The dog paused in the grassy center median of the four-lane highway, turned in a circle, and then looked briefly in Jon and Brant's direction.

"He's lost," said Brant. "Let's pick him up."

Jon leered at Brant long enough to make his point.

"We can just take him to a shelter or something," suggested Brant.

"If that dog gets in this car, you'd never want to get rid of him. You probably already have a name for him."

"Come on, Jon. Look at him. Bedford needs us."

"Bedford? Seriously?" Jon watched the dog lower its nose close to the ground and trot into westbound traffic. A truck pulling a horse trailer swerved suddenly to the right to avoid the hound and collided with a small red pick-up, sending the smaller truck off the road into the dry brown grass. The pick-up met a telephone pole head-on at full speed, clipping the pole in two. It continued slowly along in the grass, its driver bouncing limply behind the wheel, before stopping against a second pole some eighty feet from the first.

Jon threw his car into park and jumped out, leaving his door open and Brant shouting his name. He sprinted across all four lanes as traffic quickly slowed to a halt around the accident scene. Arriving at the red pick-up, Jon saw a dazed woman, probably in her thirties, looking at him through her driver's side window. Her arms hung limply at her side as blood drained down her face from her dark brown hair. Jon grabbed her door handle and pulled against the weight of the truck. Though unlocked, the door was crimped from the impact and jammed shut. Placing his foot against the side of the truck for leverage, Jon pulled again with all his strength.

The woman, watching Jon struggle with the door, began to cry. "Help me!"

"I'm trying!" said Jon. "Just hang on, OK?" Brant appeared at Jon's side. "Brant, keep pulling on the door! Try and get it open." Jon reached in his pocket, pulled out his phone and dialed 911. With the phone to his ear, he ran around the back of the truck to the passenger side. Though undamaged, one pull on the door handle told Jon it was locked.

"Nine-one-one emergency assistance, can I have your name?"

"Uh, Jon Smoak."

"What's the nature of your emergency, Mr. Smoak?"

"I'm at the scene of an accident, and I'm trying to get to a woman in her truck. She's hurt. She hit a telephone pole."

"Where is the accident, sir?"

Jon knocked on the passenger window with his knuckles to get the woman's attention. "Unlock the door!"

The woman let her head tilt to her right and blinked away the blood streaming into her eyes as she looked at Jon.

"Unlock the door!" repeated Jon, pointing at the door lock just inside the window.

"I can't move," she cried. "It hurts!"

Jon heard the emergency operator in his left ear as he held the phone against his head. "Sir? I need the address. Where are you?"

"I'm sorry. Uh...." Jon looked around him for landmarks or signs. "I'm not from around here, so...."

"What road are you on, sir?"

"We're on A1A just a few miles west of I-95." Jon held the phone away from his head for a moment. "Brant! Go get the tire iron out of my trunk! I need to break the window!" A loud explosion behind him caused Jon to drop his phone as he crouched instinctively and covered his head. Turning around, he saw white smoke hovering over the end of the fallen telephone pole. Finding his phone in the grass, he pressed it again to his ear.

"Sir! Sir!" said the operator. "What was that noise? Are you all right, sir?"

"Uh, I think the transformer on the telephone pole she knocked over just exploded," said Jon, watching the smoke grow thicker. "And now there's a fire in the grass around it." Jon could hear the woman in the car screaming and crying in fear.

"How far away from the fire are you, sir?"

"Uh, about thirty or forty feet, I guess. I don't know."

"One moment, sir. Please stay on the line. I'm sending help."

The woman in the truck was now hysterical. "Please help me! Please don't let me die!"

"You're not going to die, I promise," said Jon through the window. "What's your name?"

"Mary," sobbed the woman, the blood on her face now mixed with tears.

"Hang in there, Mary. Help's coming, OK?" Jon kept his eyes on the fire spreading quickly towards the truck. He spoke into the phone. "Ma'am? Hello?"

"I'm here, sir."

"The fire is coming towards the truck pretty fast. She must have leaked gas after she hit the pole."

"Mr. Smoak, I need you to get a safe distance from the vehicle, right now," urged the operator. "Rescue personnel are in route and will be there in three minutes."

"I don't think she has three minutes!" Jon stuffed his phone into his rear pocket and looked across the highway for Brant. He could see his car through the haze of smoke, but Brant was nowhere to be found.

"Oh, God!" cried Mary, with her eyes closed, tightly. "Please don't let me die like this! Please God! Help me, Jesus!"

Jon searched desperately on the ground for something to help him break the window, finding nothing but grass, sand, and a bag of trash from McDonalds. He looked back at the approaching fire, now just a few feet behind the truck. "Mary, I'm going to get you out of there! I need you to turn your head the other way, OK?" Mary closed her eyes and did as Jon asked. Jon reared back and threw his left elbow hard against the passenger window, shattering the glass. Reaching inside the door, he opened it from the inside handle, and climbed onto the passenger seat facing Mary. He reached over the center console, unbuckled her seatbelt, and slid his hands underneath her petite frame. As he tried to pull her towards him over the console, Mary screamed in pain. Jon let her slide slowly back to her seat as she sobbed. Cutting his eyes out the rear window, he saw no gap between the truck and the fire. Smoke now rose from underneath the truck bed. He was running out of time. Jon lifted himself up slightly, lowered his backside onto the passenger seat, and pulled his knees to his chest, his feet pointing towards Mary. Grabbing the steering wheel with both hands, he stretched his legs across Mary's lap and pressed his feet against the driver's side door.

Brant suddenly appeared outside Mary's window, breathing heavily. "Jon! I couldn't find it!"

"Brant! Pull on the door as hard as you can!" Jon straightened his legs against the door and pulled on the steering wheel with all his might as Brant pulled from the outside. The cabin began to fill with smoke as Jon strained mightily against the door. Slowly, the metal began to creak and bend as Jon screamed with effort. The door flew open suddenly, sending Brant stumbling backwards into the road. A fireman and a paramedic appeared immediately in the open door and lifted Mary, screaming, from the truck.

Jon twisted onto his stomach and crawled quickly out the passenger side door, tripping on the center console and summersaulting into the burning grass. Rolling to his feet, he scrubbed his hands through his hair to be sure he wasn't on fire and ran towards the flashing red and blue lights of emergency vehicles which now surrounded the scene. He stopped and turned back to see Mary's truck completely engulfed in flames.

"Jon!" shouted Brant as he ran towards him. "Are you all right?"

Jon looked past Brant for Mary. "Yeah, I'm fine."

"Dude," said Brant, looking down at Jon's blood soaked clothes. "No, you're not."

Jon lay on his stomach, his arms at his side and right cheek pressed flat against the white sheet of paper covering the emergency room examining table. The rubber tourniquet he wore in the ambulance still squeezed tightly around the top of his left arm. Jon watched quietly as the doctor, sitting on a stool next to his table, threaded a curved surgical needle with black suture. An African-American man in his mid to late thirties, the doctor's pleasant, but focused, expression reminded Jon of his grandmother preparing to knit a sweater as she relaxed in her front porch rocker.

"I'm going to have to place a few stitches inside this deep laceration here on the back of your arm, above your elbow," said the doctor. "I've tried to numb the area, but I'm afraid you still might feel this. Sorry about that."

"That's OK," said Jon.

"You're very lucky you didn't cut an artery, Mr. Smoak."

"That would have really ruined my day, I take it." Something about doctors brought out the dry side of Jon's humor.

"Yes, it would," said the doctor. He rolled on his stool to a nearby table, grabbed something, and then rolled back to Jon. "You could've bled to death."

"That *would* be a bad day," said Jon. His body flinched with pain as he felt the needle penetrate deep into his left triceps. Maybe it wasn't worth joking about, after all.

"Try to hold still, Mr. Smoak."

"Sorry. That really hurt."

"I told you."

"Yes, you did."

"I can give you something to make you sleepy, if you want."

"No, I'm fine," said Jon as he tried to ignore the pain. "You can call me Jon, by the way."

"OK, Jon. So, I understand you did this in a car accident."

"Sort of. It wasn't my accident. There was this dog and I saw a woman hit a telephone pole and I was helping her get out of her truck before it caught fire. I had to break her window to get in. That's how I cut my arm, I guess."

"You climbed into a car that was about to catch fire?"

"Yeah. I couldn't get her out the passenger side, so I climbed in and kicked out her driver's side door."

"Wow. Is she all right?"

"I'm not sure." Jon clinched his teeth together as he felt the needle again. "Ugh…um, they brought us here in the same ambulance. She hit her head on the windshield, I think. They had one of those neck things on her and were looking at her leg on the way to the hospital. She's here somewhere."

"I need you to relax your arm, Mr. Smoak."

"Jon."

"OK, Jon. Just try and relax for me."

"OK, I just – ouch!!"

"Sorry. That was the last stitch on the inside. That should be the worst of it."

Jon let himself exhale. "Good to know, thanks."

"That was a courageous thing you did, Jon. Helping that woman."

"I just did what anyone else would do." Jon could feel the tug and pull of the needle and thread as the doctor began to close the wounds on his arm.

"You really think just anyone would have done what you did?"

"Sure. Why not?"

"Let me ask you, when you were trying to get her out of the truck, was there a long line behind you?"

"What do you mean?" asked Jon.

"How many people were there waiting to help you?"

Jon thought of the accident scene for a moment. "Besides my friend Brant, I don't remember seeing anyone else."

"And how many cars passed by without stopping?"

"I don't know. I wasn't paying attention."

"You get my point," said the doctor. A nurse walked in the room, handed something to the doctor, and left.

"I do," said Jon. "But I just don't want to believe anyone would've let her burn up like that. Somebody would've helped her, if I hadn't."

"I doubt it. Working in this ER, a lot of the traumas I treat are inflicted intentionally by someone else. I see the worst the human race has to offer. Gunshot wounds, rapes, stabbings, beaten wives, children hit by drunk drivers. People are horrible to each other. You might be the first person I've treated who was injured trying to help someone. I guess that makes you special, Jon."

Jon couldn't think of a proper response to the doctor's compliment or to his jaded view of humanity. He lay quietly on the table, wishing he knew what to say.

"What do you do for a living, Jon?"

"I'm in advertising. Or at least I used to be in advertising. But I left that to serve God."

"Serve God? So you're in the ministry?"

"Not officially or anything like that. I'm just a regular guy who felt called to share the Gospel with people." Jon waited for the doctor's response, but nothing came. He sensed an opportunity to explore the doctor's thoughts on faith. At least he had a captive audience. "You know what you were saying about how people hurt each other?" asked Jon, flinching as the needle pressed into his arm.

"Yes," said the doctor.

"What if you had the cure for that?"

"For what? People hurting each other?"

"Mmhmm," said Jon, gritting his teeth in pain.

"I'm afraid there's no cure for that, Mr. Smoak." The light rattle of something landing in a metal bowl echoed around the room. "You had a small piece of glass just under your skin, there."

"So, you don't think people can change?" Jon asked. He tried to move his head slightly to see the doctor's face out of the corner of his eye.

"I think I know where you're trying to go with this – hold still please – but I see too much of what people are capable of doing to each other to think that simply believing in Jesus will stop it."

"Well, I wouldn't be doing what I'm doing if I didn't believe that faith in Christ has the power to change lives. I've experienced it in my own life. I mean – you're a doctor – if you knew you had the cure for cancer and could save people, wouldn't you be out telling everyone about it?"

"I've heard that analogy before. But it doesn't really work for me."

"Why not?"

"Well, for one thing, I would have to be one hundred percent certain that I had the real cure before I started giving it to other people. I would have to prove it first, test it successfully. Religion doesn't work like that. No one can be one hundred percent sure what happens to us when we die."

"I guess that's why they call it faith."

"I guess so. You have a few other small lacerations here on your elbow that I'm going to give a stitch or two."

"OK. So, what about you?" asked Jon. "What do you think happens when we die?"

"Well, my job is to try and keep that from happening, isn't it? I'm going to numb this up for you a little bit."

Jon felt a cold spray on the skin around his elbow. The stinging of his cuts quickly subsided. "Have you ever had a patient die here?" he asked, hoping to press the issue of mortality.

The doctor took a moment before responding. "Earlier this morning, they brought in a fifteen-year-old girl. She'd found her mother's sleeping pills in her bathroom and took the whole bottle. She died on the table you're lying on right now. I couldn't save her."

Jon was immediately sorry he asked. He closed his eyes and tried not to think about the young girl, lying dead on the same table. The thin sheet of white paper covering the padded vinyl did nothing to shield him from the unpleasant reality. Somewhere, Jon thought, a mother was crying in tortured agony. A tear rolled out of Jon's eye over the bridge of his nose and landed on the starched paper next to his face. He tried to turn his thoughts back to the doctor. "How do you handle something like that?" he asked.

"I guess you could say I've learned to drive without a rearview mirror," said the doctor.

"I'm not sure what you mean."

"Well, when something like that happens, I know I have to turn my focus to my next patient. Like you, for example. If I'm not at my best, one loss can lead to another. And that wouldn't be good for anyone. I'm almost finished, here."

Jon thought about his string of losses in Savannah. "Last week, I was talking with this kid in a park. He was protesting the economy or capitalism or something. I think he was really protesting his bad father, to be honest. But I was talking with him about the disappointments in his life and how accepting Christ could heal him from all the pain he was feeling. He was really lost and angry at the world. But he started to listen to what I was saying and, for a moment, I thought he was going to make a decision right there, you know. And be saved."

The doctor wiped something cold and wet around Jon's wounds. "What happened?" he asked.

"He got distracted by some other people and walked away. I lost him. He was so close, you know? And it really bothered me. I got mad at my friend who's traveling with me and kind of blamed him for it. He was part of the distraction. And then the rest of the week was horrible. We couldn't get anyone to even talk to us."

"It seems we're both in the business of trying to save people, Jon. It's not always easy, is it?"

"Nope."

"All right, there you go. All stitched-up." The doctor rose from his stool and removed his rubber gloves. "The nurse will come in and dress this for you in just a minute. She'll give you some instructions on keeping it clean and what not. Just lie still until then."

"OK."

"And I'm going to write you a few prescriptions for infection and pain. I'll leave them with the nurse." The doctor cleaned up his mess and washed his hands in the sink. He turned back to Jon as he dried his hands with a paper towel. "And lose that rearview mirror, Jon. We both have more people to save."

Jon felt a smile on his face for the first time in a week. "Yes, sir. I will. Thanks."

forty one

In All Things

"And we know that in all things God works for the good of those who love him, who have been called according to his purpose."
- Romans 8:28

Jon pushed the brushed aluminum button and waited for the large double doors to open. As he walked into the emergency room waiting area, startled looks from those seated around the room greeted him. Jon smiled politely at a curious little girl peeking over the top of a chair.

"Are you hurt?" asked the girl as Jon passed by.

"Just a little," he said. "The doctor fixed me, though."

The girl's mother whispered something in her ear, prompting her to turn around. Jon adjusted the blue cloth sling around his neck and resettled his left arm as he made eye contact with Brant across the room.

Brant rose to his feet, dropped a magazine onto his chair, and tried to contain a smile as he approached Jon. "You look like something out of a horror movie, Jonny-boy," he said, looking down at Jon's bloody clothes.

"I guess that's why everyone's staring at me."

"Ya think? How's the arm?"

"Not bad right now; it's still numb. But I need to get these prescriptions filled before we leave." Jon waved his paperwork at Brant.

"Ah, pain meds. Guess you won't be operating any heavy machinery for a while. Like, say, a BMW?"

"We need to talk," said Jon. He looked around the waiting room for an appropriate place to hold a private conversation. There wasn't one.

"Uh-oh, is our trip over?" asked Brant. "You want to go home because of your arm?"

"Just a minute," said Jon, turning towards the information counter. "Excuse me," he said to a nurse seated behind the desk. "Is there a private room around here anywhere that we could use for a few minutes?"

"There's the chapel, right down this hallway," said the nurse, leaning forward and pointing to her left. "It's usually empty. You're welcome to use that."

"That's perfect. Thank you." Jon motioned for Brant to follow him down the hall.

"This sounds serious," said Brant, losing his jovial tone.

"Well, yeah. I guess it is."

"I sent Holly a text message, by the way," said Brant. "She said she's glad you're OK and to stop trying to be a hero." Brant held up his phone for Jon to see the message as they walked. "She put a little smiley face with a tongue sticking out. See?"

"Thanks for doing that," said Jon, seeing the chapel ahead. "I'll call her later."

A small sign on the wall marked the entrance to a dimly lit room furnished like a miniature sanctuary, though it lacked any religious symbols. Four rows of chairs, three on each side of a center aisle, faced a backlit, multi-colored, stained glass window on the far wall just above a small padded altar for kneeling.

Brant followed Jon to the chairs on the front row and took a seat next to him. "So, what's up?" he asked.

"I had an interesting conversation with the doctor who stitched me up," said Jon. "And it made me realize a few things."

"Like, you shouldn't put your elbow through a car window?"

"Well, that should go without saying, I guess. But actually, we talked about trying to save people."

"He's a Christian?"

"No, I don't think he is. But he tries to save people physically and we're trying to save them spiritually. So we kind of had something in common. And sometimes we both fail at it – like you and I did last week."

"Yeah, that kind of sucked."

"It did. So I asked him how he's able to go on after losing a patient. And he said he just has to be ready for the next one. He doesn't let losing one patient cause him to lose another. He has to be at his best all the time or he's no good to anybody."

"When you say 'lose a patient,' you mean *die*, right?"

"Yeah. He actually lost someone this morning. A fifteen-year-old girl."

"Oh, my gosh." Brant closed his eyes briefly.

"I know," said Jon.

"So…he had a fifteen-year-old girl die on him this morning and he just hung around to eat lunch and stitch up your arm?"

"Yep."

Brant looked down and shook his head. "I couldn't do that."

"Well, that's the thing," said Jon. "It made me realize – we're going to have to be able to deal with losses in what we're doing, too. Just like him. Look, last week, when things got off track with David in the park, I was so bothered by it I let it affect me the rest of the week."

"I was kind of surprised you wanted to stay in Savannah the whole week, after that."

"I know. But I guess I was just being stubborn. Like we have to save at least one person everywhere we go or something."

"Or maybe you were subconsciously trying to make up for what happened with David."

"Please don't try to analyze me. I hate it when you do that."

"I'm just saying, you were pretty ticked about the whole thing."

"I know I was," said Jon. "So it's no wonder we couldn't get anyone else to talk with us. We've both been in bad moods ever since then."

Brant nodded. "I've been afraid to say anything to anybody. I didn't want to say something wrong or mess you up."

"I think we just need to move on," said Jon. "The doctor said he thinks of it like driving without a rearview mirror. You just have to put your losses behind you and focus on what's in front of you. It made me think about what Paul said in Philippians. That despite all that had happened to him and all he'd accomplished, he was just pressing on with what Christ had called him to do. We need to be like that."

"Sounds like you had a cool doctor."

"He was definitely interesting. Pretty down on people, though. He sees a lot of bad stuff come through here."

"I'm sure he does."

"He tried to convince me that we were *special* just because we helped someone."

"Come on," said Brant, "Anyone would have done what we did in a situation like that."

"That's what I said, but he wasn't buying it. Anyway, I'm sorry I've been so frustrated with you. You don't deserve that."

"No, it's all right. I totally messed up your conversation with David. Who knows, maybe he would have accepted Christ if I hadn't argued with that jerk friend of his."

"I don't know," said Jon. "But the important thing is that we don't let our failures keep us from doing our best the next time. If we'd been on our game after that happened, the week could have been totally different."

"Heck, at least maybe we wouldn't have gotten thrown out of Waffle House."

"That was bad," said Jon, laughing at himself.

"That was totally not my fault," said Brant. "I was just trying to eat. You were the one doing all the talking."

"I know. That was definitely on me." The mental picture of Brant's face as they left the restaurant made Jon start to laugh. "But I've never seen anyone cram half a waffle in his mouth before."

"I was hungry! And I was afraid to ask her for a to-go box after she told us to get out."

"Next time, I promise to wait until *after* we've eaten to witness to our waitress."

"Good rule," said Brant. "I think she definitely got the part about being a sinner, though. That's for sure."

"I know," said Jon, shaking his head. "I was pressing a bit too hard on that."

"Just a little," said Brant, holding his thumb and index finger an inch apart.

"I guess I don't make much of a witness when I'm in a bad mood. Look, from now on, why don't we just do our best and let God sort out the rest?"

"Did you mean that to rhyme?" asked Brant.

Jon laughed. "No, it just came out that way."

"Nice."

Jon looked at the nondescript altar before them and remembered the last conversation he had with Brant in a church sanctuary. He felt a similar need to reset himself before God. "You mind if we prayed for a minute?" asked Jon.

"Sure," said Brant.

"I'll start and you can jump in after me, if you want," said Jon. They both closed their eyes and bowed their heads as Jon began to pray. "Almighty God, dear Father in heaven, I want to thank you for using the doctor to fix my arm and straighten out my head while he was at it. Help us to do our best in sharing your Gospel with others. And beyond that, we just put everything in your hands, God. We know we'll face rejection and losses. We know we'll make mistakes. But we also know that you have other opportunities waiting for us. Help us to be ready, Lord, at all times to be witnesses for you. I'm sorry that I let the experience in the park last week keep us from serving you effectively afterwards. We commit ourselves to pressing on in service to you, no matter what challenges we face. Please be with us and let your Holy Spirit guide us in all that we do." Jon paused for a moment.

Brant took the cue and began to pray. "Dear God, I'm sorry I let my big mouth mess things up in Savannah. Help me to do a better job of reaching people for you and helping Jon. And please be with the woman who was in the car accident. I think Jon said her name was Mary. Please be with the doctors who treat her and let her know you love her, God. Thank you, Lord Jesus. Amen."

"Excuse me, did you just say *Mary?*"

Jon turned around to see a bald middle-aged man, dressed in jeans and a light blue workman's uniform shirt, standing up from a chair in the back of the chapel.

"I did," answered Brant, raising his right hand as the man moved towards them.

"Are you the two men who helped my wife out of her truck?" he asked, taking a seat in a chair directly behind them.

"You're Mary's husband?" asked Jon, turning in his chair to face him.

"I am. The ambulance guy told me what you did. Thank you."

"How is she?" asked Jon. "We came in together, but I don't know where they took her."

"She's in surgery now. They aren't telling me much. But she was banged-up pretty bad, I'm afraid."

"Well, we'll keep praying for her," said Jon. "My name's Jon and this is my friend Brant."

"Nice to meet you boys. My name's Granby."

"Mr. Granby, I—"

"Granby's my first name," the man said, interrupting Jon. "Granby Scott."

"Oh, I'm sorry," said Jon.

"That's all right. Granby's a family name. I get called Scott Granby all the time. Anyway, thanks for what you two did for Mary. Is your arm OK, there? Is all that blood yours?"

"Yeah, I'm afraid so," said Jon. "But it's fine. Just a few stitches. We're just glad we were able to help get Mary out before the truck caught fire. I think God was looking out for her."

The man grimaced, slightly. "Well, I don't see how you can say that," he said.

"Why not?" asked Jon.

"Well, I mean, she goes to church all the time. She prays and reads her Bible every day. I haven't stepped foot in a church in five years, but she's the one in surgery and I'm out here. If God was looking out for her, why didn't he keep from getting hurt like this? That should have been me, not her."

Jon realized an opportunity to share his faith had just fallen in his lap. "Is that why you came in here? To ask God that question?"

"I don't know why I came in here, exactly," said Granby. "I wouldn't know what to say to God, anyway. It's just not right. This shouldn't have happened to Mary, of all people. It ain't right."

Jon searched his mind for words of wisdom or appropriate scripture, but found nothing. "To be honest, Granby, I don't know why things like this happen, either. A stray dog decides to cross the road, and your wife ends up in the hospital. I don't understand it any more than you do. But I know that God does."

"Is that what happened?" asked Granby. "A dog got in the road?"

Jon nodded. "A truck swerved to miss the dog and knocked Mary's truck off the road and into a telephone pole. It happened right in front of us. I don't think she ever had a chance to slow down."

Granby's head tilted down.

Seeing the man's lip begin to tremble, Jon regretted how casually he had described Mary's accident. He remembered receiving the news of Lacey's car accident and suddenly knew exactly how the man felt. The unanswerable questions of *why* as he rolled on his floor in agony. The overwhelming, futile desire to undo what had been done. Even if it meant taking her place. He also remembered what sustained him in the days and years that followed. "Granby," Jon said, "would you trade places with your wife right now, if you could?"

Granby sniffed his running nose and looked up at Jon. "You know I would," he said. "She's the best thing in this world to me. I'd give my life for her in a heartbeat."

Jon smiled, slightly. "Granby, that's how God feels about you."

"How's that?" asked Granby.

"That's the same way God loves you. He let his Son die for you on the Cross so you could be saved from your sins. Jesus traded places with you. And it's God's love that will get you through tough times like this."

"You sound just like my wife," said Granby with a pained grin.

"She talks to you about her faith?" asked Jon.

Granby leaned back in his chair. "She's been trying for years to get me to go to church with her. Ever since we got married."

"You said you'd do anything for her," said Brant. "Why not that?"

Jon had almost forgotten Brant was sitting next to him.

"I don't know," said Granby. "It's just...." His expression suddenly hardened. "Look, I work hard for a living, OK? I work six days a week fixing heating and air units all over Nassau County. I don't feel like getting all dressed up on my one day off to hear some preacher tell me I'm a sinner. I don't need that." Granby's eyes bounced back and forth between Jon and Brant.

Jon was startled by his defensive reaction to Brant's question and had no idea what to say next.

"What do you like to do on your day off?" asked Brant.

"I *fish*," said Granby, emphatically.

"I love to fish," said Brant, turning himself in his chair to better face Granby. "What kind of fishing do you do, down here?"

"Inland salt water, mostly," said Granby, his eyes softening. "We go up in the Nassau River and around behind Amelia Island."

"I bet you find some good Redfish and Black Bass in those waters," said Brant.

"Sure do," said Granby, warming to the topic. "And a few Spotted Sea Trout every now and then, too. Depends how far inland you go. Where are you boys from?"

"Columbia, South Carolina," said Brant.

Jon felt his opportunity to reach Granby with the Gospel slipping away, just like his experience with David in Savannah the week before. He was sure Granby needed to understand and accept the love of Christ. But in a matter of seconds, Brant had turned the conversation from salvation to sport fishing. Jon's mind raced to find some way to pull them back to the matter of faith.

"My wife's parents live up in Sumter, not too far from there," said Granby. "Good fishing up that way, too."

"You bet," said Brant. "Lake Marion is my fav—"

"Granby, would you mind if we prayed for your wife, Mary?" asked Jon, interrupting out of desperation. He didn't know what to say to Granby, but he knew what to say to God.

Granby appeared surprised at Jon's question. "You mean like, right here? Like you were doing when I came in?"

"If that's OK," said Jon.

"Sure," said Granby. "I guess that'd be all right."

Jon bowed his head and closed his eyes, hoping Granby was doing the same. "Dear Heavenly Father," he prayed, "we acknowledge you as Lord over all things. You created the Universe and everything in it, God. You are everlasting and all-powerful and yet we know your eyes are on us. You care about us. Your Word says you even count the hairs on our heads. I know we matter to you, Lord. And I believe that you love us. So, it's hard for us to understand why bad things happen to us sometimes. And it's even harder when they happen to someone who loves you and worships you, like Mary. But we know that you watched your own Son suffer and die two thousand years ago. Jesus felt every nail and every moment on that Cross. And you did that for us. You love us that much. And I know you understand how much Granby is hurting right now as he waits for news on Mary. Dear God, we ask you to guide the surgeon's hands and send your healing power to her body. Fill her with strength and let her faith shine on those around her in this hospital. We ask this so that you may be glorified, dear Lord. God…you were there for me when I lost my wife, Lacey, in her accident. You were with me in the darkest hours of my life, Lord. And I pray that you'll comfort and strengthen Granby the same way, right now. Let him know that you desire a relationship with him that's more meaningful and eternal than anything he's ever known. Give him the hope and peace that comes from knowing your Son, Jesus. God, I have to believe that Mary has prayed this same thing for Granby many times. I pray that you'll hear us, Lord. And I ask that you let your Holy Spirit move in Granby's heart right now, Lord. Draw him close to you. I pray these things in Jesus' Holy name. Amen."

Jon opened his eyes to see Granby leaning over his knees, his head still bowed as he sniffed his nose.

Granby slowly raised himself up and wiped his wet face on his shirt-sleeve. "You lost your wife in a car accident?"

Jon looked into the man's probing eyes and nodded his head. "Years ago. But God got me through it, Granby. I wouldn't be here without him."

Granby dropped his gaze to the floor and rubbed his rough hands together between his knees. "I'm sorry."

Jon felt moved to put a decision in front of Granby. "Granby, I don't know why some things happen. But I'm so thankful I know Jesus when they do. And you can have the same strength and hope that God gave me, if you accept Jesus Christ as your Lord and Savior. Would you like to do that right now?"

Granby held his eyes down. "Yes, I would," he said, quietly.

"Then just pray this after me, OK?"

"OK."

Jon prayed out loud as Granby repeated after him. "Lord God, I admit that I am, in fact, a sinner. And without you there is no hope for me. But right now, I accept the sacrifice you made for me through Jesus on the Cross, Lord.

I believe he died for my sins and that you raised him from the dead. And in his name, I ask you to forgive me of my sins. And I accept your amazing grace, dear Lord. I commit myself to turning from my sins and following you from this day forward. Thank you, Lord Jesus. You are my risen Savior for evermore. Amen."

Jon opened his eyes and reached for Granby's shoulder. "Welcome to the family of God, Granby."

Granby's face was flushed with emotion as he offered his hand to Jon and then to Brant. "Thank you, guys. I can't wait to tell Mary. She's not going to believe it."

"I bet she will," said Jon.

Granby stood to his feet. "I'm going to go check with the nurse to see if they know anything. Will you wait here for a few minutes? I want you to be there with me when she wakes up."

"We're not going anywhere," said Jon, glancing at Brant.

"Great," said Granby as he turned to leave. Stopping in the doorway, he turned around. "Who are you guys, anyway?"

"No one special," said Jon, with a smile.

forty two

The Way Home

"Jesus answered, 'I am the way and the truth and the life.'"
- John 14:6

Jon sat uncomfortably on the front pew next to Brant rethinking his decision not to take his pain medicine. He had wanted his mind to be clear when the preacher called on him to speak. But as his arm throbbed in pain with every heartbeat, Jon began to regret accepting Granby's invitation to attend his baptism, offered the day before in Mary's hospital room.

"You OK?" whispered Brant.

Jon winced and nodded reassuringly as he watched Granby, wearing a white pleated robe, enter the baptismal pool behind the choir loft at the front of the sanctuary.

The pastor, standing behind Granby to his left, began speaking to the congregation. "I've known Granby Scott for some time, now. As you've heard, his wonderful wife, Mary – who is so dear to many of us – was in a serious car accident yesterday and remains in the hospital this morning. Our prayers are with her, and we're hopeful she'll be back worshipping with us, soon. But it was through that tragic event that God chose to work on Granby's heart. The Lord used two Believers, whom you'll meet in a moment, not only to save Mary's life, but to share the Gospel with Granby in the hospital. And it was there that Granby made his decision for the Lord."

The pastor turned to face Granby. "Granby Scott, have you accepted Jesus Christ as your Lord and Savior?"

282

"I have," said Granby.

"If you'll hold onto my arm," instructed the pastor. "Then on your public profession of faith, I baptize you, my brother, in the name of the Father, Son, and Holy Spirit." The pastor lowered Granby backwards into the water and lifted him quickly back to his feet. "Buried in baptism, raised to walk in the newness of life," added the pastor. The congregation applauded as Granby wiped water from his face and made his way up the steps from the pool, disappearing into a room behind the choir loft. "Please pray with me," said the pastor to the congregation. "Almighty God, you've shown us through your Word and in our lives that all things work together for the good for those who love you and who are called according to your purpose. There's no clearer example of that than what we've witnessed over the last twenty-four hours in the lives of Granby and Mary. We thank you for bringing Granby to faith through these events, and we ask that you provide healing to Mary's body. Lord, we pray that your mighty hand will be on those caring for her now in the hospital, that her health will be restored and that she will be home with her family, soon. To you be the glory, God. In Jesus' name, we pray. Amen."

Jon kept his eyes closed even after the pastor had finished praying. "Father, please help me through this pain," he prayed. "Help me to stay focused and say what you would want me to say. Like the preacher said, to you be the glory." While the rest of the congregation stood and began singing a hymn, Jon remained seated and continued praying. "Is this where I should even be, right now, God? It feels good to be in your house, but I feel like I should be out talking with people who aren't already *in* church. And I don't want to stand up in front of all these people and get their applause for things that I know you've done, not me. Please help me to share what you're doing through me in a way that glorifies you, Lord. I ask this in Jesus' name. Amen."

As Jon opened his eyes and stood for the last verse of *Blessed Assurance*, his head spun with dizziness. He blinked heavily, letting the back of his legs press against the edge of the pew to hold him steady. To his left, an elderly woman sang at the top of her lungs in a raspy, throaty voice. For a moment, Jon forgot about his arm while his mind searched for a suitable comparison to the sound of the woman's singing. A cement truck mixer, he decided.

By the time his head had finally cleared, the hymn was over. Jon turned to his left and gave a smile to the old woman. She smiled and nodded politely as everyone sat down noisily on the old wooden pews.

The pastor entered the sanctuary through a side door and walked up the three steps onto the chancel and took his place behind the pulpit. "When I went to see Mary in the hospital yesterday," he said, looking out over the congregation, "I found Granby by her side with two gentlemen, whom I had not met previously. One was wearing bloodstained clothes. His left arm was bandaged and hung in a sling. The other was smiling and eager to tell me about what had transpired around Mary's accident. Together, they shared quite a story. As I listened, it became evident to me that God's hand was on them, throughout. What triggered the series of events that led to Mary's accident yesterday – and ultimately Granby's baptism this morning – was a seemingly random, stray dog. More about that in a minute. But how God began to intervene in these two men's lives, to put them in a position to help Mary physically and Granby spiritually, started months and even years before. When Granby invited them to be here with us this morning, I asked if they wouldn't mind sharing a little of their story with us. At this time, I'd like you to meet Jon Smoak and Brant Morris. Jon and Brant, if you wouldn't mind joining me here on the stage, please."

Jon moved off the pew as polite applause spread around the sanctuary. He felt Brant's hand around his right arm holding him steady as they made their way up the steps to the pastor's side.

"But before I turn the microphone over to them," said the pastor, "I'd like to relay what these two did at the scene of Mary's accident yesterday. They are truly heroes."

As the preacher described the help they gave Mary, Jon took note of a little boy – probably nine or ten years old – sitting on the front pew, doodling with a pen on the back of a worship bulletin. Jon remembered doing the same thing when he was a boy in church, sitting next to his father and mother, biding his time until the service was over and he would be free once again to go play. Jon smiled to himself as he watched the boy swinging his legs under the pew as he drew. It was like watching a younger version of himself from over thirty years ago. The more Jon focused on the little boy, the less aware he became of anything else happening around him. He began to wonder what his own life would have been like if he had accepted Christ at that boy's age. What if someone had taken the time to really explain the Gospel to him? Just sitting in church with his parents didn't do it. What if he had grown up knowing Jesus as his Lord and Savior? What decisions would he have made differently? Would he have met Lacey? If he had, could he have led her to Christ? Would she still be alive? If someone had just taken five minutes when he was a boy to be sure he understood what church was all about, how would his life have been different?

"Jon," said Brant, elbowing Jon in the right arm.

Jon looked to his right at Brant and then at the preacher. Both men were smiling at him.

"I'm sorry, what?" asked Jon, feeling the warmth of embarrassment on his face.

"He's on pain meds," said Brant, producing a large laugh from the congregation.

"I would be, too," said the pastor, continuing the laughter. The pastor waited until the sanctuary was quiet again, before turning towards Jon. "Jon, I was asking if you would like to tell everyone what you shared with me in the hospital. About your calling to be a witness for Christ." The pastor handed a microphone to Jon.

"Oh, sure," said Jon, trying to gather himself. As he received the microphone in his right hand from the pastor, Jon studied the many faces smiling back at him from the church pews. He wondered how many of them *really* knew Jesus. Maybe this was where God wanted him to be that morning, after all. Jon cleared his throat and began to speak. "For starters, I was raised in a church, a lot like this one. My parents took me to church every Sunday. But I didn't find out until I was a lot older that sitting in church didn't make me a Christian." His eyes fell again on the little boy, his head down, still doodling. And one thought overtook Jon's mind: *What would he say to a nine-year-old Jon Smoak, if he had the chance?* He felt himself step forward and down the stairs towards the little boy. He looked at the boy's father as he approached. "Would you mind if I borrowed your son for a moment?" Jon asked.

"As long as you give him back," the man said with a smile. Those seated nearby chuckled lightly at the exchange.

Jon offered his hand to the boy, who looked up at his father.

"It's OK," the man said.

The boy scooted himself off the pew and reached for Jon's hand. Jon led him to the steps in front of the pulpit and sat down. The boy took a seat on Jon's right.

"What's your name, son?" Jon moved the microphone in front of the boy's face.

"Johnny," said the boy.

"Johnny," repeated Jon, slightly spooked by the coincidence. "That's my name, too. Do you have an H in your name?"

"Yes, sir. I'm named after my daddy. He's got an H in his name, too."

"You're lucky. I always wanted an H in my name. But the nurse in the hospital where I was born misspelled my name on my birth certificate, and my mom didn't catch it. So I'm Jon without the H."

"You can have my H, if you want. I ain't usin' it."

The congregation broke into laughter.

"How old are you, Johnny?"

"Eight and a half."

"Eight and a half," repeated Jon. "OK, Johnny. I have a question for you."

The boy looked up at Jon with raised eyebrows and a slightly worried expression.

"It's easy, I promise," said Jon.

"OK."

"Why do you think all these people came to church this morning?" asked Jon.

"Cause somebody told 'em they had to, I guess."

The church filled with laughter. The boy's father rubbed his hand over his mouth and looked down at the red carpeted floor.

"That's probably true in some cases," said Jon, "but why do you think it's important for us to come to church?"

"God," said Johnny.

"God. That's right. And what does God want us to do when we're in church?"

"Be quiet."

Jon waited for more laughter to subside before continuing. "Sometimes we need to be quiet and listen, don't we?"

"Yes, sir."

"You know, when I was your age, do you know what I did when I was in church?"

The boy shook his head silently.

"I drew pictures on the back of my worship bulletin," said Jon, with a smile.

"That's what I was just doin'!" said Johnny to more laughter from the congregation. The boy looked around the church. He appeared to be unsure why people were laughing.

"But when you get older, you learn a few things," said Jon. "And, now, do you know what I wish I had been doing back then instead of drawing?"

"What?" asked Johnny.

"Listening to my pastor."

The boy turned around and looked up at the pastor standing next to Brant and then looked back at Jon. "Really?"

"Really," said Jon. "Do you know why?"

Johnny shook his head back and forth.

"Because he's here to tell you about the best, most important thing you'll ever hear in your whole life."

"What?"

"That God loves you. That he's real and that he loves you. He loves you so much that he let his only Son, Jesus, die for you. Just so you can be with him in heaven one day. Would you like to go to heaven one day, Johnny?"

"Yes, sir. That's where my momma is. She died when I was born."

"I'm sorry to hear that," said Jon, looking up briefly at Johnny's father. "Do you know what you have to do so you can go to heaven, too?"

"I have to be good."

"How good do you have to be?"

"*Really* good!"

"Are you ever really good?" asked Jon.

"Sometimes," said the boy, sounding unsure of his answer.

"Sometimes, but not all the time?"

"No, sir. I get into trouble sometimes."

"What usually happens to you when you get in trouble?"

"No TV," said Johnny, looking at his father.

"That's right. You get punished, don't you?

"Yes, sir."

"And is your father happy when he has to punish you for something you did wrong?"

Johnny shook his head. "No, sir. Last week, I got a spankin' and he said it hurt *him* more than it did *me!*"

Jon glanced at Johnny's father and gave him a knowing smile. "That's because he loves you, right?"

"Yes, sir."

"Well, Johnny, we all do bad things sometimes. God calls that sin. And it doesn't make him happy when we sin. There's no sinning in heaven. But God made a special *way* to fix things when we sin to make sure we can go to heaven when we die. In fact, the Bible tells us that early Christians were even called *Followers of the Way*. Do you know what *Way* I'm talking about?"

Johnny shook his head.

"OK," said Jon, trying to think of how best to explain it. "Let's see…if you were out riding your bike and you got lost, you'd want someone to show you the way home, wouldn't you?"

Johnny nodded his head in agreement. "One time when I was little I got lost in the woods behind my house, and folks had to come out lookin' for me."

"And they found you and showed you the way home, right?"

"Yes, sir. My daddy found me."

"Well, Johnny, that's what Jesus, God's Son, did for us. See, because of our sin – the bad things we do – we're lost and separated from God. Like you were lost in the woods and separated from your dad. But Jesus came to earth from heaven and found us. And he showed us the way to get home – to his home in heaven. Do you know the way he showed us?"

"No, sir."

"Jesus told us we need to believe that he's God's Son and that he came to save us because we've let our sin get us lost from God. And to fix that, Jesus took the punishment for our sins so we don't have to."

"No TV for Jesus," said Johnny with a grin, this time enjoying the laughter from the congregation.

"I'm afraid it's even worse than no TV," said Jon. "God said we deserve to die for our sins. That's why Jesus had to die for us. He took the punishment we deserved."

"Oh," said Johnny, the smile gone from his face.

"But the good news is that God raised Jesus back to life. And he's alive with God in heaven today. Isn't that awesome?"

"Yes, sir, it is," said Johnny.

"So the way to heaven is really simple. If we admit that we're sinners and trust that Jesus died for us and rose again from the grave, then we'll be saved and go to heaven when we die. All you have to do is pray and tell God that you don't want to be lost anymore. That you're sorry for your sin and that you want to follow Jesus and get to know him, because he'll show us the way to live a life that makes God happy. Have you ever prayed that, Johnny?"

"No, sir."

"Would you like to do it, now?"

Johnny looked at his father, who nodded gently as a tear ran down his face. "Will I get to go to heaven one day and see my momma?"

"Yes, you will," said Jon. "And your life here will be a whole lot better, too. Because Jesus will be with you now and in heaven."

"OK," said Johnny. "I want to do that."

"Let's pray together, then. Just repeat after me and mean what you say in your heart, OK, Johnny?"

"Yes, sir."

"Dear, God," said Jon. "I'm sorry I do bad things sometimes. I know you don't like that. Please forgive me. I thank you for letting Jesus take my punishment for me on the Cross. I want to trust him to save me, God. I want to let Jesus show me the way to you in heaven. I want him to come into my life right now and guide me. And help me live in a way that makes you happy, God. Thank you for saving me, Jesus. Amen."

Jon shook Johnny's little hand and pointed him back to his father's waiting arms as the congregation stood in applause. Jon rose to his feet and walked up the stairs to rejoin Brant and the pastor. As he turned back towards the sanctuary, he saw Granby slip in through the side door and take a seat on the front pew next to Jon's Bible. As the applause faded, the congregation slowly took their seats and resettled themselves in the pews.

Jon lifted the microphone to his mouth. "And for God's glory, that's what we've been called to do."

forty three

Liam

In the morning shade of several large live oak trees draped in Spanish moss, Jon strolled casually with Brant along the sidewalk of Collegiate Loop in Tallahassee. He was careful to guard his left arm, still hanging in a sling, from the possible bump of passing students, most of whom walked heads down, focused on their smart phones, across the Florida State campus. Just beyond a large redbrick dormitory to their right, a large grass quadrangle teamed with backpack-laden students crossing the open field in all directions. "Class must have just let out," Jon said. "Might be a good time to talk with some of these kids. Let's cross the street."

Brant huffed as he followed Jon off the curb. "Jon, unless you post something on Reddit or somehow get all these kids to follow you on Instagram, I doubt you're going to get their attention. I think we're just wasting our time out here."

Jon glanced curiously at the scowl on Brant's face as they crossed the street. "Well, I guess I'm just not as pessimistic as you today, Brant." He stepped up onto the sidewalk and continued into the grass to escape the main flow of student traffic. Brant lagged lethargically behind.

"I think God can really use us here," Jon said over his shoulder. "Besides, we did OK with college kids in Charleston. Why not FSU?"

"For one thing," said Brant, "this place reminds me of Clemson's campus with all these brick buildings." He waved his index finger in the air at the buildings surrounding the quad. "And I hate Clemson."

Jon stopped and turned to face his friend. While he didn't mind Brant's sentiment towards Clemson, he'd grown tired of his foul mood. "What's up with you this morning? You've been a grouch ever since we left Denny's."

Brant placed his hands on his hips and looked around the quad, narrowing his eyes. "It's nothing I want to talk about, OK?"

"What, did they short you on cheese in your omelet this morning?"

"Fine, make fun of me. I don't care." Brant dropped his hands by his side and took two aimless steps away from Jon.

"Oh, come on," said Jon. "What is it, for Pete's sake?"

Brant stiffened as he turned around. "Look, I had a couple of frustrating texts from Kim this morning, and I don't feel like talking about it right now, if you don't mind. So can you just drop it?"

"OK, geez," said Jon, holding up his hands. "It's dropped. Whatever."

Jon walked ahead onto a sidewalk branching off from the street, angling towards the center of the grassy quad. Scanning the landscape for anyone who might have time for a conversation, his attention fell on several students standing before a young man speaking from a short wall surrounding a fountain at the center of the quad. A few steps closer, Jon could see a small black book in the young man's hand as he spoke. Jon turned around quickly and called to Brant, who was following at a distance. "Hey, I think that guy's preaching!"

"Good, he's got this covered," said Brant, with dry indifference. "Let's go someplace else."

"Are you kidding me? We might be able to help him or something. Or maybe he can help us. This is such a God thing!"

Brant turned and looked back in the direction of their parked car.

"Will you snap out of it?" asked Jon. "Come on, we can talk to those kids listening to him, right now." Jon quickened his pace slightly, leaving Brant lagging behind. As he neared the fountain, the students standing in front of the preacher turned and walked away in separate directions across the quad. "Shoot," said Jon. He turned around to find Brant walking up slowly behind him. "You're just not into the whole *serving God* thing today, are you?"

"I'm here, aren't I?" responded Brant.

Jon sighed, turned his back on Brant and continued towards the fountain. Within a brick-paved square surrounded by red rose bushes, several columns of white water shot up from the center of a large oval-shaped pool. In the knee-deep water stood six life-sized bronze statues of young women clothed in various swimwear styles of the past century. Their casual poses suggested playful relief from a hot Florida afternoon. On the retaining wall surrounding the fountain pool, the young preacher shared his message. In his mid to late twenties with closely cropped blonde hair, his yellow polo shirt hung un-tucked over his faded jeans as he spoke with a British accent to anyone in shouting distance. Reaching the edge of the brick square, Jon positioned himself next to a white bench as he listened.

"And that means all of us," said the young man. "Romans 3:23 says, 'for all have sinned and come short of the glory of God.' When I was twenty-four years old, I was a civilian defense contractor in Iraq. I was making tons of money. I could have anything I wanted. The nicest flat, the finest clothes, the most beautiful women. I had women, lots of women. I was having sex anytime I wanted. I even paid prostitutes for sex. I would have two, sometimes three women a night!"

Jon looked around him for signs of interest from students passing by.

"Listen to this guy," said Brant, appearing at Jon's right shoulder.

"Pretty cool, isn't it?"

"*Cool?* This guy came all the way from England to tell us what a miscreant he was. How is that going to win anybody over?" Brant cupped his hands around his mouth and shouted towards the young preacher. "Get to the part about Jesus!"

The preacher turned his focus towards Brant. "Oi! Just sharing my own testimony, mate."

"No kidding," said Brant. "It's all about you, so far."

The preacher glared at Brant and then looked away as he continued preaching.

"Brant, what the heck are you doing?" asked Jon. "You don't heckle a preacher! He's on *our* side, remember?"

"Sounds to me like he's on *his* side. Just listen to him brag."

"I'm sure he's just trying to connect with these kids, Brant."

"How? By making it sound fun to be a scumbag?"

Jon realized the preacher had stopped speaking and was now staring in their direction. The young man lifted his arm and pointed at Brant. "You need Jesus, brother."

"Hey, there you go!" responded Brant, clapping his hands in sarcasm. "Go with that!"

The preacher shook his head and once again turned his attention to the passing students. "I was twenty-four and was living like a king! I took drugs every day."

"What are you on right now?" shouted Brant, laughing to himself.

"Right," said the preacher. He hopped down off the wall and marched towards Brant. "Mate, if you want to talk with me about Jesus, I'd love to oblige. But if not, I'll kindly ask you to bugger off!"

"Uh…bugger off?" asked Brant. "Speak English, pal. This is America."

The young man blinked deliberately and shook his head. "All right, then. How's this: Clear off! Leave! Get lost! Is that *American* enough for you? Or should I dumb it down a bit more?"

Jon inserted himself between Brant and the young preacher. "Hey, look, we're sorry to bother you. We're out trying to witness to people, too. Just in a different way."

The preacher stepped back and looked at Jon. "And what way might that be then, Yank? Goin' round interfering with a man whilst he's testifying for the Lord?"

"I was just trying to help you," said Brant.

"Help?" asked the young man. "Why are you doing the devil's work, then? I'm trying to reach this lot for Christ!"

"So are we," insisted Jon.

"We just think you're going about it the wrong way, is all," added Brant.

Jon shook his head at the young man, disavowing himself from Brant's opinion.

"Oh, I am, am I?" asked the preacher. "And you're some sort of expert, I suppose?"

"I didn't say that," said Brant.

"Right. Well, in that case, why don't you belt up and let me go on, then? I'm trying to serve the Almighty."

"That's funny," said Brant. "All I hear is you bragging about what a big sinner you were."

Jon tried intervening again, hoping to end the debate. "Brant, if you'd just—"

"I'm trying to explain," interrupted the preacher, keeping his focus on Brant, "what a sorry sod I was before I came to know the Lord. If you'd let me finish you'd have known that by now."

"But all these kids walking by don't need to hear that," argued Brant.

"I beg to differ, mate." The preacher crossed his arms over his chest. "I believe they do."

"Whatever," said Brant. "I just don't think making yourself out to be a scumbag is going to save anyone. I'm just saying."

The young man leaned forward, waiting for Brant to continue. "You're just saying what, then?"

"What I just said," answered Brant.

The young man looked at Jon for help.

"I know," said Jon, shrugging his shoulders in empathy. "I don't get that either."

"You see my point, don't you, mate?" the preacher asked Jon. "They need to know the before *and* after, yeah?"

Brant answered before Jon could respond. "Just tell them the *after!* All they're going to remember so far is that you had sex with prostitutes in Iran."

"Iraq!" said the young man.

"Same difference," said Brant. "Just get to what matters is all I'm saying."

The preacher stepped slowly back and pointed both arms towards the fountain. "All right, show me how it's done, then."

"What?" asked Brant, taking a step backward.

"Come on, now. Up you go. Let's see you have a go at it."

"Hey, man, you're the street preacher, not me," said Brant, waving his hands.

"No, I insist, mate. You're the one waffling on about what to say to these American kids. Show me how it's done here in the States."

Jon's initial embarrassment over Brant's boorish behavior had faded. He now found himself enjoying the debate and the preacher's challenge to Brant.

"Go ahead, Brant," he said, suppressing a grin as he nodded towards the fountain. "Show him how it's done."

Brant glared at Jon and then back at the young preacher. "Fine," he said. "Watch and learn." Brant passed between Jon and the young man, muttering something under his breath as he climbed up onto the fountain wall. After making sure of his footing with the fountain behind him, he stood straight and glanced over at Jon. Jon smiled and gave him a slight nod of confidence. Brant turned his attention to the passing students. As he surveyed the activity on the quad, his body slowly became motionless, as still as the bronze statues standing behind him in the water.

While Jon waited patiently for Brant to say something, he turned to the young man. "So, what's your name?" he asked.

"Liam. What's his?" Liam nodded towards Brant, who had yet to open his mouth.

Jon felt mildly slighted by Liam's interest in Brant. "That's Brant. And I'm Jon."

"Chum of yours, is he?"

"Yeah," said Jon, reluctantly. "He's a good guy. He's just…in a mood this morning for some reason."

Brant repositioned his feet and moved himself back and forth on the fountain wall as he continued to look out over the quad. Passing students gave little notice to his presence. He took a deep breath and finally began to speak. "What my British friend here was trying to say," he said in a modest voice, "is that God loves you."

"I can't hear you, mate!" shouted Liam, cupping his hands around his mouth.

Brant glanced at Jon and cleared his throat. "God loves you!" he said in a much louder voice. "And he wants you to know that. God loves you so much he gave his only Son, Jesus, to die for you. He died, so that you can live in heaven when you die if you put your faith and trust in him. My friend and I will be right over here if you want to talk with us about that." Brant stepped down quickly and walked towards Jon.

Liam breezed by Brant without acknowledgement and reassumed his place on the fountain. He wasted no time in continuing his message. "Friends, Jesus died for you! And only Jesus can save you from your sins! Romans 6:23

says, 'For the wages of sin is death; but the gift of God is eternal life through Jesus Christ our Lord.'"

Jon noticed Liam spoke louder and with more energy than he had prior to his exchange with Brant.

"God wants a relationship with you so bad he gave up his only Son to make a way for you. John 3:16 says, 'For God so loved the world that he gave his only begotten Son, that whosoever believeth in him should not perish, but have everlasting life.' Jesus can save you from your sin and give you eternal life with Almighty God. You can trust him to save you if you put your faith in him today! If you accept Christ as your Savior, right here today, you'll never have to worry about your eternal address. You won't have to worry about going to hell. Jesus said, 'And I give unto them eternal life; and they shall never perish, neither shall any man pluck them out of my hand.' You're safe if you know the resurrected Lord! Friends, I want you to know the joy Christ has given me in my life. I want that same joy for you! Come and talk with me and my American friends, here. Let us show you how you can receive a new life in Jesus Christ. We'll be right over here."

Liam hopped off the wall and approached Brant. "Was that more of what you had in mind, brother?"

Brant smiled, humbly, and extended his hand. "That was perfect," he said, taking hold of Liam's hand and shaking it twice. "I'm sorry I gave you a hard time. That's a lot harder than I thought."

"Excuse me," said a girl appearing behind Liam. Dressed in what Jon surmised to be standard attire for FSU coeds – gym shorts, sorority T-shirt, and flip-flops – the girl shook her long brown bangs away from her eyes as Liam turned to face her. "I have a question," she said.

"Sure, love," said Liam, clasping his hands behind his back as he prepared to listen.

"Um, I really like your accent," said the girl. Her slightly hoarse voice and subdued tone made her compliment sound obligatory.

"That's not a question, now, is it?" asked Liam with a friendly grin.

"No," she said, flashing a soft smile that twitched with nervousness. "Um, it's just that…I was wondering how you can say that Jesus is the only way to heaven. What about all the other religions in the world? Are you saying they're all wrong? That everyone else is going to hell?"

"Is that what you're worried about, love?" asked Liam. "All the other religions?"

The girl shifted a step to her left, pointing her face into the slight breeze and letting it push the hair from her eyes. "No, um…I'm just saying I don't know how you can say Jesus is the only way to heaven. That seems pretty close-minded and intolerant of other people's beliefs. We're not supposed to be like that. I mean, how can you say who's right and who's wrong?"

"You're saying I'm a bit blinkered, am I?" asked Liam, rubbing his chin. "That's fair, I suppose. What's your name, love?"

"Brooke."

"Brooke, I'm Liam. And this is Brant and…."

"Jon," said Jon, again feeling snubbed.

"Hi," she said, glancing at Jon and Brant, before returning her attention to Liam.

"Brooke," said Liam, "what is it that really bothers you about Jesus being the only way to know God?"

"I just told you," she said, sounding more confident. "It's closed minded, bigoted, and intolerant. It may offend someone."

"That, it will," said Liam, unbothered by her concern. "Does it offend *you?*"

"Me, personally? Not really, I guess. I just don't understand why you'd want to offend people of different beliefs. Doesn't that hurt your message?"

"That's kind of you to worry about my message," said Liam. "But do you usually go around representing other people's feelings and beliefs?"

"I'm not trying to speak for everyone," said Brooke. "I just—"

"Well, speak for yourself, then," said Liam. "Tell me what *you* believe."

Brooke lifted her eyebrows over her wide hazel eyes. "What do *I* believe?"

"That's right," said Liam, wearing a disarming smile.

Brooke glanced at Jon and Brant as if they might know something that could help with her answer. "Well," she said, looking back at Liam, "I guess I really don't know *what* I believe."

"All right, then. Let's start with God," said Liam. "Do you believe in the Almighty?"

"I guess I believe there might be something out there, you know."

"Like what?"

"I don't know…some higher power, maybe."

"How do you know that?" asked Liam.

"I don't know. Mysteries of the world, stuff like that. Like, how did all this get here?"

"That's funny you say that. The first chapter of Romans tells us that God has made his eternal power and divine nature clearly visible in creation so that all people are without excuse. That means his presence should be obvious to everyone. You just proved that verse."

"OK, so?" asked Brooke, shrugging her shoulders.

"I'm just making sure, love, that you don't think aliens put us here or something off like that."

"No, of course not," said Brooke.

"So, can we say you believe in God, then?"

Brooke took a half step back and dragged the toe of her flip-flop across the brick pavement. "Yeah, I guess you could say that."

"And you believe he made us and all that we see?"

"I guess so. Sure. But that still doesn't change my question."

"Right. Your Jesus question," said Liam, tapping his chin with his finger. "But first, let me ask – if you were God and you made us, would you care about us?"

"Well, sure I would," said Brooke, enjoying the easy question. "If I made you I would have to care about you. And I wouldn't send you to hell, either. That's my point."

"Do you think God sends people to hell?" asked Liam.

"No, that's what *you* were saying. I'm not saying that. I think God is fair to everyone."

Liam's toothy smile pushed his cheeks higher on his face. He seemed to be enjoying his spiritual chess match with Brooke. "We'll come back to hell in a minute," he said. "But we can agree that God cares about what he's made, yeah?"

"Yeah, OK."

"The Good Book says that God loves us and wants us to know him. But we've created a barrier that keeps us from having a relationship with him. It's called sin. The Bible says God hates sin. He won't look on it. What do you think of when you hear the word sin?"

"TV preachers," said Brooke, making a sour face. "They're always, like, calling us sinners and wanting our money."

"Sounds like you watch them a lot," said Brant.

"No. God, no," said Brooke, shaking her bangs back into her face. "Never. I just...you know, everybody knows what they're like." She turned her head and let the breeze manage her hair again.

"Well, they are right about one thing," said Liam. "We're all sinners. Do you think you've sinned, love?"

"I guess," said Brooke. "But no one's perfect."

"Precisely," said Liam. "The Bible says we've all sinned. And Romans 6:23 says the wages of sin is death. That's what we deserve. That's the bad news."

"What's the good news?" asked Brooke.

"The good news is that God loves us so much he made a way for us to be forgiven of our sins. Jesus took the punishment we all deserve."

"But—"

"Not yet," said Liam, silencing Brooke with his index finger. "First, play along with me for a bit."

Brooke settled back on her heels and crossed her arms. "Fine. Go ahead."

"All right, let's say I was dying of cancer and there was a procedure where all my cancer cells could be transferred to another person. And you volunteered to be that person for me. What would happen to me if they took all my cancer and put it in your body?"

"If they put *your* cancer in *my* body?"

"Right. What would happen to ol' Liam?"

"I guess you'd live," said Brooke. "Because you wouldn't have cancer anymore."

"And what would happen to you?"

"Well, I would have your cancer, right? So...I'd die."

"Tell me, Brooke, is there anyone you would do that for?"

"Anyone I would die for?" Brooke dropped her rigid pose and ran her hands through the sides of her hair, resetting the clip on the back of her head.

"Yeah," said Liam. "What would it take for you to do that for someone?"

Brooke glanced across the quad towards Collegiate Loop. "I guess I would have to really, *really* love them," she said.

"Spot on," said Liam. "And that's what Jesus did for us on the Cross. He took our sin – our terminal, spiritual cancer – and put it on him. He died in our place. He took the punishment we deserve."

"Why would he do that?"

"You just said it, yourself," said Liam. "Because he loves you. The Gospel of John, 3:16, says—"

"I know," said Brooke, "God gave his one and only Son, yada, yada…."

"That whosoever believeth in him," said Liam, "should not perish, but have everlasting life."

"Everybody's heard that," she said.

"Right. So, the question now is, do you believe it? It's a gift, Brooke. And God's waiting for you to receive it."

Brooke crossed her arms and looked down at her red painted toenails. "But I just don't know if it's right to say that if I believe in Jesus I'm saved from hell, but everyone else isn't." She looked up at Liam. "Why would a loving God do that? Why would he save me and send other people to hell? It just doesn't seem fair to me."

"Hmm. There's that word again," said Liam.

"What word?"

"What year are you here, love?" asked Liam, skipping past the answer to her question.

"I'm a junior. Why?"

"Smashing. Do you have a favorite professor since you've been here?"

"Sure. Dr. Gunderson."

"And what does the good doctor teach?"

"I had him for Film Theory."

"Film theory? What do you read?" asked Liam.

"What do I *read*?" repeated Brooke. "I'm not sure what you're asking."

Liam laughed at himself. "Sorry, I'm still learning to speak American," he said, winking at Brant. "What's your *major*, love?"

"Oh. I'm getting a BFA in Animation and Digital Arts."

"That's cool!" said Jon. "That wasn't even a degree when I was in college."

"Right," said Liam, cutting his eyes at Jon.

Jon suddenly understood how it felt to receive the same dismissive glance he was used to giving Brant.

"So," said Liam, "do you think Dr. Gunderson wants everyone in his class to get an A?"

"I'm sure he'd probably like that. He's really nice. But it would never happen."

"Why not?" asked Liam.

"Because not everyone will do the work or go to class all the time. Some people are just slack."

"But why doesn't Dr. Gunderson just *make* them do the work and go to class if he wants them to get an A?"

"That's not how it works. He can't *make* them do anything."

"So, the students have a choice whether they want to do the work or not," said Liam.

"Right."

"I'm guessing you got an A in his class," said Jon.

"Yep," said Brooke, proudly. "He said I was one of his favorite students."

"So, how would you feel, then," asked Liam, "if at the end of the semester, Dr. Gunderson decided to give everyone an A whether they did the work or not. Or even showed up for class?"

"That wouldn't be fair," said Brooke.

"*That's* the word we were looking for," said Liam, channeling Sherlock Holmes. "Why would it not be fair?"

"Because I earned my grade. I did the work. I deserved my A."

"So you're fine with him giving some people a failing grade, then?" asked Liam.

"If they didn't do what they were supposed to do, sure. They deserve it. That's not on Dr. Gunderson. If they fail, that's on them."

"I see," said Liam. "And you like Dr. Gunderson, yeah?"

"I do, yeah."

"And you think he's fair?" asked Liam.

Brooke paused momentarily and studied the grin growing on Liam's face. "OK, you kind of trapped me there, didn't you?"

"Smart girl," said Liam. "All right, then. Finish the thought for me."

Brooke reached in the pocket of her gym shorts and pulled out a white iPhone. She checked the time and slid it back into her pocket. She refocused her eyes on Liam. "You're saying that God wants everyone to get an A – I mean, go to heaven – but it's up to us to earn it. And if we don't, we deserve what we get. We deserve to go to hell."

"Not quite," said Liam. "Do you think you can earn your way to heaven?"

"Well, I can try and be a good person," said Brooke. "I like to help people. I do volunteer work with my sorority. Last week we made gift baskets and gave them to a nursing home."

"Terrific," said Liam. "You've convinced me you're a good person, Brooke. But how will you know if you've done enough to convince God?"

"Well, I don't, I guess," she said.

"You won't," said Liam. "But it doesn't matter, anyway. Romans 5:8 says that while we were still sinners, Jesus died for us. You don't need to clean yourself up or earn your way to heaven. Jesus died for everyone just like they are. God's love is unconditional. You just have to accept his gift in Jesus. Ephesians chapter two says it's by grace that we're saved through faith. It's not anything we can do to earn it. It's a gift from God."

"So, if I can't earn it, what do I have to do?" asked Brooke. "I'm confused."

"It's the answer to your question, Brooke," said Liam. "You have to put your faith in Jesus to save you. Everyone does."

Brooke eyed the street across the quad as she considered Liam's claim. "I don't know what that means, I guess."

"It starts with belief," said Liam. "You have to believe that Jesus is the Son of God, like he claimed to be, and that he died on the Cross for your sins and then rose from the grave to prove his deity and power over death."

"That's a lot to ask," said Brooke, beginning to appear anxious.

"Think about it carefully," said Liam. "We've got time."

"I don't," said Brooke, looking around at the emptying quad. "I'm late for class."

"What will happen if you miss it?" asked Brant.

"You don't want to miss your chance at salvation, Brooke," said Jon. "It'll change your life forever."

"That's what scares me," she said.

"Brooke, you have three blokes here who've all made the same decision you're faced with now," said Liam. "And we can all tell you, there's nothing to be afraid of. It's the best decision you'll ever make."

"And we're afraid of what will happen if you don't," said Brant.

Brooke's eyes darted back and forth between the three men. She dropped her gaze to the brick pavement beneath her feet. "I've got to go," she said, abruptly. She straightened her book bag on her shoulders and walked quickly around the fountain to a sidewalk leading off the quad towards Collegiate Loop.

The three men stood in silence as they watched Brooke leave the quad and hurry across the street.

"Bollocks!" said Liam, slapping his Bible against his hand.

"I thought she was going to make a decision," said Brant.

"I'm afraid she did," said Jon.

Liam picked up a maroon book bag resting against the side of the fountain. "Right. Well, I'm off," he said. "It's been a pleasure, mates." Liam quickly shook hands with Jon and Brant and turned to leave.

"That's it?" asked Jon, surprised at Liam's sudden departure. "You're leaving?"

"Late to class, myself," said Liam, setting off across the quad.

"You're a student here?" Brant called out.

"Grad school!" shouted Liam as he hurried away across the grass. "Cheers!"

Suddenly, unexpectedly, Jon found himself alone again with Brant. The mass of students rushing to class had cleared, leaving the spacious quad empty and quiet, but for the sound of water splashing into the fountain behind them.

"So, what now?" asked Brant, scratching the back of his head.

"I don't know," answered Jon.

forty four

Trust Issues

"As the heavens are higher than the earth, so are my ways higher
than your ways and my thoughts than your thoughts."
- Isaiah 55:9

"That's a football stadium?" asked Brant, looking up at two tall brick towers framing the eight-story brick façade of Doak Campbell Stadium. "It looks more like a cathedral."

"Well, they do worship their football around here," said Jon. "Have a seat." Jon sat down on a metal park bench facing a large monument of some kind, built in the middle of a concrete pathway leading towards the stadium. The square, gothic-style, brick structure featured four arches revealing a continuous waterfall within its center. Adorning the monument's top were three bronze torches pointing to the sky some twenty feet above its base.

"Why do we always end up at fountains?" asked Brant, sitting down next to Jon.

"Search me. I'm not writing this story. God is."

"So, God told you to come check out Florida State's football stadium?"

"Yes," said Jon, deciding to go with the joke. "Yes, he did. And he also said FSU should beat Florida by seven this weekend."

"Wow, that's quite a direct line you've got there with the Man upstairs," said Brant, playing along. "Maybe we should go place a few bets on the game. Win some cash for our trip."

"Nah, that would be cheating," said Jon, pretending to be serious. "Insider information, you know."

Brant and Jon sat quietly for a moment. Jon set his gaze on the water flowing inside the fountain and let his mind wander. He imagined the open plaza before him filled with excited FSU and Florida football fans filing into the stadium to see one of the biggest rivalry games in the country. At that moment, college football – something Jon had always enjoyed with a passion – seemed so unimportant to him. And the realization made him feel like a stranger in his own body.

"Seriously, Jon," said Brant, snapping Jon out of his daydream, "you've been walking around like a zombie since we talked with Brooke and Liam forty minutes ago. And now we end up at an empty football stadium. What are we doing over here?"

Jon turned his head to look at Brant. "Honestly? I have no idea."

"Well, that's comforting," said Brant. "What happened to you leading the charge across campus to save everyone? Wasn't that you a little while ago?"

"Yeah, I suppose," said Jon, wishing the description still fit. "I just need a moment to regroup, I guess."

"From what? Brooke blowing us off?"

"No, it's not just that. I mean, yeah, that was disappointing when she walked off, but that was Liam's deal. I was just a spectator."

"So, what is it?"

Jon looked up at the Spanish moss swaying gently in the breeze as it hung from a large oak tree to his left. "I feel like…I feel like every time I'm really sure God is giving me a vision for something, it never turns out like I think it's supposed to."

"Like what?"

"Well, like Liam, today. When I saw what he was doing over there on the quad, being bold and preaching to all the students walking by. And then trying to lead that girl—"

"Brooke," said Brant.

"Right, Brooke. I was so sure that God had led us here to work with him, the three of us, you know? That would have been awesome. Think about it. He's young and on fire for Christ."

"And he's got that cool British accent," said Brant.

"Yeah. I mean we could have really reached some of these kids around here. And I'm thinking, 'Wow, God! Thanks for leading us to Liam! This is gonna be great!' But then Liam just takes off. Gone. *Cheers, mates!*" Jon shook his head. "I just don't get it. I mean, I believe God has a purpose for what we're doing and the decisions we're making. But sometimes…I just can't see it. It's so frustrating."

"Then you need to turn around," said Brant.

"Is that supposed to be some kind of deep advice or something?"

"No, it means, look behind you." Brant pointed his index finger subtly past Jon.

Jon turned to his right and saw Brooke approaching just a few feet away.

"Hi," she said, stopping in front of their bench.

Jon felt a chill run through his body. "Hey, Brooke."

"You remembered my name," she said, smiling.

"Of course," said Jon, thankful for Brant's reminder.

"He's really good with names," deadpanned Brant.

Jon gave Brant a look. "Very funny," he said, turning to Brooke. "So, what brings you over to the football stadium?"

"Oh, the Film School is in that building right there," she said, pointing to one of the two four-story brick buildings attached to either end of the stadium. "I just got out of class."

"So you made it, after all?"

"Yeah. I was pretty late, but that's OK. Is the British guy still around?"

"He had to go to class, too," said Jon. "He's a grad student here."

"Oh, cool," she said, appearing unsure what to say or do next. "Oh, well. Maybe I'll see him around. Bye." Brooke began to leave.

"Is there something we can help you with?" asked Jon.

Brooke stopped and took two slow steps back towards them. "Oh, um…." She paused as she watched a group of students pass by. She slid her thumbs under the straps of the book bag hanging from her shoulders and seemed to wait until they were out of earshot before continuing. "It's just that…I was sitting in class and thinking about what we talked about earlier – about God and heaven and everything – and I was hoping to talk to that guy again."

"I think we can help you," said Jon. "What do you want to know?"

"What happened to your arm?" she asked, looking down at Jon's left arm resting in his sling.

"Long story," said Jon.

"He hurt it saving a woman from a burning car," said Brant.

"Wow, really?" she asked, sounding impressed.

"Yeah, but it's fine," said Jon, slightly embarrassed by Brant's boast on his behalf. "Tell me what you were thinking about in class."

"Oh, um, I guess…I guess I want to know how I can be sure I'm going to heaven. I mean, I understand what he said about not earning it. I got that. But I don't understand what I need to do, otherwise. I don't even remember all the stuff he told me I had to believe."

"I bet you remember more than you think," said Jon. "Give it a shot."

"OK, well…he said I have to believe in Jesus. And that he was God's Son. And that he died on a cross for me, which I don't really get that part, but…oh, and that he came back to life."

"That about covers it," said Jon. "Do you believe all that?"

"I think I want to," said Brooke. "I just don't know how to be sure it's true."

"There's very little in this life you can be one-hundred percent sure of, Brooke," said Jon. "We just have to take some things on faith."

"But I like to know things for sure. I can't go around just believing anything people say. Where would that get me?"

"No place you'd want to be, I can assure you," said Jon.

"He means hell," said Brant.

"Oh," said Brooke, her eyes showing new concern as she looked down at Jon. "Is that where you think I'm going?"

Jon wanted to kick Brant. "It doesn't matter what I think, Brooke. It matters what God thinks. But I understand that you need confidence in what you choose to believe, right?"

"Right," said Brooke. "So why should I believe what that guy said about God and Jesus? Why should I just take his word for it?"

"OK, well, let me ask you," said Jon as an analogy came to his mind. "Have you ever been to Russia?"

"Russia? No. Why?"

"Are you sure it's there?" asked Jon.

Brooke laughed. "Of course, I'm sure."

"How do you know, if you haven't been there?"

"Well, I've read about it and seen it in pictures and movies and stuff. I mean...it's Russia."

"So you're relying on the experiences of other people who have been there, right?" asked Jon.

"I guess you could say it like that, sure."

"Well, this is no different," said Jon. "The Bible is full of stories from people who had direct experiences with God. I've read about Jesus and the promises God makes to people who have faith in him. And I know that what it says is true because I've experienced it in my own life. Liam, the British guy, and Brant can both tell you the same thing. They've experienced the love of God personally through faith in Jesus Christ. We couldn't deny his existence and power to change our lives any more than a Russian could deny Moscow exists. That's why we're out telling people about it. If you don't want to take our word for it, read the Bible for yourself. Start with the Gospel of John."

"I don't have a Bible," said Brooke.

"Download the app on your iPhone," said Brant. "You'll have a Bible in about thirty seconds."

Brooke looked at Jon, studying him for a moment. "Is it all that real to you?"

"It is," said Jon. "And when you see the truth in what we're saying, you'll feel the same way, too. But you have to experience it for yourself, first."

"Brooke, giving my life to Jesus saved my life, literally," said Brant. "I wouldn't be sitting here today if it weren't for him. I was a total mess, but he healed me. It's like night and day. It's that real."

"We're not trying to sell you anything, Brooke," said Jon. "It's your choice to accept what we're saying or not. God gave us a free will to choose. But he wants you to know him and experience his love in your life just like we have. The Bible says that God 'wants all people to be saved and to come to a knowledge of the truth.' That's what he wants for you."

Brooke took a step back and looked at the campus around her. "I just...." She stopped herself and looked down at her feet as she rubbed the rubber soles of her flip-flops against the concrete.

Jon sat quietly, giving her time to work through it.

Brooke took a deep breath and exhaled. "I want to believe," she said, still looking down as she shook her head. "I don't know what that means in the big scheme of everything…but, I do." Brooke looked up at Jon and smiled. "I believe it."

"That's good, Brooke," said Jon. "But understand that belief is just the first step."

Her smile faded. "There's more? What do you mean?"

"Receiving salvation through Christ requires faith, not just belief. In the Book of Ephesians it says, 'For it's by grace you've been saved, through faith – and it's not from yourself, it's the gift of God – not by works, so that no one can boast.' What that means is God does the saving. But we have to come to him in faith, not just belief."

A crease formed between Brooke's full eyebrows. "I don't understand the difference."

"Belief is just agreeing with something intellectually," said Jon. "It's passive. It doesn't require anything of you. Faith means you put your trust and confidence in what you believe. And that leads to action."

"It still sounds kind of the same to me," she said.

"OK," said Jon, looking around for an illustration. He saw another park bench across the sidewalk from them. "Do you believe there's a bench over there?"

Brooke turned and looked behind her at the empty bench. She then cast a smirk at Jon. "Is this another Russia thing? Because—"

"She's on to you, Jon," laughed Brant.

"I see that," said Jon. "Brooke, just stick with me for just a minute on this. I promise there's a point to it."

"All right," said Brooke. She looked dutifully at the bench. "Yes, I believe there's a bench over there. Now what?"

"Do you believe if you sat on it, that it would hold you up?"

"Sure. You guys are sitting on one just like it."

"True, but don't you want to contact the manufacturer to see how it was built or find out the maximum weight it will support or anything like that? You said you like to know things for sure."

"I do, but the fact that you're sitting on one exactly like it is proof enough for me."

"So, you're willing to put your full weight on that bench and trust that it will hold you up without you having to do anything?"

"Sure. So, what's the point?"

"That's faith," said Jon.

Brooke looked over at the empty bench. Jon gave her a moment to consider what she'd heard. He looked at Brant and winked, hoping he would stay quiet, as well.

"I think I see what you're saying," said Brooke, looking back at Jon.

"Just remember that belief doesn't require anything of you, Brooke," said Jon. "But faith does. It requires trust. Like sitting on that bench. When you put your faith in Jesus, you're putting this life and your eternal life in his hands, and you're making yourself dependent on him. You're trusting that he's the only way to be forgiven of your sins and to know God. And you're trusting him to save you through no effort of your own. And he will."

"That's how to be sure you'll go to heaven, Brooke," said Brant. "Jesus really is the only way."

Brooke nodded her head. "OK. I get it, now. I fully do."

"So, I have to ask you," said Jon, seizing the moment, "would you like to put your faith in Jesus to save you?"

Brooke hesitated before answering. "I don't know," she said, looking back towards campus.

Jon watched her carefully. A subtle frown appeared on Brooke's face as a decision wavered in her mind. He decided to give the issue a gentle shove. "What do you think's holding you back, Brooke?"

She dropped her gaze down to her feet and shook her head. "It's just kind of scary, you know? I mean…this is all so crazy. My day wasn't supposed to go like this."

Jon smiled knowingly at Brooke's disagreement with fate. He'd felt the same way just twenty minutes before, wondering why reality failed to cooperate with his plans. But now, he could see God's hand in their chance meeting by the football stadium. "Maybe it was supposed to go like this, Brooke," he said. "Only one way to really know for sure. Just say yes."

Brooke lifted her head; her eyes met Jon's. His heart pounded in his chest. He'd just thrown a Hail Mary pass towards the end zone and held his breath as it spiraled towards an uncertain fate.

Brooke's dark eyebrows floated upwards as she held her gaze. "OK," she said, plainly. "What do I need to do?"

Jon fought off the impulse to throw his hands in the air and celebrate. "You need to pray and tell God what you've just decided," he said, calmly, "that you're putting your faith and trust in Jesus. He'll hear you and save you. I can lead you in that prayer right now, if you like."

"Right here?" asked Brooke, glancing around at several students passing by. "Shouldn't we go somewhere private? Like a church or something?"

"When you joined your sorority, were there other people around?" asked Jon.

"Yeah, but—"

"And you wear your sorority letters on your shirt for everyone to see," said Jon, pointing at her light blue T-shirt with white Greek letters across the front.

"And on your book bag," added Brant, "and on your hair thing and—"

"I get it," said Brooke, narrowing her eyes playfully at Brant.

"Jesus said if you acknowledge him publicly, he'll acknowledge you before God," said Jon.

"That's in the Bible?" she asked.

"The Gospel of Matthew chapter ten, verse thirty-two," said Brant.

Jon turned his head towards Brant with surprise.

Brant shrugged his shoulders. "I've been reading."

"OK," said Brooke. "I'd like to pray, if you'll help me."

"Absolutely," said Jon. "Brant, could you let Brooke sit down for a minute?"

"Sure," said Brant, hopping up from the bench.

Brooke sat down next to Jon, dropping her book bag at her feet. "I can't believe I'm doing this," she said.

"Are you sure you want to?" asked Jon. "Because—"

"I'm sure, I'm sure."

"OK, then. We're just going to bow our heads and close our eyes for a minute. And I'm going to pray and you just repeat after me, OK?"

"I'm a little nervous," said Brooke as she waved to two girls passing by.

"Don't worry about anyone else. Just focus on telling God what's in your heart as we pray."

"OK," said Brooke.

"Here we go," said Jon, bowing his head to pray. "Dear God in heaven, I admit that I don't understand everything there is to know about you. But I come to you now, a sinner, by faith. I trust that you love me and I trust that your Son, Jesus, died for me. And I trust him to forgive me, to make me new, and clean in your sight. I put my eternal soul in Jesus' hands, Lord. And I trust him to bring me home to you when I die. I invite Jesus into my life now. And I commit myself to studying your Word and following him the rest of my life. Thank you for loving me. Thank you for saving me. In Jesus' name I pray. Amen."

Jon opened his eyes, guarding his left arm from an expected hug of gratitude from Brooke.

"Thank you," she said simply as she stood up from the bench. She picked up her book bag and swung it onto her right shoulder.

"You're welcome," said Jon, searching Brooke's face. He tried to reconcile her dispassionate response with the life changing significance of her decision. The lack of any emotion on Brooke's face or in her eyes made Jon wonder if she really meant what they had just prayed. Maybe he had done something wrong.

"Can you wait right here for about ten minutes?" asked Brooke. "I want to go get my roommate. She needs to hear this, too."

Jon's eyebrows pushed upwards on his forehead and his mouth dropped open. "I'd be happy to," he said, his mind trying to grasp what was happening.

"Awesome. Be right back." She turned and began to walk quickly away. After just a few steps, she broke into a jog as she rolled her book bag off her shoulder and tucked it under her arm. "Don't go anywhere!" she called back to Jon and Brant.

"We won't!" shouted Brant as he methodically retook his seat on the bench next to Jon. "Well, Jonny-boy," he said, casually. "Ready to admit that God might know what he's doing, after all?"

Jon smiled through a sense of humbled amazement. "I think I need a little more of that trust thing I was just telling Brooke about."

Brant laughed. "Physician, heal thyself."

"That's from the Gospel of Luke. You *have* been reading haven't you?"

"I've been reading the Gospels after you go to sleep every night. Trying to get to know Jesus."

"That's great, Brant," said Jon, leaning back against the bench. He crossed his legs and rested his hands on his lap, loosely interlocking his fingers. As he looked up at the water flowing down from the top of the brick monument, spilling onto the pavement below, Jon felt renewed. God was in control. And it felt good.

"Oh, incidentally," Jon said, turning to Brant, "are you ready to tell me what Kim said in her text this morning? I'm guessing that's what caused you to take out your frustrations on poor Liam."

"Oh, yeah," said Brant, producing an immediate frown. "I'm sorry about that. It's just that…she said she doesn't want Jacob spending Christmas at my apartment. I was supposed to have him for Thanksgiving, but I couldn't because of our trip. So we agreed to switch. But now she says it's not safe where I live, and she doesn't want him waking up on Christmas morning in an apartment with no furniture."

"But he's been to your place before, hasn't he?"

"Yeah, but the last time he was there, something was going on in the parking lot – a fight or argument or something – and I think he told his mom about all the police cars."

"Oh," said Jon, imagining her reaction. "That'll do it."

"Yeah."

"Does she know we're only going to be home a few days? When are you going to see him?"

"I don't know. That's the problem."

Jon could see the hurt and disappointment in Brant's face. And while he'd been looking forward to enjoying a short break from Brant during their trip home for Christmas, he couldn't let his friend suffer through Christmas alone. "Actually, I don't think it's a problem, Brant."

"Well, not for you, it's not," said Brant. "But unless Santa really does exist and he's bringing me a new furnished condo in a nice neighborhood, I'm not going to see my son this Christmas. And that just sucks."

"Brant, text Kim and tell her that you and Jacob are spending Christmas at my house. And if she has any questions, she can call me."

"Seriously? You'd do that for me?"

"Absolutely. We'd love to have you and Jacob. You can meet Holly and see my mom again. Although, I'm not sure she'll remember you."

"Oh, man! That sounds great, Jon."

"Awesome. It's settled, then."

"But I know Kim will want to pull up your house on Google Maps to make sure you don't live in a slum or a barn or something."

Jon laughed. "That's fine. You can send her my address. I just hope the grass was cut when they took my street level picture."

"I really appreciate it, Jon. That's huge."

"Glad to do it, Brant." Jon's eyes refocused on a group of students walking towards them in the distance behind Brant. He leaned forward on the bench to get a better view. "Oh, my gosh," he said.

"What?" asked Brant, turning around. "Whoa."

Across the parking lot adjacent to the stadium, Brooke was leading a group of four girls and two boys back towards them. Smiling as she came, she waved her hand over her head at Jon and Brant.

"Jon?" asked Brant.

Jon smiled in stunned amazement as he retuned Brooke's wave. "Yeah?"

"You say God told you to come over to the football stadium today?" asked Brant, reviving their joke as he watching the seven students approach.

"Yep," said Jon, playing along.

"And how much did he say FSU would win by on Saturday?"

"Seven," said Jon, beginning to laugh as he counted the students.

"I'd call that a sure thing," said Brant.

forty five

Dear Amy

"Do not arouse or awaken love until it so desires."

- Song of Songs 2:7

December 18

Dear Amy,

   Surprise! When was the last time you got a real letter in the mail? I'm guessing not since you and I used to write back and forth when we were in high school! Thanks for the card you sent me! It came after I left, but Holly read it to me and sent me a picture of it on my iPhone. Pretty funny! Thanks for your prayers!

   I know you're probably wondering why I haven't been on Facebook or anything since we chatted online back in September. I've had to force myself to disconnect from everything (Facebook, the news, the internet, etc.) so I could focus on what I'm doing out here and avoid everyday distractions. One of the biggest distractions is simply the thought of my "normal" life back home. I've had to redefine what normal is for me over these last couple of months. And I decided that posting my experiences on Facebook just to see who "likes" them would make what I'm doing seem kind of trivial. Besides, as long as God "likes" what I'm doing, that's enough for me. So I've been off the grid, so to speak. But that doesn't mean I haven't thought about my old friend! I can't wait to take you up on your offer for dinner and church when I get back. I'm really looking forward to seeing you again and catching up on the last twenty-five years. Whoops! I forgot – no counting years, right?!

315

The trip has been a bit of an adventure so far. Kind of crazy, actually. I've really had to pray for God to keep giving me a love for people. The kind of love that makes me care about where they spend eternity. But it's not easy sometimes. People can be so rude, even when you're trying to share the love of Christ with them. We got kicked out of a Waffle House by an angry waitress in Savannah and then we almost got arrested in Baton Rouge for "conspiracy to start a riot!" That's what one of the officers said, anyway. (Long story. I'll save that one for our dinner at Frank's.) I just keep telling myself that God loves everyone. I don't know how or why he does sometimes, but he does! I guess if he can love me, he can love anybody, right?

I just hope that what we're doing is making a difference for Christ. I've had my moments of doubt and discouragement, usually when I'm lying awake at night rethinking everything. I miss being home, too. Last night I was dreaming that I was in my own bed back home on a Saturday morning, and I could smell pancakes cooking in the kitchen (I guess my dog was making breakfast!). When I opened my eyes and saw that I was actually sleeping in my car in a rest stop in Louisiana, it was pretty disappointing. But I know God wants me to be right where I am. All this is just hard sometimes. Even harder than I thought it would be. Particularly after I hurt my arm. I got a pretty deep cut helping a lady from her truck after an accident. I had to have a lot of stitches inside and out, and it was really painful for a while. It's a lot better now, though. It's not fun to be on the road when things like that happen! But I know I can't give up on what God's called me to do. Especially with Brant along. I feel like I have to be a strong example for him. He's my age, but he's so young in his faith. But he's so bold and direct when we witness to people! Sometimes that's created problems, but other times I find myself wishing I could be more like him (I would never admit that to him!). But I do feel a huge sense of responsibility for him.

Oh gosh — I just realized you don't know who Brant is, do you? He's an old friend of mine from college who recently accepted Christ and reconnected with me at my church. He kind of asked his way into going with me at the last minute and I said yes. Why, I don't know! I was supposed to do this on my own. That's what God called me to do and I've kicked myself a few times for letting Brant come along. He can really be a pain sometimes. And he snores really loud! (We're staying in a hotel tonight and he's asleep in the bed next to mine right now.) We're just a little bit different (sarcasm there) and I've been kind of hard on him a few times. But maybe God's got a reason for why he's out here with me. I don't know. I need to give that some more thought in prayer, I guess.

Anyway, the important thing is that we've seen a few people come to faith! That's been really exciting! To feel like God is using you to share the Gospel with someone and then to see them saved right in front of you is just the most amazing, satisfying experience ever. It feels like I'm doing what I was created for. I don't know how else to explain it. At that moment when someone accepts Christ, life just makes sense to me. It's like nothing else matters. It's just amazing. And we were blessed to experience that on the very first day of our trip! The first two people we talked to in Charleston accepted Christ! Can you believe that?! I think that's really helped us stay motivated when things haven't gone so well. And that's been a lot of the time, unfortunately. But I'm so thankful that God has used us to reach the people we did in SC and Florida and Mississippi. And I'm praying he has more in store for us in Texas and on out West!

Writing this reminds me of all those letters we used to write back when we were kids. I still have all yours, you know! I found them in a shoebox in my parent's attic when they sold their home and moved in with me years ago. I'm hoping you threw my letters away as soon as you read them! Heaven knows what an idiot I was back then. I would hate to see what I wrote! But your letters always helped me get through the school year. I remember thinking that September through May was just time spent waiting until I could get back to the beach again. And see you, of course!

I hope this letter finds you and your family well and that you haven't forgotten about me! I don't have an address for you to write me back, but I just wanted you to know how things were going so far. We're headed to Austin next. We're going to visit the stadium where Cam Parsons preached when I was saved watching him on TV. I can't wait! Then we're going to fly home for a few days to spend Christmas with Holly and my mom and then fly back out here and continue west to California, sharing Christ along the way. I hope you have a Merry Christmas and a happy New Year! Please keep us in your prayers. I hope to talk with you soon!

Love,

Jonny

P.S. I hope you can read my handwriting! I don't think I've written this much since college!

forty six

Jus Soli

"Consequently, you are no longer foreigners and strangers, but fellow citizens with God's people and also members of his household"
- *Ephesians 2:19*

Jon sat in the passenger seat of his car, studying the map on his iPhone. As he directed Brant across Austin towards the University of Texas baseball stadium, his excitement over visiting the place where Cam Parsons preached the night he accepted Christ was tinged with nagging guilt. He remembered lecturing Brant about the purpose for their trip the morning they left home. It was not going to be a sightseeing trip, nor was it about having fun. It was about serving God. And yet, here he was guiding Brant towards an otherwise meaningless destination, purely for his own enjoyment. They should be looking for opportunities to engage people, his conscience told him. But his deep desire to see the very place he had desperately longed to be that night twenty years earlier – when he watched people stream down the stadium aisles to begin a new life in Christ – pushed him forward. He hoped God would understand.

"Turn left after this Popeye's Chicken," said Jon, "before you get to the Taco Bell up there. That should be East Martin Luther King Jr., Boulevard."

"How about I just turn into the Popeye's Chicken, instead?"

"How about you tell your stomach to wait?"

"How about I punch that fresh scar on your arm and make you cry like a baby?"

"Wow," Jon laughed. "Are you that hungry?"

"Suppertime equals food, man," said Brant, tapping his hands on the steering wheel as he waited in the intersection to turn left. "What's so hard to get about that?"

"I get it, I get it. Let's just go to the stadium for a few minutes then we'll go somewhere, OK?" Jon shook his head as he watched the timer on the crosswalk count down towards zero. "You're like traveling with a goat."

"A goat that's gonna punch you in the arm if you don't give him something to eat."

"Nice. You're a real pal, Brant."

"I know, right? You're lucky you know me." Brant grinned as he turned through the intersection. "OK, we're on East MLK. Now what?"

"Just keep going straight and we should run right into it."

Brant drove them along the tree-lined four-lane boulevard past a variety of small businesses and industrial warehouses. Jon checked the map on his iPhone. They were getting close.

"Are you sure UT's baseball stadium is around here? This looks all industrial." Brant slowed the car as they bounced across two sets of railroad tracks. "It's not very collegiate looking."

"If you were heading into Columbia on Shop Road going to a football game at Carolina, this is exactly what you'd see. Warehouses, repair shops, all this stuff."

"Well, that's true, but still. Hey, look at that," said Brant, pointing at a yellow traffic sign suspended over the road. "We're entering a school zone. We must be getting close."

"We're looking for a college baseball stadium, Brant, not an elementary school playground."

"It was a joke, Jon. Remember those?"

"Just watch where you're going."

Brant leaned forward over the steering wheel and looked at the small houses lining both sides of the road. Most of the old clapboard homes were ready for Christmas with Santa-themed yard art, colored lights, and foil-wrapped front doors. "Now we're just in some old neighborhood. Are you sure this is the right street? I can't imagine a baseball stadium popping up in the middle of all these houses."

"Yes, I'm sure. It should be right up here. It's just before you pass over the interstate."

"Look at all these little one-story houses," said Brant. "I guess they haven't discovered stairs in Texas, yet."

Jon decided to make an attempt at humor. "Maybe they want to be close to the ground since they love their state so much. You know like, close to the dirt? Because it's Texas…."

"Was that a joke, Jon? I'm not sure, because, one – it wasn't funny. And two – it came out of your mouth."

"Are you saying I'm not funny?" asked Jon, watching for traffic around them. "Watch out for that truck."

"I'm saying you're not funny."

"What are you talking about? I'm funny."

"Jon, if you have to say you're funny, then you're not."

Jon couldn't help growing nervous about a pick-up truck swerving back and forth in the lane next to them. "Don't get too close to that guy. He's on his phone or something. And you might want to slow down."

"Take right now, for instance," said Brant. "I don't find you amusing at all."

Jon realized he was being slightly overbearing. "Sorry. I'm just better at driving than riding, I guess."

Brant covered his mouth and coughed. "*Control freak.*"

"I heard that," said Jon, looking at his phone.

"What? I didn't say anything."

"Uh-huh."

"I just coughed, that's all," said Brant, ginning. "It's this dang dry air out here."

"Yeah, right."

Brant looked to his left as he changed lanes. "Man, look at that cemetery over there. It's huge! That's the biggest cemetery I've ever seen. They must bury every dead person in Texas in there."

Jon leaned forward to see across the road as they continued past a large grass field dotted with stone grave markers and large shade trees. The cemetery seemed to stretch away from the road as far as Jon could see. "That is big. It looks like it goes way back there, too."

"And it just keeps coming," said Brant as they continued along. "I like walking around old cemeteries. You ever do that?"

"No," said Jon. "I figure I'll spend enough time in a cemetery after I die. Why would I want to walk around in one while I'm alive?"

"Now see, that was kind of funny, Jon. Maybe there's hope for you, yet."

"I told you."

Brant turned his attention back on the road in front of them. "Uh-oh," he said.

"What?" Jon looked out the windshield and answered his own question. "We're about to cross over I-35. We drove past the stadium."

"Are you sure we passed it?"

Jon turned around and looked out the rear window. "Yep. That was it back there. Turn around."

"Shoot. I have to go over the bridge first then I'll turn around. How did we miss a baseball stadium?"

"You and your amazing cemetery."

Brant drove across the wide overpass for the interstate and turned right on Red River Street, making a U-turn before turning left, back onto Martin Luther King, Jr. As they rode across the overpass, Jon could see the stadium on the left side of the road. A five-story building of sand-colored brick, brushed aluminum, and glass sat directly across from the cemetery that held their interest the first time by.

"UFCU Disch-Falk Field," said Brant, reading the large brushed aluminum letters that spanned the top corner of the stadium. "Some name. Is that it?"

"Pretty sure," said Jon, despite having some doubt.

"It doesn't look much like a baseball stadium," said Brant. "It looks like a nice office building or something. No wonder we missed it."

"That must be the back side of the stands behind home plate. Turn in here."

Brant steered the car into the empty stadium parking lot, pulling to a stop in a space near the back corner of left field. He turned off the car. Jon sat looking out the passenger window at the stadium trying to reconcile a twenty-year-old memory with the view his eyes were taking in.

"You want to get out?" asked Brant.

"Yeah, let's check it out," said Jon, unsure exactly what he hoped to see.

Brant followed behind Jon as they walked towards the fence surrounding the field. Jon stopped at a gate leading to a pedestrian concourse behind the third-base line seats and placed his hands around the green aluminum fence rails. Brant joined him as they looked out across the ball field.

"This looks brand new, Jon. Are you sure this is the same stadium?"

"It sure looks a lot different than what I remember from TV. Of course, that was twenty years ago. That field turf is obviously new. And I don't think all these seats along the third-base line were here. Shoot, I don't know. You're right. Everything looks new."

"Well, I'm sure they've done renovations since you saw it on TV. I mean, it's Texas. They light cigars with hundred dollar bills out here."

"No, they don't."

"I bet J.R. Ewing did," said Brant.

"OK, aside from rich, fictional, oil barrens on TV, no one does that." Jon dismissed Brant's distraction and focused on the field. He sighed and leaned his forehead against the gate. Simply standing outside the fence failed to satisfy the desire that drove him halfway across the country to see the stadium. Jon stepped back and eyed the top of the six-foot high fence. "Think you can climb this?" he asked.

"If I say no, will you drop whatever idea you have in your head right now?"

"I want to get inside," said Jon.

"No."

"Why not?"

"First of all," said Brant, "when I suggested we come here, I didn't mention anything about committing a felony, did I?"

"You said you wanted to get me on the field. Besides, trespassing's not a felony. It's a misdemeanor."

"It's a crime, Jon!"

"Not a real one. Come on, let's climb over."

"That's the second thing – have you seen me? I'm not exactly in fence hopping shape."

"No sweat. I'll help you. Come on."

Brant stood glaring at Jon, hands on his hips.

"We're not going to get in trouble," said Jon. "I promise."

Brant pointed to a white and red sign attached to the fence. "Jon, it says right there, *No trespassing. Violators will be prosecuted.* Prosecuted, Jon! I don't want to end up in some Texas prison."

"You say that like we're in some third-world country."

"We might as well be! We don't know anyone out here!"

"Oh, come on. You're being ridiculous. We're just sightseeing. It's not trespassing."

"Sightseeing. *Really*, Jon?"

"Yeah, there's a difference."

"Well, I'm sure when you explain that difference to a judge he'll thank you for enlightening him."

"Oh, just shut up and climb over, will you? This whole thing was your idea."

Brant shook his head, huffed, and backed several steps away from the gate. "The one time you pick to be spontaneous, it has to be illegal," he mumbled, glancing around the empty parking lot. He ran towards the fence and jumped, pulling his torso on top of the gate with great effort. Jon grabbed his left ankle to hold him steady while Brant threw his right leg across the top rail. He teetered for a moment before carefully shifting his weight to the field side of the gate.

"OK, let go," said Brant.

"You got it?"

"Yeah, just let go."

Jon gave Brant's leg a gentle push upward and watched him tilt over the top of the fence and land awkwardly on the other side.

Brant regained his balance and looked at Jon. "Well?" he asked, slightly out of breath. "You coming or what?"

"Nah," said Jon. "I changed my mind. I'm gonna go grab a bite to eat. I'll be back in a little while."

"Get your butt over here! I'm not going to jail alone."

"Kidding! I'm kidding!" Jon laughed and reached for the top of the gate. Hopping as he pulled himself up, he grimacing briefly as the muscle in his left arm tensed with pain. Once on top of the gate, he let his weight carry him over and landed neatly on the pavement next to Brant. "See? Piece of cake."

"That's what you owe me for making me break the law – a big piece of cake."

"Come on, criminal."

Jon walked across the concrete sidewalk and sat down on a small grass hill adjacent to the third-base stands, overlooking left field. Brant sat down on the grass next to him.

"Is this better?" asked Brant.

"Yeah, I guess," said Jon, still unsatisfied. As the sun's light began to fade in the evening sky, Jon looked out at the artificial playing surface and tried to picture the scene from twenty years ago.

"Anything coming back to you?" asked Brant.

"Kind of. I remember Cam Parsons' stage was there in the outfield behind the big Longhorn logo. And there were rows of chairs covering the infield. I've always imagined myself sitting in the stands over there, just to the left of home plate, on the first-base side. I guess that's where the main TV camera was."

"Cam Parsons came to Columbia one summer back when we were in school, didn't he?" asked Brant.

"Yeah."

"You should have gone."

"Believe me, I wish I had," said Jon. "I guess that's why seeing those people accepting Christ on TV made me wish I was here. I've always wondered what my life would have been like if I had gone to that crusade when he was in Columbia."

"You mean if you had accepted Christ back in college?"

"Yeah. Do you ever think about that? If you had become a Christian when you were a lot younger, how things would have been?"

"Not really," said Brant. "I'm just happy to be one now. But I'm sure my life would've turned out a lot different. I was pretty lost and didn't even know it."

"You and me, both, brother."

"But if you *had* become a Christian back then" said Brant, "do you think you would have still married Lacey and had Holly? I mean, you don't want to just wish that away."

"No, I know. But I met Lacey sitting in a bar with you a week after Cam Parsons was in town. If I had gone to see him – and if I had gone forward at his crusade – I probably would have still been dating the girl I was seeing that summer. Heck, I might have even married her, I don't know. And I probably wouldn't have even met Lacey. It's kind of weird to think about."

"What girl are you talking about?"

"Jenny McNeil."

"I don't remember a Jenny McNeil. What did she look like?"

"You never met her. She was the lunch girl, remember?"

"*Oh,* the lunch girl! The one who dumped you because you weren't a Christian?"

"Yeah, that one."

"That's pretty funny now, if you think about it."

"You thought it was pretty funny back then, too."

Brant laughed. "Yeah, sorry about that."

"No harm. I deserved it. I just wish I could've had it both ways, you know?"

"How's that?"

"You know – I wish I could have become a Christian in college then still met Lacey and had Holly." Jon gazed out at the field for a moment, thinking about his imagined perfect life. The pleasant daydream quickly turned painful as reality crept back in. He shook the thoughts from his head. "Sometimes, I just get so tired of…regretting things. I know I shouldn't, but…."

"Like what?"

"Well, like this!" said Jon, extending his hands towards the field and dropping them onto his lap. "I mean, I get saved watching Cam Parsons on TV, which should be the most amazing thing that's ever happened to me. And it is; don't get me wrong. But here I am, twenty years later – all the way out in Austin, Texas – just because I've always regretted not going to his crusade in Columbia. I mean, what are we even doing here? Seeing this stadium doesn't change anything."

"What did you expect?"

"I don't know," said Jon, his eyes slowly scanning the stadium. "I guess…I guess I was just hoping to experience something I missed. To kind of help me fill in the blanks, you know?"

"Yeah, I get that."

"I just wish things could've been different."

"OK, so let's say you could go back in time and change one thing in your life. Would that be it? That you went to his crusade in Columbia?"

"No," said Jon. His answer was instinctive. He knew what he would change without hesitation. Jon lowered his head and laughed once, quietly. "I guess it doesn't really matter, does it? I mean, I can sit here and wish some things had happened differently. Believe me, I've spent plenty of time doing that. But in the end…life is just…the sum total of every decision we've ever made, good or bad. And there are no do-overs."

"Well," said Brant. "I guess that's why they say all things happen for a reason, right?"

"You did *not* just say that," said Jon. Brant had unwittingly challenged one of Jon's firm convictions.

"Why?" asked Brant. "You don't think everything that happens was meant to be?"

"No, I don't. And neither should you."

"Why not? I didn't just make that up, you know. A lot of people think that."

"That's because a lot of people want to feel better about sin in their life or some stupid decision they made instead of owning up to it. It's just sappy, greeting card theology. It sounds nice, but it's not true."

"Wow. OK," said Brant. He sat quietly for a moment. "But I was reading in the Book of Romans a couple days ago and it says in there somewhere that everything happens on purpose for our good or something like that."

"You're talking about Romans 8:28," said Jon. "And that's not what it says."

"What does it say?"

"It says, 'in all things God works for the good of those who love him, who have been called according to his purpose.'"

"That's what I said. Everything happens for a reason."

"No, that's not what it means, Brant."

"Well, why does it say that if God didn't mean it?"

"Look, first of all, God's definition of *good* is a lot different than ours. He sees everything in the context of eternity and what brings him glory. All *we* care about is how we feel today. Plus, it says we're called according to *his* purpose, not ours."

"But—"

"And if you say everything was meant to be, that would mean that God intends for us to commit every sin we've ever committed. And that's just not true. God hates sin. The Bible says we're supposed to be blameless and pure. Jesus even said we're to be perfect, just like God in heaven. So just because God *knows* we're going to screw up doesn't mean he *wants* us to."

"Yeah, but sometimes good *does* come from bad things that happen," said Brant. "I wouldn't have found Jesus if I didn't hit rock bottom in my own life. So, it's like all the bad stuff I did to lose Kim actually led me to accept Jesus. So God must have meant for it to happen that way."

"Wow, how Machiavellian, Brant. You really think that's how God works? He wants you to sin like crazy until you hit rock bottom as long as something good comes from it? Really?"

"I don't know. Maybe. It worked out didn't it? I got saved. Now, if I can just get—"

"Brant, just because God forgave you doesn't mean he wanted you to sin and experience all the pain you've been through. He's not a sadist, you know. Read your Bible, man."

"I am!"

"I'm sorry, I know you are," said Jon. "But look, you and I could have accepted Jesus any time before we actually did. We didn't have to live like idiots to find salvation. The truth was right in front of us the whole time. I'm just glad God always allows us to come to him and seek his will. That's when things start to work for our good and his. That's what it's all about – doing things in his will according to his purpose, not ours. His good is our good, even if it costs us everything. Get it?"

Brant frowned and looked to his left at the large scoreboard in center field. "Hmph," he said.

"Don't *hmph* me," said Jon. "You know I'm right."

"Hmph."

"Say it: Jon, you're right."

"I'm hmphing because now I can see why people want to believe everything happens for a reason. I think I was using that to justify all the bad stuff

I did as long as the outcome was good. It made me feel less guilty about everything. Like it was just all part of the plan."

"Exactly! There's no accountability in that. You just shrug your shoulders and say, 'Oh well, must have been meant to be.' But it's God's *grace* that takes away our guilt. Not some feel good philosophy."

"You're right. That's what I've been doing. I admit it. I fell for it. Crap."

"I'm sorry, I missed the first part of that. What did you say?"

"I said, 'you were right.'"

"Ah, thank you. I like the sound of that. Anyway, what were we talking about?"

Brant looked out at the baseball field. A slight grin pushed a dimple into his left cheek. "Do-overs," he said.

"Oh, yeah," said Jon. "As in, there aren't any."

"Maybe that's where you're wrong, Jonny-boy." Brant stood up. "I think I've got an idea." He brushed off his pants and began walking down the grassy slope towards the field.

"Where are you going?" asked Jon.

Brant stopped at the wall along the third base line and looked back at Jon. "I want you to go over behind home plate and sit where you think the camera was, where you imagined you would have been sitting if you had been here twenty years ago."

"Why? Are you going to take a picture?"

"Just go on over there. Hurry up."

"All right, all right." Jon stood up and walked in the direction of home plate along the concourse behind the stadium's lower section. As he walked, he watched Brant climb over the field wall and drop himself onto the artificial playing surface. Brant jogged onto the field, adjusting his steps to avoid stepping on the white foul line as he crossed over into left field. Jon laughed at his friend's respect for baseball superstition as he made his way around the stadium to the first-base side. He turned down an aisle and took a few steps towards the field before stopping. Looking around the seats and out at the field, the view seemed about right. Jon could imagine the stadium full of people, their eyes all focused on the stage in center field. And he remembered being moved by the face of a girl on TV during Cam Parsons' sermon. Her features were long lost in his memory, but he remembered her unblinking expression as she listened to the same words he heard. As he looked around the stadium, he wondered where she might have sat. And he wondered if she walked forward to the stage that night.

"Sit down!" shouted Brant as he stood on the large, burnt orange Longhorn logo behind second base. "Are you ready? Can you hear me?"

"I can hear you," said Jon, taking a seat. "What am I supposed to be ready for?"

Brant paced nervously back and forth, for a moment. He then lifted his arms in the air and began to speak, loudly. "As I look around this great stadium tonight, I see many people who are lost and on the road to hell! Everyone here needs Jesus in their lives, my friends! You may think of yourself as a good person, but that won't matter in the end. You may have been raised in the church, but that's not a ticket to heaven. Or you may know you're lost, and you're here looking for answers."

A large smile spread across Jon's face. His eyes opened wide with quiet laughter as he listened to his friend preaching from the center of the field.

"Whatever your situation," Brant continued, "I've got Good News! The Bible has the answer for you! And that answer is Jesus Christ! There's only one way to be sure you're going to heaven, friends, and that's by trusting in Jesus! The Bible says we're all sinners, but God loves us, anyway. He loves us so much he let his Son die on the Cross for us two thousand years ago. So if you want to be saved from the fires of hell and receive the gift of eternal life in heaven when you die, won't you trust Jesus and accept God's grace and forgiveness? I want you to come down here on this field right now and stand in front of this stage and pray to receive Jesus as your Lord and Savior! I'm talking to *you,* Jon Smoak! Come on down!"

Jon wiped tears of joy from the corners of his eyes, jumped up from his seat, and trotted down the stairs towards the field. He hopped over a railing, landing on the soft artificial grass, and jogged out to meet Brant just behind second base.

"How was that?" asked Brant, smiling at Jon as he approached.

"Brant! That was the most awesome thing I've ever heard, man!" Jon embraced Brant, briefly. "Thank you! That was perfect!"

"I'm glad you liked it. I just thought maybe that would help you fill in some of those blanks you mentioned."

"It does! It definitely, does." Jon turned and looked around the stadium. "I really feel like I know what it would have been like to be here, now."

"That was the whole idea to begin with!" said Brant. "So, mission accomplished?"

"Absolutely!" Jon turned in a circle, gathering in the whole scene. "Say... this is really cool out here."

"Yeah, it is," agreed Brant. "It seems a lot bigger from the field, doesn't it."

"Can you imagine standing on a stage out here and preaching to this place packed with people?"

"No, I really can't," said Brant.

"Well, you sure do a good Cam Parsons. That was amazing!"

"Actually, I was trying to be more like Liam. You'd have to be a Texan to do a good Cam Parsons. But hey, you could do it. You're kind of a virtual Texan, aren't you?"

"A virtual Texan?" asked Jon.

"Sure. This stadium is like your spiritual birthplace."

"But I was watching on TV in South Carolina."

"Hence, the virtual part. You're a Texan by second birth, Jonny-boy."

Jon laughed. "I think that's stretching the laws of citizenship just a bit, but what the heck. I'll take it."

"So, Tex," said Brant, giving Jon a shove, "can we leave now and go get something to eat?"

"Sure, partner. And, seriously, thanks again for that, Brant. I owe you one."

The two turned to walk back towards the third-base line.

"Who's that watching us over there behind the fence?" asked Brant.

forty seven

The Witness

*"Like newborn babies, crave pure spiritual milk, so
that by it you may grow up in your salvation."*
- 1 Peter 2:2

"You boys can't be out there on that field!" shouted a man from behind the stadium fence.

Jon squinted his eyes to get a clearer view of the figure, silhouetted by the streetlights illuminating the parking lot behind him. He realized he was looking at a police officer standing on the other side of the same gate he and Brant had climbed over to get into the stadium. Jon waved his hand over his head. "We're sorry, officer!" he shouted. "It's OK, we're leaving now."

"Yes, you are! Get over here!"

"*Great!*" said Brant, glaring at Jon. "I *told* you we shouldn't hop the fence. What the heck are we gonna do now?"

"Just stay calm," said Jon, trying to take his own advice as they walked towards the third base line. "Just be cool, OK? We're not in trouble. He's just going to tell us to leave and that'll be the end of it. You'll see."

"Hurry up!" shouted the officer from behind the fence.

The command startled Jon and Brant into a trot towards the short wall surrounding the playing surface.

"Maybe he'll buy us some ice cream, too. Huh, Jon?" asked Brant, growing quickly out of breath.

"I promise, we have nothing to worry about," said Jon hoping he was right.

"Well, now we do," said Brant, pointing behind him. "You just stepped on the foul line."

"Dang! There goes my no-hitter."

"I'm serious, man! This guy looks ticked. I think we're in big trouble."

They reached the wall surrounding the field, hopped over onto the small grassy hill, and walked up to the main concourse. Jon studied the imposing law enforcement figure on the other side of the fence. The officer stood inches away from the dark green aluminum rails, his right hand covering the top of his gun holster, his left gripping the front of his thick black leather belt. Standing straight and stiff in his black uniform, he wore a stern, slightly angry expression.

Jon began to share Brant's concern. Maybe they really were in trouble. "God, a little help, please," he prayed quickly in his head as they neared the fence.

"You boys are trespassing," said the policeman.

"We're sorry, officer," said Jon, trying to offer a disarming smile through the fence.

"How'd you get in there?"

"We climbed this fence. Over the gate, here," said Jon. Thinking he would just plead ignorance to the crime, he added, "We didn't know—"

"I hope you aren't going to tell me you didn't know you weren't supposed to be in there. You climbed right over a sign that says, *No trespassing.*"

"Um," said Jon, recalibrating his story. "Actually, I was going to say…we didn't mean to cause any trouble."

"Uh-huh. Can you climb back over the fence?"

"Yes, sir," said Jon.

"Then do it."

Jon grabbed the top rail and pulled himself up and over quickly, dropping to his feet on the other side. Looking back through the fence, he realized he'd forgotten to help Brant.

"Thanks," said Brant, scowling at Jon.

"I'm sorry. You want me to climb back over?"

Brant didn't answer as he took two steps backwards then rushed forward. Bounding upwards, he pulled himself onto the fence, folding himself over the top rail at the waist. He struggled momentarily to get his right leg over. Leaning to his left, he wobbled slightly before pulling his weight over the top, dropping to the ground on his heels, and stumbling backwards into Jon's arms. Jon pushed Brant upright. They both turned to face the policeman, who had backed several feet away.

"Let me see some ID," said the officer.

Jon put his right hand on his empty back pocket. "Um, my wallet's in my car," he said, pointing across the parking lot. "Can I go get it?"

"Mine is too," said Brant.

"Hop to it," said the officer, swinging his arms towards them as if he were herding ducks.

"Yes, sir," said Jon and Brant, in unison.

"What were y'all doing out there on the ball field?" the officer asked as they walked towards Jon's car.

"Well, it's kind of a long story," said Jon.

"Make it a short one, young man."

"Yes, sir," said Jon. "You see, I became a Christian watching a Cam Parsons crusade on TV that he did right in this stadium about twenty years ago. We're here from South Carolina, and I just wanted to see what it would've been like if I had been here that night. That's all."

"We were just having some fun," added Brant as they arrived at Jon's car.

"Cam Parsons, huh?" said the officer in a slightly less authoritative tone.

"Yes, sir," said Jon, opening his driver's side door.

"About twenty years ago, you say?"

"Yes, sir."

"I was at that crusade," said the officer.

"You were here?" asked Jon. The thought of talking with someone who was in attendance the very night he was saved left him instantly captivated.

"About half of Austin was here at one time or another that weekend," said the officer, looking back at the stadium.

Jon stood motionless next to his car, smiling at the living relic from his spiritual history.

"Your ID?" prodded the officer.

"Oh, sorry." Jon ducked inside his car to retrieve his wallet from the center console.

334 | Greg M. Dodd

Brant was sitting in the passenger seat, feeling under the seat and in the door panel for his wallet.

"You put it in the glove compartment," said Jon.

"Oh, right." Brant retrieved his wallet and looked up at the officer from the passenger seat. "Did you go down on the field at the crusade, officer?"

"Are you asking me if I was *saved*, young man?" The officer made quotation marks in the air with his fingers.

"Well, um," said Brant, handing his license to the officer. "I wasn't trying to…."

"Son, I was at that crusade working security all weekend. It was my job to be there." The officer studied Brant's license. "Is this your current address, Mr. Morris?"

"Yes, sir," answered Brant, standing up next to the car.

The officer looked at Brant and then back at his license. Brant shifted nervously back and forth on his feet in front of him.

"You got to take a leak or something, son?" asked the officer.

"No, sir," said Brant.

"Then stop dancing around. Stand still."

"Yes, sir," said Brant, snapping to attention like a soldier. "Sorry, sir."

The officer looked again at Brant's license. "This says you weigh 185."

Brant looked down at his round stomach and rubbed it as if he were pregnant. "I guess I've gained a few pounds since that picture was taken."

"Uh-huh."

Jon returned from the other side of the car and handed his driver's license to the officer.

"How about you, Mr. Smoak? Is this your current address?"

"Yes, sir. I still live there."

"I'll be right back." The officer walked towards his patrol car, taking Jon and Brant's licenses with him.

"Can you believe that guy was here at the crusade?" asked Jon. "This is amazing!"

"Jon, are you getting any of this? We're about to be arrested for trespassing! We're supposed to fly home for Christmas in the morning, but no! We're going to be sitting in some county jail!"

Jon ignored Brant's hysteria as he watched the policeman cross the parking lot and climb into his patrol car. "I've got a feeling God wants me to witness to this guy."

"What? *Him?*" asked Brant, pointing across the parking lot. "You're going to witness to *him?*"

"Yeah."

"Jon, you got all over me for even asking that state trooper back in South Carolina if he was a Christian. And now you want to witness to Wyatt Earp over there? Are you insane?"

"All things happen for a reason, eh, Brant?"

"Not funny, man. Not funny."

"Seriously, I've got a good feeling about this. Besides, it's what we came out here to do."

"Maybe he's already a Christian," said Brant. "Did you think about that? He was at that Cam Parsons crusade."

"He said he was just working security. We can't just assume he's saved. Just be quiet and let me do the talking."

"I want my own lawyer," said Brant, looking back at the patrol car.

"Whatever," said Jon. He felt a rush of adrenaline as he watched the officer talking on his radio behind the wheel of his car. Jon said a quick prayer, keeping his eyes fixed on the officer while Brant paced anxiously beside the car. "Lord Jesus, I'm your servant," Jon prayed quietly. "Please give me the words to say to this man. Use me to bring him to you, Lord. Help me be bold for you, in Jesus' name."

The officer opened his door, stepped out of his patrol car, and began walking slowly back towards Jon and Brant.

"Here he comes," said Jon. "I've got this."

"It's all yours," said Brant, leaning against the car.

The officer waved his hand, motioning for Jon and Brant to walk towards him.

"Come on," said Jon. The two walked towards the officer, meeting him halfway between the two cars. As the three men regrouped in the middle of the parking lot, the officer studied Jon for a moment without speaking, tapping the two driver's licenses against the palm of his left hand.

"You know, Mr. Smoak," he said, looking into Jon's eyes, "Cam Parsons was a good man. I doubt he'd approve of two grown men committing illegal entry and trespassing just to run around and play pretend on a ball field."

Brant whispered beneath his breath, "I told you."

"Did you know Cam Parsons?" asked Jon. The officer's blank stare made him feel nervous for asking. "It's just…the way you said that, it sounded like you might have known him or something. That's why I asked. I wasn't trying to—"

"I met him once," said the officer, interrupting Jon's rambling.

"You did?" asked Jon, trying to steady his nerves. "How, I mean, when…when did you meet him?"

"The week before that crusade, we got word of some death threats against him. So we met with him and some of his staff to talk about it. My chief advised them to cancel the crusade."

Jon began to feel mildly star-struck, forgetting his current situation. "I can't believe you got to talk to him. That must have been awesome."

"He was just a man, young fella. Just like you and me."

"Yes, sir," said Jon, reigning in his enthusiasm. "Can I ask what happened after that? They didn't cancel the crusade, obviously."

"Well," said the officer, letting his gaze drift above Jon's head. "I remember there was a lot going on that weekend. There was a football game early that afternoon so we were already stretched thin on men to help here at the baseball stadium that night."

"I always wondered why they held the crusade here instead of at the football stadium," said Jon.

"It was just a scheduling thing. But we told him and his staff we couldn't guarantee his safety the whole weekend, particularly when he was out there on that stage," said the officer, pointing down towards the field.

"But he preached, anyway," said Jon.

"He did. He said it wasn't for him to decide when the Lord would call him home, but he was going to serve him until that day came. He said if it happened here in Austin that weekend, so be it."

"Wow," said Jon as he considered the courage and commitment behind those words. He realized he wouldn't be standing in Austin if Cam Parsons had given into fear. He wouldn't have seen him on TV that night. And he may not even be a Christian. The inspiration gave Jon a renewed sense of boldness.

"He was a Texan, you know," said the officer.

"Yes, sir. I know," said Jon. "Officer, do you mind if I ask you a question?"

"Go ahead."

"Where would you say you are in terms of faith in God?"

The officer grinned knowingly at Jon. "Young man, you don't live your whole life in Texas without hearing about God."

Jon noticed Brant dropping his head and taking a small step back, but he pressed on. "So, what do you think about the message of salvation Cam Parsons preached?"

"Cam Parsons was a fine preacher," said the officer, firmly. "Everybody knows that."

"But do you think that Jesus is our only way to a relationship with God?"

The officer smiled. "Son, I'll leave all that up to the folks who sit in church on Sundays."

"You don't go to church?" asked Jon.

Brant cleared his throat.

"I work traffic control for a big Baptist church every Sunday morning. That's as close as I get."

"But don't you want to go yourself?" asked Jon.

"Son, if there's something you want to know, get to it," said the officer, regaining his stern expression.

Jon set his feet as he fought off his nerves. His body became tense as if he were preparing to take a punch in the stomach. "OK, has anyone ever taken a Bible and shown you how you can have a relationship with God through faith in Jesus Christ?"

The officer glanced down at his black shoes and then looked up at Jon with a smile. "No, I can't say as they have."

Jon remained tense. "Would you be interested in letting me do that, right now?"

The officer stared Jon in the eyes. "Take your best shot," he said.

"Wait right here!" Jon jogged back to his car, unlocking the trunk with his remote key fob as he approached. He opened the lid and leaned over the compartment, lifting his nylon suitcase from underneath Brant's gym bag. Unzipping his bag, he searched for his Bible underneath his clothes. Not finding it, he moved the bags around the trunk with a growing sense of panic, becoming fearful he had left it in their last hotel room. Jon stood up straight for a moment and placed his hands on the trunk lid, conscious of the policeman waiting with Brant. "Oh, duh!" he said, closing the trunk. He opened the rear passenger door and found his Bible on the floor behind the seat. Poking out from the top of its pages were slips of paper marking verses he had been trying to commit to memory. But for this opportunity, he wanted no mistakes. He would rely on God's written Word rather than his memory to share the Gospel message with the policeman.

Jon closed the car door and turned to see Brant standing alone. Across the parking lot, the policeman was climbing into his patrol car. Jon jogged quickly towards Brant as the officer began to drive away. "Brant! What happened? Where's he going? What did you say to him?"

Brant held up his hands. "Me? I didn't say anything. He just left."

"Daggum it!" shouted Jon, kicking at the pavement.

"Don't blame me, Jon. I had nothing to do with it."

Jon gripped his Bible with both hands in front of his chest. He watched the patrol car stop at the parking lot exit, turn left, and then speed away. Turning back to face Brant, he let his Bible drop to his side in his right hand. "I'm not blaming you," he said, unsure if he was being honest. "It's just that...I don't understand. Why would he just leave?" Jon watched Brant cross his arms and look down at the pavement. He suspected Brant knew more than he was letting on. "Did he say anything before he left?"

"Well, yeah," said Brant. "Here's your license, by the way."

"What did he say?" asked Jon, stuffing his driver's license in his back pocket.

Brant looked back at the stadium. "He said he liked my sermon."

"He said *what?*"

"He said he liked my sermon. I think he heard the whole thing."

"You mean he was watching us?"

"Apparently," said Brant.

Jon turned and moved a few steps towards the stadium fence as he imagined what the officer witnessed as he watched them on the field. "He was just messing with us the whole time, wasn't he?"

Brant shrugged his shoulders. "Maybe. I don't know. But he scared the crap out of me, that's all I know. Can we leave now?"

"That just *sucks!*" said Jon. Unsure where to direct his frustration, he began walking back towards his car.

"What sucks?" asked Brant, following behind Jon. "Not getting arrested?"

"I get all geared up to share Christ with him – thinking I was being all bold and stuff – and he was just screwing with me! I'd rather have someone get in my face and argue, than be patronized like that. I feel like a total *idiot.*"

"Why does it matter, Jon?"

Jon stopped to face Brant. "Why does it matter? Because it was totally pointless, that's why! It was a complete waste of time."

Brant stopped with him. "You don't know that, Jon."

"Oh, so you think it was God's will for me to get played by some cop with nothing better to do than jerk us around?"

"Oh, here we go again," said Brant, rolling his eyes.

"What's *that* supposed to mean?"

"You trying to figure out God's will…like you're reading the map on your iPhone or something. Give me a break, will you, Jon?"

"Brant, discerning God's will in what we do is important. If you—"

"Look Jon," interrupted Brant, "I think as long as you're doing what the Bible says to do – and you were – I don't see what the big deal is. God's not going to be mad that you tried to witness to that guy." He continued on towards the car, leaving Jon behind him. "You make all this *way* too complicated sometimes," he said, looking back over his shoulder.

Jon shook his head dismissively and moved towards the car. "That's because it *is* complicated, Brant." As he opened his car door, Jon remembered when he was young in his faith, like Brant. "Maybe one day you'll understand."

"Oh, you mean I'll understand enough to be all confused and frustrated like you? No thanks." Brant opened the car door and lowered himself onto the passenger seat. "Besides, what about 'faith like a child' and all that?"

Jon settled in behind the steering wheel and returned his Bible to the floor behind Brant's seat. "It's not that simple, Brant. You see—"

"No, I think it is that simple, Jon. God loves us. Jesus saves. Do what the Bible says. What's so complicated about that?"

Jon opened his mouth to counter Brant's argument, but his mind had no response. God loves us. Jesus saves. Do what the Bible says. A sense of humility began to shrink his spiritual arrogance as he started the car. Jon hated to lose an argument, particularly to Brant, but he knew he had done just that. He took a deep breath and let go of his frustration. Turning his head, he looked at his friend with a new sense of curiosity. "Brant, I think your simple theology would put a serious dent in the Christian book industry."

"Well, I don't want to put anyone out of work," said Brant.

"I think they're safe for now," said Jon with a smile as he started the car. "Anyway, thanks again for pretending to be Cam Parsons for me."

"I was happy to do it. Even if it meant being psychologically tortured by Wyatt Earp back there."

"That Earp's one tough hombre," said Jon trying to lighten the mood with his best Texas accent. "Why don't we go rustle up some grub at a local eatery, eh cowboy?"

"You buying?" asked Brant.

"I reckon so," said Jon, narrowing his eyes as he continued the bit.

Brant shook his head. "The cowboy thing isn't working for you, man."

"Oh, come on," said Jon. "You said I'm a virtual Texan."

"I know. But you sound like Andy Griffith trying to do a bad Clint Eastwood impression."

"Ouch. I'm just striking out all around tonight."

"You shouldn't have stepped on that foul line. I tried to tell you."

"I'm sure that explains everything," said Jon.

"Well, if it makes you feel any better," said Brant, "before the cop left, he did say one more thing."

"What's that?"

"He said, 'Tell your buddy to keep trying.'"

forty eight

Seeds

"Listen! A farmer went out to sow his seed. As he was scattering the seed, some fell along the path, and the birds came and ate it up. Some fell on rocky places, where it did not have much soil. It sprang up quickly, because the soil was shallow. But when the sun came up, the plants were scorched, and they withered because they had no root. Other seed fell among thorns, which grew up and choked the plants, so that they did not bear grain. Still other seed fell on good soil. It came up, grew and produced a crop, some multiplying thirty, some sixty, some a hundred times."

- Mark 8:3-8

Jon plopped into his seat and finished typing the text message to Holly he had started as he boarded the plane. *Just boarding now in Austin. I'll let you know when we leave ATL for home.* Waiting for her reply, he imagined her typing with her thumbs faster than he could type on a standard keyboard with ten fingers. A moment later, the ring tone of an incoming text made Jon smile.

Yay! Praying 4 u!

Seeing his battery running low, Jon turned off his iPhone and slipped it into the pocket of the seat in front of him.

"I bet you ten bucks you forget that," said a college-aged girl as she dropped a book bag onto the aisle seat next to Jon.

"Nah, I'm too addicted to it to leave it anywhere," replied Jon, looking up as she stuffed a bag into the overhead compartment. Printed in white on the front of her royal blue T-shirt were two large letters – *YL* – above the words *Costa Rica*. Jon recognized the logo of Young Life, a Christian youth service organization. "I like your shirt," he said.

"Thanks!" said the girl as she moved the book bag onto her lap and sat down. "It's a Young Life shirt."

"I see that," said Jon. "Did you go to Costa Rica with them?"

"Yes, sir," she said, removing a set of red on-ear headphones from her bag. "I just finished working on a service project there. We built a basketball court for a community ministry in Talamanca. It was so cool. The kids were so excited."

"That's awesome. My name's Jon."

"Hey, Jon. I'm Katelyn. Merry Christmas."

"Merry Christmas to you, Katelyn." Jon shook her hand gently. He had prayed for an opportunity to witness to someone on the flight, but maybe God just wanted him to compare faith notes with another Believer. "Do you get to share Christ with the kids while you're working on projects like that?"

"Um, not really. We don't go out evangelizing door to door or anything. We just try and create an environment where kids will want to come and then the mission there can teach them about Christ. But they definitely know why we're there and what we're about."

"That's really cool," said Jon.

"Yeah, I love it." Katelyn smiled as she wrapped the headphones around her neck and plugged the cord into her iPhone.

Jon let Katelyn settle in for their flight as he tried to imagine a group of young people building a basketball court in a remote Central American village. Her sincere enthusiasm contrasted his own attitude towards church service projects when he was a teenager, roughly equating them with prison camp labor. No kid in his right mind would willingly give up free time for unpaid work that benefited a total stranger, he believed at the time. The few times his parents had enrolled him in youth service projects, he just assumed he was being punished. Yet Katelyn served willingly and for the right reasons. As Jon smiled at his youthful stupidity, a gray-haired man in a tailored business suit stopped at their row and lifted a thin leather bag into the bin over Jon's head.

The man took off his suit jacket, folded it neatly, and placed it in the bin with his bag. Shutting the compartment door, he looked down at Jon.

"Morning," he said, pointing past Jon to the empty window seat. "That's me."

"Looks like you get the window," said Jon, with a smile as he pulled his legs close against his seat to let the man squeeze by. He suddenly felt underdressed in his faded jeans and black V-neck sweater.

"It's not first class, but I'll take it," the man said, dryly, as he took his seat next to Jon.

As the remaining passengers made their way to their seats and got settled, a flight attendant rattled through her preflight announcements in robotic fashion as another walked the aisle closing the overheard compartments. Jon turned to check on Brant, who was seated across the aisle a row behind him. While failing to make eye contact, Jon could see Brant was already in a conversation with an elderly priest seated next to him. "Oh, gosh," Jon thought to himself, "I hope he behaves himself over there."

The plane rolled slowly onto the runway, swinging its nose around to the left before coming to a stop. The pilot gave final instructions to the flight attendants as Jon closed his eyes to pray. "Dear God, just a quick prayer to say thank you for the chance to go home and see Holly and my mom for Christmas. If it's your will, God, I just ask that everyone on this plane arrives safely where they're going and that they'll experience your glory and love this Christmas. Please help me to see opportunities to be a witness for you on this flight, Lord. Just give me the words to say and the courage to say them. Thank you, God. In Jesus name, I pray. Amen."

Before Jon could open his eyes he felt the sensation of rapid acceleration. His body shook with the plane's rough vibration as their speed increased down the bumpy concrete runway. Any time now, Jon thought. A smooth, quiet, upward turn pushed him deep into his seat as the plane's wheels left the ground. The feeling reminded Jon of being on a ride at the fair. Closing his eyes again, he thought of his very first roller coaster ride on the old wooden *Swamp Fox* in Myrtle Beach. He had overcome intense fear and a fair amount of teasing from his older cousin, Caleb, to place himself into the metal car and let the safety bar lock in front of him. After that first terrifying ride, it was all he wanted to do the rest of the summer. It was the same summer he met Amy, he remembered. As the plane continued its ascent, Jon wondered what she was doing and if she'd received his letter. He knew he would face temptation to contact her while home for Christmas, but committed himself against it, still wary of where his interest may lead him.

"Headed home or just leaving?" asked the man seated next to the window.

"Hmm?" replied Jon, shaking the thoughts of Amy from his head. "Oh, I'm on my way back home for Christmas."

"What do you do for a living?" the man asked with a directness that made Jon feel like he was being interviewed.

"I'm a creative director for an ad agency," answered Jon, enjoying a small remnant of professional pride. He hadn't seen himself that way since leaving home and realized he missed the identity his career provided.

"Advertising...interesting," said the man, leaving his intention for the word *interesting* firmly ambiguous.

"How about you?" asked Jon.

"I'm CEO of a chemical engineering company out of Atlanta."

"Wow," said Jon, feeling smaller than he had just seconds ago. "So, I'm guessing you're probably not used to flying in coach are you?"

"It's been a while, to be honest. But I needed to be on this flight, and first class was full. Are you based in Austin?"

"South Carolina," Jon answered, hoping he wouldn't hear *interesting* in response.

"Oh, really?" The man turned slightly towards Jon and smiled for the first time. "We own a house on the beach in Litchfield. We vacation there every summer."

Jon was happy to hear a reference to something familiar so far away from home. Although, he'd always viewed Litchfield as Pawleys Island's rival just across the north inlet. Litchfield just seemed more commercial and touristy than Pawleys. "I love Litchfield," Jon fibbed. "I grew up going to Pawleys Island. My mom is from Georgetown."

"We love Georgetown," the man said. "It's a nice little town, once you get past the paper mill smell, of course. Good restaurants, too. We eat at The Rice Paddy almost every time we're down there."

"That's a nice restaurant," said Jon. As long as he could remember, The Rice Paddy had been in business on Front Street in Georgetown. An upscale white tablecloth kind of place where rich old people dined, Jon had never eaten there. But the man seemed to fit their clientele. "We eat at the River

Room a lot," said Jon. "It's more casual, but nice. It's just across Front Street. On the river, of course."

"I've seen that over there. We'll have to try it sometime."

"It's good." Jon was beginning to like the man seated next to him. "Make sure you try the sautéed pound cake for dessert. It's amazing."

"That's probably close to what they're having in first class right now," the man joked.

"No doubt."

"So, were you visiting a client in Austin?" the man asked.

"No. Actually, my friend and I," said Jon, pointing over his shoulder towards Brant, "are traveling around the country sharing the Gospel with people."

"You mean like the Gospel from the Bible? That Gospel?"

"Yep, that's the one."

"Interesting," said the man, nodding his head forward as he looked at the back of the seat in front of him. He was clearly masking deeper thoughts behind the word, leaving Jon to wonder. "Doing that on your Christmas vacation, are you?" asked the man.

"Actually, I'm on a leave of absence for a few months. We're just flying home for Christmas. Then we'll head back to Austin in a week to get the car and keep driving west to California. We'll try and reach as many people as we can and then head back home sometime in March. That's the plan, anyway."

"You took a leave of absence from your job to do that?"

"Yep."

"And I assume you mean an unpaid leave of absence."

"That's right."

The man chuckled. "You must be independently wealthy."

"Hardly," said Jon. "I'm using money from my retirement to fund the trip and cover my bills while I'm gone."

"Wow. What about your friend?" The man peered over the top of the seats towards Brant. "Does he work at the same agency you do?"

"Brant? No, he's just an old friend. He's living off a severance package right now so he was free to go with me."

The man paused for a moment. "I have to ask, what possessed you to take time off from your career and dip into your retirement fund to go do something like that?"

To be asked that question by a CEO made Jon feel slightly more uncomfortable than usual. He knew it wasn't a good career move by any measure, but his answer was still the same. "Well, I felt it was something I was called to do."

"By whom?"

The man's question told Jon he had the witnessing opportunity he'd prayed for, after all. "God, of course," he said, noticing the man's raised eyebrows. "You seem surprised."

"I don't know you well enough to be surprised," the man said. "I just think it's kind of…."

"Crazy?"

"Actually, I was thinking irresponsible. No offense."

"None taken," said Jon, swallowing his pride. "I've heard it all, believe me."

"I'm sure you have. How accepting was your company to you taking time off like that? Did you tell them why you were leaving?"

"Oh, I told them. I got the official approval I needed. Company policy and all. But unofficially, my boss pretty much banned me from coming back to my job. She said I'd be taking out the trash if I had the nerve to come back."

"And you went, anyway?"

"It was something I had to do. It's a matter of faith." Jon paused for a moment to picture himself, wearing a cleaning crew uniform, taking the trash out of Amanda's office. "I think some things in life are more important than your job title," he said, more for his own counsel than for the man seated next to him. But aware that he'd just downplayed job titles to a CEO, Jon added, "No offense."

The man laughed. "None taken. Look, I don't mean to get in your business or anything – I'm as religious as the next guy – but you may have just committed career suicide. You realize that don't you?"

"Oh, I know. Believe me, I know. But I just have to trust that what I'm doing is what God wants me to do. The rest will sort itself out later."

"Wow," said the man, shaking his head. "That's a lot of trust."

"That's what faith is," said Jon, hoping to tell him more.

"Well, I hope all that works out for you." The man turned his head and looked out the window.

The flight had just begun and Jon's attempt to explain his calling and perhaps share his faith had come to a condescending end. The man seemed to have more empathy with Jon's boss, Amanda, than for his desire to serve God. And he apparently had no interest in discussing matters of faith. Jon looked to his left at Katelyn. Her headphones covered her ears and her eyes were closed. He wouldn't mind learning more about her Young Life experience, but hated to interrupt her time relaxing. Jon considered the prospect of sitting in awkward silence for the next two hours with only an airline magazine for entertainment. Reminding himself that simple, casual conversation was still an option, Jon turned his head to the right. "So, how long have you lived in Atlanta?" he asked the man.

The man pulled his attention away from the view outside the window. "About four years," he said, struggling to get comfortable in his seat. "We used to be headquartered in Austin, but my company bought a competitor that was based in Norcross, just outside of Atlanta. They had some executive talent there and a better technical infrastructure than ours, which was one of the reasons we bought them. So I moved my office to Atlanta temporarily to oversee the transition, and we just stayed there. I moved our corporate headquarters there two years ago."

"Interesting," said Jon, trying out the vague response for himself. The intentional ambiguity gave him a brief feeling of power over the conversation. "Do you travel a lot?"

"Back and forth to Austin mostly. I was there this time for a funeral."

"Oh, I'm sorry. Someone in your family?"

"No, it was one of our employees."

"Oh, no."

"Yeah. He worked in our IT organization that supports our research facility in Austin."

"What happened? Some kind of accident?"

"He had an aneurysm," the man said, plainly. "Died in the office, sitting at his desk. He was on the phone with his wife when it happened."

"Oh, my gosh," said Jon, picturing the scene in his mind. "How old was he?"

"He was about your age, I'm guessing. Forty-four. Had a wife and two kids. One in college."

"That's just terrible."

"Yes, it was."

"Well, I'm sure his family appreciated you going to his funeral."

"Oh, it's just part of the job, really. Not that I didn't want to go. I didn't mean it like that. But it was a pretty traumatic experience for the folks in our Austin office. I just wanted to make sure they were OK and staying focused. We brought in grief counselors to talk with everyone."

"You said you were religious," said Jon, recalling the man's words from their first attempt at conversation. "Does that help you deal with tough situations like that?"

"I'm sorry?" asked the man, appearing confused by Jon's question.

"You said a few minutes ago that you were as religious as the next guy," said Jon, trying to steer the conversation back to faith.

"Oh, right, right. Well, this was work related, so religion didn't really play into it."

"Can I ask you what it means to you to be religious?"

"Sure," said the man, repositioning himself again in his seat. "First, I suppose it means to believe in God, of course. We belong to a church and all that. My wife is pretty active in the Sunday school class that we belong to."

"That's great. What about you?"

"Oh, I go," he said, glancing over his knees at the floor. "I'm there with her most Sundays. Well, maybe about half the time, I suppose." He looked at Jon and smiled. "I go when I can, how 'bout that?"

Jon laughed, appreciating the man's progressive honesty. "I'm sure you're a busy man. Do you ever find time to get involved in any way? With your Sunday school class, maybe?"

"Not really. They asked me recently to serve on a committee to plan some landscaping around the back of the church property. I went to one meeting, but it was a waste of my time. You don't need a committee to plant some bushes. Just do it."

"I guess they were just trying to get people involved."

"I suppose. But my time is a little more valuable than that. I'm doing pretty good just to make it to the service on Sundays."

"They should just be happy you're there when you can make it," said Jon, doing his best to hide his sarcasm.

"Exactly! That's what I tell my wife."

Jon's subtle humor had inadvertently led the man in the wrong direction. "Seriously, I hate to tell you this, but God doesn't need you to do him any favors."

"I'm sorry?"

"You really are just wasting your time if you're not going to church for the right reasons."

"OK, I'll bite. What do you think are the right reasons?"

Jon saw an opportunity to pull Katelyn into their discussion. "Well, let's ask Katelyn."

"Who's Katelyn?" asked the man.

Jon turned to his left and tapped Katelyn on the knee to get her attention. She lifted her headphones away from her ears and smiled politely, her eyebrows raised in anticipation of a question.

"Katelyn, can we ask you something?" asked Jon.

"Sure," she said, still holding the headphones close to her ears.

"We're talking about faith and church. Can I ask why you're serving with Young Life in Costa Rica? What motivated you to do that?"

"Oh, sure," she said, placing her headphones on her lap and pausing the music on her iPhone. "Well, I guess I just want to share God's love with people. I want them to know that he loves them. And it's all about relationships, you know? I mean, the best way for someone to learn about Jesus is for me to treat them like Jesus would. So they experience his love, kinda. It's like, when I do things for the people there, I feel like it points them to Jesus. But it's not about what I do for them. It's about what Jesus does through me for them. I don't know if that makes any sense." She turned her head away as a loud conversation across the aisle distracted her, momentarily. Looking back at Jon she said, "I kind of forgot what your question was."

"That was perfect, Katelyn. Thank you," said Jon. He recognized Brant's voice as one of those coming from across the aisle behind him. Jon lifted his head to see over Katelyn's seat and saw Brant in a debate with the priest next to him.

"I'm just asking, why don't you?" asked Brant, loudly.

"I serve my congregation, young man," responded the priest in a firm, but controlled tone.

"But if you serve God, you should want to share Christ with anyone, not just your congregation. You should know that! Don't you read your Bible?"

Jon cringed. The passenger seated directly in front of the priest raised himself up and peered over the seat at Brant. "Hey buddy, back off!" said the man. "You don't talk to a priest that way."

"Why not?" asked Brant.

Jon wondered if he should get involved to calm the situation. Before he could decide, he heard the footsteps of a flight attendant moving quickly up the aisle towards Brant.

"Is there a problem here?" she asked.

"This clown here is giving the Father a hard time," said the man in front of Brant.

"Father, would you like to move?" asked the attendant. "We have an empty seat in first class if you'd like it."

"I'm fine right here," said the priest, calmly. "Thank you, miss."

"How about I move instead?" offered Brant, looking up at the flight attendant.

"He acts like a jerk and gets a seat in first class?" asked the priest's defender.

"He's not going to first class," said the flight attendant. "Come with me, sir," she said to Brant. "We have an empty coach seat up near the bulkhead."

Brant stood up into the aisle, opened the overhead storage compartment and pulled his backpack onto his shoulder, making eye contact with Jon.

"What are you doing?!" asked Jon in a hushed tone.

The flight attendant turned her attention to Jon. "Are you flying with him, sir?"

"Um...," said Jon, hesitant to admit he knew Brant. He wasn't sure if Brant was in trouble and didn't want to be included if he was.

"Yes, we're flying together," stated Brant, looking sorely at Jon.

"Would you like to move with your friend, sir?" asked the attendant.

"Uh, no thank you," said Jon.

"Thanks a lot, *Peter*," said Brant and followed the flight attendant towards the front of the plane.

Jon couldn't help but grin at Brant's reference to Peter denying Christ. Apparently, Brant was reading his Bible more than he realized.

"How do you like that?" asked the man next to Jon. "They told me first class was full."

Jon ignored the man's interest in first class accommodations as he watched Brant make his way up the aisle.

"Was that your buddy?" asked the man.

"Yes," Jon admitted.

"He seems like a handful. I kind of like that."

"He's just…passionate sometimes, that's all. We've known each other since college." Jon watched Brant as he struggled to make room for his backpack in a full overhead compartment near the front of the plane. "Well, actually, we just reconnected after about fifteen years or so at church."

"So, *that's* how your trip came about," said the man, as if he'd just solved a mystery. "It's something through your church."

"No, honestly, it came to me through prayer and God's Word."

"It was *your* idea, then."

He still didn't get it, Jon thought. "I like to think it was God's idea. I wouldn't have dreamed this up on my own, I promise."

"But I'm sure your church had something to do with it, right? Nobody would just go off on their own and do that."

"My church really didn't have much to do with it, at all. The people I talked to there really weren't even onboard with the idea at first."

"I don't understand. If your church didn't ask you to do it, why do it?"

"Because it's not about me and my church. It's about me and God."

"What's the difference?"

Jon laughed at the breadth of the question. "Wow, where do I start? I might need a minute on that one."

"Take your time. It's a two hour flight. My name's Geoff, by the way."

"Is that with a J or a G?"

"G-e-o-f-f. Geoff Holland."

"Hey, Mr. Holland. I'm Jon Smoak. That's Jon with a J."

"I think I could've guessed that," said Geoff, smiling. "Nice to meet you Jon. And please call me Geoff. I hear *Mr. Holland* enough. It would be nice to hear my first name every once in a while."

"Fair enough," said Jon. He paused for a moment, trying to decide where to take their conversation. "So…you see church and God as being the same thing?"

"Well, not literally, of course. There are lots of different churches and religions. But they all recognize God in some way."

"*A* god, maybe, but there's only *one* way to know the one true God and that's through Jesus Christ."

Geoff tilted his head and grinned as if he knew something Jon didn't. "Jon, in my company, we like to show respect for diversity. We don't espouse the belief that one religion trumps all others. Who am I to tell my Hindu employees that their religion doesn't count because they don't believe the same thing I do?"

"And what is it that you believe?" asked Jon, trying to keep the focus on Geoff rather than Hinduism.

"Me?"

Jon affirmed his question with a nod of his head.

"Well, I believe in God, of course. But I don't claim to own a monopoly on what it takes to get to heaven. I think God has revealed himself in many different ways to many different people. That's why we have so many religions in the world. The Mormon faith, Islam, Hindus, Judaism, etcetera, etcetera. But it's all the same God. I respect that, along with the right not to believe in anything. I run a large company, and I have to respect and value the differences in all people."

Jon resisted the strong temptation to argue the fallacy in Geoff's pluralistic theology. He wanted to learn Geoff's core beliefs instead of his company's policy on diversity. "And what do you think about the Bible?" asked Jon.

"Well, I think it's…it's a record of…." Geoff attempted to cross his legs, but gave up quickly after hitting his knee on the back of the seat in front of him. "I think it's a collection of writings that were captured by certain people over time…trying to explain things they couldn't understand any other way. Like Creation or natural disasters, for example. Or what happens after we die."

"Do you think the Bible is God's Word?" asked Jon.

"Well, it's certainly *about* God. But if you're asking me if it's written by the hand of God, so to speak, I would have to say no."

"Interesting," said Jon for intentional affect. "So, who do you say Jesus was then?"

Geoff smiled. "I see where you're trying to lead me on this. And I appreciate what you and your friend are out doing – what's his name?"

"Brant Morris."

"Brant," repeated Geoff. "But you don't need to do that with me."

"I'm sorry, Mr. Holland – Geoff. I was really just interested in what you think about things. You're an experienced, successful person, and I was just curious. But I don't want to make you feel uncomfortable. Like you said, it's a two hour flight."

"I'm not uncomfortable," claimed Geoff.

Geoff pulled the airline magazine from the seat pocket in front of him. Jon watched him quickly flip through its glossy pages, stopping on several random ads, before returning it to the seat pocket. Maybe it was time to back off, again. The last thing Jon wanted to do was create a tense situation for the rest of the flight or force Geoff to move. He wondered how Brant was doing. He hadn't seen or heard any evidence of controversy in Brant's new section. Maybe he'd fallen asleep, Jon hoped. To his left, Katelyn sat with her eyes closed, her headphones still covering her ears. Lacking anyone to talk with, Jon wished he had brought something onboard to read. In preparation for the trip, he had imagined himself in deep discussions about God and salvation with those seated around him. He never thought about having time to read. But now, he sat quietly with nothing to do. He closed his eyes and wondered if he could fall asleep.

"You know, when I was younger," said Geoff.

Jon opened his eyes and turned his head to listen.

"I guess I was a sophomore in college," Geoff continued.

"Where did you go to school?" asked Jon.

"Georgia Tech. That's where I got my bachelor's, but I got my master's degree in chemical engineering from MIT."

"Wow," said Jon. "That's impressive."

"But while I was at Tech, my roommate got caught up in a…I guess you'd call it a revival. This thing that was going on at the time around campus. A lot of hysteria about God and what not. You know, the whole Jesus Movement back in the early seventies." Geoff looked at Jon for confirmation.

"I've heard about that, sure," said Jon, wondering where Geoff's story was leading.

"To me," said Geoff, "the whole thing seemed like a lot of people acting emotionally instead of thinking through things rationally. So I stayed out of it. But I remember, one night I came back to the dorm after being out with some friends, and my roommate was holding a Bible study with some other students on the floor of our room. They asked me to join them. But I just stepped over them and grabbed a beer out of the fridge and headed back out. He told me the next day they prayed for me after I left." Geoff stared vacantly at the seat in front of him with a somber expression on his face. "He was a good guy."

"Your roommate?"

"Yeah. His name was Tim."

"Did you guys ever talk about faith?"

"I guess that's what made me think about him," said Geoff. "He asked me the same thing you did a few minutes ago. Who did I think Jesus was?"

"What did you say?"

"Oh, I don't remember. That was forty years ago," said Geoff, with a small chuckle. "But I remember him quoting something to me from C.S. Lewis."

"It was probably what he said in *Mere Christianity*, that Jesus was either a liar, a lunatic or the Son of God."

"I think that was it. Tim had that book. What's that all about?"

"Well, we know from the Bible that Jesus claimed to be the Son of God," explained Jon. "That means, logically, either he was a liar or just some crazy person – that's what a lot of people of his day thought he was – or he really was who he said he was. Those are the only three options Jesus left us with. It's up to you to decide which one you believe. Was he a liar, a lunatic or the Son of God? It's not an emotional issue. It's straightforward reason. Maybe that's what your roommate was trying to help you see."

Geoff sat quietly for several minutes. Jon prayed silently as he looked down at the floor. "God, help this man to see his need for you." He searched his mind for Scripture, something he could share that would fit the context of their discussion. Jon heard himself speak before the words formed fully in his head. "You know, in the Gospel of Matthew – and I think in Luke, too – the Bible tells us that Jesus asked Peter the same question: 'Who do you say I am?'"

"What did he say?" asked Geoff.

"He said, 'You're the Messiah, the Christ, the Son of God.'" Jon looked into Geoff's eyes. For a brief, uncomfortable moment, he saw a searching intensity, almost fear, in the blue eyes staring back at him.

Geoff turned his head away and gazed out the window at the clouds passing beneath them. Jon waited for his response, certain that God was working on Geoff's heart. He began to feel excitement over the possibility of leading this important businessman to Christ. What an impact Geoff could have on the lives of those around him.

"I think I'm going to see about that seat in first class," said Geoff. "Excuse me."

Helplessly, Jon watched Geoff stand up and squeeze past him into the aisle. Geoff gathered his coat and leather bag from the overheard bin and walked up the aisle towards the front of the plane, disappearing into first class. For several minutes, Jon held his eyes on the blue curtain that separated the two sections and waited prayerfully for Geoff's return. Maybe there was no empty seat in first class after all, he hoped. Or maybe Geoff would have a change of heart and want to continue their discussion. But Jon's hope diminished rapidly with each passing moment; he finally gave up.

Jon unbuckled his seatbelt, lifted the armrest to his right, and scooted over to the empty window seat. Leaning his elbow on the armrest, he let his chin rest on the palm of his hand. He pressed his forehead against the acrylic window and prayed silently as he stared into the limitless sky. "God, what am I doing wrong? I can't seem to say or do anything that makes a difference to anyone. I'm trying, but I just…you give me these opportunities and I just blow them. I haven't reached anyone in *weeks*."

The truth in Jon's prayer made him feel worse. Looking out the window, he searched for the ground below, which appeared in faint glimpses through the wispy, white vapor. A sudden break in the clouds revealed a living map of roads, buildings, and neighborhoods surrounded by the green and brown checkerboard of farmland. He considered the thousands of people going about their lives beneath him. "God…is this what you see when you look down on us? So many people down there need Jesus…but I'm just one person, God. How can I possibly make a difference?"

"Excuse me," said Katelyn.

Jon turned to his left and saw Katelyn holding her headphones in her lap as she looked at him with a shy smile. "Hey, Katelyn."

"Um, I didn't mean to eavesdrop on your conversation with that man or anything, but I just wanted to tell you that I think it's really cool what you tried to do."

"Oh, I didn't know you could hear us," said Jon, pointing to her headphones.

"I had the music off," she said. "I hope you don't mind. But I was kind of interested in what you were talking about."

"No, I don't mind," said Jon. "But I don't think you heard much. I'm afraid all I did was make him want to sit somewhere else."

"You never know. My team leader in Costa Rica says it's all about planting seeds. Maybe you planted a seed with him that will grow into something. I'm just saying. So don't give up hope. That's all I wanted to say." Katelyn's dimples showed on her cheeks as she smiled at Jon.

"I appreciate that, Katelyn." The hope the young girl offered pushed a brief swell of emotion onto Jon's face. He hoped it didn't show. "And I'm glad we got to sit together. Good luck with Young Life."

"Thank you, sir." Katelyn placed her headphones back on her ears. "I hope the rest of your trip goes well."

"You, too." Jon closed his eyes and prayed himself to sleep.

The plane rolled to a hard stop at one of Atlanta's hundreds of terminal gates. After a moment of collective anticipation, Katelyn and other passengers around Jon sprang to their feet at the sound of a bell chime and began rifling through overhead compartments. Jon pulled his iPhone from the seat pocket in front of him and remained seated at the window, willing to wait until the plane's doors opened to begin his exit.

"Guess I owe you ten bucks," said Katelyn, smiling and pointing to the iPhone in Jon's hand.

"Oh, yeah," said Jon, remembering their bet. "Actually, I think our bet made me remember it. So let's call it even."

"Deal," said Katelyn. She stood up and maneuvered her way into the aisle. "It was nice meeting you."

"Nice to meet you, Katelyn. Good luck."

Despite his nap, Jon felt tired. Or maybe just defeated. He looked over the seats to find Brant, but the aisle full of impatient travelers obstructed his view. After several minutes of quiet waiting, the line to exit the plane began to move forward. Jon sat hoping for a gap in the steady flow of people and luggage. A very pregnant woman, swaying back and forth as she walked up the aisle, made eye contact with Jon and nodded for him to join the procession. "Thanks," said Jon, standing up. He grabbed his coat from the overhead bin and made his way off the plane.

Walking up the enclosed ramp, Jon hoped he wouldn't run into Geoff Holland once inside the airport. He imagined the man angrily telling him to stay away. Or perhaps, since Geoff had the rest of the flight to consider their conversation, he would confront Jon and give him another lecture on the value of religious diversity. Either way, it was an encounter Jon hoped to avoid.

Entering the gate lobby, Jon saw Brant standing beside a waist-high trashcan. The two made eye contact as Brant waved his hand. Next to Brant stood Geoff Holland. A flash of anxiety ran through Jon's body. Both men watched Jon as he made his way towards them. Other than coincidence, Jon struggled to find any possible reason why Brant was standing with Geoff. Regardless, there was no avoiding him.

As Jon approached, he spoke to Geoff first, hoping to defuse any potential confrontation. "Geoff, this is my friend Brant Morris."

Geoff looked to his right at Brant then back at Jon and smiled. "I introduced myself just a moment ago when I saw him standing here," said Geoff. "I was hoping to find you."

Here comes that lecture on diversity, Jon thought.

Geoff offered his hand to Jon and shook it firmly. "Jon, I want to apologize for my quick exit from our conversation earlier. That was very rude of me."

"Oh…well," said Jon, unprepared for Geoff's apology. "That's OK. I know I was…." Jon wasn't sure how to describe his unsuccessful attempt at sharing his faith.

"My opinions don't really get challenged much anymore," said Geoff. "I guess I reacted poorly. But you gave me a lot to think about, and I want to thank you for that."

Jon remained dumbfounded as he watched Geoff reach into his suit pocket and pull out a white business card and pen. After writing something on the card, he handed it to Jon. "Here's my card. That's my personal cell phone number on the back. If I can ever do anything to help you boys, please don't hesitate to contact me. Maybe I'll see you at the beach sometime, Jon."

"That sounds great," Jon mustered from his dazed mind as he looked up at Geoff.

"Thank you, sir," said Brant.

"Merry Christmas," said Geoff. He gave Jon a smile and left, quickly disappearing into the sea of people moving in every direction around the gate. Jon stood looking at the card in his hand, unsure of what just happened.

"Hey, man," said Brant. "What did you say to that guy?"

"Not much," said Jon, replaying his conversation with Geoff in his head.

"Well, you did better with him than I did with that priest," said Brant as they began to walk towards their next gate. "Do you know what he said to me when he passed by a minute ago?"

"I can't imagine," said Jon.

"He said, 'Pearls before swine, young man. Pearls before swine.'"

Jon broke into laughter. "He really said that?"

"Yeah, right back there," said Brant, pointing back at the trashcan. "Was he calling me a pig?"

"That's classic," said Jon, enjoying the smile across his face as he shook his head.

"What does that even mean?" asked Brant.

"I wouldn't worry about it, Brant. You know, there aren't too many people who would tell a priest he needs to read his Bible."

Brant shrugged his shoulders. "Well, I was just saying."

Jon laughed and grabbed the back of Brant's neck. "Yes, you were," he said. "Let's go home."

forty nine

The Dog That Saved Christmas

"Therefore encourage one another and build each
other up, just as in fact you are doing."
- *1 Thessalonians 5:1*

"Look at *this* house, Mom," said Jon as he steered Holly's 4Runner into his neighborhood. He slowed so she could enjoy the thousands of tiny white Christmas lights outlining the shape of the large brick home. In the yard, glowing strings of light wrapped around Palmetto trees, bushes, and three rattan reindeer, posed to graze on the green winter ryegrass. He glanced over to see his mother nodding off in the passenger seat. Jon smiled with envy. The rush of decorating his entire house the day before Christmas left him wishing he could close his eyes, as well. Having just returned home from Texas the day before, he'd seriously considered skipping the annual chore of dragging his artificial tree from under the house and sorting through all the ornaments, lights, and keepsakes stored in his attic. But the thought of hosting his mother, Brant and Jacob, not to mention Holly, in an undecorated house just wasn't acceptable.

As Jon turned onto his street, he could see the two strands of white lights glowing in the garland he'd hung from his own front stair railings. The small display made him glad his mother had slept past the showplace at the front of his neighborhood. He gently nudged her knee to wake her. "See the lights on my front stairs, Mom?" he asked, turning into his driveway.

His mother opened her eyes and took notice of Jon's modest attempt at decorating. "Oh, look at the pretty lights on the stairs," she said. "I love the red bows, too. You always do such a nice job decorating for Christmas."

"Well, I learned from the best," Jon patted his mother's knee as he came to a stop in his garage.

"Whose car is that?" she asked, pointing to the silver Toyota Corolla parked underneath Jon's basketball goal.

"That's my rental car. We drove that home from the airport last night. Brant must already be here with Jacob."

"Who?"

"My friend Brant. He and his son Jacob are staying with us for Christmas, remember?"

"Oh, yes. I just haven't seen that car before. Did you buy it for Holly?"

"No, ma'am. You're in Holly's car. That's just a rental car from the airport. My car is in Texas." Jon could see the confusion on his mother's face as he turned off the 4Runner. "Don't worry about it, Mom. Let's just get you inside. Holly's got supper all ready for us."

"What are we having?" she asked.

"We're having chicken and rice perlo with green beans, squash casserole, macaroni and cheese, and sweet potato casserole. And for dessert we have a sixteen-layer chocolate cake with vanilla ice cream."

"Oh, my goodness gracious," said his mother. "Holly cooked all that?"

Jon laughed. "No, ma'am. We ordered it from a restaurant here in town. They prepare everything. All we have to do is just pop it in the oven. It's a lot easier than trying to cook everything from scratch."

"Well, it all sounds wonderful to me," she said.

Jon hopped out of the 4Runner and jogged around to open his mother's door and help her from the car. As she slowly found her footing on the garage floor, Brant opened the door to the house and stood smiling in the doorframe waiting to greet them. Jon guided his mother up the three brick steps and into the house as Brant moved slowly backwards with their progress, stretching his hands forward should Jon's mother need assistance. Once inside, Jon reached behind him and closed the door.

"Mom, this is my old friend from college, Brant Morris. You might remember him from my wedding."

"Hi, Mrs. Smoak," said Brant, giving Jon's mother a gentle hug. "Merry Christmas. It's good to see you again."

Jon's mother studied Brant's face with an uncertain smile.

"Mom, Brant was the groomsman who took the microphone from the band at our reception and tried to sing that Frank Sinatra song."

Brant tried to smile through his embarrassment. "Thanks for bringing that up, Jon."

"What was the song, again?" asked Jon, remembering Brant's inebriated performance.

"*The Way You Look Tonight*," said Brant, reluctantly.

"Oh, yes," said Jon's mother, nodding her head. "I remember, Brant. You don't still try and sing, do you?"

"No, ma'am," said Brant, cutting his eyes at Jon.

"Well, that's good," she said, prompting laughter from Brant and Jon.

"Brant's traveling with me on my little mission trip thing, Mom. Remember?"

"Oh, yes. How nice."

"Mrs. Smoak, I want you to meet my son, Jacob. He's in there on the couch in the den. Jacob, stand up so Mrs. Smoak can see you." The boy remained seated with his back to the kitchen and waved his hand above his head without turning around. "I'm sorry about that," said Brant. "He must be playing a game on his phone or something."

"Merry Christmas, Nana!" said Holly, walking into the kitchen from the dining room.

"Hello, precious," said Jon's mother as she received a hug from Holly. "My, how you've grown-up since the last time I saw you."

"I saw you last week, Nana."

"Oh, that's right. Well, you're just as pretty as you can be. Jon, every time someone comes in my room and sees Holly's picture in the frame you gave me, they always say, 'Who is that? Is that your granddaughter?' They think she looks just like a movie star."

Holly blushed. "I look like such a dork in that picture."

"Hey, I took that picture," said Jon. "I think it looks great."

"Ugh," said Holly. "Anyway, everything is all warmed up and ready, Dad."

"OK, let's eat, then. I'm hungry," said Jon. "Mom, why don't you come in here and sit down. Holly's got the dining room table all set for us."

Jon's mother moved slowly through the kitchen towards the dining room. "Oh, I just love eating at my mother's old table," she said. "I grew-up eating at this table."

"I know," said Jon. "And it's still hanging in there."

"Jacob, come on, Son," said Brant, calling into the den. "Let's eat."

Jon pulled a chair out from the end of the table for his mother. "Mom, you sit here on the end next to me so I can help you if you need it. Holly, why don't you sit at the other end? And Brant and Jacob, you two can sit across from me."

"You sure you don't have name tags for us to wear, too, Jon?" asked Brant. Jacob giggled slightly without looking up from his father's side.

"Yeah, Dad," said Holly. "Just let everyone sit wherever they want."

"That's fine," said Jon. "I was just trying to help." Despite the half-hearted protest against his seating arrangement, everyone took a seat at the seventy-year-old maple table, precisely where he had suggested. On top of a red tablecloth covering the table's worn finish, Holly had filled every empty space with serving dishes full of food.

"Mom, would you like to bless it for us?" asked Jon.

"It's your house, Son. I think you should bless it."

"OK, then," said Jon. "Let's pray. Almighty God, we worship you here tonight on Christmas Eve as we gather together to celebrate the birth of your Son, Jesus. We thank you for such an amazing gift and the price you paid for our salvation. Thank you for this time together with family and for this wonderful food. Please bless it to our bodies and us to your service in Jesus' name. Amen."

Jon inched forward, the dry wood of his chair creaking loudly as he positioned himself closer to the table. Anytime he sat down on one of his dining room chairs, Jon always braced himself for the possibility of it collapsing underneath him, knowing it would happen eventually. When his grandmother passed away twenty years earlier, Jon's mother had insisted that he take her old table for his first home with Lacey. Sentiment had long ago blinded him to its well-used condition. And it remained an antique fixture in his otherwise modern home.

"This all looks amazing," said Brant. "You did a great job, Holly."

"Thank you, sir. It was fun."

The five helped their plates, passing the serving dishes clockwise around the table until each plate was full. As everyone began to eat, conversation came to a halt. Besides an occasional comment about how good the food tasted or how much there was of it, the meal proceeded in noticeably awkward silence. Jon's primary concern centered on his mother, who frequently struggled to keep food steady on her fork. He finally assumed the task for her, alternately feeding her and himself.

"So, Holly, you go to Carolina?" asked Brant.

"Yes, sir," said Holly.

"Good. That's good."

"Mmhmm."

Jon knew Brant was already aware of Holly's college situation and was simply attempting to make conversation. But the social void quickly returned, amplifying the sounds of forks clanging on plates, Brant chewing and Jacob slurping milk from his glass. Jon knew a simple way to at least get Holly talking. "Holly's got a new boyfriend, Mom," he said.

"Dad!" said Holly.

"What? You do, don't you? The boy from the coffee shop. What's his name again?"

"His name's Brighton. And he's not my boyfriend. We're just talking."

"About what?" asked Jon.

"No, I mean we're just friends. We like each other, but we're not dating."

"In our language," said Brant, "that means they're dating, Jon."

"Sure sounds like it to me," said Jon. "You bring him up all the time, Holly."

"Apparently not enough for you to remember his name, Dad. Besides, I told you, we're just friends."

"Have you kissed him, yet?" asked Brant.

Holly bounced her eyes back and forth between her father and Brant. "Um…yeah, but…."

"They're definitely dating," said Brant.

"Thanks for clearing that up, Brant," said Jon, smiling at his daughter.

"No problem."

Holly huffed and filled her mouth with a fork-load of macaroni and cheese.

"Is he a nice boy, Holly?" asked Jon's mother.

Holly swallowed and took a sip of iced tea. "Oh, yes, ma'am. He's very nice. And he's very polite. You'd like him, Nana."

"What's his name?" she asked.

"Brighton," said Holly.

"Your grandfather's roommate in college was named Brighton," she said.

"Was that his first name or last name?" asked Holly.

"His first name. His last name was Foster."

"Oh, my God," said Holly. "That's Brighton's last name. How weird is that?"

"Holly, you must have mentioned it to Nana sometime recently," said Jon. "I think she's just a little confused."

"I haven't, Dad. I promise."

"I'm not confused, Son. Brighton Foster was your father's roommate when I met him in college. Your father was at South Carolina, and I was at Columbia College."

"Are you sure his name was Brighton Foster, Mom?"

"How could I forget a name like that?"

"Well," said Jon, stopping himself from explaining the obvious.

Holly looked down at her iPhone. "It was Brighton's grandfather," she said.

"How do you know that?" asked Jon.

"I just texted Brighton. He's actually Brighton Foster, the third. His grandfather went to Carolina back in the fifties. Brighton's at his grandparents' right now."

"Ask him if his grandfather remembers Frank Smoak," said Jon.

"Hang on," said Holly, typing with her thumbs and waiting a brief moment for a reply. "Yep. He said they were roommates."

"Wow," said Jon. "You were right, Mom."

"Brighton says they were having the same conversation at their house about my last name. He said his granddad is sorry to hear about Papa passing away. I just told him about that."

"Brighton Foster was a good friend to your father for a number of years," said Jon's mother.

"I never heard Dad mention him."

"Oh, they had a falling out over something right before you were born, Son. In fact, your father had planned to name you after him. You were going to be John Brighton Smoak. But he changed his mind after their argument."

"You're kidding," said Jon.

"No, I'm not."

"What was their argument about?" asked Jon. "Do you remember?"

"It's been so long ago. I don't recall. But I don't think they ever spoke again after that."

"That's sad," said Jon.

"OK," said Holly. "This is kind of freaking me out a little. It's like finding out Brighton and I are related or something."

"For Pete's sake, Holly, you're not related," said Jon. "I think the whole thing is kind of cool."

"Of course you do," Holly said. "You're not dating him."

"I didn't think you were either," said Brant.

"I'm not," said Holly, appearing sheepish.

Brant smiled at Holly. "It's a small world, isn't it?"

"Too small."

Jon chuckled at his daughter's discomfort as he scooped a few green beans onto his mother's fork. As he leaned towards her, she opened her mouth to speak.

"You know, Son, Brighton Foster was the reason your father became a Christian."

"What?" asked Jon, setting the fork and green beans back onto her plate. "Seriously, Mom? I thought Dad was always a Christian."

"No one's born a Christian, Son."

Embarrassed, Jon tried to correct himself. "I didn't mean it like that. I meant I thought he was a Christian growing up."

"Brighton invited your father to church with him when they lived together at school. That's when he started taking an interest in faith. As a matter of fact, that's where I met him."

"I thought you met Dad at a Carolina basketball game."

"That was our first date. But I met him at church."

"At the church Mr. Foster invited him to?"

"Yes. I met him at a student ice cream social at First Baptist downtown. That was where all the Columbia College girls went to meet USC boys back then."

"You and Dad went to a Baptist church? That's a hoot. I never knew that."

"Oh, yes," she said.

"But y'all were Methodists as far back as I can remember," said Jon.

"That was because of me," she said. "I grew-up in a Methodist church in Georgetown, and your father had only been going to First Baptist a short while. We got married in my home church and just stayed Methodists our whole marriage."

"Wow. Brighton Foster brought you two together by inviting Dad to church and now his grandson is dating your granddaughter. That's just amazing."

"We're not dating," said Holly.

"Jon, your father used to know a Brighton Foster when he was in college," his mother said. "They were roommates."

Jon's enjoyment of their conversation ended with the sudden reminder of his mother's frail short-term memory. "Yes, ma'am," he said. He could see signs of fatigue in her wrinkled face and cloudy eyes. "Are you finished eating, Mom? You want anything else? Some dessert, maybe? We have cake."

"No, thank you, Son. I've had more than enough."

"Would you like to go rest in the recliner in the den for a little while? While we clean up?"

"That sounds fine," she said.

Jon helped his mother from the table and guided her around the Christmas tree into his den, steadying her by the elbow as they moved slowly by the couch to his recliner. He eased her into the chair and turned on the television. "You just rest here for a few minutes, Mom, and I'll be right back." Jon unfolded a blanket from his couch and placed it gently over his mother's legs. "*It's A Wonderful Life* is on, Mom. Is that OK?"

"Oh, that's fine," she said, leaning back in the chair. "Can you turn it up a little, Son? I can't hear what they're saying."

Jon pointed the remote at the TV and turned up the volume. "Is that loud enough?"

"What?" she asked.

"I'll take that as a *yes*," he said and placed the remote control on his mother's lap. He returned to the dining room to find Holly and Brant serving dessert plates loaded with thick slices of chocolate layer cake and vanilla ice cream. "Just what I don't need," said Jon. "But what the heck. It's Christmas, right?"

"Exactly," said Brant. "Nice to see you eating like a normal person for a change, Jon."

"It happens every now and then," said Jon. Using his fork, he cut equal parts of cake and ice cream and scooped the bite into his mouth. The lack of sweets in his regular diet only made them taste better when he finally indulged. "Oh, my gosh. That's so good."

"See?" said Brant.

"OK, this is weird," said Holly, scowling at her iPhone. "Brighton says his Aunt Megan says to tell you hello, Dad."

Jon exchanged looks with Brant. "Megan who?" he asked.

"Yeah, who's Aunt Megan?" Brant asked Holly.

Holly shrugged. "His aunt is all I know."

"Ask him what her last name is, honey" said Jon.

Holly typed into her phone. "Her maiden name was Foster, but she's married now."

"Megan Foster?" asked Brant, looking at Jon. "From MindShare?"

A fast-moving wave of twenty-year-old memories washed over Jon. The Wofford football game, flirting smiles in the hallway, chatty visits at his desk, an answered prayer for help. "Wow," he said, with a quick shake of his head.

"Like I said, small world. Eh, Jon?" asked Brant.

"Right now, it feels about the size of a grape."

"Who is it, Dad?" asked Holly.

"Just someone Brant and I used to work with a long time ago," said Jon. "Ask Brighton to say hello for me."

"And me, too," said Brant, turning his eyes to Jon. "You know she's the one who introduced me to Debbie, don't you?"

"No, I didn't know that," said Jon.

"Who's Debbie?" asked Holly.

"Brant's first wife."

Holly dropped her iPhone on the table beside her dessert plate. "OK, my head's about to explode. Can we talk about something else, please?"

Jon laughed and relaxed in his chair. "Gladly," he said. He looked across the table at Brant's son, Jacob, staring quietly at his cake and ice cream. Jon realized the boy had been excluded from all conversation during dinner. "So, Jacob, what grade are you in?"

"Fourth," said the boy, without shifting his gaze.

"Do you have a favorite teacher?" asked Jon.

"Dad, it's Christmas Eve," said Holly. "I doubt the kid wants to talk about school. I know I don't."

"Oh, right. Sorry about that. So, what are you hoping Santa will bring you for Christmas tonight, Jacob?"

Brant shook his head quickly and enlarged his eyes at Jon. "Santa's going to leave Jacob's toys at his mom's house tonight," he said, his mouth full of cake. "He'll see them when he gets home tomorrow. Won't you, Son?"

Jacob had yet to touch his dessert. "I want to go home," he said.

"Jacob, would you like to go watch a Christmas show?" asked Holly.

Jacob shook his head back and forth as he stared at the ice cream melting into his cake.

"No?" asked Holly. "Not even *A Charlie Brown Christmas*?"

"He doesn't like that one," said Brant.

"Why not?" asked Jon.

Brant rolled his eyes discreetly at Jon.

"The kids on that show are mean," said Jacob. "My mom says bullying isn't nice."

"There you go," said Brant.

"Oh, for Pete's sake," said Jon, with a laugh. "It's Charlie Brown. They all turn nice in the end, don't they?"

Jacob looked up at Jon. "You mean when they're singing at Snoopy's dog house?"

"Yeah," said Jon. "Hark the herald angels sing, glory to—"

"But they still call him a blockhead for getting that little tree," said Jacob.

Jon shrugged his shoulders. "Well, yeah, but…."

"Those kids *are* pretty mean to old Chuck, aren't they, Son," said Brant, patting Jacob on the back.

"I guess I never really thought of it that way," said Jon. "I just always thought it was funny."

"How about *Elf*?" asked Holly. "Does your mom let you watch that?"

"That's one of our favorites, isn't it, buddy?" asked Brant.

Jacob looked down at his plate without responding to his father's question.

"You want to go upstairs and watch it in our playroom?" asked Holly. "There's a big TV up there and lots of my old toys to play with."

"You're a girl," said Jacob. "I don't want to play with girl toys."

"I've got Legos. Do you like Legos?"

"You play with Legos?" asked Jacob, beginning to show interest.

"I did when I was growing up. They're not just for boys, you know."

"Honey, I closed-up Elvis in the playroom to keep him away from the tree," said Jon. "Be careful with the Legos. He might chew them up or swallow one."

"We'll be careful," said Holly.

"Who's Elvis?" asked Jacob.

"That's my dog," said Holly. She glanced at her father. "Our dog, I mean."

"You have a dog?" asked Jacob, taking a bite of his cake. "What kind is it?"

"He's an Anatolian Shepherd," said Holly.

"An Ana-what?" asked the boy, shoveling a spoonful of soft ice cream into his mouth.

"An Anatolian Shepherd. He looks like a...well, he's kind of weird. Do you have a dog?"

"I'm not allowed," said Jacob. "My mom says they pee on everything and chew up furniture."

"Well, she's right about that," said Jon. "But it's just when they're puppies. They grow out of it."

"Can we go see him?" Jacob asked Holly.

"Is that OK, Mr. Morris?"

"Sure, Holly," said Brant. "But be careful, Son. Don't let him jump on you."

"I won't," said Jacob, pushing himself away from the table.

Holly grabbed Jacob's hand and led him through the kitchen and up the stairs to the playroom over the garage.

"The last thing I need is for him to go back to his mom's house with dog scratches all over him," said Brant. "I'd never hear the end of it."

"He seems like a nice kid, Brant."

"He hates me."

"What?"

"I don't mean that literally. It's just that…he was really upset about coming over here. I had to physically carry him out of his mom's house with him crying and Kim standing there watching. Not exactly a Hallmark moment on Christmas Eve."

"Oh, wow. I'm sorry, man. I thought this would be a good thing for you guys."

"It's not your fault. I appreciate you having us here. But I just think Kim has made me out to be some sort of absentee father since you and I left on our trip. I've tried to stay in touch with him. But whenever I call, he doesn't answer or doesn't want to talk. And he never responds to my text messages."

"He's got his own phone?" asked Jon. "He's ten."

"An iPhone. They all do, nowadays, Jon. Get with it."

"I guess I'm behind the times. Holly didn't get her own phone until she was…oh wait. She was in fourth grade. She was ten. Never mind."

"You see?"

"Yeah, but it wasn't an iPhone, for Pete's sake. It was just an old flip phone."

"What kind of father let's his own daughter go around with uncool technology like that?"

"It was cool enough nine years, ago, believe me." Jon scraped the last bit of cake from his plate and cleaned the fork in his mouth. "That was ridiculous."

"See what you're missing the other 51 weeks out of the year?" asked Brant.

Jon could hear feet rumbling down the stairs from the playroom. Jacob landed in the kitchen and rushed into the dining room in his sock feet, sliding to a stop on the hardwood floors. "Dad, can I have a drink of water?" he asked, breathing heavily.

"Sure, bud," said Brant, reaching for his son's empty glass on the table.

"That one had milk in it," said Jacob. "Can I get a new glass?"

"I'll get it," said Jon, pushing away from the table. He made his way into the kitchen, followed closely by Brant and Jacob. Jon pulled a clean glass down from his cabinet and filled it with ice water from the refrigerator door. "Here you go, sport," he said, handing the glass to Jacob.

"Why are you out of breath, Son?" asked Brant, pushing sweaty, blonde hair off of Jacob's forehead while the boy drank. "What have you been doing up there?"

"Wrestling with Elvis! He's awesome. It's so much fun. He tried to bite my whole head!"

"Jon?" said Brant, quickly.

"Relax. Elvis won't hurt him. He just plays a little rough sometimes."

Jacob took a long drink, handed the glass back to Jon and turned to go back up stairs. Brant caught Jacob by his shoulders and turned him towards Jon. "What do you say to Mr. Smoak?"

"Thank you for the water," said Jacob. He freed himself from his father's grasp and hurried onto the stairs.

"Hey, Jacob," said Jon, causing the boy to stop and turn around just a few steps up from the kitchen.

"Yes, sir?"

"Has your dad told you about the time he saved a woman from a burning car?"

"Huh?" asked Jacob.

"He saved a woman from a burning car," said Jon, cutting his eyes briefly at Brant. "He didn't tell you about that?"

"When did you do that, Dad?" the boy asked, letting himself slide one step down towards the kitchen.

"Uh…that happened a couple months ago," said Brant, looking at Jon. "But it was really—"

"It was amazing," said Jon. "Like something out of a movie!"

"What happened?" asked Jacob, stepping back down into the kitchen.

"Well, you know your dad and I are traveling across the country to tell people about Jesus, right?"

Jacob looked at his father. "Mom said you were off on vacation instead of looking for a job."

"She told you that?" asked Brant.

"It's not a vacation Jacob," said Jon. "Your dad's working with me to help people understand how they can know God through Jesus and go to heaven when they die. It's super important work and your dad is doing a great job at it."

"Oh. So, when did he save the lady in the car?"

"Well, we were driving through Florida a couple months ago and we were in our car waiting to turn onto a highway when this dog crosses the road and causes an accident right in front of us. And this woman's pick-up truck hits a telephone pole and starts a fire! So your dad and I jump out of our car and race over to her, but she was trapped inside her truck and couldn't move! So I got in the truck from the other side, but I couldn't get her door open to get her out. And the fire was getting closer and closer to the truck! Smoke was all inside and I couldn't see anything. I didn't think we were going to make it! Then all of a sudden your dad just grabs her door from the outside and rips it open!"

"You did?!" asked Jacob, looking up at his father.

"He did!" said Jon. "And then these firemen pulled the lady out just before her whole truck burst into flames!"

"Wow!" shouted Jacob. "That's like Captain America or something!"

"It was!" said Jon. "Your dad saved that lady's life! He's a hero!"

"Jon," said Brant.

"That's awesome, Dad! I can't wait to tell Mom that story! She's not gonna believe it!"

"I can hardly believe it, myself," said Brant, looking at Jon.

"Dad, you want to come upstairs and play with Elvis and watch *Elf* with me and Holly?"

"Sure, Son. I'd love to."

"You have to come see all of her Legos. She has *so* many. It's amazing!"

"OK."

"And can we stay up late and build stuff? Just you and me?"

"As late as you want, pal."

"Yay!" shouted Jacob as he turned and ran up the stairs.

"You coming, Jon?" asked Brant.

"You guys go ahead. I'm going to clean up a bit and watch the movie with my mom for a little while before I put her to bed."

"Need any help cleaning up?"

"Absolutely not. You go be with your son."

"OK," said Brant as he began to climb the stairs. "Hey, Jon, I appreciate what you just did there. I owe you one."

"Hey, after what you did for me in the stadium in Austin, let's just call it even. OK, Captain America?"

Brant laughed. "Ok. But seriously, man, you saved our Christmas."

"Well, I think Elvis deserves at least some of the credit for that."

"Thank God for Elvis, then. Anyway, Merry Christmas, Jon."

"Merry Christmas, Brant."

fifty

Single Purpose

*"But one thing I do: Forgetting what is behind and straining
toward what is ahead, I press on toward the goal to win the prize
for which God has called me heavenward in Christ Jesus."*
- *Philippians 3:13*

A steady mist hung in the cool air as Jon walked with Brant towards the church entrance. Jon hadn't spent a Sunday morning in his own church in three months. And he was about to enter the Single Again Sunday school class for the first time since turning his world upside down in front of its members. His stomach ached with nerves as he walked with Brant in between cars in the full parking lot. Looking up at the two-story brick building, the church seemed bigger than Jon remembered.

"They're not going to ask us to say anything in there are they?" asked Brant.

"Well, that's kind of why we're here," said Jon. "Steve and Phillip asked if we'd come to Sunday school while we're home for Christmas and share how our trip's been going. And I said we would."

"Well, I'll just leave all that to you."

"Why? Are you shy all of a sudden?"

"I just don't like public speaking, that's all."

"Wait a minute," said Jon, stopping on the sidewalk. "*You* have a fear of public speaking?"

Brant didn't stop. "I didn't say I was afraid of it. I just don't like it, that's all."

"People don't like public speaking *because* they're afraid of it," said Jon, now trailing behind.

Brant turned around to face Jon, walking backwards. "So, basically, you're calling me a chicken?"

"Bak, bak, bak," said Jon, folding his wrists under his armpits and flapping his elbows like wings. He discovered making fun of Brant to be the perfect, if not accidental, stress reliever.

"Fine. Whatever, dude." Brant turned his back to Jon and walked on towards the church while Jon continued his chicken imitation behind him. "You know everyone is probably wondering who that idiot is in the parking lot doing the Chicken Dance."

"Aw, come on, Brant. I'm just kidding." Jon jogged a few steps to catch up as they neared the church entrance. He smiled at the two gentlemen holding the doors open for them. "Good morning," he said as they entered the education building. "Besides, man, I saw you get up on that fountain at FSU and speak to those kids. And what about your big Cam Parsons sermon in Austin? That was awesome! So I know you can do it if you want to."

Brant stopped just past the welcome desk and pulled Jon over to the opposite wall. "Those kids at FSU weren't listening to a word I was saying. I knew that. They were all just walking by on their way to class. And it was just you in that baseball stadium. And technically the cop, but I didn't know he was listening. But standing in front of a Sunday school class full of people...." Brant lowered his voice as an older couple passed by them. "Everyone in there's been a Christian a lot longer than me, you know. The thought of them just sitting there staring at me is terrifying."

"Wow, so you really *are* scared."

"Fine. I admit it – I've got a fear of public speaking, OK, Jon? Feel better now?"

"I just think it's funny, is all. It's so...not you."

"Well, it *is* me. So if you don't mind, I'd rather you do all the talking."

"Fine," said Jon, turning to walk down the hall. "Come on. I'll introduce you as my mute sidekick."

"I'm not your sidekick. We've talked about that."

"Oh, that's right – you're Captain America."

Brant gave in to a smile on his face as Jon stopped at the closed door of his Sunday school room.

"Here we are," said Jon. "You ready?"

"Sure, whatever."

Jon looked through the small window in the door. "Oh great, Phillip's already started his morning announcements. We were supposed to get here early."

"Oh, well. I guess we should leave."

"Stop being such a wuss," said Jon, opening the door.

"Well, there's our guest of honor now," said Phillip, standing behind the small, wooden podium. "Perfect timing. Come on in, guys. Happy New Year! We were just getting started."

Jon started to sit down in one of two empty chairs just inside the door.

"Have a seat right up front here, guys," said Phillip, waving them forward and pointing to several empty front-row chairs directly before him. Brant followed Jon to the front of the room and took a seat next to him in front of the podium.

"Most of you know Jon Smoak, and I believe some of you may have met his friend Brent Morris."

"Brant," said Steve, standing off to the side of the room.

"Brant Morris," said Phillip. "I'm sorry, Brant. I don't know why I can't remember that. But Jon and Brant have, for the last several months, been on a mission trip to spread the Gospel wherever the Lord leads them. But they've flown home for Christmas from…."

"Austin," said Jon, looking up at Phillip.

"Austin, Texas, that's right. And we've asked them to come share what God's been doing through them. So, Jon and Brant, if you guys would come on up." Phillip clapped his hands as he backed away from the podium, prompting the rest of the class to join in a brief applause.

Jon rose from his chair and moved behind the podium as Brant positioned himself to his left. "Hi, I'm Jon and this is my friend Brant. Um, for those of you who were here the last time I stood in front of you, I promise: No crying today." Jon paused for a moment as polite laughter echoed around the room. "As Phillip mentioned, we've been out on the road looking for opportunities to share Christ with people. And all that really started right here a few months ago. The Lord convicted me of letting my faith become a meaningless routine of activities rather than a relationship with him. And in struggling through all that in prayer, I asked God an open-ended question, which I've learned can be a little dangerous. I asked him how I could serve him. The answer was pretty startling. It led me to Matthew 28:7, which says, "Go quickly and tell his disciples he has risen from the dead." I believe God was impressing upon me a sense of urgency to really do what that verse says – to go and tell people about Jesus and to do it now.

"There are a lot of lost people out there who desperately need to hear the Good News of salvation through faith in Jesus Christ. So I committed myself to doing just that. I took a six-month leave of absence from my job and, the night before I left, I had dinner with my friend Brant, here. And he asked if he could join me on my trip. So, the two of us headed west, witnessing to folks along the way. And we've been blessed to see several people make decisions for Christ. And I've got to tell you, the feeling you get from allowing God to use you to lead someone to salvation is…it's hard to put into words. I told a friend of mine it feels like you're doing what you were created to do. I've never experienced that in my career or anything else. Being a father is a close second, but seeing God change lives right in front of you is just an amazing experience."

Jon could see a hand raised towards the back of the room. He didn't recognize the man's face. "You have a question?"

"Yeah, how receptive have people been?" the man asked. "Have you had anyone just reject you outright?"

"Oh, absolutely," said Jon. "We've had our share of rejections. The Gospel can be flat out offensive to some people. If you think about it – if you take its message seriously – it means you have to accept that the way you're living, or what you currently believe, is wrong and that your current path has eternal negative consequences. A lot of people just don't want to hear that."

"Like in Baton Rouge," said Brant.

"You want to tell them about that?" asked Jon, hoping to draw Brant out of his fear.

"No, you go ahead," said Brant.

"What happened in Baton Rouge?" asked Phillip.

"Well, let's just say you don't want to challenge a group of LSU fans outside of a restaurant after a football game on the issue of drinking too much. That didn't go over too well."

"I can imagine," said Phillip, above laughter from the class.

"It was our fault, really," said Jon.

"My fault, actually," said Brant, raising his hand.

"We kind of lost our message that time," said Jon, "and things got a little out of hand."

"And a few people didn't like it when I told them they were going to hell without Jesus," said Brant, looking down at the floor.

"That caused a bit of a ruckus," said Jon. "The police got involved and threatened to arrest us. Actually, I think they were trying to rescue us. It was a little intense there for a few minutes. But we've seen the opposite happen, as well. People being receptive to God's message and making decisions of faith that changed their lives. It's been really cool to see."

"But how do you even approach someone?" a woman asked. "Initially, I mean. How do you start a conversation about faith with a total stranger?"

"I think that was the biggest question I had going into all this," said Jon. "I know Steve will tell you – the best way to share Christ is through your existing relationships. With people who know you and see the way you're living your faith. It's much more difficult to initiate a conversation with someone you don't know and have it be a meaningful discussion. But I think every situation has been different for us. We've tried canned approaches. You know, "Can I talk with you about Jesus?" And so forth. Some folks will say yes and some will say no."

"And some will cuss you out," said Brant, drawing more laughter.

"We've had that happen," said Jon. "But the thing I've learned is that if you make yourself available to serve God and are looking for opportunities to share your faith, he'll put you in situations to do that. Some of the most successful conversations we've had with people were those we didn't even plan or seek out. They just happened. God prepared the circumstances and we were ready when he did. First Peter 3:15 says, 'Always be prepared to give an answer to everyone who asks you to give the reason for the hope that you have.' I think that's the secret." Jon paused and looked around the room. "Any more questions?"

"I have one," said a woman Jon knew.

"Sure, Sylvia."

"How do you think your life will be different when you come back and go back to your job and normal routine and everything?"

"Wow," said Jon. "I don't know. Right now, it's hard to even think about that. But I do have bills to pay and a daughter in college, so I'm sure I'll have to get back in the grind at some point. But I hope I'll never stop looking for chances to be a light and witness for Christ." Jon looked to his left. "Brant, how about you?"

"I don't have a job, so I can't answer that."

"He's an IT guy," said Jon. "So if you know of any jobs out there, please let him know."

Phillip stepped forward. "Are there any more questions for Jon and Brant?"

Jon looked around the room again for any raised hands, but saw none.

"When do you guys head back out?" asked Phillip.

"We're actually heading to the airport right after church," said Jon.

"Well, thanks for coming and sharing with us this morning."

"Thanks for having us," said Jon.

The class applauded as Jon and Brant began to move back towards their seats.

"Before Jon and Brant sit down," said Steve, moving to the center of the room. "Come on back up here for a second, guys."

"Oh, that's right," said Phillip. "Steve and I want to make an important announcement. I almost forgot. Go ahead, Steve."

Steve walked over and stood in front of the class, resting his elbow on the podium. "Thanks, Phillip. Before Jon left on his trip, he asked to meet with Phillip and me to discuss what he felt God had called him to do. He also wanted to get some advice on how to witness to people, something he'd never done before. That seems funny to say now, after hearing their story. But Jon and Brant are proving what God can do when we truly seek his will, listen for his direction, and then actually do what he calls us to do, regardless of the cost to us. Phillip and I have talked a lot since that meeting with Jon. And we've prayed about how we, as a class, can better follow the example God has given us through these two men. So, with that as background, I'll turn it back to Phillip for the announcement."

"Thanks, Steve." Phillip pointed his remote control at the projector and advanced his PowerPoint presentation on the screen behind him to the next slide. "Beginning with the New Year, the *Single Again* class will be known as the *Single Purpose* class. Our single purpose will be to disciple single adult Believers to reach non-believers in our community. We will grow our faith and knowledge of the Lord through Bible study and prayer. And we'll seek to make him known to those who need to hear his message of salvation through Jesus Christ."

Steve moved in front of the podium to address the class. "Phillip and I believe this is more than a simple name change. The name, Single Purpose, represents our desire to actively, intentionally seek God's will for our lives. And we'll start by focusing on what he's already revealed to us in Scripture. So often we get caught-up in the question of '*What's God's will for me?*' that we ignore what he's already told us to do. And a central part of what he's commanded us to do is to go out into the world – outside these church walls – and make disciples of Christ. I want to thank Jon and Brant for their example and inspiration for this new direction for our class. After a lot of prayer and discussion, we really feel this is the direction God has placed on our hearts as leaders of the class. Does anyone have any questions?"

A man holding a cup of coffee and a doughnut in the back of the room asked, "Will we still get to do social activities like Beach Day and the New Year's Eve party?"

"Absolutely," said Phillip. "We may even choose to have more social activities, if they help us in our mission to reach people around us. But we're not a dating service for single Christians."

Several people in the room, including Jon, shared a brief laugh in appreciation for Phillip's assertion. It was clear to Jon that Phillip's perspective had changed dramatically since he'd been gone. Where Phillip used to soak in laughter from the class, he now simply waited for it to pass so he could continue.

"The focus for those events should be," said Phillip, "how can we use them to reach others for Christ, so that he is glorified and is made known to others? Steve and I hope we'll all experience the joy that can come from challenging and encouraging one another to grow our relationship with the Lord and allow ourselves to be used by him. Steve, did you have anything else you wanted to add before you began your lesson?"

"No, I think that covers it," said Steve.

"OK," said Phillip, turning to Jon with a smile. "Jon, I'm afraid of what might happen, but would you do us the honor of opening our time of study in prayer?"

Jon laughed along with the rest of the class. He hadn't thought about being asked to pray and was mildly surprised. "I'd be happy to," he said. He put his hands behind his back, bowed his head and closed his eyes. "Dear Heavenly Father," he prayed, "we come before you now to study your Word and grow in our knowledge and understanding of your will and how we can put our faith into action. Lord, I thank you for this class and the leadership you've provided over it. I pray that you will use everyone in here to glorify you by sharing your love and message of hope and salvation to those around us. And God, if there is anyone here in this room, right now, who doesn't know you as their Lord and Savior – or maybe they're just not sure – God, I pray that your Spirit will move in their hearts and they will seek you this morning – here now or in worship – and come to know the assurance and peace and joy they can only find in Jesus. Please speak to us now through your Word as Steve brings our lesson. In Jesus' name, amen."

Jon and Brant took their seats again on the front row as Steve picked up his iPad from his chair and placed it on the podium in the front of the room. He cleared his throat and began his lesson. "Today, we're going to look at the story of Lazarus and the rich man in the Gospel of Luke, chapter sixteen, verses nineteen through thirty-one. In these verses, Jesus gives us a behind the scenes look at hell. The title of our lesson, is *Hell Needs a Comeback*. Today, in pulpits across the country and even in many of our seminaries, the topic of hell has largely disappeared. Most people simply don't want to hear about it. And even fewer believe in its existence. A recent poll found that only forty-three percent of Americans believe in the existence of hell as a place of eternal suffering after death. And less than two percent of respondents to the same survey believed they would go there. This belief seems to run counter to what Jesus said in Matthew 7:13-14, when he said, 'wide is the gate and broad is the road that leads to destruction, and many enter through it. But small is the gate and narrow the road that leads to life, and only a few find it.' Jesus clearly flips the percentages.

"Unfortunately, the majority of people in this country are on the road to hell and don't even know it. Failure to believe in hell does not change the fact that it exists any more than failure to believe the sun will rise tomorrow will keep it from happening. Belief, or lack of it, cannot alter truth. And unless we, as Christians, do a better job of proclaiming the whole Gospel, including what Believers are saved *from*, we are dooming an entire generation to a false sense of eternal security.

"Christians often soft-pedal the existence of hell for various reasons. But I believe the primary reason is that if we truly accept as fact that the lost people around us – including many we know and love – are going to a real place called hell unless they accept Christ, we would be bound by every sense of morality, ethics, duty, and love to tell them how to avoid that horrible fate. And that obligation scares us. Cam Parsons once said, "I cannot proclaim the wonders of heaven without warning of the fires of hell." Folks, hell is in need of a comeback. So, Brant, you go right on telling people about the eternal dangers of rejecting Jesus Christ. Don't be shy, my friend."

Jon felt a nudge against his arm and turned to see Brant's smiling face.

"See?" whispered Brant.

"Yeah," whispered Jon. "Now, if we can just get you up in front of a crowd."

fifty one

Back In The Saddle

"For I know the plans I have for you,' declares the LORD, 'plans to prosper you and not to harm you, plans to give you hope and a future."
- Jeremiah 29:11

Jon tapped his foot to *A Fire I Can't Put Out*, by George Strait, mouthing the words as he studied the variety of mounted hunting trophies hanging from the oak-paneled walls of the Buck-N-Bull Saloon. Framed pictures of camouflage-clad hunters, posing with their kill, covered any wall space not occupied by stuffed animal heads or mounted antlers. His dinner was losing its warmth on the plate before him, but Jon waited patiently for Brant to return from the restroom before he began eating. His empty stomach growled above the sound of the music as he watched six bearded men at a nearby table devour large servings of barbequed ribs, hamburgers, and steaks. As Jon's gaze passed over the bar, he caught the attention of his waitress, inadvertently summoning her to his table. A slender, modestly attractive woman in her thirties wearing blue jeans, cowboy boots, and a white T-shirt, she perfectly matched Jon's imagined stereotype of a Texas saloon waitress.

"Did everything come out OK?" the waitress asked with concern in her voice.

"Yep, looks great," said Jon. "I'm just waiting on my friend to start eating. He's in the restroom."

"Oh, good. I thought something was wrong with your order. Let me know how you like those fish tacos. They're my favorite."

"I will."

"Again, my name's Sophie. Just holler if you need anything."

"Thanks, Sophie."

Brant returned to the table as Sophie departed, grinning as if he'd just heard a joke.

"What's so funny?" asked Jon as Brant took his seat.

"You've got to go to the bathroom. They have the largest buffalo head I've ever seen mounted in there over the urinals! Can you believe that? Who puts a buffalo head in the bathroom? I was so busy staring at it, I almost missed!"

"Do I have to hear a report from every visit you make to the bathroom?" said Jon, pouring sweetener into his iced tea.

"Hey, I'm just saying." Brant scooted his chair up to the table and widened his eyes at the large burger surrounded by french fries, which overflowed from his plate. "Wow, this looks amazing. Were you waiting on me to start eating?"

"I was waiting, so we could pray first."

"Oh, thanks. You wanna do it this time or should I?"

"I've got it," said Jon, bowing his head over his plate. "Dear Father in heaven, we thank you for our safe flight back to Austin so that we might continue the work you've called us to do. Please guide us and let your Spirit work in us and through us as we seek to bring others into a relationship with you, Lord. Use us for your glory, God. And we thank you for this food. In Jesus' name, we pray. Amen."

"Amen," said Brant. "Look at this burger, man! I guess everything *is* bigger in Texas." Brant's burger dripped with chili and melted pimento cheese as he lifted it with both hands towards his mouth.

"Are you really going to eat all that?" asked Jon.

"You know it. I'm starving. I haven't eaten anything since we left your house this morning."

"I guess that chicken sandwich I bought you at the airport in Atlanta doesn't count."

"That was just a snack," said Brant. He sunk his teeth into his burger and moaned with satisfaction.

Jon shook his head and bit off the end of his first grilled fish taco. He was happy to be back in his normal healthy discipline, after eating anything and everything while he was home for Christmas. Brant, on the other hand, appeared equally happy to be indulging himself, as usual.

"OK," said Brant, his cheeks still full. "Why is there a stuffed monkey on the shelf behind the bar?"

"That's not a monkey," said Jon, looking towards the bar. "It's a baboon."

"How can you tell?" asked Brant, still chewing.

"Look at its butt. And see how long his snout is? Baboons have longer snouts, like dogs. And shorter tails, too."

"All right, I'll rephrase the question. Why is there a *baboon* on a shelf behind the bar?"

"I have no idea," said Jon, scooping his fork under a slice of grilled zucchini. "I guess they ran out of bulls, deer, rams, and jackalopes."

"And buffalo," added Brant. "Say, why do you know so much about monkeys and baboons?"

Jon finished chewing and took a sip from his glass of iced tea. "We used a baboon in a TV spot for a client last year. We went through two monkeys and three baboons before we finally got one to do what we wanted."

"You got to work with real monkeys?"

"Yep. I mean, we had a trainer and several handlers, but yeah."

"That's so cool! What was the commercial for?"

"Toilet paper."

"Are you serious?" Brant set his chili-cheeseburger back on his plate and laughed with delight. "Toilet paper? With a baboon?"

"Yep," said Jon. Brant's hearty reaction made Jon laugh with him. He obviously fell into the ad's target audience.

"So, did you have him sitting on a toilet and everything?"

"It was a she. And yes, we did. The spot actually won an award." As Jon described the commercial to Brant, the memory of its creation cycled in the background of his mind. Filming the spot had been the most difficult and frustrating experience in his career with Crescent-Tango. An untrusting, impatient client, constantly intervening in the creative process, made every decision a battle and pushed the project far over budget. And despite the intended humor in the commercial, the pain of making it had kept him from enjoying the final result. But Brant's joyful appreciation was contagious, and Jon finally felt free to revel in it.

Brant leaned back in his chair to stretch his stomach and catch his breath. "Oh, man. I can't believe I never saw that on TV."

"It's on YouTube. I'll show it to you later."

Brant continued chuckling to himself as he dipped his french fries in ketchup and ate them, two at a time.

"I hope you think it's this funny after you see it," said Jon.

Brant shook his head and wiped his mouth with a napkin. "I want your job, man. I bet making that commercial was a blast."

"Actually, it was pretty...." Seeing the smile on Brant's messy face stopped Jon from sharing the frustrating truth behind the experience. Why ruin a good story, he thought. "It was pretty cool. Yeah. It was fun."

"That's awesome," said Brant. "So, have you thought about what we're going to do after this?"

Jon pushed a slice of avocado into his second fish taco with a fork. "I thought we'd drive on to El Paso tonight and start out fresh there in the morning."

"No. I mean when our trip is over. What do you think you'll do?"

"Didn't I already answer that question in front of our Sunday school class this morning?"

"Yeah, but that was in front of the class. What do you really think you'll do? Seriously."

"To be honest...I'm trying not to think about it. I'll worry about all that in a few months, I guess."

"What if Croissant-Mango doesn't give you your job back?"

"It's Crescent-Tango."

"Crescent-Tango, sorry. I knew it was something weird like that. What kind of a company name is that, anyway? It sounds made-up."

"It's an ad agency, Brant. What do you expect?"

"Ah, good point. Anyway, if they won't take you back, what are you going to do?"

"Are you trying to stress me out, here? I'm trying to have a nice meal."

"A nice meal?" asked Brant, looking around him. "Jon, we're in a place called the Buck-N-Bull Saloon and there's a stuffed baboon over there staring at you. People don't come here to have nice meals."

"You got me there. But at least they had these fish tacos. They're not that bad."

"Eat some *real* food will you?"

"You call that massive, death burger real food?"

"Yes, I do," said Brant taking another large bite. "So, anyway, what are you going to do when we get home?"

"I told you, I don't know," said Jon, beginning to feel pressured. "Will you stop with the questions?"

"I'm just making conversation, Jon. It's what normal people do."

"Normal people don't talk with their mouths full of food," said Jon. "Why don't you just go back to talking about baboons and toilet paper?"

"Are you saying I'm not interested in adult conversation?" asked Brant.

Jon dropped his hands on either side of his plate. "Geez, man! We sound like an old married couple or something!"

"I was just wondering what your plans are, Jon. That's all. I'm not trying to make you mad or anything."

"I told you I don't want to think about it right now. Just let me eat." Jon stabbed three zucchini slices with his fork, stuffed them in his mouth, and focused his irritation at a boar head, hanging across the room.

"But it's just three months from now, you know," said Brant, refusing to move off the topic. "I would think you'd have some big plan, already."

Jon dropped his fork loudly onto his plate. "I don't have one, OK? I don't have a big plan. I have no plans. There! Are you satisfied?"

Brant looked down at his mound of french fries for a moment. "Not even a spreadsheet with all your options listed out, with pros and cons for each one?"

"I don't do that," said Jon, diverting his eyes to the baboon.

"Uh-huh," said Brant.

Jon looked back to see Brant smirking and tapping a french fry on his plate.

"OK, I have a list of options," admitted Jon. "But it's not in a spreadsheet."

"Where is it?"

Jon sighed. "It's in an app on my iPhone."

"I knew it! See? I *know* you, man!"

"Lucky guess," said Jon, feeling exposed.

Brant laughed with satisfaction as he tossed the french fry into his mouth. "So, if advertising doesn't work out for you, maybe you could be an evangelist or something, Jonny-boy. You ever thought about that? Who knows, you could be the next Cam Parsons."

"I really can't see that happening, Brant," said Jon, reaching for his iced tea.

"Why not?"

"Because, I have to go back to work. It takes money to live, remember? Besides, I'm no Cam Parsons. I'm not even in the same…*species* as Cam Parsons."

Brant took an oversized bite from his chili-cheeseburger, stuffing two french fries soaked with ketchup into his mouth as a chaser. With his friend's mouth occupied, Jon took pleasure in the break in conversation and let his mind reflect on Brant's off-hand suggestion. As he placed the last of his fish tacos in his mouth, he imagined himself standing on the edge of a stage, before a stadium full of people, preaching the Gospel. Just for an instant, the vision seemed almost believable…even plausible. The thought of reaching more than one person at a time seemed so much more efficient than what they had been doing.

"I'm serious, man," said Brant, his mouth still full of food. "You should think about it. You'd be good at it."

"An evangelist," said Jon, listening to the sound of the word.

"Yeah. Why not? It's the same thing you're doing now. Just with more people."

"But how would I even get started doing something like that? I'm going to run out of money before too long as it is. And evangelists don't charge admission, you know. It takes lots of donations and support. And people who actually want to listen to them."

"Start small," said Brant, with a shrug of his shoulders. "Then you just need some rich person to fund you while you build your ministry, that's all."

"Oh, that's all," said Jon, pretending to be relieved. "Thanks for the tip, Brant. Speaking of rich people…let me give this to you now while I'm thinking about it." Jon pulled a small white card from his wallet and handed it to Brant.

"What's this?"

"It's the business card from that guy I met on our flight home for Christmas. Geoff Holland. He runs a big chemical engineering company out of Atlanta, and it sounded like they have a lot of IT people. He said to call him if he could ever help us, remember? You should give him a call about a job. They have a big office right here in Austin. That's his cell phone number on the back."

"You sure he'll remember me?" asked Brant. "We just spoke for a moment after we got off the plane."

"Believe me, he'll remember you. Just say you're the guy who argued with the priest on his flight from Austin. He'll know who you are."

Brant grinned. "OK, thanks. I'll definitely call him. I wouldn't mind living in Atlanta."

"What about Austin?"

"Are you kidding? I wouldn't live here as a ghost."

"Why not? Austin's a nice town."

"Nah, Texas isn't my thing."

"What's wrong with Texas?" said their waitress, Sophie, appearing at the table.

"Oh...hi, Sophie," said Brant, slightly startled.

"What don't you like about Texas?" she asked, folding her wrist against her hip as she looked down at Brant.

"Nothing," said Brant, backpedaling quickly. "Nothing's wrong with Texas. It's me, actually. It's *my* fault. I'm just not cut out for the Southwest climate. It's the dry air. You know...it makes me...sleepy."

Jon fought against the impulse to laugh at Brant's conjured effort to avoid insulting Sophie's state pride.

"It makes you sleepy?" asked Sophie.

"It's a rare condition," said Jon, intentionally locking Brant into his ridiculous story.

"That's right," said Brant. "This is my doctor, Jon – I mean – Dr. Smoak. He travels with me in case I get...."

Sophie raised an eyebrow at Brant. "Sleepy?" she asked.

"Right, in case I get sleepy. Isn't that right, Dr. Smoak?"

"Yes, that's correct," deadpanned Jon. "In fact, just last night, Mr. Morris here became extremely sleepy and lost consciousness for approximately eight hours. He didn't wake up until this morning. It's definitely the dry air."

Brant covered his mouth to contain his laughter.

"Are you guys for real?" Sophie asked, putting her hands on her hips.

"No, we're really not," said Jon, ending the ruse with a smile. "We're just messing around. Sorry about that."

Sophie giggled and blushed, fanning her face with her ticket book. "I was about to say – that's about the weirdest thing I've ever heard!"

"It can't be as weird as the story behind that baboon," said Brant, pointing his thumb over his shoulder.

"What baboon?" asked Sophie.

Brant turned and pointed behind the bar. "The one right there!"

Sophie turned her head and looked up at the stuffed baboon. "Huh. Look at that. I never noticed him before."

"What?" asked Brant. "It's a baboon! How could you not notice a baboon?"

"Honey, there's so many dead animals on the walls in this place, it gives me the creeps. I just try and ignore 'em all. They're kind of gross, if you ask me."

"Well, I guess I can see that," said Brant.

"If you don't mind me asking," said Sophie, "if y'all aren't from Texas, where are y'all from?"

"South Carolina," said Jon.

"Oh! I was born in Charleston!" she said. "My daddy was stationed at the naval base there while he was in the Navy."

"How long have you lived here?" asked Jon.

"In Austin, only about two years. But I grew up in Fort Worth after my dad got out of the service. What are y'all doing out here from South Carolina?"

"We're glad you asked," said Brant, placing his elbows on the table. "We're going around telling people—"

Jon kicked Brant under the table.

"Ouch! Geez, Jon!"

"We're just here on business," said Jon, cutting his eyes at a very confused Brant. "You wouldn't happen to know a good church we could visit while we're here, would you?"

"Oh, you can come to *my* church! It's Grace Hill Baptist, about five miles out 290, west of here."

"Are you a member there?" asked Jon.

"Yes, sir. It's wonderful. We see folks getting saved every week. Well, almost every week. If you come next Sunday, I'll meet you there and introduce you to our pastor, Rob Stoneridge. He's such a good Bible teacher. He tells it like it is, straight from God's Word. You'll love him. You *are* a Christian aren't you, Dr. Smoak?"

"Hmm?" asked Jon, momentarily confused by the title. "Oh, I'm not a doctor. He was just kidding about all that."

"Oh."

"But yes, we're both Believers. We're both Christians."

"Oh, that's wonderful," gushed Sophie. "I just love meeting folks who love Jesus as much as I do."

"Well, it's our pleasure to meet you," said Jon. "And thank you for inviting us to your church. If we're in town, we'll be sure to come visit."

"I would be so excited if you do. If you let me know you're coming, I can meet you. Just call the Buck-N-Bull and leave a message for me. My name's Sophie."

"Right. And I'm Jon and this is Brant."

Brant waved. "Hey, Sophie. As I was about to say a minute ago," he said, scowling at Jon, "we're out doing God's work ourselves. We're driving across the country talking with folks about Jesus."

"Oh, wow! I think that's wonderful. God bless you, both. I'll add y'all to my prayers. Can I get you boys anything else? Some more tea? Some dessert, maybe? We have homemade key lime pie and Oreo cheesecake."

"I think we're done, Sophie," said Jon. "Thank you, though."

"OK, I'll just leave your check at the bar whenever you're ready."

"Thank you." Jon paused for a moment, until Sophie was out of earshot. "Well, that was refreshing, huh? We actually met a real Christian. In a saloon, no less."

"What the heck did you kick me for?!" asked Brant.

"I'm sorry. I meant to tell you about an idea I had."

"For what? Causing me pain?"

"No, for starting a conversation with someone and feeling them out about where they are faith-wise. I figured if we ask them to recommend a church and they can't, we'll know we have an opportunity to witness to them."

"Oh, I get it," said Brant. "And if they can, we know they're a Christian."

"Well, not necessarily. But at least we'll know a little about them and we can start to ask them questions from there."

"That might work," said Brant. "I like it."

"Cool. So let's don't forget to try it again, sometime."

"I won't forget. Thanks to you, I'm going to have a painful reminder on my shin for the next few days."

"I think you'll live," said Jon, standing up from the table. "You want to get the tip and I'll grab the check?"

"That works," said Brant. "Say, I wonder if they'd sell us that baboon."

"That's OK. One baboon in my car is enough. I don't need another one."

"Ha-ha, very funny, Jon."

"See, I told you I was funny."

"And now you just ruined it."

fifty two

Single Again

Jon lowered the sun visor above his head to shield his eyes from the set-ting sun. The empty two-lane highway, stretching west before them, drew a straight line across the Texas Hill Country. "We'll be picking up I-10 before too long," said Jon, glancing to his right to make sure Brant was awake. He hadn't said a word in the last half hour, though Jon could see his eyes were open behind his dark sunglasses. "Looks like we'll be in El Paso sometime around midnight," said Jon.

Brant grunted.

Jon checked behind them in his rearview mirror. "I think we're the only car on the road right now," he said, trying again to make conversation. "I guess not much goes on out here on a Sunday night."

Brant remained silent.

"I guess all this dry air is making you sleepy, huh," joked Jon.

Brant groaned and placed his hand on his stomach. "I don't feel so good."

Jon looked over at Brant with little sympathy. "Well, maybe you shouldn't have eaten that jalapeño-chili-pimento-cheese-burger with all those fries for dinner back at the Buck-N-Bull. Why do you do that to yourself, man?"

"Because it's so good. Why do you think?"

"It's not so good now, is it?"

"Yeah, but still," said Brant, reclining his seat back a few inches. "It was worth it."

"You should've had the grilled fish tacos," said Jon, glancing over at his ailing friend. "I tried to tell you."

"Christmas was just last week and you're already back on your healthy diet," said Brant as he fumbled with his cell phone. "Live a little, will you?"

"I'll live a lot longer than you, I know that. I can hear your arteries hardening from here."

"Crap," said Brant. "I forgot to charge my phone again. When we get near civilization, I need to get a car charger." Brant tossed his phone in the passenger door compartment, closed his eyes, and put both hands on his stomach. "Ugh, I feel like an animal is doing flips in my stomach."

"Well, you did order it rare. Maybe it's still moving around in there."

Brant adjusted his seat upright. "Seriously, I think you're going to have to pull over."

Jon tapped his brakes to turn off the cruise control. "You think you're gonna throw up?" he asked, thinking of his car interior.

"No," said Brant with a grimace. "It's the other end."

"Oh, you have *got* to be kidding me." Jon pressed his foot on the brake as he eased the car onto the side of the road. "What are you going to do for toilet paper?"

"If the baboon in your TV commercial could figure it out, I think I can manage something."

"The baboon in my commercial had toilet paper!"

"Just let me worry about it. Hurry up and stop, will you? Come on, come on!" Brant unbuckled his seat belt and opened the door as the car rolled to a stop in front of a dirt road extending at a right angle away from the highway. He jumped out, leaving the door open behind him, and ran down the dusty road.

"Just get as far away from the car as possible!" shouted Jon, only partially joking. The less he had to know about Brant's stomach issues the better. "Keep going!" He laughed as he watched Brant disappear into a group of Ashe juniper and blackbrush trees. Jon lifted his foot off the brake and tapped on the gas just enough to swing the passenger door closed before stopping again. "This may take a while," he said to himself.

Deciding to stretch his legs while he waited, Jon turned off the car and got out. The silence of the open Southwest Texas terrain made Jon wonder briefly if his ears were clogged. Standing beside his car, the evening air felt cool on his face as he marveled at the red, yellow, and orange sunset painted across the sky over the rangeland before him. Looking to the south, dark clouds of an isolated thunderstorm cracked lightening down into the distant horizon. And behind him to the east, stars were already visible in the quickly darkening sky. Jon turned slowly in a circle, glancing back and forth in all directions. He knew in a few moments the scene would be gone and the sky would give way to darkness, but he enjoyed the beauty while it lasted.

The sound of Brant's approaching footsteps ended Jon's communion with God's creation. "Oh, man," Brant sighed loudly, rubbing his stomach.

"I don't want to know," said Jon, holding up his hands.

"I think they may want to put one of those roadside historical markers here," Brant said, proudly. "Or maybe a warning sign for hazardous waste. That was ridiculous."

Jon laughed as he fished his keys from his pocket. He could see Brant was feeling better. "You worked up a whole stand-up comedy bit while you were over there, didn't you?"

"I've got more if you want to hear it."

"I'm sure you do, but I'll pass," said Jon as he opened his car door. He stopped and looked at Brant across the roof of the car. "Are you safe to ride with now or do I need to put on a hazmat suit?"

"I'm good," said Brant, hopping into the car.

Jon settled in behind the steering wheel. "I have to ask, did you…you know, clean up after yourself out there?"

"Of course, I did. I just tore up my boxers and used that for TP."

"Oh, good thinking. That's exactly what the baboon did in our commercial."

"Seriously?"

"No. I'm kidding. Baboons don't wear boxers."

Brant laughed. "You're right. They wear briefs. Like Curious George."

"Curious George didn't wear underwear," said Jon. "He was naked."

"No, he wasn't."

"Yes, he was. I read all those books to Holly when she was growing up. He was naked." Jon pushed the ignition button, but the expected hum of the engine waking up didn't follow. "Uh-oh."

"What do you mean, *uh-oh*?" asked Brant.

Jon pushed the button again with the same result. "I mean, uh-oh, like… we might be in trouble." He pushed it several more times, but the car failed to respond.

"You're kidding right?" asked Brant. "This is a BMW."

"So what?"

"You don't see BMW's broken down on the side of the road, Jon."

"Well, you might see one now," said Jon, pushing the ignition button again.

"Did you put your foot on the brake when you pushed the button?"

"I know how to start my own car, Brant."

"Then why won't it start?"

Jon stared at the lifeless, disloyal, instrument panel. "I don't know." He closed his eyes and let his head fall back against his headrest. "Why, God?" he asked out loud.

"What do you think it is?"

"I have no idea," said Jon, managing his frustration. "Just be quiet for a sec and let me think."

"Why don't we open her up and see? Maybe it's just a loose wire or something. I'm always fixing stuff on my Jeep."

"This is *not* some old Jeep," said Jon, imagining Brant randomly pulling wires and cables under his hood. "And unless you're a certified mechanic, you're not touching anything."

"I sure as heck can't make it much worse, Jon!" said Brant, raising his voice, slightly.

"Trust me, you can." Jon tried to remain calm to counter Brant's growing anxiety. "Besides, I don't want to mess up my warranty."

"We're stuck in the middle of Nowhere, Texas and you're worried about your *car warranty*?! Are you kidding me?"

Jon picked up his iPhone and turned on the screen. "Look, I'll just Google a towing service. There has to be one around here somewhere, if not back in Austin. They'll send a tow truck for us, and we'll be out of here in no time." Jon looked at his signal strength indicator on his phone. "*Great.*"

"What?" asked Brant.

"No service."

"Oh, come on!"

"Well, Brant, if you'd remember to charge your phone every once and a while, maybe we could use yours!"

Brant unbuckled his seat belt, got out of the car and slammed the door. Jon was glad to be alone for a moment. He couldn't think with Brant openly venting his stress. But the momentary silence did nothing to spur any ideas in Jon's mind. They were stuck. He looked at Brant sitting with his back to him on the front of the car and wondered what to do. With no apparent options, Jon got out of the car and joined Brant, leaning against the front edge of the hood. The two sat in silence for a moment, staring down the empty road.

"I told you we should've taken my Jeep," said Brant, folding his arms and crossing his legs.

"Brant, if we had taken your Jeep, we wouldn't have made it out of Columbia."

"Well, I'd rather be stuck on the side of the road in Columbia than in the middle of the daggum desert!"

"That makes no sense, whatsoever," said Jon. "And technically we're not in the desert. Just relax. I'm sure we can flag someone down."

"Oh, that should be easy! Let's see." Brant stood up and took a few steps onto the vacant highway, looking in both directions before turning back to Jon. "*Who*, Jon?" he asked, waving his arms in the air. "We're on the one road in America with no traffic!"

"Brant, I don't know what to tell you," he said, lowering his voice. "Just have a seat and calm down. Someone is bound to come by soon. OK? I don't know what else to tell you."

Brant walked back to the car, took a seat next to Jon and sighed. "I'm sorry. This just freaks me out a little. I don't like being stranded out in the middle of nowhere."

"I don't know anyone who does. I'm just as frustrated as you."

The two sat quietly for several minutes, waiting for a car to pass by.

"You think maybe we should pray about it?" asked Brant.

398 | Greg M. Dodd

Jon felt humbled by Brant's suggestion. Prayer should have been his first option. "Absolutely," he said. "Do you want to start?"

"Me?" asked Brant.

"Sure. Go ahead."

"OK," said Brant. The two bowed their heads as they sat on the hood of the car and Brant began to pray. "Dear God, this kind of sucks right now. We're stuck here in the middle of nowhere. Of course, you know that. But we know that you want us to tell people about Jesus and be witnesses for you. So we just ask that you provide someone to help us get going again, so we can do that. Please forgive me for getting mad with Jon. I know it's not his fault. Even though he should've had his car serviced before we left."

Jon felt Brant's elbow bump against his ribs.

"That was a joke, God," said Brant. "I'm just frustrated. But I pray that whatever comes from this situation will give us a story to tell about how much you love us and how awesome you are, God."

Brant paused and let Jon pray. "Heavenly Father," said Jon, "we know that you work all things together for the good of those who love you, according to your purpose. Like Brant said, we pray that even in this circumstance, you'll direct us in your path so that we might glorify you in some way, God. And just for the record, Lord, you know I had my car serviced before we left. In Jesus' name, we pray. Amen."

Brant chuckled at Jon's prayerful rebuttal. "So now we wait?"

"Yep," said Jon. "Now we wait."

The sun's light was completely gone from the clear sky as the two sat in silence on the highway. Though the moon had yet to rise from the horizon, light from the millions of stars above illuminated the landscape around them.

"So, how much did you tip Sophie?" asked Jon.

"I don't know. A few bucks. Why?"

"Well, we represented ourselves as Christians, that's all. I just hope you didn't stiff her on the tip."

"I didn't stiff her. I left a good tip."

"How much?"

"I told you, a few bucks."

"Please tell me it was at least fifteen percent."

"I don't know. If you're so worried about it, why don't *you* leave the tip next time? I'm sure you've got an app for that on your fancy iPhone."

"I don't need an app to figure out – hang on." Jon paused as he heard the sound of a car approaching behind them. "Here comes someone."

"I got it," said Brant. He turned around and stepped a few feet into the road, waving his arms over his head. The car moved into the left lane and sped by without slowing down. "Nice," said Brant, dropping his arms as he watched the car's taillights speed away. He took his place again beside Jon on the hood of the car.

"I don't think you made it clear that we needed them to stop," said Jon.

"What are you talking about? I was waving like a mad man."

"It looked like you were waving *hello*. I wouldn't have stopped for you, either."

"Well, next time why don't you do more than just sit there?"

The two sat without talking for several minutes. Jon began to consider the idea of walking back towards Austin. If nothing else, perhaps he could find cell coverage along the way to make a call for help.

"So, can I ask you a question?" asked Brant, breaking the silence.

"Sure. We seem to have plenty of time."

"How come you never remarried?"

Jon turned and looked at Brant. "Why would you ask that?" he asked, evading the question with a question.

"I was just wondering. Seems kind of odd to me."

"Odd?"

"Yeah," said Brant. "I know you're not gay or anything."

"That's very reassuring. Thanks, Brant."

"So, what is it then? Why didn't you ever get remarried?"

Jon looked down the road stretching into the darkness. He didn't want to talk about the subject, but couldn't think of a graceful way out of answering Brant's question. "Oh, I don't know," he said. "I just got busy, I guess. Work, Holly, my parents…you know." He hoped his casual answer would satisfy Brant's curiosity.

Brant placed his left heel onto the bumper of Jon's car. "I call bull-dookie on that, dude."

"Bull-dookie? Really?" Jon chuckled at the choice of words as he pushed Brant's foot off his bumper.

"Yeah, bull-dookie. I'm trying to clean up my language. Anyway, what's the real reason?"

"That *is* the real reason. Unless there's something you know that I don't."

"Oh, come on, Jon. You got busy? I'm not buying that. If you wanted a relationship, you would've had one. It's as simple as that. Someone like you would have to *try* not to meet someone."

"What do you mean *someone like me?*"

"You know – good job, nice house, nice car, in shape, not bald. Pretty much the opposite of me, except the bald part. I'm just saying, you shouldn't be hurting for dates, man."

"So, you're saying that I didn't *want* to get remarried?"

"Yeah, I guess that's what I'm saying. I'm just wondering why you chose to be alone all these years, that's all."

Jon had run out of countering questions and was beginning to feel cornered. It was a topic he rarely let himself explore, much less discuss with other people. And he knew how persistent Brant could be once he made up his mind to pursue something. He tried to end the intrusion quickly. "Brant, we're not going to go there, OK?"

"Not going to go there? Did you get that from Holly? At least bull-dookie is original."

"Let's just change the subject, OK?"

"Why? I'm just asking why you didn't want to get remarried. It's not that hard of a question, Jon."

Jon sighed. "You should have been a prosecuting attorney."

"The witness will answer the question," said Brant, in a deep, authoritative voice.

"The judge says that, not the attorney," said Jon, hoping to keep Brant on the tangent.

"Just answer the question, Jon. Come on, man. It's me." Brant smiled at Jon. "I'm not some stranger off the street."

Jon thought for a moment about opening up and talking honestly with Brant. Why was it so hard? Maybe some things are just too personal. And this felt like one of those things. But now that the question had been asked, Jon doubted he could completely avoid the answer over the next few months as they made their way to California and back. He decided to try and give Brant an honest answer. "I, um…."

"You what?" prodded Brant.

Jon turned to look at Brant. The brief eye contact filled Jon with anxiety. "I don't want to talk about this." Jon stood up from the car and took a few steps away from Brant.

"Oh, come on!" said Brant, looking up at Jon. "I've told you how screwed up my life is. You can't answer one simple question? What else do we have to do out here in the middle of nowhere?"

"It's not a simple question, Brant." Jon knew the question *was*, in fact, a simple one. It was the answer he was afraid of.

"Does it have to do with Lacey?"

"Of course it has to do with Lacey," answered Jon, feeling pulled in a direction he didn't want to go.

"You couldn't see yourself with anyone else, is that it?"

"No, that's not it," said Jon, looking away from Brant. His initial anxiety over the question was quickly turning into annoyance.

"Are you going to make me play twenty questions, or are you just going to tell me?"

Jon glared at his friend. "Why does it matter, Brant? What difference does it make?!"

Brant huffed and placed his left foot on the bumper, again, frowning as he stared straight ahead down the highway. "Just forget it, Jon. Geez. Excuse me for trying to be a friend, man."

Jon looked at Brant and wondered how to respond. The headlights of an approaching car briefly lit everything around them as it sped by, leaving them again in the darkness of the highway. Neither Jon nor Brant acknowledged the car or the missed opportunity to be rescued. Jon knew Brant was trying – in his own clumsy way – to be his friend. And he realized Brant might be the only true friend he really had. Jon lowered his head, closed his eyes for a moment and dropped his guard. "It's my fault," he said.

"No, that's OK," said Brant. "I shouldn't have asked. It's none of my business. We can talk about something else. Baboons or something."

Jon took a seat again beside Brant on the hood of the car. He fixed his gaze on the red taillights disappearing over the dark horizon. "No, I meant Lacey's accident. It was my fault."

Brant turned and looked at Jon. "How could it be your fault? I thought she fell asleep driving by herself."

"She did. But it wouldn't have happened if I'd been with her like I was supposed to be."

"Jon, it's been a long time, but I thought I heard you were home taking care of Holly that night. Wasn't she sick or something?"

"No, she wasn't sick. I don't know how that story got out there, but I never corrected it. People were saying all kinds of stuff at the time."

"Still, you can't blame yourself like that, man. It was an accident."

"You want to know the truth, Brant?"

"Well, yeah," said Brant, with a nervous laugh. "That's usually what I hope for when I ask someone a question."

Jon breathed in deeply and exhaled. "That night, we had an argument while we were getting ready to go to a party. I tried to tell her about...I mean, I tried to explain my faith to her. I was a new Christian at the time. And I was such an idiot about everything. I didn't know how to talk with her about it. She got mad and I got frustrated. Then she left me alone at the house with Holly. She went to the party by herself. And I just let her go. I just...watched her leave. It's my fault she died."

"Jon, why do you keep saying that? She fell asleep. That could happen to anyone."

"She was drunk, Brant." Jon turned towards Brant and looked him in the eyes.

Brant paused for a moment as he studied Jon's face. "I didn't know, Jon. I know people wondered about that, but...I mean, *I* wondered...."

"I knew she'd be drinking at the party," said Jon, looking ahead into the darkness. "And I still let her go without me. I remember...I was actually happy I got to stay home that night. I knew she would still be mad at me when she came home, but I didn't care." Jon felt a deep, aching emptiness inside his chest. "Back at the baseball stadium, you asked what I would change if I could go back and change anything. I would have gone with her. I should have...." Jon closed his eyes.

"Hey, Jon, I didn't mean to make you…."

Jon tried to shake the emotions welling up in his head and rubbed his hands against his face. "No, it's all right. I've been trying to avoid talking about this for eighteen years. I even stopped talking to God about it a long time ago. I knew he forgave me, but…."

"So…is that the answer to my question? Why you never remarried?"

Jon took a deep breath to gather himself. "Well, yeah. I guess it is." He tried to see himself objectively for a moment. "Maybe I was just scared to try again. I think I just kind of hid behind raising Holly and taking care of my parents. Staying busy with them was always a good excuse not to get involved with anyone."

Brant sighed and shook his head. "Didn't you get lonely, man?"

"I used to. It was horrible those first few years. Then I kind of got numb to it. I stopped expecting things to be any different. I just accepted the possibility that I was never going to be with anyone else, you know? If being Holly's dad was all God wanted me to be, I was fine with that. I failed as a husband, but I could still be a good dad, you know?"

Brant shook his head again. "No offense buddy, but that's just about the biggest cop-out I think I've ever heard."

"*What?!*"

"You heard me, Jon. All that's just a convenient way to avoid experiencing life while you look like a martyr doing it. 'I'm just a poor widower raising my daughter. Boo-hoo.' I can't believe you, man."

Jon's face flushed with anger as he stood up in front of the car to face Brant. "*What the hell, Brant!* I thought I was talking to a friend here!"

"You are, Jon! But it sounds to me like you needed a friend to kick you in the ass a long time ago! You've wasted eighteen years of your life feeling sorry for yourself. So you made a mistake! We all make mistakes! Life goes on, man!"

Jon's blood pressure skyrocketed. He lunged forward and grabbed Brant's shirt in his fists and shoved his back against the hood of the car. Brant let his arms flop to his side, his palms open in defenseless submission. Jon leaned over Brant's face, pulling him up by his shirt. "I killed my wife, you son of a bitch! Don't you get that?!" He shoved Brant against the car, turned his back, and walked away down the dark empty road.

Brant stood to his feet in front of the car. "Jon! Where are you going, man? You didn't kill anyone! Lacey was an adult! She knew what she was doing! She's the one who made the mistake, Jon, not you! She got drunk. She drove the car. She hit the tree. It's not your fault!"

Jon spun around and walked quickly back towards Brant. "Don't you tell me it's not my fault!" Jon dug his fingernails into his palms. His chest heaved with emotion as he stopped an arm's length in front of Brant. "You have *no* right to tell me that!" he shouted, pointing his finger in Brant's face. "You, of all people! You didn't even come to her funeral!"

"I did, too, Jon," said Brant, plainly.

Jon recoiled and dropped his hands to his side.

"I was there," said Brant.

Jon stood motionless, staring at Brant. The revelation conflicted with eighteen years of unspoken resentment. "I didn't see you there," he said, suddenly unsure of himself.

"That's because I didn't want you to see me. I'd been a total ass to you. I may be a jerk, Jon, but I didn't want you to have to deal with my baggage at your wife's funeral."

Jon began to pace back and forth in front of the car like a caged animal. He wanted out of the conversation. It had gone too far. Brant's intruding questions had given new life to the pain Jon had buried so long ago. He wanted to escape and just be alone. But in the wide expanse of the Texas landscape, there was nowhere to hide. He was stuck with Brant. "Why did I even bring you on this stupid trip in the first place?!"

"Maybe because you knew you couldn't do it by yourself," said Brant.

"The hell, I can't! All I've done is clean up your mess every time we talk to somebody! You don't have a clue how to reach anyone!"

"Oh, whatever, man! I think you're just pissed-off that I'm taking away the crutch you've been leaning on all these years."

"What crutch?!"

"Your guilt, Jon! Hello! You talk about God's grace all the time, but you don't have a clue how to live in it!"

"I don't have to take that from you, Brant!"

Brant took a step forward as Jon retreated around the left corner of the car. "You know what? I think you hang on to your guilt because it keeps you safe, doesn't it?! No risk, no pain. Right, Jon?"

"Shut up, Brant!" yelled Jon, jabbing his finger in the air at Brant.

"No, I'm not going to shut up, Jon, because you need to hear this. You need to start living, man! Why can't you see that?"

"Why can't you just shut the hell up?! You have *no idea* what I've been through!!" Jon swung his fist through the air as he made his point.

"News flash, Jon! *Everybody* hurts! You think you're the only one who lies awake at night punishing himself over every stupid thing he's ever done? You think it's easy living with two failed marriages, no job and a kid I hardly ever see? The only reason I didn't put a bullet in my head five months ago was because the faith I saw in you twenty years ago gave me hope. So I'm not going to sit here and let you get away with this crap!"

"Get away with what?! What are you talking about?"

"I refuse to let you be less than who I thought you were, Jon. I looked up to you because of your faith. It gave me hope that there was something better out there. Something more to life than just…." Brant took his eyes off Jon for a moment as a hint of sadness crept into his voice. "And now you want to sit here and tell me how weak you are? Bull-crap! I'm not going to let you do that to me, Jon! You're *not* going to do that!"

Jon turned his back to Brant and took several steps into the empty highway. The weight of responsibility being pushed upon him was too much to bear. "Brant…just leave me alone."

"You know what, Jon?" asked Brant, leaning against the front fender. "I think that's your problem – you *want* to be alone. Because it's easier that way, isn't it?"

That was enough. Jon turned around and pointed angrily at his friend. "Shut up, Brant. I'm telling you, man, just shut up! This stupid…whatever you call this, is over!"

Brant pushed himself off the car and stretched his arms wide open. "Jon, you got me out here to do God's work, well here goes! You said you felt called to go on this trip because you were coasting in your faith, right? Did you ever stop to think you were coasting because you refused to let God bless you with somebody who could love you? Hiding behind your guilt, afraid of getting hurt, afraid of making mistakes. You said a minute ago you got numb to everything. God didn't put us here to be numb, Jon. He put us here to live!"

"Yeah, and look at you! Great example you are. You're the biggest screw up I know! You expect me to take advice from you?"

"OK. Fine. I deserve that. I *am* a screw up. And I know I've failed – a lot. But at least I've tried, Jon. The good times I had with Kim and Jacob, I wouldn't trade them for a million bucks. And now with Christ in my life, I feel like I can do anything!"

"Well, good for you, man," said Jon, clapping his hands in flippant support. "Are you finished now?"

Brant dropped his head and sighed. "Jon...you won't take advice from me. I get that. But maybe you'll take it from yourself."

"What's that supposed to mean?" asked Jon, guardedly curious.

"Back in school," said Brant, the corner of his mouth sliding up into a grin, "do you remember what you said that day we skipped our religion exams to go play golf?"

"We skipped an exam to go play golf?" The brief thought of their days in college cooled some of Jon's anger.

"Geez, man," said Brant, shaking his head. "You're memory is like Swiss cheese, sometimes."

"Well, what did I say?"

"You were talking about that tee-shot you hit across the water on that dogleg-right par four. The one that landed on the edge of the green. You had a chance for an eagle, remember?"

In his mind, Jon could see a white ball flying across the blue sky towards a putting green. He remembered watching it with his arms extended in the air as it landed just a few feet from the pin. A subtle smile began to form on Jon's face. "I remember that shot. But then I three putted for bogie, didn't I?"

"Yep."

"I sucked at golf," said Jon, folding his arms across his chest as he sorted through his memory. "I don't know why I bothered playing."

"I'll tell you why," said Brant. "After we came off 18 that day, you were still talking about that shot. You said that's all it took to keep you coming back – one good swing that you could talk about in the clubhouse at the end of the day. It didn't matter how bad the other hundred were. What happened to *that* guy?"

"You really remember me saying that?"

"Yes, I do. It didn't mean much at the time. I thought you were just bragging."

"That's because I was," said Jon.

"Yeah, but the point of it stuck with me. You don't know how many times I've used that to pick me up after I've done something stupid or failed at something. I'd just tell myself, *keep swinging*. Just keep trying. The next time might be the one I get to talk about, you know? It's the difference between living and just existing, man. You need to get that back."

Jon began to feel ashamed of how he'd treated Brant. He may be difficult sometimes, but he truly was trying to help him. "Maybe I should listen to myself more often," joked Jon.

"Maybe you should. So, come on, man. You don't want to be alone forever. It's time you started acting single again."

Jon laughed to himself. "Maybe Phillip and Steve had the right name, after all."

"Phillip and Steve?" asked Brant. "Oh, the Single Again class…name change thing. Yeah, maybe so."

Jon walked back to the front of the car and sat down on the hood. Dating. The thought led his mind straight to Amy.

"So, are you with me?" asked Brant, sitting down next to Jon. "What's it gonna take to get you back in the game? I know there's a girl out there for you. How about I fix you up on a blind date? I bet Kim's got single friends."

"No blind dates," said Jon, remembering his last one. "But…there is this one girl."

"Ah-ha! I knew it! Who is she?"

"Her name's Amy. I've known her for a long time. Since I was twelve, I guess."

"Twelve? I never heard you mention her when we were in school."

"She was a summertime friend down at Pawleys when I was growing up. We fell out of touch after we both went to college. She went to Clemson the same time I started at Carolina. We just recently reconnected."

"Let me guess – Facebook."

"Yep. She sent me a friend request about a week before we left. She's divorced now and living at the beach. She wanted me to come down and take her to dinner."

"And?" asked Brant.

"I couldn't before we left. I had already committed myself to this."

"You kill me, man," said Brant, laughing. "I'm pretty sure God allows people to have dinner together, Jon. We could've left anytime. Why didn't you take her out?"

"Because…it's different with Amy."

"Why, what's wrong with her?"

"Nothing's wrong with her. Why do you always say that? No, it's just that…I had it pretty bad for her growing up, but I never said anything."

"Why not?"

"Because I'm an idiot," said Jon. He immediately held up his hand to stop Brant from adding his agreement.

"I wasn't going to say anything," said Brant.

Jon looked out into the distance and smiled to himself as an image of Amy, standing on the beach in front of him, came to his mind. "I remember, she had this look she used to give me. It would just totally hook me every time. We'd be talking on the beach and I was always trying to impress her, you know. And she'd be listening to me go on and on. And every now and then she'd give me this little look with her eyes and a subtle little smile, you know? Like she knew something I didn't."

"I'm sure she did."

"What do you mean?"

"That look meant she knew you liked her, Jon."

"What would you know about it?"

"Apparently, more than you."

"Well, anyway, we never went out. And then when we connected on Facebook, we did the chat thing for about two hours. And it was like no time had passed at all. It was like we were eighteen again. I was hooked all over again. But I knew if I went down there and took her out and we hit it off, I would never be doing what you and I are doing right now."

Brant looked around at the dark Texas landscape. "Yeah, this is great."

"You know what I mean," said Jon. "I wouldn't have gone through with it."

"So where did you leave things with her?"

"I'm supposed to call her when I get back and take her to dinner down at the beach. I mailed her a letter when we got to Austin, before Christmas, just to stay in touch."

"You mailed her a letter?" asked Brant. "Like…with a stamp?"

"Yes, a real letter with paper and a stamp and everything."

"Did you hit your head and forget about the Internet, cell phones, FaceTime…."

"I'm just trying to keep my distance, so I can focus on what we're doing. That's all."

"Ah, well, there's a shocker – you keeping your distance. That's what we just finished arguing about, you know."

"I know. What can I say?"

"Well, is this Amy a Christian girl? Because you swore those off once before, if I remember right."

"Funny guy," said Jon, amazed at Brant's memory. "She's actually a preacher's daughter."

"Oh, I see!" said Brant.

"Not in the bad way. She was the first real Christian friend I ever had. She's awesome."

"Well, all right, then." Brant clapped his hands once and rubbed them together. "We need to get your car fixed so we can save some more folks then get you back home for your date with Amy. Sound good?"

"Sounds like a plan," said Jon with a smile. "And I'm sorry I called you a son of a bitch."

"It's OK. I've been called worse. I've got two ex-wives, remember."

"Ah, good point."

Sitting on the car with Brant, Jon began to feel a small sense of relief. Even hope. Soon, he realized, he would be free to see Amy without reservation. And he would do his best to leave the past behind him. "Oh, hey, you mentioned blind dates, earlier," Jon said. "You're not going to believe this, but I got fixed up with this one girl who told me that—"

"Hang on," said Brant. "I think I see someone coming on the other side of the road."

fifty three

A Witch And A Wedding

"Being confident of this, that he who began a good work in you
will carry it on to completion until the day of Christ Jesus."
- *Philippians 1:6*

Jon closed the door to the motel office and found Brant leaning on a chain-link fence surrounding an empty concrete swimming pool in the front parking lot. He pointed down the row of faded red motel room doors. "We're this way. Room sixteen."

"Did you see that sign?" asked Brant, picking up his bag from the ground. He pointed towards the entrance of the Green Cactus Motel. "It says *Ultra-Modern Rooms*. Maybe we'll have free Wi-Fi, Netflix, and our own Xbox in there."

"Very funny," said Jon. "I bet that sign's been there for at least fifty years. They probably meant air conditioning and black and white TVs."

Brant joined Jon on the concrete sidewalk that stretched between the parking lot and the guest rooms. "At least they had a room for us, though," he said.

"Brant, do you see any cars in the parking lot?"

Brant rotated his head to his left and let his body follow in a complete circle. "No."

"I had to wake the guy up in the office to get us a room," said Jon. "I don't think they're used to having customers around. At least not the ones who stay for more than a couple of hours, anyway."

410

The sound of a truck door closing drew Jon's attention across the parking lot. The truck driver who'd rescued them from the side of the road hopped down from his cab and headed towards the motel office.

"Goodnight, Tom!" shouted Brant, waving his arm over his head. "Thanks, again!"

The driver either didn't hear Brant or chose to ignore him.

"I sure hope that guy doesn't ditch us here in the morning," said Jon, watching the man walk across the parking lot. "We need to get into Austin to find someone to tow my car to a dealer. I hate that it's just sitting out there on the side of the road."

"Tom won't ditch us," said Brant.

"Is that his name?"

"That's what he said."

Jon paused in front of a guest room window. Cupping his hands around his face, he tried unsuccessfully to see inside the dark room through a narrow part in the curtains. He had never stayed anywhere with such modest and dated accommodations.

"Not quite the Vendue, is it?" asked Brant.

"No," said Jon. The more he saw, the more he wished he were sleeping in his car on the side of the road. Jon stepped back and looked down the sidewalk, counting the remaining rooms. "I don't think this motel even *has* sixteen rooms."

"It's probably around the corner," said Brant. "It wraps around to the right."

"What were you saying about that truck driver?" asked Jon as they continued down the sidewalk.

"I just said I don't think he'll leave us. He seems like a nice enough guy."

"Sorry, if I don't share your optimism."

"I admit he's a little grouchy," said Brant, "but he did pick us up out there in the middle of nowhere. Besides, he's probably just happy to have someone in his cab to talk to."

"Yeah, as long as you don't bring up Jesus. He made that pretty clear, didn't he?"

"Yeah, but still, I don't think he'd leave us over that. He liked talking to me about NASCAR, didn't he?"

"Thanks for that, by the way," said Jon. "I was afraid he was going to dump us back out on the side of the road there for a minute. Until you brought up…who was it?"

"Jeff Gordon."

"Yeah. Man, does he hate that guy."

"Most Dale Earnhardt, Jr. fans do. When I saw his little number 88 magnet I figured that would give him something to talk about."

Jon rounded the corner of the building and stopped in front of the first door. "Here we are. Number 16." He inserted the key into the doorknob, turned it to the right and pushed the door open with his shoulder. "I can't remember the last time I actually got a real key instead of a magnetic card for a hotel room."

Brant slipped past Jon into the room and flipped the light switch, turning on a lamp between two double beds. "This isn't bad," said Brant, looking around the small room. "Beats sleeping in your car on the side of the road."

Jon sniffed the room's sour, musty air as he tossed his nylon suitcase on the bed closest to the door. "At least my car doesn't stink. What is that smell?"

"I think that's an air freshener called *Cheap Roadside Motel*," joked Brant. "I think they all use it." He dropped his bag on the carpeted floor between the two double beds and let himself fall backwards on the bed, landing with a thud. "Ugh! This bed's as hard as the floor." He pushed himself towards the pillows and reclined against the painted wood headboard. "So, anyway," he said, positioning a pillow behind his back, "you never finished your blind date story."

"What? Oh, yeah," said Jon, sitting down on the edge of his own firm bed, facing Brant.

"What did you say her name was?" Brant leaned over to dig his cell phone charger out of his bag.

"I don't think I did, yet," said Jon as he tried to remember the girl's name. "I think it was Julie. Or Janet. Something with a J. I'm not sure."

Brant plugged his phone into the wall. "You went out with a girl, and you're not sure what her name was?"

"It doesn't matter."

"I'm guessing there wasn't a second date."

"You're jumping ahead."

"Sorry."

"Anyway," said Jon, "we're sitting there in Café Caturra, over in Forest Acres, waiting for our food, and—"

"Wait, when was this?" asked Brant, adding another pillow behind his back.

"Um, it was over a year ago, at least. Anyway—"

"I didn't know that place had been open that long."

"It's been there a while. Do you want me to finish the story or not?"

"Oh, sorry." Brant crossed his legs and clasped his hands behind his head. "What did this girl look like?"

"Um." Jon looked away at the blank wall behind the TV to focus his memory. "She wasn't bad, actually," he decided, picturing the girl's face in his mind. "Pretty attractive, really. Hazel eyes and kind of auburn-colored hair. Nice smile, too. But she had this kind of alternative look thing going on with her hair and clothes. She worked in a hair styling place down in Five-Points."

"Cute, but edgy," said Brant. "Got it. Go ahead."

"OK, so, we're sitting there and she asks me, 'So, what do you believe?' And I said, 'About what?' I had no idea what she was talking about. And she says, 'About religion. What are you?' And I said, 'I'm a Christian. What about you?' I thought she was going to tell me she was a Methodist or Catholic or something. And she says, 'Well, I'm kind of into the Dark Side.'"

"Uh-oh," said Brant, letting a grin creep across his face.

"Yeah. So I said, 'You mean like in *Star Wars*?'"

Brant's stomach shook with laughter. "You really asked her that?"

"I did," said Jon, laughing. "I didn't know what she was getting at. And then she said, 'No, like witchcraft. I'm a witch.'"

"Whoa!" said Brant, sitting up on his bed. "She really said that?"

"Yep! 'I'm a witch.' Just like that. I mean, seriously – what do you say to something like that?"

"Check please! That's what I'd say."

"My thought exactly! But I couldn't just get up and leave. We hadn't even got our food, yet."

"So, what did you do?"

"I talked about my job in advertising the rest of the dinner. It was the first time I've ever tried to be intentionally boring on a date."

"I thought that would just come naturally for you, Jon."

Jon had to laugh. "Good one."

"Thanks." Brant smiled with satisfaction and leaned back on his pillow. "Julie the witch…that's hilarious. So, what did she order?"

"To eat? Oh, I don't know." Jon tried to remember. "Salmon, I think. Why?"

"Witches eat salmon? That's like regular people food."

"Well, it's not like she flew there on a broom, Brant. What would you expect her to eat?"

"I don't know. Bugs and frogs and stuff."

"Bugs and frogs," repeated Jon. "You think I'd take a blind date to a restaurant that serves bugs and frogs."

"If you were trying to impress a witch you would."

Jon laughed and shook his head. "Why do I let you get me into these conversations?"

"You're the one who went out with a witch, dude. Not me."

"Anyway, the point I was trying to make – however this started – was that I swore off blind dates after that."

"Ah. Well, I can't say I blame you. Who would fix you up with a witch, anyway?"

"This girl in our graphic design department at work named Lauren. The witch does her nails or hair or something, and Lauren thought we'd hit it off, I guess."

"I'd like to know what Lauren thought you had in common with a witch. Didn't she know you're a Christian?"

Jon was momentarily stumped by the question. "I guess not," he said. He stood up from his bed and dug his toiletry bag from his suitcase. He thought about Brant's question as he walked into the bathroom and turned on the light. Maybe Lauren didn't know he was a Believer. But they had worked together for three years. What did that say about him?

"So, did you have sex with her?" asked Brant, calling out from his bed. "The witch, not the girl at work."

Jon leaned his head out of the bathroom door and peered at Brant. "What's wrong with you?"

"You're stalling."

"No, I didn't have sex with her," said Jon, pulling himself back into the bathroom. "Or with the girl at work, either."

"I was just kidding. Although, it would make your story a lot more interesting if you told me you had slept with a witch, once."

"Twenty years from now, I'm sure that's how you'll remember it." Jon fished his toothbrush and toothpaste from his bag.

"Hey, maybe she put a curse on you, Jonny-boy."

Jon leaned towards the mirror to see Brant's reflection through the door. "That might explain a few things," he muttered to himself as he squeezed toothpaste onto his brush.

"What was that?" asked Brant.

"Nothing," said Jon, grinning as he stuck the toothbrush into his mouth.

"So," Brant called out from the bedroom, "did you witness to her after she told you she was a witch?"

Jon stopped moving the toothbrush for a second. He heard the question, but didn't like the answer that came from his memory. Rather than answer Brant with a frothy toothbrush in his mouth, Jon continued brushing his teeth, staring at his own troubled expression in the mirror. He spit into the sink, wiped his face with a hand towel, and walked back into the room.

"Did you hear me?" asked Brant, still reclining against his headboard.

Jon sat down on his bed with his back to Brant. "Yeah, I did."

"Cool, what did she say?"

"No, I meant I heard your question."

"And? Did you share your faith with her?"

Jon took off his shoes, placed them on the floor next to his suitcase, and pushed himself back against his pillows. "No, I didn't. To be honest, it never crossed my mind. I remember just wanting to get dinner over with, so I could take her home."

"Ah-ha!" said Brant, pointing at Jon with a large smile on his face.

"And drop her off — not sleep with her," said Jon, shaking his head. "Seriously, why didn't I think to share my faith with her? That really bothers me. I mean, until you asked me that, I'd never even thought of my date with her in that context. It was just a funny story. How could I have missed that?"

"Well, you said you were just going through the motions for a long time," said Brant. "Maybe you just weren't thinking like you are now."

"I hate to admit it, but yeah, I guess so." He thought for a moment about his dinner conversation with the girl. "What a missed opportunity, though. You know?" he said, looking at Brant. "I wonder how many other chances God's put in front of me over the years that I totally missed seeing like that."

The two sat quietly for a moment.

Brant shook his head slowly as a grin crept back across his face. "Wow…Jonny-boy went out with a witch."

"Would you like her number?" asked Jon as he punched both his pillows to test their firmness.

"No, thanks. I don't need another witch in my life. Having Kim as an ex-wife is enough."

Jon turned the small clock on the nightstand between the two beds so he could see the time. "It's almost eleven," he said. "I'm going to sleep." He slipped off his jeans and folded them neatly across his bag on the floor. Straightening the waistband of his boxer shorts, he turned down the bed and slipped his sock-covered feet under the thin sheet.

"Mind if I leave the light on?" asked Brant. "I'm going to stay up and read for a while."

"Behind in your comic books, are you?"

"Ha-ha," said Brant, dryly. "Actually, I'm reading the book you gave me on how to lead others to Christ."

"Oh, cool," said Jon, feeling a touch of guilt for underestimating his friend. "See you tomorrow."

"Good night," said Brant. "Don't forget to charge your iPhone."

"Oh, thanks." Jon rolled over, reached in his bag for his charging cable, and plugged his phone into the outlet behind the nightstand. Turning his back to the light from the lamp, he pulled the sheet and comforter over his shoulders and closed his eyes. The face of his blind date appeared again in his mind, sitting across the restaurant table, smiling at him. "Why didn't I?" Jon questioned in his head. He tried to imagine a better response to her claim of being a witch than what he remembered saying at the time: "I heard the salmon's good here." She couldn't have been more lost and yet he didn't think once about trying to lead her to faith in Jesus. He could have changed her life. But instead, he had turned her into a joke.

Jon realized he was holding his eyes closed so tightly that his cheeks were beginning to cramp. He tried to relax the muscles in his face and slowly exhale as he prayed. "God, I'm sorry. I hope you'll put another Believer in that girl's path to help her. Please give her another chance to know you, God. I'm not even sure if I remember her name right. But I know you know her, Lord. You love her and gave her a chance to spend time with a Believer – me – and I let you down. And I'm sorry I didn't even realize it until now."

Jon wishfully played out a faith conversation with the witch several times in his head, before finally drifting off to sleep.

A loud noise somewhere in the dark hotel room woke Jon. Lifting his head from the pillow, he could see light from the bathroom leaking through the doorframe. Jon heard Brant's voice, raised and muffled, followed by the crack of something plastic hitting the tile bathroom floor. Jon looked at the clock and saw the time, 12:42. He tossed the covers off his body, swung his feet to the floor, and moved slowly in the dark towards the bathroom door. "Brant?" he said through the door. "You OK in there?" No sound came from the other side. He knocked gently with his knuckles. "Brant?"

"Yeah. It's unlocked. You can come in."

Jon opened the door slowly to find Brant sitting, fully dressed, on the floor of the walk-in shower. His cell phone lay in front of his feet in three broken pieces. He breathed heavily through his nose as he stared at the shower wall, his face wrinkled with distress.

"What happened, man?" asked Jon. "What's wrong?"

Brant sat with his back pressed against the shower wall, his legs bent before him and arms stretched forward over his knees. With shaking hands, he pressed a wad of bloodstained toilet paper against his right index finger.

"How'd you cut your finger?"

"On that stupid phone."

Jon looked at the broken cell phone pieces next to Brant's feet. "So, what's going on, Brant?"

Brant took a moment before responding, putting pressure on his cut with the toilet paper. He took a deep breath and let it out. "Kim's getting married." Brant removed the tissue to see blood still oozing from his finger.

"What?" asked Jon.

Brant let the back of his head rest against the shower wall. "Yep. She's getting married."

"Brant, I'm…sorry," said Jon, trying to understand Brant's reaction to the news.

"She sent me a text message. Can you believe that? A text message. We've only been officially divorced for three months and she's already getting married. And that's how she tells me. She wanted me to know I won't have to worry about paying alimony anymore. Like that's what matters to me."

Jon didn't know what to say. He knelt down on the bathroom floor next to the shower.

"You know," said Brant, "the funny thing is, I didn't mind paying the alimony. I felt like I was doing something good every month. Being responsible, you know? It was the only official connection I still had with her."

"Do you know who she's marrying?"

"Some doctor is all I know. James something. Or maybe that's his last name, I don't know. I'd show you the text, but…I threw my phone into the shower."

"Yeah, I see that. Brant, I've got to tell you I'm a little confused. I honestly didn't know you still…."

"What? That I still cared about her?"

"Yeah. I mean, you never really talk about any of that stuff. And the only time you mention Kim is when you're making an ex-wife joke or something. Just tonight, you kind of compared her to a witch."

"I know. But I didn't mean that. I guess ex-wife jokes are just too easy to pass up sometimes. It's my way of talking about her without really talking about her. If that makes sense."

"Well, you can be honest with me. You don't have to pretend for my sake."

"I appreciate that," said Brant.

"So, you still have feelings for her?"

"I never stopped having feelings for her. I love her. She's the one who left. And I don't blame her. But I just thought…I guess I started to hope that, maybe – with all the changes in my life – that she'd see me differently since I accepted Christ, you know? I thought if she saw that I'm not drinking anymore and that I'm out doing something good and decent…that maybe she'd…maybe, we could be a family again." Brant looked up at Jon. "I miss my son, Jon." He dropped his head and wiped his eyes. "Jacob actually sent me a text after I dropped him off at Kim's Christmas Day and said that he was proud of me for what you and I are doing. He told me that. It gave me hope that I could be the dad he needs me to be. Like you are with Holly." Brant looked down at the pieces of his phone. "Crap, now I can't even look at his text anymore." He closed his eyes and banged the back of his head against the shower wall, twice.

Jon looked at the broken phone. "Maybe we can fix it."

"It doesn't matter," said Brant. He closed his eyes, pushing a tear down the side of his face. "I've screwed up so bad, Jon. I've lost everything that ever mattered to me. And I suck at being a Christian, too."

"No, you don't, Brant."

"Yes, I do. You even said so. I've got nothing to share. I just argue with people. My life sucks. How can I convince anyone that they should have what I have? Look at me. I'm a nobody. I'm an unemployed divorced jerk, sitting in a cheap motel shower with a broken cell phone. Hey everybody! You should accept Jesus and be like me! I've got nothing, Jon. Why should anyone listen to me?" Brant stretched out his right leg and kicked the pieces of his cell phone across the shower floor.

"Brant, I know you're hurting," said Jon. "I can see that. But everyone who knows Jesus has a story worth telling. Your life matters. God's changed you. I can testify to that. You're not the person I knew a long time ago. What God's done with you in just a few months is amazing. But you're still going to have to deal with some of the consequences from your life before. And it's going to take some time for you to see the fruit in your life that'll come from your faith in Christ. But it will come."

Brant shook his head back and forth gently against the wall. "I don't see it, Jon. I don't see it."

"Brant, I promise – it will. Actually, that's God's promise, not mine. Philippians 1:6 says, 'being confident of this, that he who began a good work in you will carry it on to completion until the day of Christ Jesus.' You know what that means?"

"It probably means *Brant sucks*."

"No, come on. Listen to me. It means that God's never going to give up on you. He's got a plan for your faith and he's promised to finish it. You have to trust him on that. God is where your hope comes from. Not from Kim, or me, or anyone else."

Brant turned his head and looked into Jon's eyes. "Are you sure you want me along with you out here? I feel like you think you'd do better without me, sometimes."

Jon suddenly felt uncomfortable. "What makes you say that?"

"Well, you pretty much told me that in the desert. And you get pretty irritated with me sometimes."

Jon felt he had no other option but to be open with Brant. "Brant, I'm sorry for what I said out there. But listen to me. I've been beating myself up for inviting you along because I didn't really think it through or even pray about it first. It all happened so fast. I've actually asked God to forgive me for making that decision on my own without talking to him first. So, yeah, I have wondered if I made a mistake in bringing you along."

"Crap, Jon. Are you trying to make me feel worse or what?"

"No, let me finish. This is hard for me to say...I know now that I was wrong about all that. I was seeing it all wrong. Like I was the one who controlled everything. Like this was all about me and what God wanted me to do. But I know now that this was God's plan for both of us. Not just me. Heck, I wouldn't even be doing this, if it weren't for you."

"Oh, right," said Brant, rolling his eyes away from Jon.

"I'm serious," said Jon. "God used you to help me see what I was missing in my faith. That's why we're out here. It's because of you, Brant. God is working through you in a big way. And I don't want to see you get discouraged." Jon reached out and grabbed Brant's forearm. "I need you, man. OK?"

Brant glanced briefly into Jon's eyes before looking down at the aqua colored tiles of the shower floor. "You know, back when we were in college, if someone had come into Oscar Ray's, pulled us off our barstools and said,

'One day, these two idiots will be serving the Lord God Almighty,' I would have laughed them out of the bar."

"I would've helped them out the door, myself," said Jon.

"But here we are."

"Yep. I've always said God's got a good sense of humor."

"Yeah," said Brant. "I just wish I wasn't the butt of his jokes, so often."

Jon laughed with his friend. "I guess we've both been through a lot since college. But hey – God brought us back together when we both needed it the most. I guess that's why it's called *Amazing Grace*."

Brant leaned forward and crossed his legs. "Jon, would you mind if I prayed for a minute? I think I need to say a few things to God."

"Sure," said Jon. "You want me to leave you alone?"

"No, you can stay and pray with me, if you want."

"Sure, man."

Jon closed his eyes as Brant began to pray out loud. "Dear God, I'm really hurting right now. But what I need to ask you isn't about me. It's about Kim and Jacob. God…I had my chance to be a good husband and a good father and I blew it. You know that. I was a mess, Lord. I don't know how I got to be like that, but you saved me from all that was wrong in my life. You fixed me. But I guess it's too late to fix things with Kim. I admit to being angry about how Kim is moving on without me. And I guess I was a little mad at you for a minute. I just thought everything would work out differently – happy ending kind of stuff. I'm sorry I was mad at you. And regardless of how I feel, Lord, I want to ask you to watch over Kim. Help her to be a good mother to our son, Jacob. I pray that you'll give me opportunities to show him what a difference you can make in his life. And, Lord, I ask you to…I ask you to, um…bless Kim's marriage. Oh, God…it hurts to even say that. I just wanted one more chance with her, God. Just one more chance. But if that's not what you want for me or for her, then I pray that you'll be with her and her new husband, James, or whatever his name is. Help them seek you in all that they do. And help me to keep them in my prayers, Lord. And God, I thank you for my friend Jon. I wouldn't even know you if it weren't for him. He's the best friend I've ever had, and I have you to thank for that. Help us make a difference for you, Lord. Help us to reach people tomorrow in Austin as we wait to get Jon's car fixed. Thank you, God. I love you. In Jesus' name I pray. Amen."

"Amen," said Jon, wiping tears from his face. "Thanks, man."

"Sure, bud," said Brant, drying his face with his shirt. "Sorry I woke you up."

"No, that's OK. I was having the weirdest dream, anyway. I'm glad to be out of it."

"Let me guess. You were flying around on a broom with Julie, the witch, eating bugs and frogs."

Jon laughed at the thought. "That *would* be weird, but no," he said.

"Well, what was it about?"

Jon paused for a moment, trying to recall the details of his dream. "Well, I was dreaming that I was home. I was standing in my den. But the house was full of water, for some reason."

"Your house was full of water?"

"Yeah, like full up to the ceiling. But everything else was normal. The furniture was all there with pictures and stuff. And I was standing in the middle of the den watching it leak out under the doors and down the air conditioner vents on the floor. The weird thing is that it seemed like the water was *supposed* to be in the house, and it was a problem that it was leaking out. And Elvis was swimming around the coffee table, barking at me."

"He could bark underwater?"

"Yeah. And you were there, too."

"I was in your dream?"

"Yeah. You were outside on the back patio, banging on the French doors, screaming something at me."

Brant nodded and snapped his fingers. "I bet you heard me yelling at my phone in here while you were dreaming."

"Maybe," said Jon. "The weird thing is that I wasn't holding my breath or anything under water. I was breathing normal. And the water was really warm, like a bath."

"Are you sure you didn't wet the bed in there?" asked Brant.

"I didn't wet the bed. What am I, six-years-old?"

"You wet the bed when you were six?"

"No!" said Jon. "Anyway, let me finish. This is weird."

"Sorry, go ahead."

"All right, so...I decided to swim upstairs."

"Sounds like you dreamed you were Aquaman. You've got a classic hero complex, dude. That's why you want to save everybody."

"Thank you for that diagnosis, Dr. Freud."

"Where was Elvis during all this? Chasing catfish in your den? Get it?" Brant laughed at his own joke.

"Catfish. I get it. Ha-ha. I don't know where he was; he wasn't there anymore. So, anyway, I swim to the top of the stairs. And I reach up and pull the little rope to open the attic, thinking that's a way out, you know? And then all the water goes rushing down the stairs, like a toilet being flushed. So I held onto the rope and I felt myself being pulled up into the attic. And when I got to my feet, I was standing on the beach. Like at Pawleys or somewhere."

"An attic that opens onto the beach?" asked Brant. "That *is* weird."

"Yeah, but it didn't seem weird in my dream. It was supposed to be there. And I'm standing there on the beach, looking around, you know? It was early morning and the ocean was really smooth. I think the sun had just come up. And my dad was there. No one else. Except he looked all young and different. But I still knew it was him, you know? And he was standing by the water, with waves rolling in behind him, just smiling at me." A distant smile formed on Jon's face as he thought of his father in his dream.

"And?" prompted Brant. "Did he say anything? Like, 'How's it going, Son?' or 'Did you remember the sunscreen?' Anything like that?"

"Nope. That was the end of it. I guess that's when I heard you yell or throw your phone. I woke up and came in here."

Brant stared blankly at Jon for a moment. "Thanks, Jon."

"For what?"

"Just when I think I'm the one who's really screwed up, you come through and let me off the hook with a story like that."

"Well, what do *you* dream about?"

"Not weird stuff like that. That's like something out of a Stanley Kubrick film."

"I didn't say it was *that* weird. Seriously, give me something you've dreamed about."

"All right," said Brant, sitting straighter against the shower wall, "a few nights ago, I dreamed there was a puppy stampede running through my old yard in Shandon."

"A puppy stampede?" asked Jon, pushing his eyebrows up on his head.

"Yeah, I was looking out my window while I was using the bathroom, and all these puppies came running around the corner of my house and into the front yard. There was like…a hundred of them. Then they all jumped into my cousin's car on the street, and he drove away." Brant looked at Jon, waiting for his reaction.

"I think you just won the prize back from me," said Jon, standing to his feet. "I'm going back to bed. Are you done in here?"

"You go ahead. I think I'm just gonna sit here for a little while."

"All right," said Jon, turning to leave the bathroom. "Just holler if you need anything." He started to pull the door closed behind him.

"Hey, Jon," said Brant.

Jon leaned his head around the bathroom door and looked at Brant, still sitting on the shower floor. "Yeah?"

"Thanks."

Jon smiled at his long-time friend. "Anytime."

fifty four

Happy Birthday

"The ship was caught by the storm and could not head into the wind; so we gave way to it and were driven along."
- Acts 27:15

Jon fought against his compulsion to breathe. The air in the eighteen-wheel truck cab assaulted his senses with the odor of spent cigarettes, mildewed seats, and Tom's garlic breath. Even after enduring the foul atmosphere for an hour, Jon couldn't decide if breathing through his mouth – and tasting the pungent mix on his tongue – was worse than taking it all in through his nose. He alternated between the two and half-heartedly prayed for sinus congestion. But he was thankful that Tom, a weathered-looking cranky man in his fifties, had allowed them back in his truck for the drive into Austin. And as he bounced next to the door in the torn vinyl seat he shared with Brant, he thought through the logistics of getting his car repaired. He would need to find a towing service willing to drive from Austin all the way out Highway 290 to where it broke down and then to a dealership somewhere in Austin. And he would need to find a hotel – a real one – for at least one night, possibly two. Maybe it was all God's way of telling him they had left Austin too soon. Maybe God had a plan for him to share Christ with someone else there. And maybe he should try again with Tom, for starters. "Tom, I'm curious," Jon said. "We were just a couple hours outside of Austin when we stopped at the motel last night. I'm surprised you didn't just drive on into town."

"I was out of hours from driving all weekend," said Tom.

"Out of hours?" Jon asked.

"DOT rules," said Tom. "I can only drive so many hours a day and so many days in a row before I have to go off duty for a while. That's why we were late getting started this morning, too. They say it's a safety thing, but all I know is it keeps me from getting home when I want to."

"Do you live in Austin?" asked Brant.

"Heck, no. I live in Yuma, way back the other way in Arizona."

"Hey, Tom," said Jon, "I'm sorry if it bothered you yesterday when I was asking you about Jesus. It's just something that Brant and I feel we're called by God to share with people. I didn't mean to offend you."

"Called?" asked Tom. "Called by your own imagination, more like it."

Jon could see Tom was just as hostile at the mention of Jesus as he was the night before. But he felt compelled to continue. "You don't think God calls some people to serve him?"

"Think what you want, sonny. I don't care."

"But I know you think there's a God," said Jon. "You said so last night."

"Sure. All this stuff had to come from somewhere. But don't give me any of that fairy tale crap about Jesus, again. Dying on a cross and coming back to life. Give me a break. I suppose next you're going to tell me about the Easter Bunny or the Tooth Fairy."

"So you don't think Jesus was a real person?" asked Jon.

"Nope."

"The Bible sure has a lot to say about him," said Jon.

"The Bible is just a bunch of made up stories that suckers like you buy into. It's just an excuse for you to tell me how to live."

Jon tried to ignore Tom's insults and focus on his message. He leaned forward slightly to see around Brant. "But if you believe in God, how are you going to know anything about him if you don't read his Word, Tom? That's how he reveals himself to us."

Tom huffed as he downshifted his truck as they approached an exit ramp off 290 in Austin.

Jon looked out the window briefly in an attempt to get a feel for their location. They appeared to be taking the exit for Interstate 35. Jon remembered crossing over I-35 when they were looking for the baseball stadium. He turned back to Tom. "Have you ever even read the Bible, Tom?"

"Look, fella—"

"It's Jon."

"Whatever," said Tom. The diesel engine clattered loudly as he accelerated up to speed on I-35. "I don't need no Bible or no one else to tell me where I'm going when I die."

"And where is that, Tom?" asked Jon.

Tom chuckled once to himself. "Hell, probably."

"And you're OK with that?" asked Jon.

"It don't matter. What happens, happens."

"But this is what I was trying to tell you last night, Tom – Jesus could save you from hell. And you wouldn't have to worry about where you'll go when you die."

"Do I look worried about that to you?"

"Well, no you don't. That's what concerns me."

"You can keep your concern. And Jesus, too, for that matter. He's about as real as Santa Clause."

"I promise you, Tom," said Jon, "Jesus *is* real."

Tom pointed his finger over his steering wheel at the concrete road ahead of them. "You see that? That's what I see every day. *That's* what's real to me."

"Tom, Jesus walked this earth just like you and me," said Jon. "He lived and died for you. And he still lives. I know because he lives in me."

"I told you yesterday, fella, I ain't interested in no Jesus! And if you don't shut up about him, I'm gonna pull over and—"

"Hey, Tom," said Brant, waving his hand in front of Jon. "It's OK. Really. I'm sorry about my friend Jon, here. He just gets a little carried away with the whole Jesus thing."

Before Jon could react to Brant's disloyal apology, he felt his friend's elbow nudge him in the ribs.

"Tell me about it," said Tom. "What's his damn problem?"

"He's just a little focused," said Brant. "You know."

"He's a damn nuisance is what he is." Tom leaned forward and looked at Jon. "You're a damn nuisance, fella."

"I heard you the first time, thanks," said Jon, waving his hand.

"Feeding me all that crap about...Jesus this and Jesus that. If it weren't for your friend here, I'd have left both your asses back at the Green Cactus this morning."

"We're NASCAR buddies, aren't we, Tom?" asked Brant.

"Amen to that, brother."

"We get it, don't we?"

"Yes, we do." Tom lifted his foot off the accelerator and steered the truck off the interstate. "This is my exit, boys. I've got to drop my load at our distribution center on the east side. Then I can take you wherever you need to go."

Jon began to relax, knowing they would soon be able to start the process of getting his car off the side of the road and into a service center. And while he was disappointed in his failure to maintain a conversation with Tom, he was thankful Brant knew how to keep them from getting kicked out of his truck.

"Hey, there's a billboard for the Buck-N-Bull," said Brant, pointing out the windshield. "We ate there yesterday."

"Best burgers in Austin," said Tom.

"I believe it!" said Brant. "I had the pimento cheese burger with chili and jalapeños. It rocked."

"I had the fish tacos," added Jon.

"Figures," said Tom, without taking his eyes off the road.

Jon decided to just keep his mouth shut until he got out of the truck.

"So, let me ask you something about racing, Tom," said Brant. "If you like Dale Earnhardt, Jr., I'm guessing you were a big Dale, Sr. fan, too, right?"

A toothy smile wrinkled Tom's rugged face. "You ain't never lied, my friend. Best driver ever lived."

"He won a lot of races didn't he?"

"Seventy-six of 'em. Would've won a whole lot more if he hadn't got himself killed like that at Daytona."

"Yeah, that was sad. I hated to see that."

"Sonny, I didn't work for a week after that. Worst day of my life."

"Yeah, there was nobody like the old *Intimidator*," said Brant, shaking his head.

"Damn straight," said Tom. "They didn't call him that for nothin,' you know. The last thing any driver wanted to see in his rearview mirror was that old black Monte Carlo bearing down on him." Tom leaned over his steering wheel as if he were Dale Earnhardt taking aim at the car in front of him.

"He sure put a lot of guys into the wall, didn't he?" asked Brant.

"Hey, like they say, *rubbin's racing.*"

"Yep. You know, I've always wondered, though, do you think he meant to wreck all those guys on purpose?"

Jon leaned forward and looked over at Tom. He could see the man's expression change as he thought of how to answer Brant's question.

Tom's forehead wrinkled as he tilted his head and guided the truck along the straight two-lane street. "No, I don't think he meant to do it," he said. "Anybody will tell you – Dale was a true Southern gentleman. He was just a competitor, that's all. If you got in his way, that's your fault." Tom seemed satisfied with his answer.

"So then," said Brant, "you think all those wrecks were accidents?"

"Accidents happen in racing all the time, sonny. That's just the way it is."

"I'm confused, Tom. You said he was the best racecar driver ever."

"He was."

"But if they were all accidents…."

"What's your point, fella?" asked Tom, cranking his head towards Brant.

"Well, it's just that if Dale Earnhardt *meant* to cause all those wrecks, that means he was a dirty driver and had to cheat to win, right?"

"Now, hold on just a minute!"

"But if he wrecked all those guys by accident," Brant continued, "that means he was just a bad driver who couldn't control his own car. So which is it, Tom? Was Dale dirty? Or just a bad driver?"

Tom hit his breaks hard just before an intersection, despite having a green light. Jon and Brant braced themselves against the dashboard as the truck's tires screeched to a stop on the asphalt. "That does it!" said Tom. "Get out!"

"Tom, I'm just saying, if he's such a good driver, how do you explain all those wrecks?"

"Get out of my truck!"

"Oh, so it's OK for you to say Jesus Christ is like the Tooth Fairy, but I can't say anything bad about Dale Earnhardt?"

"I said '*get out of my truck!*'" shouted Tom, pointing to the passenger door.

"NASCAR's not a religion, Tom," said Brant. "You need Jesus, my friend."

"Get your *damn* stuff and get your asses out of my truck, *now!*"

Jon could hear car horns blowing behind them and opened the passenger-side door. "Come on, Brant. Let's go."

"All right, all right."

Reaching down to the cab floor, they grabbed the bags each had brought with them from the car and climbed down out of the truck. Brant looked up into the cab with a smile. "Thanks for the ride, Tom." Tom hit the gas before Brant could close the door and drove through the intersection as the light turned red over his trailer.

Jon watched their ride pull away down the street, leaving them stranded once again. He pulled his bag onto his shoulder and looked at Brant. "I really should be mad at you right now, you know," he said.

"I know. But he deserved it. He was being a total jerk to you."

"No argument there, but still." Jon rotated in a circle to take in the area in which they were now abandoned. Single-story homes with small yards, each enclosed by chain-link fences, shared the street with a bar, a used car lot, and a car wash. The modern design of a new three-story apartment building on the corner behind Jon seemed out of place with the decades-old structures surrounding it. He was at a loss for which direction to go next. But driven by a simple desire to make progress of some kind, he stepped off the curb to cross Cesar Chavez Street. He turned back to see Brant looking in the other direction. "Let's see what's down this way," Jon said.

Brant took a few quick steps and pulled even with Jon as they crossed the street. "I guess that wasn't a very Christian thing for me to do to Tom back there, was it?" asked Brant.

"No, not really," said Jon, stepping up onto the sidewalk. "But honestly, once I figured out where you were going with all that Dale Earnhardt stuff, I had to stop myself from laughing."

Brant's face came alive with delight. "Did you see Tom's face? *Get out of my truck!*" Brant's broad smile gave way to his hearty laugh. "I thought his little head was going to explode!"

"Poor guy," said Jon, enjoying Brant's amusement. "That's probably the last time he picks up two stranded motorists."

"I wouldn't doubt it. And by the way, I didn't mean all that stuff about Dale Earnhardt. I liked him. I was just trying to push that guy's buttons."

"Well, I think you did a pretty good job of that."

Jon and Brant stopped at a four-way intersection at the end of the next block. Stop signs on each corner, instead of a traffic signal, told Jon they were moving further away from the business district.

"So, anyway," said Brant. "Where to now?"

"I don't even know where we are," said Jon.

"Well, that sign across the street says that's the East Austin Neighborhood Center, whatever that is. And we're at the corner of East Second and Comal Street."

"Thanks for reading for me, Brant. But that doesn't seem to help very much." Jon reached in his pocket and pulled out his iPhone. He pressed the power button with no result. "And my phone's dead, too."

"I thought you charged it last night."

"I did. But I guess the switch that turned off the light must have turned off the wall outlet, too."

"So, we have no cell phone, no car, and no idea where we are."

"I think that about sums it up," said Jon. "But at least we're not out in the middle of nowhere, anymore." He looked across the street at the Neighborhood Center. "Maybe we can go in there and borrow a phone to call a cab."

"I say let's get something to eat," said Brant.

"How did I know you were going to say that?"

"And I'm buying," added Brant.

"Wow, *that* I didn't see coming."

"Well, it *is* your birthday, isn't it?"

Jon stepped back and looked at Brant. "How did you know that?"

"Holly told me at your house Christmas Eve when we were upstairs watching *Elf* and playing with Legos. I wanted to do something nice for you today, but my options are obviously limited."

"I appreciate that, Brant. I really do. Thank you."

"I tell you what, Jon – since I feel bad about getting us kicked out of Tom's truck, why don't we find somebody to witness to before we eat?"

"*Before* we eat?" asked Jon. "Who *are* you?"

"I'm your best friend," said Brant, punching Jon in the shoulder.

Jon shoved Brant off the curb. "Yes, you are," he said. For the first time, Jon felt truly settled about his friendship with Brant. The past was gone. He was glad – even thankful – that Brant was with him. He truly had a brother in Christ.

"And look at that," said Brant, nodding his head to draw Jon's attention across the street. A young Hispanic man sat alone on a bus stop bench facing the street in front of the Neighborhood Center. "There's the perfect candidate."

"Hang on, Brant. Let me get my Bible out of my bag, first. I want to be ready with Scripture this time."

"You know what, Jon? Why don't you let me take the lead on this one?"

"Seriously?"

"Yeah. I think I'm ready."

"All right, Mr. Morris. He's all yours. But I've got my Bible just in case we need it."

"Sweet. This'll be my birthday present to you, Jonny-boy." Brant slapped Jon on the back.

"Brant, after the luck we've had the past twenty-four hours, seeing someone saved would be the best birthday present ever."

Brant and Jon crossed the street and hopped onto the sidewalk a few yards from the young man.

"Hola," said Brant. "¿Cómo estás, mi amigo?"

"You speak Spanish?" whispered Jon as they approached the bus stop.

"You just heard all I know, right there. Let's hope he speaks English."

fifty five

Don't Stop

*"But Stephen, full of the Holy Spirit, looked up to heaven and saw
the glory of God, and Jesus standing at the right hand of God. 'Look'
he said, 'I see heaven open and the Son of Man standing at the right
hand of God.' Then he fell on his knees and cried out, "Lord, do not
hold this sin against them.' When he had said this, he fell asleep."*

- Acts 7:55-56, 60

The loud pop of the gun firing sent a searing burst of pain through Jon's
left ear as the bullet hit his chest like a sledgehammer. A brief sensation of
being weightless ended when the back of his head bounced off the ground
a second later. When his eyes opened, Brant's blurry, panicked face hovered
over him. His screams stabbed in Jon's left ear like a knife.

"Jon! Jon! Oh, God, no. Jon! Stay with me, man!"

Jon struggled to speak. "Brant...get your knee off my chest...I can't
breathe."

"That's not my knee, buddy. He shot you in the chest!" Brant looked
frantically around him as he pulled his shirt off over his head and pressed it
against Jon's bleeding chest. "Help! Somebody, please! Help!"

Under the trees behind the Neighborhood Center, they appeared to be
alone. A dog barked rhythmically in a yard nearby.

"Brant...I think I'm fine." Jon could feel wet grass underneath his back
as he tried to move and wondered if he was lying in a mud puddle. "I'm
just...."

"Just be quiet, Jon." Brant stood to his feet and turned to his left and right. "Somebody call 911! We need an ambulance! Help! Help!" The roar of a passing bus momentarily drowned out Brant's pleas for help.

"Just use my phone," Jon said, weakly.

"Your phone's dead, buddy. Remember?" Brant dropped to his knees again and pressed his shirt hard against Jon's chest. "Just hang on. I won't leave you."

Jon closed his eyes.

"Oh, God, please don't let this happen," cried Brant. "Please, God, no."

"Brant?" whispered Jon, his eyes still closed.

"I'm here, buddy."

"He already has one," Jon said, softly.

"Jon, what are you saying? Who has what?"

"OK, OK," said Jon. Opening his eyes slowly, Jon turned his head to see his Bible lying on the ground next to his right hand. He moved his fingers underneath it and lifted the bound edge, leaning it against his hip. Jon turned his eyes towards Brant. "You're supposed to take this."

"What, Jon? Your Bible? No, that's yours, buddy. You just stay still. You're gonna be all right, OK?" Brant looked towards the street. "*Help!!* Oh, God, please don't do this."

"He said," whispered Jon. "He said you'll know what to do." Jon smiled softly. His eyes closed again.

"Who Jon? I don't understand. Just lay quiet, OK? Hang in there. I'm gonna get you some help. Just stay with me." Brant looked up again towards the empty street once more and cried, "Help! Somebody! Help!"

"Brant," said Jon with all the strength he could gather.

"Yeah, buddy? I'm here, Jon. I'm not leaving you." Brant leaned over Jon's face.

Jon looked into his friend's anguished eyes. "You did good, Brant. That was good. Don't stop. Tell Holly…."

Brant's face slowly faded into darkness.

fifty six

The Harvest

"Peacemakers who sow in peace reap a harvest of righteousness."
- James 3:18

Amy navigated through the musicians as they unplugged their guitars and made their way off the stage. Walking to the front and center of the large platform, she turned on her wireless microphone and looked out across the smooth artificial grass and dirt of the baseball infield. Applause from the thousands sitting in the stands tapered off as she prepared to speak.

"Hello Austin!" Amy shouted, waving both her arms in the air. A short roar of approval from the crowd rang out across the stadium. "We're so thankful that you've come to worship with us tonight and hear God's Word preached in this beautiful stadium. You know, my husband has been sharing the Gospel of Jesus Christ around the country for the past fifteen years in venues large and small, but we always feel so blessed to come home to Austin."

A round of applause filled the stadium again as Amy smiled at the crowd.

"So, we just want to say thank you for welcoming us here tonight. You have a very special place in our hearts. And I also wanted to let you know that last night, on this very field, we saw over a thousand people come forward to accept Christ and begin a new life following him. And who knows how many more around the world made the same commitment in faith while watching online. We're just amazed at what God is doing here in Austin this weekend. And in just a moment, my wonderful husband…." Amy paused as the crowd cheered. "Before my wonderful husband delivers his message tonight, he's going to come out here and introduce a very special man. A man who has shared God's message of hope and salvation to hundreds in the most trying of circumstances. You're going to want to hear this man's story. But first, please give a big Texas hello to my husband, Brant Morris!"

Brant walked up the side stairs and on to the stage as the stadium echoed with cheers and applause. Removing the white cowboy hat from his bald head, he waved it in the air. "Hello, Texas!" The crowd roared even louder. He handed the hat to Amy, gave her a hug and waited for the crowd to grow quiet again. Amy found her way off the stage as Brant began to speak.

"It's been a few years since we've been here in Austin," he said, looking out over the crowd. "But as Amy said, you have a special place in our hearts. The love and support we've received from this community over the years has meant a lot to us in our ministry to bring hope to a lost world. And we sincerely thank you for allowing us to bring the Gospel message here this weekend.

"You know, God has a way of meeting us in strange places sometimes. Isaiah 61:3 says, 'He will bestow on us a crown of beauty instead of ashes, the oil of gladness instead of mourning, and a garment of praise instead of a spirit of despair.' Sometimes when things seem the most hopeless, when you are at the bottom looking up, God can meet you there and give you hope. For example, I met my beautiful wife, Amy, at a funeral, of all places. God brought us together at a time when we were both grieving the terrible loss of a close, mutual friend twenty years ago. It was a low point in our lives. But from that meeting, God gave us beauty for ashes, gladness for mourning, and praise for despair.

"It's in that thought that I want you to meet someone very dear to me. Marcello Soto and I have a friendship that spans the last twenty years. Way back to when I had hair. And what I've seen God do in this man's life has been a constant source of faith and encouragement to me." Brant turned to his right and waved his friend onto the stage. "Today is a very special day in Marcello's life, and I'd like him to share his story with you now. Marcello, it's all yours."

A middle-aged Hispanic man – muscular and thin – wearing jeans and a black T-shirt, with the words "Jesús Salva!" printed in white letters across his chest, walked to center stage and hugged Brant. The two men exchanged words as the crowd welcomed Marcello with polite applause.

"Don't be afraid, brother," said Brant in Marcello's ear. "Just share the truth."

"Sí, mi hermano," said Marcello. He turned toward the audience and flipped a switch on the wireless microphone control on his hip. "Hola! ¿Cómo está?" said Marcello as he looked around the quiet stadium. "Don't worry, I speak English," he said, drawing scattered laughs from the crowd. He paused for a moment, took a deep breath, and then continued. "Mr. Morris said he and I have been friends for the past twenty years. That's true, but there's a lot he didn't tell you. He didn't tell you that for those twenty years, I've been in prison. I just got out yesterday. So he's right. Today is a special day for me. It's my first full day of freedom since I was nineteen years old. And Mr. Morris didn't tell you how many times he came to visit me or wrote to me during those twenty years. Probably because it was too many to count. And he didn't tell you how I came to know Jesus Christ as my Lord and Savior. Or how I came to own the Bible I hold in my hand. That's the story of how he and I met. And I'd like to share that with you now.

"When I was nineteen, I lived right here in Austin. I went to Eastside High, not too far from this stadium. My family, we didn't have much. When I was growing up, my father and my uncle ran a small produce business delivering fresh vegetables to restaurants around town. My brothers and sisters and I worked every day before and after school to help my father. We got by with what we had. But by the time I finished high school, I wanted more. We had no money for college, and I was tired of working for my father. I wanted the stuff that working in fields and delivering produce couldn't buy. I felt like life owed me more than that. So I started stealing and selling drugs. I didn't care who got hurt or who I sold them to. It didn't matter. I was in it for me.

"One day, I was sitting at a bus stop over on East Second Street. And these two white men walked up and asked to talk to me. One of them was carrying a Bible. I could tell I wasn't going to make any money selling drugs to them." Marcello paused as a few laughs from the crowd drifted across the stadium. "So, I decided I was going to steal from them. They were both well dressed and trusting. Easy targets. One of them asked me if I knew Jesus and started telling me about what I needed to do to be saved. So, I pretended to be interested long enough to get what I wanted.

"As he talked to me, I led them around the back of the Neighborhood Center. I showed them my gun and told them to give me their wallets, cell phones, and watches. The man who was talking did what I asked, but the man with the Bible didn't. He just wanted to tell me how Jesus could change my life, instead. He told me Jesus was what I really needed, not money or drugs. And that God loved me. This made me angry. I told him that God didn't care about me or my family. That my life meant nothing to anyone, including God. I was just a meaningless number. He told me I was wrong, that God loved me so much that he sent his only Son, Jesus, to die on the Cross for me. Then he told me I could be forgiven for every bad thing I'd ever done and start a new life with Jesus. I didn't believe him. I told him he didn't know all the bad things I'd done and that God couldn't forgive me.

"I pointed my gun at him and told him to give me his wallet and cell phone or I was going to kill him. He said that even if I took his life right then, God would still forgive me if I accepted Jesus in my heart. He offered me a deal. He said I could have anything he had, but I had to take his Bible first. He told me if I read John 3:16 and still wanted his money, he'd give me all he had. He started to hand me his Bible and a car horn blew on the street. I jumped and my gun went off and shot him in the chest."

Marcello stopped and looked down. The stadium was completely silent.

"That's how I met Mr. Morris," he said. "The man I shot, the man who tried to give me his Bible, was his friend Jon Smoak. He died right there a few minutes after I ran away. Mr. Morris was the man with him that night. They arrested me two days later and charged me with murder. I plead guilty to manslaughter and was sentenced to thirty years, but I could be paroled after twenty. A month after I was in prison, Mr. Morris came to see me with Mr. Smoak's daughter, Holly." Marcello pointed to Holly standing next to Brant near the side of the stage, her arm wrapped around Amy's waist. "They told me they forgave me for what I did. And then Mr. Morris told me that I forgot something the day I tried to rob them. He pulled out Mr. Smoak's Bible, the one he tried to give me before I killed him. Mr. Morris said, 'Let's finish the deal.' He opened the Bible to the Book of John and held it up to the glass so I could read John 3:16. I read, 'for God so loved the world that he gave his one and only Son, that whoever believes in him shall not perish but have eternal life.'

"Mr. Morris asked me if I was ready to ask God to forgive me of my sins and accept Jesus as my Lord and Savior. I told him yes, and he led me in a prayer. My life changed forever that day. They let me keep Mr. Smoak's Bible, and I read it every day. I began sharing what I learned with other inmates, about God's love and mercy, and offering them a chance to know Jesus. In the twenty years I was in prison in Beaumont, I saw over two hundred men accept Jesus as their Lord and Savior, including three guards. Mr. Morris came to see me several times a year. He wrote me letters. He encouraged me and gave me things to read to strengthen my faith. And a month ago, he testified on my behalf at my parole hearing.

"I'm here today by the grace of God and the faithful witness of two men. And I'm here to tell you, it doesn't matter what you've done. God loves you and can forgive you of your sins, tonight. He wants you to know his Son, Jesus. He offers hope for the hopeless. Believe me, I know. Mr. Morris, I thank God for you every day.

"And Mr. Smoak…." Marcello looked into the evening sky and held Jon's Bible over his head as tears streamed down his face. "I'm sorry for what I did to you. You were God's faithful servant, and I owe my eternal life to your obedience in sharing the Gospel. And I thank you for this Book. It means more to me than anything I'll ever own. And I'll keep it safe until I see you in heaven, my brother."

As Marcello turned to walk off the stage, Brant, Amy, Holly, and Jacob met him and wrapped their arms around him as applause rained down from the crowd.

"Thank you Marcello," said Brant. "God bless you, my friend."

Epilogue

The warm dry sand moved underneath Jon's bare feet as he shifted his weight and took a step forward towards the ocean. The beach was empty. No people. No birds. No footprints on the sand. And, but for the sound of small gentle waves rolling gracefully onto the shore, completely quiet. Jon breathed in his surroundings, mesmerized by its beauty. Looking out over the smooth, blue water, he saw the radiant shape of a man beginning to form above the waves. Jon stepped back and shielded his eyes from the increasing glow with his right hand. The figure's white light reflected off the water, shining brighter than the sun. Jon closed his eyes and covered them with both hands.

"Jon," called a deep, magnificent voice, which seemed to emanate from all directions.

Jon fell to his knees and pressed his forehead into the sand, trembling with fear. As he wrapped his shaking arms around his head, the weight of a gentle hand came to rest on his back.

"Well done, my good and faithful servant," said the voice. "Rise and follow me, Jon."

Jon lifted his eyes to the figure standing before him. "Jesus...my God. My Savior."

"Enter into the Kingdom of Heaven, Jon."

Jon rose slowly to his feet and took a step forward. Feeling the presence of someone by his side, Jon turned to see a familiar, but youthful, face smiling back at him. *"Dad?"*

"Welcome home, Jonny."

About The Author

Greg Dodd lives in Columbia, South Carolina with his wife, Caroline, and their Anatolian Shepherd, Desmond. He earned both his bachelor's and master's degrees from the University of South Carolina and works as an IT professional for an energy-based holding company. Greg and Caroline teach a Sunday school class for newly married and engaged couples and enjoy vacationing on Pawleys Island.